COBY'S SEARCH

BY
PHILLIP TUCKER

www.philliptucker.com.au

ACKNOWLEDGEMENT

Thank you to my friends and family, for putting up with me while I wrote this book. Special thanks to Caz and Lindsey, for their hard work in turning hundreds of pages of writing into a readable book.

COPYRIGHT © PHILLIP TUCKER 2017

CONTENTS

HANOI

The tarmac squealed as the Air America Dreamliner turned into its bay and shuddered to a halt at Hanoi's International Airport. The passengers, who were mostly tourists, excitedly reached for their seatbelts. This anticipation of the release was halted, as the sound system squawked. It warned them first in English and then in Vietnamese, to keep their belts fastened and to remain seated. Several muted clicks meant the warning went unheeded.

In row seven of business class, a tall elderly African American man stirred at the announcement in Vietnamese. It awakened forgotten buried memories as he slowly stirred from his deep sleep. His hands involuntarily moved to his face wiping his eyes, as he sought to clear his vision. Focusing, Senator Cornelius Henderson took in his surroundings.

"I'm still on the plane from the US," he murmured, body relaxing as his demons sank back into distant memories.

Watching his fellow passengers, he observed a false calm had settled over them in their enforced confinement. They looked to him like athletes at the blocks, focused, filled with adrenaline, waiting for the moment when the gun went off. A 'ding' like noise sounded above him, as the seatbelt light extinguished, causing that imaginary gun to discharge. The passengers sensing gold surged to their feet, vying for space, moving for the exit door. At the same time, some tried to tidy their appearances, while frantically grabbing luggage from the overhead lockers.

Smiling at his own mind's dramatisation of the event, he too unbuckled his belt. Standing, taking in the scene around him, reminded him of his own need to be presentable. On the seat beside him, he found his suit jacket laid out neatly awaiting his inspection.

"That son of mine thinks of everything," he whispered out loud, wondering where his son who had sat next to him had gone. Looking around for him in the turmoil, he spotted Michael towards the front. He was there talking to one of their many minders. At over six foot three inches tall, his son Michael had presence. He'd been voted an all American at University, proving himself in the classroom and on the football field. Which of these was the most

4

important, could be argued. Ruggedly good looking, his only downside was his overly serious facial expressions.

"A typical senator's look," Coby surmised. "He needs to love and be loved. Otherwise, I'll never get to play with a grandchild." Coby whispered. As if reading his mind, Michael looked towards him. Giving him a curt nod, he continued his discussion with the minders.

"Who am I to talk about family?" Coby mumbled to himself, as he sat back down.

Most of the passengers tidying themselves in business class were familiar to him. Many worked for the Foreign Affairs or Trade Departments of the American Government. Some, mingled amongst them were of course security. To him, they always looked slightly disturbed, as they stood or sat talking to themselves. In truth, they were conferring with their team handlers, through their personal communications gear. He'd on occasion noticed the small black earpieces or the miniature microphones they carried on their ties. Despite his knowledge of this, he conceded that the talking to themselves gave them an intense, unbalanced look.

"Good morning Senator Henderson!" was shouted from the crowd. Someone had noticed he was awake. Smiling, Coby waved back. Subconsciously, he again felt his face for any stubble left over from his shave earlier that morning. Luckily his face was still smooth, one of the so-called perks of getting older. Adjusting a small mirror on the portable table in front of him, he grabbed his comb to tidy his hair. Grey streaks peppered his once boyish dark brown hair, giving him a statesmanlike appearance.

"You mean an old fart look." He told himself, as looking down the walkway, he saw a woman of about thirty something, watching him before turning away. "Well, maybe not that old." He chuckled. Like his son, Cornelius Henderson or Coby as he was nicknamed, was just over six feet tall. In his hey-day, he'd been quite a handsome man or so his wife Glenda told him. Now she said he had a unique statesman-like appearance, which meant old fart to him.

"Hey, Senator Henderson! Says here in 'The Times' that the President is worried you might stand against him next year!" Stanley one of his PR people yelled out from ten seats back. This caused several people to stop what they were doing and look his way.

"You talking to me or my son, Stanley?" Coby replied, trying to deflect the question.

"You know I'm talking about you Coby, I mean Senator," Stanley shot back, knowing he was trying to dodge his question.

"Stanley if they said I was touring with the Rolling Stones next year, you'd buy a ticket. Stop believing those stories. I'm retiring!" Coby yelled back, causing an outbreak of merriment.

"Sure, you are," someone else called out, causing them all to laugh harder. Smiling, knowing no one would believe him anyway, he again checked his appearance. Confident he was ready, he glanced out the window, to find his vision blocked by the mobile stairway. Curious, Coby moved to the opposite side of the plane, sitting down in a vacated seat. Shading his eyes against the glare, he stared out the window, as Hanoi Airport stared back at him.

"God, how long has it been?" He murmured, trying to remember this strip of land outside the enemy's Capital city. "An enemy no longer," he reminded himself.

It had been over thirty something years since he was last in this God forsaken country. Coby, the Commie killer, had been his nickname; even had it on the side of his Super Saber fighter-bomber, compliments of his ground crew.

"Let's hope they greet me and don't shoot me," he whispered, remembering the price the enemy put on his head back then.

Moving back to his seat, he sat down again, waiting for his son's return. Through a crack between the stairs and the plane, Coby could see two Vietnamese Army Officers by their shoulder boards, conferring with the ground crew. The uniforms were still the same he remembered, although luckily, he hadn't seen many up close.

"Just those two on that beach." Closing his eyes, he remembered another time and another life.

DA NANG, 1970.

He'd been just twenty-one when he'd first touched down at Da Nang airfield in central Vietnam, in those days a little south of the North Vietnam border. Being one of the youngest and also one of only a handful of black Americans to serve as a fighter pilot in Nam, gave Coby a lot to prove. Young, dumb and full of cum, was how his commanding officer Colonel John Douglas had described him after his first mission. Coby hard-faced, remembering that patrol, knew he was lucky to be still alive.

Like most life-threatening situations in Nam, it started with a fuck up. A detachment of Marines had been ambushed by a company of North Vietnamese regulars, on a raid along the coast, fifty miles behind the lines. Why they'd gone on the raid, no one could say, but they were trapped. Coby was on his first patrol flying wingman for an arse-licking racist named Captain Charles Benson, when they'd received a call for help. Their Area Command Centre immediately permitted them to head north to assist.

Benson, the senior officer, checked the location of the marines before answering. Seeing it was close to a known anti-aircraft hotspot, he reported he was low on fuel and was about to return to base. Benson suggested they call in another group or call the reserve wing at their base. Coby, listening in, broke into the transmission, telling the Command Centre that he had plenty of fuel. Silence followed, as high command weighed up sending a rookie over the border, on his own.

Checking what was available they found out that the Marines, wanting complete secrecy had gone in without a request for air support. Air power in the area was therefore minimal. The only aircraft available at that moment were Medivac choppers.

"Well they're going to get a workout," General Johnson growled to his staff, angry at the Marines' stupidity. Knowing without immediate air support the Marines would be chopped to pieces, General Johnson the Area Commander, had no other option but to send him in.

"Okay rookie, you go give them hell," Johnson ordered, getting a," Will do," response from Lieutenant Coby. Putting down the microphone, Johnson happy with his decision, glanced around his Command Centre. He observed his staff had a lot less confidence in the rookie than he did. Worried, he took Captain Benson's advice, ordering Coby's base to have the reserve wing launch and head north to the Marines' position.

Their prep time, plus the flight time to the Marines' location, meant they wouldn't arrive for almost thirty minutes. Johnson knew it could all be over for the Marines in half of that. Keeping his smile in place, he stood watching his staff and listening to the engagement going on to the north.

"Shit I hope to God that you pull it off kid," he whispered to himself, continuing to smile confidently.

Benson in the meantime was ordered to return to base and refuel, then return to assist the reserve wing. Turning south, Benson was fuming over his wingman playing the hero. Angry, he decided to put Coby in his place, forgetting they were both still sharing the frequency with command.

"You're a fool Lieutenant! Heroes die here all the time, even niggers," Captain Benson chuckled and swung away, leaving Coby alone with his decision.

"I've got enough fuel, Sir. I'll make it," Coby replied, ignoring the nigger remark.

"They'll chew you to pieces Lieutenant. Your head's going to be swinging in the wind, outside some gook villager's hut tonight." He sniggered. Coby remained silent and didn't reply. Instead, he increased speed towards the Marines' location.

Back at the command centre, Johnson and his staff listened to Benson's remarks in silence. All eyes now turned toward General Johnson. Without a word, he nodded to his staff and walked into his office, slamming the door. Picking up his field phone, he had the switch operator connect him to the Da Nang Airbase Commander.

Coby, checking his fuel gauge, worked out he had twenty minutes over the target area. Five minutes out he switched to the Marine battalion's frequency. Hearing multiple desperate calls for help, he asked for their positions. The desperate Marines didn't ask who he was. They just repeatedly confirmed in a solid garble of voices, that they had all retreated to the beach and were dug in, awaiting pickup. Looking out to sea, Coby could see the Navy was bringing in armoured floating troop transports, but they were copping heavy mortar and ground fire from the ridge above the Marines. Telling them to keep their heads down, Coby started his inward run.

Making sure no friendlies were still on the ridge, Coby came in low from the south. His ordinance consisted of two five hundred pound bombs and two canisters of napalm. Knowing he couldn't be sure of the enemy's exact positions, he chose napalm. Dropping the two canisters along the high ground, he hugged the ground along the coast to avoid return fire. It was his first in-country drop and luckily for the Marines, dead on target. The ridge became a burning pile of vegetation. Firing on the Marines, immediately ceased, as whatever was left of the enemy, retreated.

With the sudden drop in enemy fire, the Marines, not waiting, rushed down to the beach and started to load onto their transporters. Coby, checking his fuel, saw he was approaching the point of no return, so he turned away, heading for home. Smiling at his success, he saw a giant fountain of sand balloon up from the beach near the Marines.

"Damn, they've got artillery down there," he said aloud, as his radio came to life. The Navy Commander this time asked if he could silence the gun so that they could chopper out the more seriously injured. Stupidly he responded with a, "Will do!" before turning around, coming in again from the south.

The gun was easy to spot by the cloud of smoke it created, as it rhythmically lobbed shell after shell onto the beach. The anti-aircraft gun hidden in the jungle beside it wasn't. As Coby came in for his textbook run, the anti-aircraft gun opened up. Committed, Coby continued, dropping one of his five hundred pounders. For his efforts, he received thirty hits along his left wing and tail assembly. To make it worse his bomb missed, slamming into a paddy field beside the gun. Angry, feeling like an idiot for staying, Coby turned around coming in from the north. Deciding to eliminate the AA battery first, he primed his twenty-millimetre cannons.

He began firing as he charged in again. Saturating the entire area with rounds, he got lucky, seeing the AA position disintegrate and burst into flames before he turned north again. With no ground fire this time, he dropped his remaining bomb right down

9

the gun's throat. Secondary explosions mushroomed into the sky as he banked hard left in the direction of home.

"Stick that up your arse!" he yelled, receiving thanks at the same time from the Navy. After returning a, "You're welcome," he glanced at his fuel gauge. His eyes nearly popped out of his head when he saw how much gas he'd used!

"Holy shit, shit, shit! What do I do now?" he babbled to himself, fear making him ease off the throttle.

No matter how he worked it out, he wasn't going to make it. Thinking back to the Academy, Coby remembered a guy stretching his fuel by gaining altitude then gliding in. The story at the time was about a small Cessna two-seater propeller plane, not an overweight fighter-bomber, with holes in it. Deciding he had nothing to lose, he put his fighter's nose up, slowly gaining height.

Back at his base, Colonel Johnson, his commanding officer, looked at the clock to Coby's position on the radar.

"He's fucked! Notify air and sea rescue, and get some choppers in the air," Colonel Douglas ordered, his men scrambling. "What's his distance from here now Airman?" Douglas asked the radar operator.

"He's ten miles out due north, at seventy-five thousand feet," the airman replied.

"Seventy-five thousand! What the hell's he playing at?" Douglas asked the room.

"Maybe he's going to jump?" Captain Benson suggested sarcastically. Having returned to base, he'd complained of a fault with his steering, so his plane had been grounded. His ground crewmen were busily checking the problem, having found nothing yet. The two reserve fighters had been scrambled and were now over the Marines flying cover. Douglas stared at Benson seeing him as General Johnson had.

"Why don't you go help your ground crew with that steering problem Captain?" Douglas, affronted by his Commander's tone, left. Turning back to the radar screen, Douglas smiled, remembering a story from the Academy. At seventy-five thousand feet, Coby's fighter plane became a million-dollar glider. The engine's continuous noise, which up till then had been so reassuring, spluttered and died. An eerie silence settled as the usually hidden sound of the wind, whistled against the airframe.

Checking his bearings, Coby dipped the nose, starting his descent.

"Base, this is Angel Two, starting my approach," Coby calmly announced, watching the airspeed increase as his altitude decreased.

"For a second there I thought you'd lost the ability to speak Angel Two. Anything else we should know?" Colonel Douglas' voice leapt through his speaker.

"The mission was successful, although I took several hits to the left side of the aircraft," Coby answered, putting a good slant on his mission.

"Good for you Lieutenant. Can you give me a fuel update?"

"It appears a little low Sir," Coby fenced, seeing the airfield come into sight.

"I'd hazard a guess and say it's non-existent. You'd better not damage that plane Lieutenant Henderson, or you'll be cleaning latrines for the rest of your miserable fucking life!" Douglas screamed into the radio.

"No Sir!" Coby snapped back, as sweat broke out on his forehead, the radio going silent. Ahead, Coby saw the perimeter come into view. Seeing he wasn't going to clear it, he glanced at his speed. Judging he had just a little more speed than needed, he lifted the nose of his plane, feeling the speed drastically drop off. His only break today was that the runway faced north to south, meaning he could come straight in. Watching the fence, fairly confident he'd make it, he flicked the landing gear down. Glad it worked electrically and wasn't dependent on the engines, he heard it shudder down into position. His speed, of course, dropped off again, causing the plane to vibrate uncontrollably, as the wheels barely cleared the barbed wire fence.

"That was close," he murmured, as he hit the dirt in front of the runway. "Shit!" he screamed in fear, trying to lift the nose, causing the plane to catapult back into the air. Coming back down again, this time on the tarmac, Coby breathed a sigh of relief. Braking lightly, wiping his forehead again, he taxied the fighter towards the maintenance area, stopping fifty metres short. The fire tenders seeing he wasn't on fire, returned to their hangar, as a jeep roared up beside him.

In its wake followed a tow vehicle for the plane. Placing a ladder beside his cockpit, a ground crew member climbed up and opened his canopy.

"Welcome back Lieutenant." The Corporal, according to his stripes, grinned.

"Good to be back," Coby stammered as he again wiped sweat from his face. Dead tired, he staggered out of his plane and down the ladder. Standing unsteadily on the tarmac, trying not to fall over, he was greeted by cheers from the ground crews, in the adjacent hangars. Surprised, feeling lucky just to be alive, he managed a wave back, too drained to get excited. Any euphoria abruptly ended, when he saw Captain Benson appear from one of the hangars. The crewmen, seeing Benson, melted away, their dislike evident.

"You got lucky you glory hunter! I'll make sure you don't get another chance to do something as stupid as that again!" he spat out, his anger at Coby's success visible. Coby, knowing Benson was trying to provoke him, did not comment moving past Benson.

"You owe me a salute Lieutenant!" Benson thundered, making many of the ground crew turn around. Coby hid his anger, swiftly turned and gave a salute.

"Sorry Sir," he answered in a flat voice, then turned and walked on.

"That's better! Remember to do it next time boy!" Benson chuckled. Turning he saw the crewmen watching him, contempt written on their faces. "Get back to work you slackers!" he bellowed, walking away.

At the air base's command centre, rumours of the dressing down of Coby by Benson spread like wild-fire. Douglas picked up the dissent from the enlisted men at Coby's treatment, knew he had a decision to make. In his office, he looked at the report from his maintenance chief on Benson's plane. The chief mechanic couldn't find a problem with the steering, and there were over two hours of fuel in the tanks. Picking up his phone, he ordered both Captain Benson and Lieutenant Henderson to his office.

Thirty minutes later, found the two officers in Colonel Douglas' waiting room in their uniforms, having changed out of their flight gear. There they silently waited, while both tried to avoid looking at the other. That was quite a task considering the waiting room was only large enough for the Colonel's secretary, a Corporal, his desk and three chairs. Benson had already filed a report, citing Coby's recklessness in endangering his aircraft, by going on a mission without the proper fuel requirement.

He had also thrown in his not saluting a senior officer as well. Smugly he sat opposite Coby, expecting the young pup to get his arse kicked. Looking at the Corporal, he saw him look down at a light flashing next to his phone.

"The Commander will see you now Lieutenant Henderson," the Corporal announced from behind his desk. As Coby stood, Benson unable to restrain himself, sniggered.

"Say goodbye to your career nigger." Benson grinned, as Coby without a backwards look, knocked on Commander Douglas' door and walked in. Behind him, the Corporal who was also an African American, sat typing, ignoring Benson and his remark. Benson, picking up on his attitude, lost his grin.

"How does an Officer get a coffee around here Corporal?" he snapped, as the Corporal slowly looked up from his work.

"He goes outside to the canteen and gets it himself, like everyone else here Captain," the Corporal politely informed him and returned to his work. Captain Benson, knowing he couldn't touch the Commander's assistant, stood and left. The Corporal watched him leave then got up from his desk and tapped on Colonel Douglas' door. Hearing a, "Come in," he stuck his head inside.

"Sorry to disturb you Sir, but would either of you like a coffee?" he asked. Both men said in unison, "No, but thanks anyway." He closed the door and walked back to his desk smiling.

When Coby entered Douglas' office, he took in how neat the room was. Douglas, looking up from his paperwork, signalled for Coby to sit down. That was easy, as there was only one chair. Silence settled over the room as Douglas continued to write. Coby getting distracted stared out the window and saw his plane moved to a hangar for repairs.

"She's shot up pretty badly Lieutenant. You were lucky!" Douglas suddenly spat out, having seen the direction of Coby's eyes. Startled, Coby took a second to reply.

"Yes Sir," Coby stuttered, avoiding Douglas' glare.

"Benson has made some accusations. He wants you busted out of the Air Force. Anything you want to say in your defence?" Douglas asked, watching Coby closely. Although the younger man didn't reply, he saw anger in his eyes. His hands, which remained at his sides, balled into fists, then relaxed. Seeing Coby wasn't going to say anything, Douglas continued, "Between you and me, I think Benson is a coward and has no right to give lectures on being an officer to anyone. That aside, you pushed the envelope today and luckily got away with it.

"You're young, dumb and full of cum, which is great if you're out screwing some piece of arse, but it has no place in a fighter jet. Here lives are saved and lost by this squadron being up there hurting the enemy. Your plane might have been destroyed. Instead, it was damaged and is now offline. What if something big occurred now after we've lost a valuable asset? Do you understand me so far Lieutenant?" Douglas asked his face emotionless.

"Yes Sir," Coby answered. Deep down he knew Douglas was right.

"Then get out!" Douglas growled. Coby surprised, thinking there'd be more, swiftly saluted and turned to go out the door he entered. "Not that door, the other one," Douglas barked, as Coby fled. Douglas watched him go, hid a smile. "He'll go far," he mused, as again he looked at the letter from his Commander, General Johnson. Johnson had recommended Coby for the Silver Star for bravery. The Commander of the Marine force had also recommended him for going beyond his duty and saving his men's butts, as he put it. General Johnson himself had asked to present it, meaning he was getting it, no matter what anyone said, especially Benson.

Benson's remark about, "Heroes die here, even niggers!" was viewed as not only racist by the General, but unbecoming of an Officer. He wanted him gone. The fuel situation in his tank was what Douglas was angry about. He had returned with over two hour's flying time of fuel, meaning like Coby, he could've helped. Two planes would've flattened everything in half the time, making Coby's job a lot easier and safer.

Instead of doing three runs, either plane, as the wingman, would've spotted the artillery piece as well as the AA gun. Instead, he'd run home and avoided any risk to himself. Finished thinking about it, he told the Corporal over the intercom, to send Benson in.

"Sit down Captain," Douglas ordered. Benson, sensing trouble was coming, went on the offensive.

"I don't know what that nig. I don't know what Henderson told you Sir, but it's bullshit." Benson decided to keep race out of it.

"He didn't tell me anything Benson. This is all to do with you. General Johnson has ordered that you be transferred to Alaska, to join the Tenth Bomber Squadron based there. You'll be assigned to search and rescue duties," Douglas told him, his face still giving nothing away.

"That is outrageous! Only burnouts and pilots who have lost it are transferred to that base!" Benson barked, jumping to his feet.

"You're dead right Captain. Now I don't have to explain why you're going. Now get the fuck out of my sight!" Douglas shouted, as Benson, not bothering to salute, turned and left through the same door, passing the Corporal.

"Enjoy your trip, Sir." Benson too upset to say anything in reply slammed the door.

Two months and more missions than a pilot ever thought he'd fly, found Coby in his dress uniform. He was waiting for General Johnson and his staff to arrive. Lined up along outside the airfield's hangars were the men of the 202nd fighter wing. From the ground crews to the command centre staff, everyone was there. Coby had never felt more alive, knowing the reason for the General's visit. Colonel Douglas had dropped it on him only two days earlier.

Over dinner at the mess, he'd yelled across the room for everyone to press their Sunday best, Lieutenant Henderson was getting a medal. Coby had been struck dumb, as the mess exploded cheering. They all knew about that mission and what he'd done. They all knew he deserved it. Standing up, he thought over what to say, as the room grew quiet, waiting for his response.

"Thank you all. I might be getting this medal, but this whole unit deserves it. You all did your part to get me there and back.

Without you guys I wouldn't be getting it," he stammered, emotion making his voice tremble.

"Bullshit! There's no way I have been stupid enough to save those squids!" one of his fellow Officers yelled out, causing the room to break up. Colonel Douglas silenced the room by standing.

"Whatever you've got to drink, grab it now," he ordered, raising his glass. "To Lieutenant Henderson the Commie Killer," he toasted, the room echoing his words. Now he stood nervously with those same men waiting for the General.

On cue, the convoy made up of mostly reporters, entered the base. Driving sedately, they headed towards the assembled air wing. The entourage stopped short of the men, letting the General's car overtake the others. It came to a halt in front of Colonel Douglas.

"Attention!" Douglas shouted, as the General flung open his door and stepped out. The Colonel was just about to welcome him, when two other officers, a Marine General and an Admiral also climbed out.

"Sorry to pull this on you Colonel. But these two old warhorses insisted on coming as well. You don't mind, do you?" General Johnson asked, waving to the reporters. In the background, the Admiral and the General chuckled at their introduction.

"Of course, not Sir. Would they like to inspect my men with you Sir?" he asked, sweating.

"That would be great Colonel. After you gentlemen." General Johnson smiled, waving to the media at the same time.

Thanking Douglas, the two senior officers joined Johnson, walking along the first line. It turned out to be a great day for the men, as the three senior officers mingled with them swapping stories. They asked questions about their jobs and where they were from, as the cameras clicked away. After an hour of enjoying themselves, General Johnson asked Coby to come out front. In was then the General pinned the Silver Star on Coby's chest, as the cameras flashed.

"Congratulations son, you went above and beyond to save those Marines. Your country is proud of you!" Johnson exclaimed. Both the other senior officers shook his hand, having been told by their men of his bravery. They were just about to leave when the Marine General turned to him.

"If they give you a hard time here Lieutenant, you're always welcome over at the Marines!" he yelled out.

"Not a chance in hell General! He belongs to the 202nd!" Colonel Douglas loudly replied, his men cheering.

"Senator! Dad! Are you okay?" A distant male voice interrupted Coby's daydream. Looking up, he saw his son Michael and a hostess anxiously looking down at him.

"Yeah, I'm fine. I was just getting some shut eye, while the tourists depart." He smiled, standing up. Looking around, he realised the plane was indeed empty. "Well let's get going, son. We have that treaty to work on."

"Are you sure you're okay?" Michael asked, unsure of his father.

"I feel great son. Stop fussing over me," Coby lightheartedly answered, putting on his coat.

Deplaning, Coby found a large contingent of media and Vietnamese officials waiting near the terminal entrance. Opposite them, on the tarmac, stood an honour guard. Coby walking down the mobile stairway looked toward the officials. He saw they'd arranged their platforms so that the visiting American delegation would have to look up to them during introductions. He also noticed many looked to their watches regularly, conveying the impression that they had much more important things to do than greeting this delegation.

Grinning, waving to the crowd beyond the officials, Coby left the planned greeting path, deciding to view the troops of the honour guard. Taking his time, Coby wandered down the lines, talking to the soldiers, an American interpreter helping out. This surprised many of the soldiers and the gathered dignitaries who stood in the hot sun waiting.

"Dad, the Vietnamese representatives, are waiting," Michael whispered in his ear.

"Let them, son. We don't want to appear over-keen or submissive, do we?" he softly replied. Reaching the end of the line, Coby looked towards the gathered officials as if seeing them for the first time. Signalling the honour guard with a 'well done' wave, he walked swiftly towards the dignitaries.

"Welcome to you Senator Henderson and Senator Henderson. My name is Twain. I am my country's chief negotiator." Twain smiled, getting over repeating the Senators' names.

"Thank you, Twain. I realise it's difficult to introduce my son and me when we have the same title."

"Yes Senator, it does have its drawbacks," Twain replied.

"Well call me Coby and my son Michael. That should make it easier."

"Thank you, Sir, but as it is an official visit, we must stick to protocol." Coby nodded in understanding, as Twain led him down the line of Officials, introducing them individually. While shaking hands with the welcoming committee, Coby saw an old Vietnamese General closely watching him, as he made his way along the long line of dignitaries.

"I'm sure I know that man, but from where?" he whispered to Michael, as the Vietnamese official negotiator welcomed both Senator Coby Henderson and Senator Michael Henderson to Hanoi.

Speeches and pleasantries over, Coby found himself talking to the many faces of the Vietnamese Government. Unlike America's Government, the Vietnamese Government had party members who also served in the Armed Forces. Many of them knew he was a decorated war hero and wanted his views on Vietnam now. Like the gifted politician he was, he gave away very little. As time passed by, Coby noticed the General he'd seen earlier nodded whenever they glanced at each other. Curious as to how he knew him, he wandered over.

"Coby Henderson," he said putting out his hand, which the General shook.

"I am General Chew, but my friends call me Chew."

"Well let's hope we can be friends." Coby tried through the fog of time, to recall where he'd seen him before. "I suspect, like me, you served in the war?"

"Yes, I was a Captain back then. I served in many areas during the fight for a reunification of Vietnam."

"I know you, don't I?" Coby whispered as the General of all things winked.

"As a sign of friendship, can I offer you and your son a lift to your hotel?" the General suggested, catching Coby off guard.

"That's very kind of you," was all Coby got out, as Michael, having overheard the General's offer, interrupted.

"You can't do that Dad! I mean Senator Henderson! It would be a breach of protocol if you went with the General before the treaty is worked out!" Michael reminded him. Curious, Coby waved his son's worries away.

"I don't think the General can brainwash us both in the thirty minutes or so that it will take us to reach the hotel," he answered, as those around them laughed. Michael surprised by his father's acceptance, relented, accepting the lift with a smile as well. Twenty minutes and a lot of handshakes later, found both of them in a limousine with the General and the Vietnamese chief negotiator, quietly motoring along the main road towards Hanoi.

"No one mentioned the chief negotiator for Vietnam would be here as well?" Michael snapped, breaking the silence.

"You haven't changed a great deal Senator Henderson," the General said smoothly, ignoring Michael's accusation.

"I give up, General Chew. Where'd we meet?"

"On the shore of Halong Bay. You had crashed and were waiting to be picked up," the negotiator cut in, smiling.

"My God, you're that kid, aren't you? You're the General here's son?" Coby chuckled, as Michael sat mystified.

"What the hell's going on Dad?"

"It's a long story son." Coby lost his smile, before continuing. "Thank you for letting me go that day General. You could easily have captured me you know?"

"You saved the life of my son Twain. How could I do anything other than let you go?" The General shook his head and raised his hands.

"Still you took a chance, and for that, I thank you," Coby pointed out, as silence spread through the vehicle.

"Are you talking about when Bud Van Clef got the Medal of Honor?" Michael interrupted.

"I saw the American with you got a medal. He should've been shot," General Chew put in, leaving Michael in shock.

"What does he mean by that Dad?"

"Bud tried to kill his son and me as well. The General here shot him, just when he was about to finish us both," Coby confessed, leaving Michael even more confused.

"I'll explain later Michael. For now, let's enjoy the view," Coby suggested, stopping any more conversation, as the car made its way through the streets of Hanoi. An uneasy silence enveloped the vehicle till their arrival at the hotel. Chew finally spoke.

"We will see each other at the conference."

"Of course, although we'll leave out Halong Bay?" Coby suggested.

"Yes, that is something we can agree on. Instead, I look forward to talking to you about old times when you were stationed here."

"No, that's one thing that won't happen, General. Some things are better left buried in the past," Coby answered, his eyes distant. Climbing out of the General's car, General Chew surprised them by getting out too. The reporters outside Coby's hotel, seeing them, snapped away.

"Till we meet again Senators." The General offered his hand. Taking it, Coby nodded with understanding, till the General re-entered the car and drove away.

"Would you mind explaining what's going on?" Michael whispered, anger in his voice.

"Not here son. Let's wait till we get to the room," Coby warned, as a group of reporters approached. Like a pack of hyenas, they wanted to know what Coby and Michael, both Senators, were doing getting a lift with a Vietnamese General and Twain the senior negotiator for the Vietnamese.

"Gentlemen, the General offered us a ride as a sign of good faith. What would you expect us to do? Refuse?" Coby explanation silenced the mob.

"But doesn't protocol suggest you only socialise after the treaty is worked out?" one reporter pointed out.

"Look, the General was just being a proud dad. Or didn't you know the Chief negotiator named Twain is his son? He saw Michael was my son and wanted them to know each other. It was no big deal. Now if you don't mind I need a drink and a nap. I'm not getting any younger standing here," he joked. With a smile, he walked into the hotel foyer. The reporters having a new angle for a good story on the two opposing sons, melted away.

Inside the elevator, finally alone, Michael stared at his father. He was one of the country's most popular Senators, a Presidential candidate some were pushing for, yet rumour said he was retiring. He'd served his country for over twenty years in the Senate, yet he'd never considered running for the top job.

"That was quite a display of working the dog back there dad."

"Yeah, sometimes giving them something surprises them. If I'd said our discussion with the General was private, they'd have snapped at us like dogs all the way to our rooms. Telling them something unexpected surprised them. The line about the drink and sleeping made them back off, thinking I'm old and needed to rest. It doesn't always work, but most of the time they cut you some lack,"

"Is the problem with Bud the reason why you never ran for President?"

"It has a lot to do with it son. Let's get inside our room before you say anything more," Coby warned, as the lift opened on their floor. Standing there on his own was Paul Devon from the New York Times.

"Good afternoon Senators. I see you got a lift with General Chew and his son? Did that have something to do with Trevor?" he accused. Michael protectively moved between him and his father.

"We haven't seen or heard from Trevor for a life time Paul. So back off!" Michael barked, suddenly angry at the mention of his stepbrother. In the background, Michael saw a secret service agent closing on them.

"So, you didn't know he lives here in Vietnam?"

"No, that's news to me, Paul. I didn't know where he went after prison," Coby confessed, his hurt apparent.

"You know I've been investigating his story, Senator. I for one now believe he was innocent," Coby seemed torn at hearing the reporter's words.

"Is everything okay Sir?" the Secret servicemen barked making Paul jump, as he hadn't seen his approach. Michael was just about to answer, when Coby stumbled and collapsed, his son catching him.

"Are you proud of yourself Paul? You two help me get him inside!" Michael ordered a worried look on his face.

"I'm sorry. I thought the Senator should know that I believe Trevor is innocent," Paul told him, as they placed Coby in a lounge chair.

"Time to leave," the Secret serviceman commanded, gripping Paul's arm.

"Trevor went to jail for murder nearly twenty years ago. What possible proof could you possibly have?" Michael growled.

"A sworn confession from the man who did it," Paul retorted. Coby having heard started to struggle for breath. Michael had heard enough and made a gesture to the Secret service man, pointing toward the door. Paul, not resisting, was steered towards it.

"No, let him stay! I want to know what he knows!" Coby pleaded, gesturing for Paul to take a seat. The secret serviceman releasing Paul looked to Michael.

"Dad, you can't possibly believe him?"

"Let him talk son, please?" Coby coughed. Michael, seeing the look in his father's eyes, relented.

"Okay, dad. Jim, you can wait outside. I'll call if there's any trouble."

"No problem Sir," Jim the secret service agent replied. He gave Paul one last 'you're dead if you try something look' before he left.

"Okay, Paul. What's this so-called evidence you've got?' Michael snapped, as he sat down next to his father. Paul, opposite, dragged a chair around and sat down facing them.

"Well as you know, Trevor was seen at the demonstration at the University you were visiting. He was also seen to throw the rock. I have talked to a lot of witnesses who were there at the protest. A few who were close to Trevor, say he was badgered into throwing that rock. Some said when he threw it, it smashed a window, twenty feet to your right."

"I remember hearing a window break," Coby whispered.

"When I questioned two others, they admitted to me, off the record, that Billy Weldon, the organiser of the anti-black rally at the University, had also thrown something. One claimed it was a piece of brick from a wall he was leaning against. This was the first time I heard that a brick was thrown. I went to the police and for a price looked at the evidence. The coroner in his summation pointed out that a piece of brick had been used."

"Why wasn't that brought out in court?" Michael asked astounded.

"Because Trevor pleaded guilty. He thought he was the one responsible," Coby answered, guilt making him tremble uncontrollably. Michael, seeing his father's condition, shouted out to Jim, who burst into the room. One look at Coby made him speak into his headset summoning an ambulance.

Twelve hours had passed before Coby awoke. Looking around, he saw Michael asleep in a chair near the window. Beside him on another chair, Paul the reporter sat typing away on his laptop unaware he was awake.

"You've got quite a story, haven't you?" Coby groggily asked, as Paul jumped and shook Michael.

"You scared the shit out of us!" Paul replied as Michael sprang toward Coby's bed.

"Are you okay? The whole world is praying for you and the hospital is surrounded by the press." At the sound of Michael's voice Jim, another agent, appeared at the door.

"Jim, you can tell the people out there he's okay," Michael instructed, as Jim spoke into his headset before he and another agent closed the door, remaining outside.

"It was just a shock, Michael. All these years I thought Trevor was a murderer and now this?"

"It's true Senator. I went to Billy's house. He's dying of liver failure, from too much moonshine. I put it to him what I'd found out. He just laughed. He admitted throwing the brick, even joked about putting that rich kid in jail. The guy's going to die an arsehole," Paul told them, seeing the look of shame on their faces for their past treatment of Trevor.

"We have to find him and tell him!" Coby groaned, trying to get out of bed.

"Hey, you're not, going anywhere," Michael informed him, pushing him gently but firmly back down.

"There's a lot you don't know son about Trevor, my first wife and his father," Coby confessed, having held it in for years.

"Now isn't the right time," Michael indicated to Paul.

"No, you're wrong son, now is a perfect time."

WHERE IT BEGAN

The story of his being awarded the Silver Star for bravery made headlines back home in America. The war hadn't become bogged down yet, and the people supported their involvement, even with the growing list of casualties and body bags. The fact that he was black stirred the people and showed that they were all equal in this action as a people. On one of his few furloughs back to the States he was mobbed by people and became a news item. The black groups struggling for equality at the time saw him as a beacon for equal rights.

Universities in many States still segregated students by colour. On one of his visits home, he was asked to speak at a local University. When he arrived, he was barred from entering the white only area, having to use the basketball court instead of the University Auditorium. This appeared in many papers, raising concerns in Washington. The movement for equality wanted him to make a stand and demand change. At this stage Coby, a young pilot, was too involved in his day-to-day fight for survival, to think about the problems back home, so he let it slide.

At one of his public engagements, he was introduced, to his local State Senator, George Van Clef. The Senator was worried by the war, pointing out that if they weren't winning, they were losing. Despite what the American armed forces and their allies were achieving, Coby had to agree with his assessment. The Senator also told him his son had just passed his pilot's training and would be heading for Nam. He asked if he ended up in his unit for Coby to look after him. At first, Coby hesitated, before explaining.

"Senator, in combat there are no guarantees. When your number is up, it's up. No matter how good you are, shit happens." Seeing the Senator take on a worried look, he sought to reassure him. So, against his better judgment, he promised to keep an eye on the Senators son if he ended up in his unit, but that was all. Senator Van Clef feeling better thanked him before leaving. Coby, in the future, would look back and wish he'd never talked to him.

Eight months and twenty days was the time Coby had been 'in country'. He still had the edge, but like many, he saw the war stretching out forever. Looking towards the command post, he saw several officers talking with the now Lt Colonel Johnson. Spotting him, Johnson signalled for him to join them.

"Captain Henderson, just the person I was looking for. This is Lieutenant Broderick Van Clef or as he likes to be called Bud. I believe you've met his father?"

"Yes, Sir. He's our State Senator back home."

"Bud's one of four recruits posted to our wing. Your wingman, Captain Jones under your training, is now ready to lead, so both he and you will have two of the recruits. I thought Bud here could fly with you."

"No problem Sir, although I will miss Jones. He knew all the right bars in town." Coby smiled, causing the others to snigger.

"Well I'll leave you two to get acquainted," Johnson suggested, moving off.

"Welcome aboard Bud. Today I'll give you a rundown on the bird you'll be flying. Tomorrow we'll take her up and do a patrol of the border. Any questions?"

"No Sir, and thanks again for this chance," Bud answered, following Coby to the hangars.

Bud was a pin up boy for all that was good in America. At just over six feet tall, with blonde hair and ruggedly handsome, he had the world at his feet. Top of his class at University he also played in the University's football team. There he had excelled, and many thought he'd turn pro and avoid the draft. Instead, he'd joined the Air Force 'to do his bit', as he called it. The talk was he was destined to follow his father into politics. Many thought he could go all the way to the Oval Office.

Coby found him a quick learner. He didn't fraternise with anyone, strictly flying. Coby, on a few occasions, had asked him to come along with the other pilots for a drink. He was polite but always refused, admitting he wasn't much of a drinker and had a young wife back home who wouldn't be happy. That aside, Coby found he had the makings of a first-class fighter pilot, always supporting him on patrols. After a month of training, Coby gave him the lead, and he became the wingman.

Fourteen successful missions later found them about a hundred miles north of the border, patrolling the no-fly zone. Bud, till then, had done everything by the textbooks and Coby, pleased, was thinking it was time for Bud to train his own wingman. His thoughts were interrupted when he saw movement amongst the trees. Signaling Bud, they turned, coming back for another pass. There, heavily camouflaged, they saw a convoy of armoured vehicles on a track above the coastal plain.

"Angel One. Have a look to your right below the ridge," Coby radioed Bud.

"I see them Angel Two. Are they ours?"

"Too far north, and the tanks appear to be Russian."

"Do we call it in?"

"Yeah just in case, but I think we'll get the first run at them," Coby told him changing frequency. "Angel Two to command, can you hear me?"

"Loud and clear Angel Two. What's up? Over."

"I've got a column of armour a hundred clicks north of the border, grid 213 by 543. I'd say they're Russian tanks. Over." Several minutes passed while Command worked out who was in the area.

"You're right Angel Two. They're not ours. Can you light them up? We'll send the big boys over."

"Will do! We'll leave a fire burning for them. Over." Coby smiled, switching back to Bud's frequency.

"Angel One, we have the okay to light the position up for some B52s that are coming in. You take out the end vehicles. I'll hit the front," Coby informed him.

"Will do," Bud replied, his voice sounding excited.

"Take care Angel One. We will rendezvous south of the target when we're finished," Coby warned. Gaining height, the two fighters separated. Coby coming around saw movement from the column as the vehicles moved off the track, their infantry deploying. Lining up the lead vehicles, Coby switched on his guns, opening up as he came in fast. Hitting several of them, he saw secondary explosions, as at the end of his dive he released his two five hundred pounders. Straightening out, he flew just above the trees, before climbing back to five thousand feet.

Glancing back, he saw both ends of the column burning, which meant Bud had dropped his bombs as well. Ground-fire could be seen reaching towards him, but at this height a hit was unlikely. To his surprise, he saw Bud making another pass.

"What's he up to?" he asked himself, as multiple flashes on his wings indicated he was firing. "He's targeting the infantry, why?" he asked himself, as up above the tiny shapes of B52s could be seen approaching.

"Angel One, the big boys are here. Head back to base," Coby ordered.

"Yes, Sir!" echoed Bud's voice, as he swiftly gained altitude to join him. Together they headed south. After landing, Coby walked over to Bud's aircraft. It had been peppered with small arms fire along the right wing. Coby pulled Bud aside and voiced his concerns.

"What were you doing back there strafing those soldiers?"

"They were moving away from the vehicles. I thought the bombers might miss them," Bud answered pushing him away. For the first time, Coby saw anger in his eyes.

"Those bombers levelled the entire area. There was no need to risk yourself or the plane," Coby pointed out. For several seconds Bud stood glaring at Coby, contempt written on his face. Suddenly, as if remembering his place, Bud forced himself to calm down. He even managed a smile.

"Sorry Captain, I guess I got carried away," he apologised and started to walk away.

"Look Bud it's no big deal, but you've got to follow orders to the letter when you're up there. Your wingman must always know what you're doing." Coby smiled back, trying to lighten the situation. He remembered his own trouble going alone on his first mission.

"No problem Coby, it won't happen again," Bud assured him moving off towards their billets. Coby watched him go, confused. Was he just carried away or was it something else? Letting it go, Coby went to the Command Centre to file his report.

A week after their attack on the column, Coby found out that Bud and he would receive a medal each for the raid. For the next three months Bud remained paired with Coby, although when not flying, the two barely saw each other. Bud now had his own circle of friends, all white. Coby, through the enlisted men's scuttlebutt, heard rumours of racist remarks from the group. Coby having no problems with Bud doubted the rumours.

Christmas that year saw the 202nd Air Wing rotated home for a short break and an introduction to their new fighters. The F5 Phantom was the new workhorse of the American Air Force. Being a different set up from the old Super Saber's meant they all had to be retrained. This would take a month for even the most experienced pilots.

On arrival back home, Coby and Bud received a ticker tape parade through their State capital. Their so-called heroic deeds in destroying the column had received far more publicity than Coby thought they deserved. Welcomed home by Bud's father, Coby was invited to stay with them for a few days after Christmas. Coby noticed that Bud remained silent during his father's invitation.

"Do you want me to come, Bud?" Coby asked, seeing anger flash again in Bud's eyes.

"Of course, I do. We're brothers in arms fighting a common enemy!" Bud exclaimed, many of the reporters writing down what he'd said, as the cameras whirled. Accepting, Coby left to be with his own family.

Coby's mother and father lived in a small county outside the capital of Georgia. His father was a plumber and a good one. Coby was their only son, so coming home for Christmas meant a lot. Unlike Coby, his parents had seen the dark side of racism. For most of their youth, they had both worked on farms, being paid below the basic wage. When his father had gone his own way and started a plumbing business, only the black population would use him. Still, he survived, even managing to put his son through University.

When Coby announced that he was staying at the Senator's house, his parent's response was happy but muted. Asking why they had a problem, his dad had pointed out that the Bud Van Clef had always been one of the loudest supporters of segregation.

"That was in the past dad. The war has changed Bud's views," Coby assured them, getting a lukewarm response. Hiding his misgivings, he decided to go anyway.

After a small Christmas celebration with his parents, their extended family and local friends, Coby left for the Senator's home. The house was deserted when he arrived, as the Senator and his son were out hunting. Shown inside by the Senator's wife, he was taken to a room on the second floor, at the opposite end of the house from the family's bedrooms. Still, the room was far superior to anything he'd slept in and even had its own bathroom. Showered, Coby felt refreshed, so he decided to go for a walk around the property.

At the rear of the Senator's home, he found a tennis court and a pool. The pool like most swimming pools was rectangular, surrounded by a manicured hedge. As Coby approached it, he glimpsed a small child aged around four years old, run along the side of the trimmed hedge next to the water's edge. Seeing no adults around, Coby panicking, dashed towards the pool. Jumping the hedge, he grabbed the child, moving him away from the edge of the pool.

"That was close son. You could've drowned!" he told the boy, who looked at him innocently.

"I don't think so. But thanks anyway," a woman's voice merrily answered. Next to Coby on a beach chair, hidden by the hedge, lay a woman in a brief bikini. Coby figured that she was about twenty something years old and one of the most beautiful women he'd ever seen.

"God, I'm so sorry! I thought the boy was on his own," Coby confessed, embarrassed.

"You must be the fighter pilot named Coby that Bud's been serving with?"

"Yeah, he started training with me, and now he has his own wingman." Coby smiled, his eyes devouring her body.

"My name's Diana, Di to my friends." She couldn't help but notice Coby's eyes starting to stray.

"Glad to meet you Di." He continued to smile, trying not to look at her breasts as he bent down to shake her hand. Knowing he couldn't stop ogling her, he decided to get away from her. "Well, I better get going and have a look around the property while I wait for Bud and his father to return."

"I'd suggest checking out the old wharf behind the tennis court before you do the circuit. At this time in the afternoon, it's alive with many different types of birds," she suggested.

"Sounds good. I'll check it out, then wander around the property following the fence line. By the way, how big is the property?"

"About one hundred acres. You should walk around it easily in an hour, even if you get lost." She replied with a small smile playing on her lips.

"I should be alright, and the walk will keep me busy, till the Senator and Bud get back."

"They could be late. When they are out hunting, time means nothing." Coby saw her smile slip as if there was more to tell.

"Anyway, I'll see you at dinner," he answered, leaving. Reaching the end of the tennis courts, Coby secretly looked back to the pool. Diana was standing up holding her son, talking to Bud's mother. She was taller than he first thought and highly arousing as she stood unaware of the effect she'd had on him.

"You're a lucky man Bud," Coby whispered to himself, his mind reeling as the vision of her near naked body, made him glad he'd hadn't stayed any longer with her.

As Diana had said, the wharf was indeed alive with birds. Coby felt an attachment to these fellow flyers, as they soared into the air to hunt, before gracefully returning. They seemed unfazed by his approach as if somehow, they sensed his love for their ability to fly naturally. After slowly sitting down on a rough wooden bench at the beginning of the wharf, he sat mesmerised as the parent birds swooped down into the river. Retrieving small fish for their young, they returned to feed their children, who sat noisily chirping on the wharf railing. He grinned as they confirmed that youth no matter what species, are oblivious to anything except eating and playing.

Looking east, he saw the sun start to dip, so leaving his fellow 'pilots' he reluctantly moved off to complete the property circuit. Beneath the rows of old oak trees, Coby had the impression he was walking on a sea of gold. The leaves, with a rich brass colour, thickly covered the ground, in some places up to his ankles. Diana's image haunted him as he strolled aimlessly along, enjoying the afternoon sun. There was something fragile about her, she was so open, so?

He couldn't find the words to give her the reverence she deserved. Coming over a rise, he saw her.

She was sitting on the trunk of a fallen tree, beside the river that bordered the property. She was now wearing a wraparound dress, over her swimsuit with a see-through blouse that revealed her bikini top. On seeing him, she waved, a friendly gesture that drew him to her. 'Why is she here?'' His mind raced as he approached her.

"Hope you don't mind my intruding on your walk?" She patted the log beside her, indicating he should sit down.

"Not at all, beauty like this should be shared. Where's your son?"

"He has an afternoon nap at this time every day. I left him with his nana. She loves to watch him sleep."

"How long have you been married to Bud?" The question seemed to surprise her, as her eyelids flickered rapidly as if she was reminded of a distant but vivid memory.

"I was eighteen when we married. We had always been childhood sweethearts." Her eyes became distant as if she remembered a special moment. Looking at him, she regained her focus. "And what about you Coby? Is there a girlfriend out there somewhere in love with you, waiting for a call?"

"No, unfortunately. Between studying at University and the Air Force I never had much the time for serious relationships," He realised there had been plenty of one night stands especially in Nam, but he figured they didn't count, as love hadn't been part of it.

"Tell me, does Bud behave himself over there?"

"Of course, he does. I've never seen him once with another woman," Coby answered, a little surprised by the question and his defence of a man he had little to do with.

"Let's keep moving before we lose the light," she suggested getting to her feet, ending the moment.

Most of the time they walked in silence, broken only by Diana's sudden spotting of a rare bird or elusive animal. Her voice became a melody to Coby, which he moved along with, always wanting to hear more. This rhythm of movement they shared, led to the occasional brush of her body against his. Like a static charge, it sent a tingle through him, torturing him, as only something unattainable or forbidden can.

Stealing an occasional sideways glance at Diana, Coby drank in her beauty. The rise and fall of her breasts through the top she wore was like torture for him. Her bikini did little to hide them as Coby each time reluctantly looked away. At one stage, overcome with desire, he had the urge to pull her to him and crush her lips with his. Cursing his morality, he refrained, knowing she was a fellow airman's wife. Still, for some reason unknown, he sensed she wanted him too.

As the music continued to flow wordlessly between them, Coby felt his bottled-up emotions trying to fight their way free. The realisation that he shared his fears and triumphs with no one echoed through his soul, as he looked at this beautiful woman, wanting to confess everything to her. Walking beside her, Coby concluded that he was desperately lonely and needed someone to confide in. Looking down, he was surprised to see his right hand trembling slightly.

Embarrassed, he quickly put it in his pants pocket, focusing on walking, not wanting to ruin his time with Diana.

"Are you okay?" Diana softly asked. Coby guessed she'd seen his hand for she sounded concerned.

"Of course, I am Di. Who wouldn't be here?" Coby forced a smile increasing his pace, not wanting to fall apart in front of her. Diana watched him move ahead before increasing her own pace to catch up. Once next to him again, she noticed his pace slowed back to their previous leisurely stroll.

"You can talk to me, Coby. I'm a good listener," her soft voice whispered. Reaching across, she lightly held his right arm. This gesture forced Coby to withdraw his hand from his pocket. Coby, silently looking down, noticed his hand no longer trembled, as he held her hand, entwining his fingers in hers.

"Thank you, Di, but I'll be alright. It's just that the war takes its toll. Being here with you makes me realise what I'm missing," he confessed, feeling her fingers tighten on his. Diana's breathing was suddenly louder as Coby's proximity made her blood race. "What am I doing?" she silently asked herself.

Since their first meeting at the pool, Diana had felt a wanton desire to be with him. It was ridiculous! She scolded herself. She'd only just met him. As she lay on her beach chair talking to him, knowing she was practically naked in her small bikini, she hadn't covered herself. Instead, she'd let him devour her with his eyes, loving every minute of it. When he'd left, she felt ashamed. It was then that Emily her mother-in-law had appeared. Picking up Trevor, she'd asked if it was okay if she gave Trevor an afternoon treat before putting him to bed. Diana made her promise not to spoil him too much, as Emily carried a happy Trevor towards the house.

Diana guiltily stood watching Emily, as she playfully tickled Trevor, making him giggle uncontrollably.

"Thank God she didn't come sooner," Diana whispered, wondering what Emily would have thought if she'd seen her brazenly showing herself to Coby. Lying back down on her towel, she tried to think of something else. It was useless, as the sun shone down, warming her. The image of Coby appeared every time she closed her eyes. It had been a long time since Bud had looked at her as Coby had, she remembered. Maybe that was it. Coby looked at her the way Bud had when they'd first met.

Getting up, she walked to the pool and dived in, cooling herself off. Climbing out, she toweled herself down, putting on her wrap around dress and sandals.

"It's a walk I need," she whispered, walking away from the house. Cutting across the property, she reached the back-boundary fence. Sitting down upon a fallen tree, she listened to the birds singing as she rested. Guiltily looking around, she knew why she had chosen this spot. It was because after telling Coby to visit the wharf by the river, he would follow the fence along the boundary past here.

"God, what am I doing?" She scolded herself watching for movement along the riverbank. After five minutes, Diana, feeling guilty for shamelessly waiting for Coby, decided to leave. She was about to get up when along the river bank she saw Coby approaching. Realizing that she knew little about this man, she was assailed by doubt.

"What if he tries to make love to me? "she whispered to herself, knowing how remote this spot was on the plantation. A vision of him ripping her clothes from her body, made her stand up. "He hasn't seen me yet. I can still leave or hide," she thought, her body trembling with both fear and desire. Caught by her indecision, she watched him approach, until he saw her, smiled and waved. Relaxing, knowing he was an honorable man, she patted the log beside her, indicating he should sit down with her.

What they'd talked about she had no idea. Her only thought was of their closeness. Sitting there, she kept imagining her clothes being ripped off, which made her flush. Fortunately, her tanned face hid her embarrassment. In the end, either she or Coby brought up Bud, ending those flashes of visions.

They'd walked along the boundary wrapped in their thoughts, broken only by her nervous pointing out of birds and animals, which distracted her from what she wanted to talk about and do. It was then she noticed his trembling hand. Shell-shocked, they called it. She had seen soldiers who had returned from Vietnam with the same tremors. It was then she took his hand. 'What now?' she asked herself, wanting to stop and make love to a man she didn't even know! Instead, looking ahead, sensing the house was near, she broke their embrace.

Coby, losing her hand, looked at her then directly ahead. As the Van Clef house came into view, he seemed briefly lost. Diana was the first to break the silence.

"Thank you for sharing your walk with me Coby." She smiled, and her hand touched his once more, in a more than a friendly handshake.

"I will always remember it Di," Coby answered, continuing to hold her hand. Wanting to say something more, she mouthed words that didn't come. Pulling her hand free she turned and left him to walk on alone.

Coby drained by his emotions, not knowing what to do or say, kept on walking. Near the front veranda, he noticed the Senator sitting there.

"Well, you've finally returned Captain. How do you like the property?" Senator asked.

"It's magic Sir. Thanks again for inviting me," he replied. Out of the corner of his eye, he saw Bud watching him from the porch on the front veranda above them. Waving to him, he saw Bud give a brief nod, before going back inside.

"Come up here and share a drink with a tired old man and I'll tell you about the world of politics." The Senator chuckled, as Coby gladly joined him. Pouring himself a drink, Coby looked down at his hands, relieved to see them both steady again.

The following day the Senator had a party at his home. Coby found his dress uniform had been picked up from his parents' home so both he and Bud could wear them at the party. Many fellow Senators flew in from Washington. They crowded round the two pilots, vying for photo opportunities with the two heroes. Many engaged Coby over the course of the war, wanting his viewpoint. Guardedly he'd answered them, giving the prepared line his commander had issued them with. "Yes, we had some setbacks, but we'll stay the course and support our allies," was one of his favorites.

Senator Van Clef knew the truth. The country was publicly being bled to death on National TV. He believed the US should cut and run, get out before the war became a complete disaster. Despite the man's arrogance, Coby considered him correct in his opinion. Of course, he never publicly backed him, having seen what happened to officers who spoke out. Diana was there as well with Bud's son. She hung off Bud's arm, smiling happily, giving the public impression of the perfect family. As time passed Trevor, Diana and Bud's son was taken inside by his nanny so that the couple could enjoy their night.

For the party, Diana had worn a long cream dress, with a matching wide brimmed hat. Hats were popular in the south where temperatures could be quite high. Watching her mingle with Senators and local people alike, Coby noticed she had a slight limp. At first, he thought her high heel shoes were the problem. As the afternoon progressed, it became evident, that she was in pain. In the end, she left the party, indicating that she wasn't feeling well. As dinner time approached, Coby excused himself to change.

Taking a short cut, Coby went up the rear stairs through the kitchen toward his room. Down the hallway, he saw one of the maids examining Diana's right leg. She'd pulled up her dress to her waist revealing her black underwear. At any other time, this would've attracted his looks, but not this time. To his horror, he saw black welts about an inch wide running horizontally across the back of her legs. Coby stood opened mouthed, recognising the marks. Someone had whipped her.

As if sensing, someone was spying on her, Diana looked past her maid and saw Coby standing there. Their eyes locked, as Diana sobbed and turned away from him in shame. The maid, sharing her pain, pulled her head to her shoulder, holding her, letting her cry. Coby unable to do anything, continued to his room. After changing out of his uniform, Coby quickly packed and carried his bag to the car. He was just about to leave when Senator Van Clef intercepted him.

"What's wrong Coby? Why are you leaving?" To his surprise, Coby saw he was genuinely upset.

"Look Senator, you seem on the level, but Bud's got a dark side."

"I don't understand Coby. What's wrong?"

"Bud's wife has marks on her legs. I saw one of the maids attending to her. When I was a kid, I saw marks like that on black people's backs after being whipped."

"We don't know for sure that it was Bud and why would he do it anyway?"

"Who else would it be and the why I wouldn't know. Just talk to him, Senator. You're his father." The Senator looked crestfallen, stood there, trying to work out an alternative reason for what had occurred. In the end, Coby's explanation seemed the only plausible one.

"I'll talk to him and make sure it stops. Can we keep this between you and me for now?"

"Of course, Senator. I'll tell no one, but he needs help," Coby warned, starting his car.

"Thank you, Coby. You keep safe over there and remember what I said about this war. I have a feeling it's going to end badly," he confessed, as Coby nodding his understanding, drove away. As he drove through their front gates, in his rear vision mirror, he saw the Senator still standing in the driveway.

Pulling up out front of his parent's house, Coby found his parents sitting on the front porch, enjoying a cool breeze on a warm balmy night. Coby grabbing his bags walked to them and sat down.

"I thought you weren't coming home till tomorrow?" Coby's mother asked as Coby kissed her on the cheek.

"Too many politicians Mum. I haven't got much in common with them. So, while they were all talking politics, I snuck out. I'd rather be here with you two anyway," Coby lied, getting a kiss from his mother in return.

"I'll get you some cake." His mum smiled fondly at him, then hurried inside.

"Why did you really leave?" Coby's father whispered, watching the door.

"Saw something I shouldn't have Dad. Let's leave it at that," Coby answered, his father nodding his head, accepting his son's explanation.

"How long till you head back to Nam son?" his father softly asked.

"Another four days Dad. We have still got time for some fishing." Coby watching his father saw his eyes start to mist up.

"We're both worried about you being over their son. Many of our friends have sons over in Nam as well. Some have died. Just be careful. Your Mum's scared, as am I." His father choked out, as his mother could be heard approaching. His father wiping his eyes forced a smile and made room for her. In silence, they eat cake, no more was mentioned about the war or his stay at the Van Clef's plantation.

The trip back to Nam took longer than expected. After being certified to fly Phantoms, the wing had to fly them across the Pacific to Hawaii, then to the Philippines, before the last leg back to Da Nang. After completing the crossing in three days, the 202nd arrived at Da Nang airfield. Below, they saw evidence of fighting all over the airfield and the surrounding countryside.

The Vietcong in their absence had launched an offensive, and the south had been caught napping. They had suffered horrendous casualties and been rudely woken up. Where before coming and going from the base had been just a question of showing your ID, now personnel had to pass through two checkpoints, each covered by tanks. Two outer circles of razor wire surrounded the perimeter, inside those two barriers; and the ground being sowed with mines.

Landing, the pilots found morale had been shot to pieces. The ground crews felt unsafe, and everyone carried a weapon. A sense of defeat hung over the base, lifted slightly by the arrival of the new planes. The F5s were tough and could take a beating and still get you home. They could also carry a larger range of weaponry at a far greater speed, making them a match for the Russian Migs that the North Vietnamese were supposedly flying.

The talk was that the Russians were supplying pilots as well, as losses to the North's Air Force had been severe and too costly to replace. Coby had his doubts, although it could explain why the Migs never came south. This side of the border, there was the chance that one might be forced to eject and be captured, something the north and their allies wouldn't want. On several of his missions, he'd seen a couple of Migs in the distance, but they always retreated, never engaging the numerically superior allied air forces.

During their training in America, Bud had moved on, having been promoted to Captain. Now he flew with his wingman, avoiding Coby and keeping within his select group of friends. On the odd occasion when they ran into each other during briefings, Bud was polite and always nodded. His eyes though always reflected suppressed anger, barely held in check for whatever unknown reason.

Operations resumed as soon as the 202nd hit the ground. Patrols, which had been a walk in the park, now became a cat and mouse game against the surface to air missiles. The enemy had infiltrated the mountainous areas around Da Nang, making even taking off and landing subject to sporadic weapon fire. Not only could they fire on the airfield, their observation posts relayed information about fighter movements and directions to their command centre. It had led to more than one raid being ambushed by mobile missile batteries, which deployed ahead of their suspected courses.

These enemy positions received priority, as the airbase had to be secured before they could mount an offensive of their own.

Infantry backed by air cover were used to locate each Observation Post. Once located, they were destroyed by artillery or air strikes. It took over a month of continuous sorties to break the enemy's back, but it was worth it. During this time, Bud became more talked about than Coby. Not just for the number of raids, but his tendency to strafe the enemy mercilessly.

Rumors of villages hit and noncombatants killed by Bud and his wingman became worrying. High Command distracted by the unrest all over the country, seemed either unwilling or uncaring as complaints about the bombing of civilians grew. This caused a major split in the 202nd air wing, dividing it into two camps. There were those who didn't care who got killed as long as the US won, and there were the ones who were shocked at the civilian death toll. The Commander, Lt Colonel Johnson, had been just about to act and transfer Bud's group of pilots when everything changed.

HIGH COMMAND

The top brass, fearing the war was sliding into the unwinnable category, decided to 'up the ante' and bomb the north. Summoning the 202nd air wing, Commander Johnson was brought up to date about what his unit would be expected to achieve. To say he was far from happy was an understatement. At the next mission briefing, he told his men what was going on.

"Gentlemen, the focus of keeping the border and the skies south of the demilitarised zone clear, are over. As from tomorrow, the North Vietnamese supply chains are our primary targets. The brass wants their soldiers' ability to wage war strangled, so it's open season on gook ammo dumps and strongholds. Anything that could be used to help them fight was to be destroyed. Any questions?" Douglas asked.

"Sir, what about anti-aircraft batteries and missiles sites? The north is full of them," a pilot asked, getting some grumbling support.

"We'll be sending in some ground attack aircraft to pulverise them and jammers to run interference with their missiles' guidance systems. They'll sort out most of the opposition. Still, be extremely careful. There's bound to be some that survive," the Colonel warned them before the meeting broke up. Coby saw that Bud's group was overjoyed by these developments. Bombing indiscriminately would now go unpunished, if reported at all. Coby's group, on the other hand, felt an ominous tone in this escalation of the war.

Coby rocketed down the main coastal road, leading south from the port of Haiphong in the north. Fearing invasion, first the French and then North Vietnamese had fortified every river crossing with concrete machine-gun pillboxes. These had become constant sources of anti-aircraft fire. The plan to neutralise the enemy's anti-aircraft response had fallen far short of expectations. Losses had grown to such an extent, that the 202nd prime objective was to dampen down the enemy's anti-aircraft positions, instead of attacking more important targets.

In charge of two wings of paired planes, Coby, today, was to play the part of the bait. He would fly straight towards the port city of Haiphong and draw the enemy's angry attention, while the other three planes watched, tailed behind and sought targets. The plan worked well, sometimes too well. Looking at his left side wing, Coby saw several holes, dangerously close to his fuel tanks. Those had come from a small island off the coast, which was supposedly uninhabited. His wingman Lieutenant Denison had taken care of them, but not before they'd sprayed Coby's plane with some sort of multi-barreled machine-gun.

"That's the price of doing business," the Colonel had told him, after another such operation. In theory, they held all the cards. Speed and surprise were with them on these operations. The problem was, it only took a single bullet, hitting the right spot at the wrong time, to end their existence. The telltale flash of tracers passing his cockpit brought Coby back to the present. Another enemy gun emplacement had fired on him, giving away its location.

Turning away, dodging from side to side, Coby watched his three guardian angels dive down from above firing on the gun emplacement as they came. Pulling up, the last Phantom dropped two bombs on the target, shockwaves spreading out as they hit. A crater beside where the gun emplacement used to be, showed one had missed. The other had hit beside the gun and with their ordinance that was all they needed.

"Good work team. That's one that won't cause any more problems!" Coby shouted into his microphone, just as something reflected in the sky above him. Gazing up, using his hands as a shade, Coby froze. There, peeling off right and coming down fast, were six fighters.

"Enemy fighters at twelve o'clock!" Coby screamed, as his three companions went to afterburners, accelerating. As much as being jumped by six enemy fighters scared Coby half to death, there was also the thrill of finally facing an enemy pilot in air combat. Fighter pilots lived to prove themselves against their adversaries. Coby hoped that this would be his chance. As they dove towards his group, Coby came to the conclusion that the enemy must've decided to make a stand and give some of the punishment back.

"Drop your ordinance and engage. And remember to watch your leader, wingmen!" He added, as, on cue, his wingmen appeared behind him.

Increasing speed, Coby watched the distance between the oncoming jets shrink as flashes on the enemy planes meant they'd launched their missiles.

"Rolling to the right!" Coby informed his wingman, as peeling to the right he rolled his plane over coming out of a half circle behind the enemy planes. Flicking on the missile tracking system, he heard the infrared tracker start to growl. Not thinking, just reacting, he launched two missiles before turning away. His wingman had trouble copying his manoeuvres but managed to launch two missiles moments later before following. To his right, Coby saw two of the enemy fighters had split his second wing. High above the Phantoms, a third pair started to dive, while the two isolated Phantoms were distracted.

Warning the two Phantoms, Coby came in fast, dividing his fire, targeting both of the first two fighters. This made them both turn away giving his trapped wing a chance to escape. Lieutenant Denison, Coby's wingman, fired a burst at the diving enemy planes as well, causing one of the luckless pilots to turn right in front of Coby. Not hesitating, Coby fired a long burst, raking the enemy plane from tail to cockpit. The pilot seeing his plane was finished, hit the silk and jumped.

The thump of metal hitting metal, sounded behind Coby, warning him. Rolling over, going into a tailspin, Coby looked for who was shooting at him. Over his shoulder he saw the ugly nose of the surviving Mig fighter from the dive, right on his tail, bearing down on him. Denison caught off guard, had veered away, having chased after another Mig that was tailing the other two Phantoms. Coby, now on his own, tried desperately to shake his tail. Looking back, he saw the enemy pilot copying his every move. He had a bad feeling that this pilot was no rookie.

"He's flying that plane like it was part of him," Coby said out loud, pulling every trick in the book to try and shake his adversary. His shadow he noticed counted every one of his moves, playing with him. "Shit, he's got to have been flying fighters for a long time to be this good," Coby concluded, going to afterburners and diving. Two minutes felt like two hours as the two planes twisted and turned trying to get the upper hand. "I've got to shake this bastard before he finishes me!" Coby cursed, as several machine gun rounds punched holes in his left wing. Rolling over again, he put his nose up and climbing instead of diving. The Mig caught off guard, dived for a split second before correcting.

"You didn't see that coming?" He laughed, getting a bit of distance on the Mig. Looking back, he stopped laughing as he saw the Mig launch another missile. Not even having time to curse, Coby flipped over corkscrewing into a dive. The missile confused by the tactic, flew past, diving towards the ground. "I've had enough of this shit," Coby growled lowering his flaps, killing his speed. The Mig completely caught off guard this time, managed briefly to fire a burst of machine-guns rounds, before it sailed past.

Coby again feeling the impact of enemy fire, throttled forward, firing a long burst of his cannon, while he had the chance. The Mig even though it was hit, still managed to roll over and tried to loop behind him. His opponent would've gained the upper hand with this manoeuvre, except that he'd allowed his speed to drop, following Coby's stunt with his flaps. That, combined with the damage he'd received, allowed Coby to copy his tactic coming out of his rolled behind him. Lining him up again, Coby opened fire.

One minute, the enemy aircraft was jigging about the sky trying to avoid his fire. The next it was a fireball, heading towards the ground. Drenched in sweat, Coby thankful he'd survived the encounter searched the surrounding skies. He was surprised to see the sky empty of enemy planes, only his three fellow Phantoms in sight.

"Looks like they bugged out? Anyone hurt?" Coby asked, his breath coming in huge gasps as his adrenaline continued to pump.

"I'm not hit personally, but my ride's not doing too well," Captain Bill Green, informed him, sounding worried. Moving closer to Bill's plane, Coby checked it over. He could see lots of damage, but nothing that should stop him getting home. He was just about to reassure him when he saw a faint mist escaping from his left wing.

"Your plane looks okay Bill, but you're losing fuel from your left wing. Try and transfer fuel to the right-wing fuel tank if possible," Coby suggested.

"That's just great. Why is it always me?" Bill answered.

"If it makes you feel any better Captain, mine will be going to the metal shop too I'd say," Lieutenant Denison cut in.

"Okay everyone, we'll all brag about our battle damage when we get home. Let's all gain some height. I found in the past that it helps," Coby advised.

"God, I thought one of those Migs had me, until you blew him out of the sky Coby," Captain Green confessed, starting to climb through twenty thousand feet.

"Did anyone else get one of them?" Coby asked, having forgotten for a moment that he'd shot down two. No one answered, so he continued. "Me getting two, is an achievement for us all, considering there were six of them."

"You got three not two Captain," Lieutenant Steward, Captain Green's wingman interjected. Coby tried to think of the third and came up empty.

"Are you sure Lieutenant? I can't remember seeing another one hit."

"When we first engaged, you fired off two rockets, before diving and strafing those two Migs that were after us. When I turned to get out of the way, I saw one take a missile right up his jet engines exhaust. The thing just fell apart, although the pilot got out," Steward informed him.

"Yeah, I saw the guy eject, although I wasn't sure who got him?" Denison put in.

"Holly shit! You came out here today to be bait and end up being an ace. I can't believe it!" Bill chuckled, the others congratulating Coby.

The return to base was not a walk in the park. After sending a report of the engagement and damage they'd received, the four planes limped back toward the border. Bill voiced his concerns about not making it, as his fuel gauge dropped. From reports, they all knew that downed American pilots just disappeared, their fate unknown. He told Coby bluntly that if the worst happened, he'd rather crash land, then jump and hang defenselessly, while Charlie peppered him. Coby agreeing made the decision and swung out over the sea following the coastline.

Doing this increased the distance they'd have to fly, although, if Captain Green had to use his parachute or ditch into the sea, he could be swiftly rescued. Twenty miles short of the border, Captain Green's plane coughed and died. Bill, in the end, decided to ditch into the sea. Taking his plane down, he skimmed the water's surface, until it suddenly touched. The impact made the plane bounced several times along the surface, before nose-diving into a wave. Pulling back the cockpit's canopy, Green inflated his small life raft and threw it out.

Jumping into the sea, he swam to the raft and climbed in. His three guardian angels flew protection above him, after sending out a mayday message. Coby, even though his plane was damaged, refused to leave Bill. Instead, he waited patiently for help to arrive. Looking at his fuel gauge, Coby knew the other two planes like himself were getting low on fuel.

"You two head back to base. I'll stay and can keep an eye on Captain Green," Coby assured them.

"Your plane is a shot up a lot more than mine is Captain. If any one should stay, it should be me," Lieutenant Steward pointed out.

"It wasn't a request Lieutenant. Get those planes back to base," Coby ordered. The two pilots without another word, peeled off, heading south.

"What's going on up there Captain Henderson?" Colonel Johnson's voice sounded through his radios speaker.

"Just sending two of my planes back to base Sir."

"You only lost one plane Captain. That means there should be three planes returning, not two."

"Captain Green's in the water. I'm not leaving him till I see a rescue craft."

"You get that plane back here straight away Captain."

"You're breaking up Sir; I didn't get that last bit. I'm losing you."

"Bullshit Captain! Don't try that shit with me!" The Colonel exploded, although there was no answer to his anger. Looking around the command centre, Colonel Johnson saw some men turn away to hide a smile. Lowering his microphone, he glared at them.

"What the fuck are you all looking at? Find something to do or I will!" he bellowed, making the men cringe, some leaving. Picking up his mike again, he continued, "When you get back Captain, that radio better be broken!" He growled, leaving the command centre for his office. Once there he sat down and chuckled. Picking up his phone, he called General Douglas to tell him about Coby becoming an ace.

Out to sea, Coby slowly circled Bill hoping by the time he got back to base Colonel Johnson would have cooled down. The only worry he had with Captain Green's location was his proximity to the shoreline. Coby estimated the shore was only about a mile from his location. All it took was one lone enemy soldier to see the rubber raft bobbing off the coast and bullets would start kicking up the water. Twenty minutes of patrolling the area and watching his fuel drop, found a vessel coming towards them.

It was a US navy patrol boat, which had responded to their call. A relieved Captain Green was picked up, the boat immediately heading south. Coby feeling relieved, return to base.

Arriving, he found the base a sea of reporters. Over the years, only a handful of pilots had engaged a Mig, let alone shot one down. Shooting down three in one engagement, making the pilot an instant ace, was unbelievable. The ground crew lined the runway as the Coby's plane thundered overhead, doing a fly past. Taxiing to a stop next to the two other planes from the mission, he jumped down from his plane after breaking off the radio headpiece.

Lieutenants Denison and Steward rushed to bear hugged him, as the ground crews ran out and surrounded them. Everyone wanted to know what had occurred including the media who joined the ground crews. Some even asked if the enemy pilots had been Russian. Seeing his men were being swamped, Colonel Johnson intervened. Gathering some of the base's security detail, he had them shepherd the three men to the mission hut, which also was the debriefing room. Once there, he had the media wait outside while he debriefed the airmen.

"Well Coby you've done it this time," Johnson started, before Coby cut him off.

"I didn't have any choice, Sir. The radio broke off in my hand. Here it is." Coby gave it to him. "That aside Colonel, I would not have left Captain Green until he was rescued, even if it meant ditching into the drink myself," Coby answered defiantly.

"I didn't mean that Coby. I meant shooting down those Migs, you idiot. The top brass wants to milk this victory for all it's worth. There's even talk of a medal from the President himself."

"It was a team effort, Sir. Without Captain Green, Denison and Steward things would have been very different," Coby pointed out, sounding relieved.

"Sir, that's not true. Captain Henderson was all over those Migs. Sure, we helped, but the victory belongs to him. He's a born fighter pilot!" Lieutenant Steward interjected.

"Well said, Lieutenant. Now you three get back out there and tell those reporters what happened. Just be careful that you don't say too much!" Johnson smiled and left.

"Shit! I thought I was in for it!" Coby confessed after the Colonel left, causing the others to laugh.

"You pushed your luck today, Captain. Your plane had by far the worst damage. You should've had either Denison or me cover Captain Green," Steward interrupted him, as they walked towards the media.

"That's the privilege of rank Lieutenant. You get to do stupid things because you can. Now let's get this over with and no bullshitting," he warned, as light bulbs started flashing.

At the mess hall that night a party was held to celebrate the victory. Coby, centre stage and plied with drinks, sat happily while the two Lieutenants didn't allow the truth to get in the way of their story. By eleven that night the celebrations were coming to an end when Captain Green staggered in. The patrol boat that picked him up, had been well stocked with booze. Green by the looks of him had fully enjoyed his return trip.

Cheering erupted as he staggered over to Coby hugging him. Coby would remember this night, as one of the best nights of his life, as he stood amongst the men of 202nd fighter group. Looking across the room, he saw even Bud raise his glass, as the pilot next to him whispered something, making him laugh. Returning the gesture, Coby raised his glass, to see Bud turn away joining a conversation with his small circle of like-minded pilots.

"Watch that one," Captain Green beside him whispered, after seeing the polite toasting between Coby and Bud. "He's out to make a name for himself Coby, and unlike you, he doesn't care who gets hurt while making that name."

"He does the job Bill. He might be a little over the top, but he is a good pilot,"

"Mark my words Coby. He'll be burning up after this to prove himself. Just keep away from him if you can. While you're here, he'll always be second best, and it's eating him up. God, you think you'd played up with his wife, the way he looks at you. Just be careful."

"Okay Bill I'll watch him, but for now, let's have another drink." Coby attempted to change the subject. Bill looked at him as if to say more, to warn him. Chuckling, he too moved on, ordering another drink. Coby somehow got back to his billet, having tied it on. Taking off his clothes, he collapsed onto his bed, lying on his back thinking. Bill's words kept echoing through his diminishing consciousness.

Was this all about Diana? The whipping and the anger, was it all to do with him going with Diana on that walk? It made sense even though it seemed petty. Bud knew he'd only just arrived and met her, so thinking they'd slept together was pretty unbelievable, no matter how much Coby had wanted to. Was it something deeper, far eviler Coby mused? He was black. She was white. What was his reason?

He'd been warned Bud was a racist but had refused to believe it. Could that be the cause of those looks? Closing his eyes, he drifted off, forgetting his worries, his dreams again filled with Diana.

Two weeks and twenty missions later, found Coby remembering Bill's words. Flying a ground attack mission, to support a Marine incursion into the north, Coby, letting Denison fly lead, ran into trouble. As the wingman, Coby was following Denison for a strafing run on an enemy position, when his engines started to sputter. Turning away, he climbed towards the coast at the same time signalling Denison and Captain Green and his wingman, that he was in trouble. Denison immediately turned and followed him. Captain Green and his wingman stayed to finish the mission, promising to follow when they were relieved. Radioing in the problem and asking for assistance, Denison watched Coby's plane slowly lose altitude.

"Stay calm," Coby spoke out loud, as his engines died.

Cursing, he tried to restart them. Three times the starter whirled, as Coby prayed the engines would answer. "Come on you bastards wake up!" he screamed, as traces flashed by his cockpit. "God, I'm that close to the ground that even the everyday Vietnamese grunts are shooting at me." He snorted, as Denison's plane screamed by, his guns chewing up the surrounding countryside.

On the fourth try, the engines caught, exploding into life. Pulling up, Coby tried to get some height. The ground fire grew in volume, as heavy weapons joined in, trying to stop the wounded bird from getting away. A loud bang, followed by pain in the back of his head, ended his optimism, as the engines again started coughing. Going to afterburners, Coby in panic used his precious reserve fuel in a desperate attempt to reach the safety of the south.

"Captain, ease up, or you won't make it!" Denison's alarmed voice sounded through his headset. Calming down, Coby cut the burn.

"Denison, I've been hit bad. What's my bird look like?" Coby asked as his breathing became ragged.

"You've got a lot of damage behind your cockpit and some smoke. Other than that it looks flyable. Where are you hit?"

"In my back and head, I'd say," Coby replied, as he became aware of a warm wet feeling, flowing down his back. "Yeah I can feel blood running, but I can still move my hands and feet."

"Well if that's all, maybe we should go back and help the others?" Denison suggested.

"Yeah Captain Green's most probably complaining already about how we left him to do all the work," Coby groggily answered.

"No, he's here beside you wondering what the fuss is all about. Your engine is running, so why did you leave?"

"Just getting old I suppose," Coby replied as his eyes fluttered, his concentration fading. Denison, behind him, watched Coby's plane start to dip over to the right.

"Captain straighten up! You're going over to the right!" He received no answer.

"Coby wake up!" Bill shouted, as Coby, his head clearing over-corrected before straightening.

"God, I must've passed out," Coby told them his voice sounding sleepy.

"Try to move around and increase your oxygen," Bill suggested. Moving his back brought a surge of pain making him scream out.

"Oh, shit that hurt!"

"That's good! Pain will keep you awake Coby," Bill assured him, having heard the scream.

"The airstrip is in sight, Sir. Can you see it?" Denison asked. In the distance, Coby saw the blur of the tarmac coming up quickly to his right.

"Yeah, it's a little to my right. I'll correct now," he answered, changing his heading. After several minutes had passed, Captain Green's voice boomed again through his headset.

"Reduce speed, Coby! You're going too fast!" Coby was fumbling for the thruster control to reduce speed when the engines died. Checking the fuel gauge, he found he still had plenty. After the fourth try, he concluded it wouldn't start.

"It won't start Bill, but from here I should be able to glide in. I'm becoming an expert at that," his voice a mere whisper.

"Well, you won't have to worry about ground speed Coby. You're going fast enough, but I'd put wheels down if I were you," Bill suggested. Dizzy, Coby fumbled again for the wheel controls.

"Straighten up Captain! You're going over to the left!" Denison warned. Shaking himself, Coby's vision cleared, as he started his approach.

On the ground, Colonel Johnson watched apprehensively, as Coby's plane swung right then left, fighting to stay level. The fire crews were already out in positions as his plane hit the ground hard. Skidding sideways on one wheel the plane straightened, all three wheels down. The Colonel was just about to say, "Thank God," when Coby's plane turned suddenly left, leaving the tarmac. It hit the soft grassy area beside the airstrip, the front wheel collapsing, as the plane flipped over onto its side.

"Oh God no! Get me a jeep Sergeant! Let's get out there!" the Colonel shouted. In the distance, he could see the rescue crews arrive at Coby's plane.

By the time the Colonel got there, the other three planes had landed. They too joined the growing crowd, gathered around the wreck of the once invincible fighter plane. It took twenty minutes to cut Coby free, while all the time foam was being sprayed, on what was left of the fighter. His injuries were critical, so he was airlifted straight to a military hospital in Saigon. The Colonel, after he'd gone, stood with Coby's ground crew, looking at the wreckage of the plane.

"I want to know what the fuck happened to that plane men! The engine stopping is one thing, taking four tries to start them again is something else. Get to it, or you'll be all out of a job!" the Colonel ordered, before returning to his headquarters. Walking straight into his office, he slammed the door behind him and sat down, trying to calm himself. His Corporal, who'd been promoted to Sergeant, entered and placed a cup of coffee in front of him and waited. When no comment was forthcoming, he spoke.

"How's Captain Henderson?"

"I'm not sure. He's pretty banged up," the Colonel confessed.

"He'll be alright. The guy's indestructible."

"No one's luck lasts forever Sergeant. There's always a butcher's bill to be paid to the God of War, and he doesn't care who pays it."

"His ground crew took it pretty hard Sir?"

"Yeah. I chewed them out over the plane's airworthiness. I might have been a little too hard on them."

"They know you're just upset like everyone else. They'll get over it, Sir." The Colonel nodded and pulled out a letter, handing it to the sergeant. After reading it, the sergeant looked thunder struck.

"My God the Congressional Medal of Honor! Does he know Sir?"

"No. I was going to tell him at mess tonight. I've been sitting on it for two days, waiting for this series of missions to end. I feel such a fool; he should've known."

"Like I said he's a fighter. He'll be all right," the sergeant assured him, moving to the door.

"Thanks for your insight mother superior," the Colonel replied, managing a smile.

"Anytime Sir."

Coby spent thirty days in the hospital recovering from his injuries. A piece of metal from the rear of the cockpit had lodged in his back. It had stopped short of his heart, coming to a halt beside his spine. The surgeons had worked for four hours, carefully removing the jagged piece of metal, knowing a slip could make him a paraplegic. Two days after the operation, the lead surgeon came to visit him. Removing the weights that had prevented him from moving, the surgeon asked him to move his toe.

It would always be one of his most terrifying and exhilarating moments of his life when that toe moved freely.

While he'd been recovering in hospital, his ground crew had spent every waking hour trying to find out the fault. One engineer, in the end, had visited Coby in the hospital. His explanation had led them to the fuel supply system. Coby had also told him to tell the crew he didn't blame any of them, which made them search even harder. The engine was all but destroyed, so they salvaged one of the fuel tanks. Taking it apart, they examined the insides.

Very little fuel remained, but they hoped to find out if contaminants in the fuel were responsible. Instead, they found blobs of grease lining the walls. Shocked and angry, they now knew it was no accident. Colonel Johnson when he was informed went ballistic. Calling in the Officer in charge of the base security, named Captain Graven, he wanted to know how some saboteur had managed to get through his security. The officer angrily pointed out that a saboteur wouldn't have just targeted one plane. He would've gone for as many as he could. He also would not have used grease, when explosives and fuel were much more efficient and on an airbase, plentiful.

In the end, both men concluded that someone on the base had carried out the sabotage. Why they didn't know. Calling an assembly of all personnel, the Colonel informed them about what had occurred. He asked that if anyone had seen anything to come forward. Most were horrified at what they saw as an attempt on

Coby's life by one of their own. Morale sank to a new low following this news.

That afternoon after he'd finished work, one of the ground crew came to see the Colonel. He wasn't completely sure he'd seen anything, but he did see one of the pilots near Coby's plane.

"Spit it out Private. Who did you see?"

"A Lieutenant named Brigham, Sir. He was on the maintenance ladder near the left wing of Captain Henderson's plane," the Private nervously told him. Brigham, the Colonel knew, was Bud's wingman. It wasn't much, so the Colonel asked the Private not to spread it around until he checked. The Colonel for a second opinion asked Captain Green to his office. When Captain Green arrived, he could see the Colonel was worked up about something. Once he was seated, the Colonel told him what he learned.

"You've got be kidding Sir! An officer, sabotaging a fellow pilot's plane, it's unheard off! To tell you the truth, I find it hard to believe," Green answered. Then a thought came to him. Johnson noticed the look on his face.

"Have you got something to add Captain?" he snapped.

"Not really Sir. It's just that group Bud hangs around with; they hate Coby. It's not only because he's black, but it's also that he is such an outstanding pilot. But it's not just a racist thing Sir. I think there's something personal, going on between Coby and Bud."

"Have you any proof?"

"No Sir."

"Then let's just keep an eye on them. Other than that we can't do anything until we're sure. And don't tell the men. They're liable to go ape shit if they think Bud's group is going after the black pilots." Johnson warned, wanting to avoid any more racial tension.

"We've got to do something, Sir?"

"Forget the 'we', Captain. Leave this to me. I know you're close to Coby, but this has to be carried out the proper way. Am I understood?"

"Yes Sir," Green answered and left.

"Sergeant, get in here!" the Colonel yelled out.

"Yes, Sir."

"Between us two, I've got a problem. It seems one of my men has threatened to hurt another. How do you think I should react?"

"For the good of the air wing, I'd say he should be transferred to an air transport unit. He can still fly, but he'll know he's been punished."

"Who said it was a pilot?" The sergeant stood as if turned to stone but didn't answer. The Colonel, seeing he wasn't going to talk, continued. "Lieutenant Brigham hasn't got what it takes to be a fighter pilot. Maybe he'll make a good Hercules pilot, flying cargo planes instead. Transfer him to the 337th Airlift Squadron in Guam immediately! He'll be happier there."

"Sounds like a good decision Sir," the sergeant replied neutrally.

"Get Lieutenant Brigham in here pronto. I'll give him the good news."

"I'll go get him now Sir," the Sergeant answered, a slight smile creasing his face as he hurried out.

By the time Coby returned to the airbase, a lot had happened. News that he was to receive the Medal of Honor did much to boost morale. Lieutenant Brigham's sudden departure, although rumoured to be because of Coby's accident, was viewed as just the Air Force's way of handling problems. The big news was Coby wouldn't be the only one going to Washington. Bud, while breaking in a new wingman, had just about single-handedly stopped an offensive, earning him the Silver Star.

He'd been patrolling an area of rugged mountains, west towards the border with Cambodia. Briefly, something reflected sunlight, which made him turn for another look. Amongst the trees, he spotted a group of heavily laden trucks, motoring along a well-camouflaged road. They were flying at twenty thousand feet at the time, and the convoy was unaware they'd been spotted. Turning for another pass, Bud watched in disbelief as the convoy turned into what appeared to be a dead end valley.

Looking more closely, he saw the walls of the end cliff open and the vehicles drive into it. The door then promptly closed.

"Hey, Gordon did you see that?" Bud asked his wingman. The Lieutenant at the time was having trouble predicting where Bud would turn next, let alone looked down.

"No Sir, what was it?"

"I'd say a secret base or an ammo dump. Either way, we're going in."

"I haven't bombed anything yet Sir."

"Well now's the time Lieutenant. Just follow me down and drop your bombs, where I drop mine. That shouldn't be too hard."

"Yes Sir," Gordon answered, sounding as if he was going to wet his pants. Switching frequencies Bud informed headquarters of his discovery. In reply, they told him there were no known friendlies in the area, so he was given permission to plaster the position.

The valley walls were steep, so they'd have to come down at a steep angle to get a shot at the hidden base. Diving, picking up speed rapidly, Bud thundered out of the sky, followed timidly by his wingman. Almost immediately ground fire erupted from the valley walls. Several bangs meant the ground fire was extremely accurate as Bud continued downwards. In seconds the valley wall with the hidden entrance filled his sights as the flashes of anti-aircraft fire sparkled around the whole valley. Bud, knowing it wouldn't get any better, released everything he had.

Pulling up the stick he felt the plane shudder as free of its heavy ordinance it accelerated away. Four five hundred pound bombs behind him hurtled towards the hidden cave entrance, as Bud cleared the valley and raced away.

When the first shockwave hit him, Bud felt the entire plane vibrate, before nose-diving into a spin. Behind him, the horizon became a fiery red then dark brown, as the mountain valley roared into the air. It was as if a volcano had erupted, the valley walls crumbling as the mountain expanded, before retracting, crumbling in upon itself. Gaining control of the plane, Bud couldn't believe what had happened. The entire mountain was gone, replaced by a depression filled with a pile of rocks.

"Wholly shit did you see that?" Bud said out loud.

"Yes Sir, although I'm amazed you're alive."

"How come you are Gordon? You were supposed to be behind me. You should be dead," Bud pointed out, having only now remembered his wingman.

"When they started shooting at us, I was hit, so I turned away. I've still got my bombs."

"Any other time, I'd have your arse for not following me down Lieutenant. This time we'll make an exception, as you're still alive."

"Will we make another pass Sir?"

"Why? There's nothing left. I doubt even the AA gunners survived on those hills. They must've had a shitload of explosives down there. I've never seen an explosion that big before," Bud admitted, wondering what was down there.

"Are we going back to the base now Sir?"

"Yes Lieutenant, I think we earned our pay."

The enemy position contained nearly the entire North Vietnamese Army's reserve ammunition for a coming summer offensive. The attack still took place, but without ammo, it soon ground to a halt, with heavy losses to the Viet Cong. High Command had been ecstatic, showering praise on Bud and the air wing. Bud even seemed to have softened his attitude towards Coby, being there to welcome him home.

"The Medal of Honor! God, the girls, will go crazy for you now!" Captain Green screamed out above the noise in the mess hall, the night of Coby's return. Toasting Coby yet again, Captain Green even raised a glass to Bud, forgetting past troubles.

"Boy, I wish there were more Migs around. I'd like to get a shot at one," Gordon chimed in, trying not to fall on his face.

"Be careful what you wish for Lieutenant. It might come true," Bud warned, hoping he'd get away with his fake change of heart.

"I got lucky Lieutenant. I was in the right place at the right time. If I hadn't seen them coming down, we mightn't be here," Coby admitted, the alcohol taking its toll.

"Bullshit. It was your instincts that made the difference. You looked up because you're a good pilot Coby. That's what it's all about!" Captain Green interjected, toasting Coby yet again.

As the night drew to an end, Bud, having had more than he should have, stopped at a latrine for a piss. Leaning against the wall with one hand to support him, he felt a pistol press itself against his temple.

"You fooled the others tonight Bud, but not me. I catch you near Coby's plane in the air or on the ground, and I'll shoot you down you cocksucker," Bill warned, before pistol-whipping him across the back of the neck.

Waking twenty minutes afterwards, Bud found his uniform soaked with urine, from where he'd been laying in the urinal. He got up shakily and looked around before sneaking back to his billet. Grabbing another uniform, he tossed his soiled one in the bin, before showering. Clean, he returned to his bed sleeping. The next morning as he walked to the mess with his group of friends he saw Captain Green approaching.

"Sleep well, Bud?" Bill asked as he walked by, as if nothing had happened, making Bud furiously stare after him.

"What was that all about?" a friend of Bud's asked.

"Nothing that can't wait!"

After a lot of enforced rest, and two months of waiting, found Lt Colonel Johnson, Bud and Coby, plus many other servicemen and women, marching up the driveway towards the White House. They were greeted by flashing bulbs as the media tried to capture the soldiers at their finest. In synchronised formation, they came to the wooden platform, erected outside the White House, where the President and his wife watched and waited. The passing servicemen and women saluted, turned and did a loop before they came to a halt.

"Company! Right turn!" a sergeant screamed. Turning to the right, they all stood at attention, facing the platform. The President came forward and inspected the men and women, who represented nearly all the services. Demonstrators from the anti-war movement which was in full swing at the time were barred from entering the grounds during the presentation. Instead, they made their presence known through chants and loudspeakers, along the boundary fence.

Like many members of the armed forces, Coby was offended that the servicemen were the targets of all this hate. These men were serving their country, like millions of others had through the ages. If anyone was to blame, it was the politicians who sent them overseas. They should be the ones targeted, not the ones following orders. But the servicemen were easy targets. In their uniforms, they stood out.

"It's a sorry day when servicemen can't come home to parades without this nonsense," Senator Van Clef confessed, as he walked up and stood beside his son.

"That's democracy for you, Sir. We mightn't always like it, but it's what we fight for," Lt Colonel Johnson replied, happy to be there, away from the war.

"Well, for now, let's think about why we're here. Demonstrators or not you three have earned those medals. No one can take away that!" the Senator exclaimed, waving for the cameras.

The medal ceremony was a solemn occasion. President Nixon had just taken office and being a military man himself, wanted to present the medals personally. The constant heckling from the demonstrators annoyed him, although he did his best to ignore them. The medal presentation was scheduled by order of medal merit. The "lesser" ones, although still incredibly hard to earn, were awarded first. Lt Colonel Douglas received a Bronze Star, for a raid he'd led to rescue a downed pilot. Coby didn't know the full details, but rumours suggested that against orders he'd piloted a chopper and rescued a downed pilot just over the border.

It seems with a major raid going on up north; they couldn't spare a Medivac chopper for an hour. Douglas, wanting his pilot back safely, didn't want to wait. Commandeering a chopper, that was being repaired at the base, he put together a crew and headed north. They luckily found the pilot and rescued him, while he was on the run from a platoon of enemy soldiers. He should've received at least a Silver Cross for his bravery, but High Command hadn't been happy with a Lt Colonel risking his life. Douglas didn't care what he got. He'd rescued his pilot, and to him, that was all that counted. Still, as Coby watched, he saw how proud Douglas was to get that medal.

The next group was the one Bud belonged too. These men had earned the Silver Star, the second highest medal level you could earn. In his dress uniform, Bud looked every bit the all-American hero. All the participants received a rousing cheer from the gathering. Bud, who was well known, received a louder response from the crowd. Last, to be presented, Bud joined the crowd of onlookers and was joined by Diana and Trevor.

Bending down, Bud let his son touch his medal, as the media fought for the perfect shot of the perfect family. To the outside world, they had everything going for them. Coby, watching, knew differently. 'God, he could pull it off and become the President someday,' Coby thought, as he saw the drill sergeant nod for him to start moving.

Marching towards the platform, as the drill sergeant had taught him for the last week, Coby sensed the cameras swinging in his direction. That day he was receiving the only Congressional Medal of Honor. Rarely was this medal presented for outstanding bravery.

"Ladies and gentlemen, we now present the Congressional Medal of Honor to Captain Cornelius Henderson," echoed from the address system. Coby, stiff as a board with stage fright, briskly walked up onto the platform.

The crowd, seeing a black Air Force officer climbing onto the platform stilled. Even the demonstrators who had been so vocal became silent. Coby had never felt so humble and yet so proud, to be standing in front of the President, while his armed feats were read to the audience. Coby didn't remember much of what was said until the President lifted the Medal of Honor by its long ribbon, over his head and placed it around his neck. It hung down next to the Silver Star from his first mission and the Bronze star he'd earned with Bud.

"Congratulations Captain! Your country applauds your bravery under fire," President Nixon announced, shaking Coby's hand.

"Thank you, Sir. It's an honour," Coby replied, wondering if he should've answered, before saluting his Commander. The crowd, hushed during the presentation roared their support. Even the demonstrators clapped, if not despondently. In the crowd, Bud, standing with his family, had a hard time hiding his contempt.

"Is everything okay Bud?" Diana asked, noting his look.

"Of course. Why wouldn't it be?" He smiled back, his eyes full of suppressed anger. Diana guessing the problem didn't say anything further, just continued to play the loving wife. Across from them, Coby walked down from the platform to be greeted by his mum and dad, plus a handful of relatives, some he hadn't seen for years.

"You made us all proud son!" his father managed to get out, as he cried, hugging his son.

"Just be careful from now on Coby. You take such risks over there," his mother said softly touching his arm, as a reminder that he was her son first before country.

"He's a fighter pilot. He doesn't know what careful is!" Lt Colonel Douglas loudly proclaimed with a grin, having heard Coby's mother. He joined her and the rest of Coby's family, in celebrating his bravery. It would be Coby's last fond memory of Vietnam.

The next stop was a press conference where Coby mainly fended questions about the course of the war. Finished, feeling drained, he excused himself, in need of some fresh air. His parents had left, travelling back to one of their relation's homes where they were staying, on the outskirts of Washington. Coby had arranged to meet them there later that night at a party in his honour. For now, Coby just wanted to sit and think, so he walked around the grounds of the White House, looking for a quiet spot to take a break. Finding a bench behind a large oak tree, he sat down to rest.

There was a cool breeze blowing from the north, as Coby silently watched the responsive trees stretch, straighten and bend again. It became hypnotic as Coby, with a yawn, drifted off, his long day catching up with him. How long he'd been asleep for, he wasn't sure until he became aware of a voice whispering musically to him.

"A penny for your thoughts?" a familiar melody asked from behind him. Coby was dumbfounded to find Diana standing there, holding her son's hand. She looked every bit as sensual as she had the first time he had seen her. Coby at first couldn't find the words to answer, as Diana sat down beside him, Trevor hopping onto her lap.

"How are you, Diana? Did you see the presentation? Bud looked good getting that medal," Coby fumbled, hating to bring Bud into any conversation.

"Yes, I'm sure it will help his career path. It's funny you mentioned Bud getting his medal and not your own. The Medal of Honor is an incredible honour to have bestowed on you. From what I've heard you deserved it ten times over; let alone the others you are wearing."

"Everyone over there who serves deserves a medal, Diana. You have no idea what it's like."

"That's what I like about you, Coby. You're always looking after the others who don't get the recognition. Some might consider them unimportant." Coby didn't hear all she said, only the part about liking him.

"Where's Bud? I bet you're all going out for some slap up celebration with the Senator?" Coby sensing something was happening between them, tried reluctantly to prevent it.

"Bud and the Senator have already left. They're meeting with some of the Senator's influential friends to discuss Bud's future. I'm to meet them later at the hotel. Bud doesn't like me involved in politics." Diana sounded disappointed. A silence developed between Diana and Coby, as Trevor moved towards Coby, fingering his medals. Knowing fate was now in his control, and he didn't want to stop it, Coby spoke up.

"How about we go for coffee?" he suggested, his heart racing.

"I'd like to Coby, but Bud has a problem with me being seen with you," Diana whispered, looking embarrassed.

"Is it because I'm black?" Coby snarled, as Trevor picking up his voice's anger, moved back to Diana's side.

"No, not really. The problem is, he thinks something is going on between us," she softly replied, her eyes downcast, not looking at him.

"Is there?"

"No, of course not, we hardly know each other," she replied, as her face flushed.

"Then let's have a coffee somewhere private, just the three of us." Diana for several seconds studied him, before relenting.

"Okay, I know a place." Writing out the address, she handed it to him. "I'll meet you there in an hour." She nervously smiled, before picking up her son and moving back towards the White House. Coby in her absence stared at the address. It wasn't a coffee shop. It was the address of a home here in Washington.

"What am I doing?" he asked himself.

Paying the cab driver who for the tenth time repeated how proud he was of him, Coby alighted. In his dress uniform with the Medal of Honor swinging from his neck, he looked anything but discreet. Walking up to the door, he rang the doorbell waiting. Moments later Diana opened the door.

"Before you ask, this is my sister's house. They're away on holiday in Europe, and I promised to call in and check to see if everything was okay," Diana explained looking sheepish. "I thought since you were worried about being seen with me, this was a good place."

"Diana I'm worried what your husband might think, not about being seen with you. Coming here if we are discovered, would be worse than if we had gone to a coffee shop with Bud at the next table."

"I'm sorry Coby. It's just that during our walk, I felt we'd made a connection. Bud saw us, which is why he reacted so badly and beat me. I suppose in a way, it's my fault."

"In no way was it your fault, Diana. We were just walking together and nothing else! No one has the right to whip or punish someone like that. The guy needs help!"

"Well, we're here now. Let me make you that coffee." Diana smiled, changing the subject. Coby knowing he was crossing the line, entered. Following Diana, he walked through the lounge into the kitchen. Opening the back door, Diana led him outside. At the rear of the house was a small porch. Coby sitting down took in the view, as Diana prepared coffee. He wasn't sure how long he'd sat there, but looking up he saw Diana standing inside the door looking out at him.

"Are you okay?" she asked, as Coby shot out of his chair and opened the door for her, before answering.

"Yes. It's just being here so far from the war; you realise how important little things are, like sitting on a porch waiting for a woman to join you for a coffee." He smiled, as Diana with a tray loaded with cups and jugs squeezed passed him. Laying out a tablecloth on a small table, she arranged the cups pouring them both a coffee. A comfortable quiet settled over the two as they sipped their coffees, looking over the rear yard. All the adjoining yards had no fences, which created a park like quality. Two large maple trees dominated Diana's sister's yard.

"The maples don't look that old. Were they here when your sister moved in?"

"No, Greg, my sister's husband, is a Canadian. Before moving to Washington with her, Peggy had the two trees planted so he wouldn't get homesick. They're ten years old and are already monsters. It takes Greg a full day to clean up the leaves in the fall. Peggy says he enjoys every minute of it." Diana giggled.

"I never was much for gardening. Always thought it was time-consuming. I'd rather fly," Coby admitted absentmindedly, his love for flying still his passion even in war.

"You'll have to take me up someday?"

"That I can promise you." Coby laughed, as again silence descended, broken finally by Diana.

"Is this a mistake?" she whispered her eyes misting up.

"No Diana, it's one of the best days of my life. The problem is you're married to a man I serve with. Personally, we don't have a friendship, and it angers me that he beat you. But we're brothers in arms, fighting for what we believe to be a just cause. Many would think I was betraying him by just being here, let alone falling in love with you." Coby stopped talking, as he considered the gravity of what he'd said to her.

Diana at first didn't reply. She sat looking at Coby as her eyes again misted up. She wondered if he'd just flippantly said the words and didn't really mean them.

"Coby, I," she got out as Coby stopped her.

"I know what you're going to say, that it's absurd, that we don't really know each other that well. It's just that since the day when we walked together, I've been infatuated with you. You've captured my heart, Diana. I'm in love you," he stammered, and timidly reached across, placing his hand on hers, as if the very act betrayed them both.

"I feel it too Coby. I know it's wrong, I'm a married woman, but I'm drawn to you and want more than anything to be with you," she confessed, tears running down her cheeks. Coby felt his heart pump wildly, as he felt her soft trembling hand enfold his. Standing, he pulled her up from her seat and towards him. Wrapping his arms around her waist, he held her body against his, as a small moan escaped her lips. This soft sound made him momentarily stop.

Fearing he was moving too fast and that she might pull away, he ended the embrace. Looking into her eyes, he saw her smile, as the realisation that the moan, was of her willingness to surrender to him, not fear. Seizing the moment, he again pulled her to him, his need for her becoming unbearable. Tilting her head back, he kissed her lightly on the lips, the sensation rocking him, as he savoured her capitulation to him.

Her lips he found were so soft, so fragile, that he held himself back, scared that he would crush them. Her hand, resting on his shoulder pulling him to her, reassured him, as he hungrily flattened his lips against hers. Their passion grew as Coby's hands roamed over her body, each movement making Diana moan and press herself against him, wantonly enjoying his maleness. Suddenly as if remembering where she was and what she was doing, Diana broke away from him.

Trembling with both arousal and shame, she wept as tears flowed down her face.

"I have to go Coby. I want to stay but I can't!" she pleaded as she backed away from him, her eyes looking haunted with guilt.

Coby, his heart pounding, stood speechless, his pent-up emotions and pain trying desperately to break free. He wanted more than anything to beg her to stay with him, to continue that kiss or even just hold him. Anything would have been better than leaving him alone. In that instant, he became aware that he needed someone to share his pain and that frightened him. Up until this moment, he'd been able to hide his psychological wounds from his constant combat inside the regimented life of the Air Force. Now with his growing love for Diana, his fear of dying without a wife or children or a life for that matter, made him wonder how long he could go on without help.

Looking at her, he tried to find the words, to explain his pain. Instead, he sadly nodded his acceptance of the situation, unable to reply for fear of ruining what he had received in the way of love from her. Without a word being spoken, they picked up their discarded cups placing them back on the tray. Carrying them to the kitchen, Diana washed while Coby wiped. Once everything was put away, silence returned. Coby overwhelmed with want, pulled Diana to him. This time the kiss was full of suppressed hunger, as Coby pushed her back against the wall. They fervently enjoyed what they both saw as their last moment together. As before, Diana broke the embrace.

"Please Coby, don't make it any worse than it already is?" she cried, pushing him away.

"I don't want to leave you, Diana. I want to make love to you," he confessed. Reaching for her, he pushed her up against the wall, pulling at her underwear.

"No Coby! Please not here and not while I'm married!" she pleaded. Coby heard her through his lust and hesitated, before stopping. "I want you to Coby, but now would make it seem like I was cheating on Bud. I know he doesn't deserve my loyalty, but he is my husband, and until I end my marriage, we will have to wait." She sadly pointed out, holding back tears. Coby for several seconds stood facing her, unable to answer. His heart was racing like a fire truck, as he gulped down mouthfuls of oxygen, to try to placate the adrenalin surging through his system. Gradually calming down, he backed away from Diana slightly, until he regained enough control to talk.

"Promise me at least that will you will keep in contact, that you'll write to me?" Coby groaned, his body trembling with suppressed hunger for her.

"Yes, I'll write, although I'll use a different name just in case," she promised, as guilt crept into their moment.

"What's your full name?"

"Diana, Annette Van Clef."

"Then use Annette. That way I'll feel a bond with you," Diana agreed, as Coby stole one last kiss.

Coby left first after calling a taxi. He felt both elated and at the same time frustrated by her. Frightened, he knew how close he'd come to ripping the clothes from her body, in his need to have her in the kitchen. It frightened him how much he wanted her, even to the point of forcing himself upon her. He'd luckily kept control, although next time it might be different. Somehow, he knew she would've let him and that's what drove him crazy, knowing she wanted him too.

"Next time I won't be able to stop," he said out loud, as the taxi driver looked back at him.

"Do you want me to stop Captain?" he asked, having only heard part of Coby's ranting.

"No keep going, I was just thinking about something else."

"I bet you were. Those medals must make the women go wild?"

"Not as much as I'd like," Coby answered, the driver chuckling.

Arriving at his hotel to change before meeting his family, he found a small media contingent, waiting for him. Asked how he'd spent his day after receiving the medal, he'd told them that he'd spent it in quiet contemplation, remembering brothers in arms who hadn't been as lucky. Moving passed them, he was just about to enter the hotel when a reporter asked a question, which would change his life forever.

"Captain, what do you think of segregation at our Universities and in the country overall?" The question at first surprised him. Having not been told to avoid it, he answered.

"Black soldiers and white soldiers live and die together in war. In the past, we segregated our forces but not today. If we are to move forward as a nation, it must be with equality for all Americans, no matter what their colour or background," Cody replied. To his surprise, some of the media clapped.

Across town, Senator Van Clef was attending a fundraiser for another member of congress, when a TV screen showed Coby outside his hotel. Wearing his uniform with the Medal of Honor hanging round his neck, plus his two other medals pinned to his right coat pocket gave him a movie star like quality. The room was full of some of the wealthiest people in America, but all conversation stopped when he was asked the question on segregation.

Whoever was on the camera, knew their stuff. Not only was it a clear picture, but it also zoomed in now and then to Coby's Medal of Honor and his face. It gave the whole speech a professional look. Senator Van Clef's views on segregation were different from most of the Senators from the southern states. He'd seen the ugliness of racism first hand as a child and secretly wanted it stamped out. Many of his constituents didn't see it that way, so like his fellow Senators, he avoided the subject.

Looking around the room, he noticed many clapped as Coby finished speaking. When he first met Coby, he had seen straight away that the kid had Presidency written all over him. That was quite a vision, considering Coby was black. He remembered chuckling about it, thinking how incredible it would be to have a black president. Then he'd soberly thought about it.

"Why not?" he'd said out loud, thinking about the groundbreaking moment it would be for America. Looking at his son who was also watching, his heart sank when he saw the sneer on his face.

"That Captain's got a big future, Bud. You mark my words son. He's going places."

"He's just an uppity nigger, who can fly a plane," Bud smirked, liquid spilling from his glass as he spoke. The Senator stood there as if time had stopped. He thought back to Coby's remark about Bud needing help after finding he'd whipped his wife. The Senator, angry, tried to talk with him, but found him unbending, convinced he had done nothing wrong. The problem with Bud was that he'd spent too much time in private schools with his rich friends. Living a pampered, if not isolated existence, he'd become a bigot, judging everyone by colour and their social standing.

"Go home, Bud. You've had too much to drink!" his father ordered. Bud sneered at his father as he left. The Senator watched his son use his charm on the other people in the room, as he made to leave. These people would some day back his campaign for a Senate seat and then with luck, a run at the Presidency. He began to strongly suspect that Bud didn't deserve it at all.

"I've failed him as a father!" Senator Van Clef sadly concluded, knowing he'd spent too much time away in Washington, instead of being a father to Bud.

"Are you okay Senator?" Robert Charles, his press secretary, asked. Robert had been his press secretary for five years. A Harvard graduate with a political axe to grind, he'd met the Senator while attending a rally for equal rights. Robert's parents were Mexican by birth and had crossed the border searching for a better life. With hard work, they now lived the American dream, putting Robert through college and then University, something unheard of in their hometown south of the border.

When he first met Senator Van Clef, he thought he was just another Southern redneck politician, hiding his hate of all things not white. Debating him on equality he'd attacked the Senator accusing him of covering up the racism in his State. To his surprise, he found the Senator was honestly offended, his true beliefs in equality visible for all to see. Later, after the debate, the Senator sought him out to offer him a job helping him change people's generational views. Robert accepted and never had reason to question his decision.

On several fundraisers, he'd met Bud, or Broderick, which was his birth name. He'd found him a little aloof as if talking to Robert offended him somehow. He put it down to his being uncomfortable with the media attention at these functions, having probably been told by his father to keep a low profile. At one such fundraiser, Robert had been in his father's office, which adjoined the conference room. Bud with some of his University friends, were in there drinking. Someone mentioned the Senator's press secretary, which made him stop and listen.

"How can your old man put up with having a Border crosser working for him?" one voice enquired, as the others sniggered.

"My father always had a soft spot for Wetbacks. I can assure you if I make it into the Senate, he'll be the first out the door!" Bud's angrily replied. The others sniggered and hooted their support. "We'd better get back to the gig. There's money to be extracted from the gullible," Bud said chuckling, as he and his friends rejoined the party.

Robert stood there shaken by what he'd heard. Angry, he thought about going to the Senator and having it out, then resigning. He hadn't, knowing he admired the Senator and this matter would hurt him deeply. Instead, he kept his distance from Bud hoping the bigot would trip himself up, ending his chance of a political career. Instead, he'd firmed as a future nominee for a Senate ticket, something Robert hoped to stop. Now as he watched the exchange between Bud and the Senator, he wondered if the Senator himself would stop his son.

"I'm okay Robert. I'm just disappointed in my son."

"Why? Bud is intelligent and looks good in that uniform. He'll go far with a little support," Robert pointed out, watching Bud leave, hiding his true thoughts.

"Would you vote for him?" the Senator asked, watching Robert hesitate. "Exactly! You see Robert, you know him personally. The people don't."

"Senator, with his military background and his looks, he could go all the way to the White House. Don't worry, he'll mature once he's back home," Robert lied, although his doubts echoed through his voice.

"He's not fit to be President, Robert. You know that, as well as I do. Let's leave it for now. I've got to get re-elected, and this war is starting to hurt my support."

"You'll get back in, or I'm out of a job," Robert grinned, trying to lift the senator's mood.

"I wished you'd been my son Robert. You make me proud to be an American," Senator Van Clef confessed, putting his hand on Robert's shoulder as they walked out together. It was one of the best moments of Robert's life.

Back in Nam, Coby felt what he always did whenever they returned from America. The clouds of defeat were rolling in from the north. The South Vietnamese forces had become bogged down by corruption. Funds which were desperately needed to buy weapons and ammunition were being syphoned off by greedy commanders. They sought to fatten their coffers then flee the country before the end came. Now America and its small group of coalition partners seemed to be fighting the north on their own, while the wealthy in the South fled. Da Nang was still relatively secure, although constant mortar attacks and the occasional artillery peppered the airfield. For the first time, Coby concluded that he didn't want to be here.

There was also Diana. She seemed to be everywhere, filling his dreams day and night. There were so many unasked questions in their relationship if you could call it that. Would she leave Bud for him and what part in her thinking would her son Trevor play? Also, there was the colour issue. Diana seemed okay with his being black, but many people would have a problem. Sure, society was changing for the better, but the black-white situation in America had always been tricky. Even his parents might have a problem with his being with a white woman. He smiled and shook his head, thinking racism went both ways.

On the flight back, Coby had been seated next to Colonel Douglas, while Bud was towards the back with some news correspondents from the States. Luckily, he seemed unaware of his meeting, or as he hoped, his first date with his wife. He could still remember that kiss, so fragrant and yielding, yet so tantalisingly unobtainable. It left him frantic for another. The Colonel seeing him deep in thought broke into his daydream, to give him some secret if not worrying news. He told him of an upcoming raid high command was planning. It was a bold, dangerous move.

The plan was for four planes to breach the air defences of North Vietnam towards the Chinese border, where it was believed the Communist leadership of the North would be meeting with its backers. The bunker where the meeting would take place was a forward position facing China, and the military liaison officers from both China and Russia would be present. More importantly, Ho Chi Minh, the leader of North Vietnam would also attend, making its targeting a priority.

This was the first time the Military had intelligence on the elusive leader, supplied by a leak in Moscow. Coby figured high command was desperate to come out of Vietnam with a win. Killing the North Vietnamese popular leader might cause a leadership vacuum. The North would have many contenders, destabilising the country for some time. Worse case the country would remain divided, with the Americans going home, maybe not winners, but not losers either.

The Colonel warned that anti-aircraft batteries of missiles and guns would be everywhere. It would be no walk in the park.

"Why don't you use B52s? They'd pulverise the entire area?" Coby interrupted wondering why four Phantoms.

"The proximity to the border with China means we can't afford to hit anything on China's side of the border. The war is going badly enough, without China coming in boots and all," the Colonel pointed out, resuming his clandestine briefing.

For the task, it was decided that Coby and Captain Green would fly decoy, while Bud and Captain O'Neil would bomb the target. Coby and Captain Green would still be armed with bombs, just in case, the other two didn't make it. Otherwise, their primary job was to be decoys, to protect Bud and O'Neil's arses. Finished, the Colonel asked Coby's opinion of the raid.

"It seems a bit risky Sir. A lot of things can go wrong even before we reach the target. Are we doing that bad?" Coby whispered.

"Soldier to soldier, we're killing ten of them for every man we lose, but it isn't about how many we kill. It's about who can take the punishment long term. In a war, we'd drive north and wipe them out. Here in a police action, we can only defend. The American people want their sons home. They don't want them dying here for what they see as a corrupt government. If we don't pull this off Coby, I think we'll be going home losers."

"Well then, we better get it done," Coby replied managing a smile as well.

"That's the spirit! We'll start planning the raid once we hit the ground," Douglas answered, as Coby returned to his daydreaming about Diana.

True to his word, Colonel Douglas once they'd landed at Da Nang, ordered Coby and the pilots involved in the operation to begin planning and training for it. The mission, of course, energised Bud. He would have overall command, despite Coby's seniority. This was because he was handling the primary objective of the mission, the bombing. Although Coby had his misgivings, as time passed, he recognised Bud's experience in ground attacking targets was invaluable.

The plan was for Coby and Green to come in dumb as if doing a recon patrol along the coast then along the border with China. They would, of course, attract all the attention, while Bud and his wingman at tree height, travelled up the border with Laos and come in from the west. Timing was everything, which caused a problem. Since secrecy was paramount, no recons or practice runs were allowed. Bud seemed unconcerned by this, while Coby worried about the unknown. As the day of the attack grew nearer, Coby's gut instincts warned him the raid wouldn't go as planned.

4 am with the light just starting to break through the darkness saw the twenty serviceable Phantoms of the 202nd fighter wing, wheeled out onto the tarmac. A massive raid on Hai Phong Harbor by thirty B52s supported by sixteen Phantoms from the 202nd would help cover Bud and Coby's wings.

As the planes thundered down the runway, Coby watched Bud and his wingman head inland rapidly leaving the main force, moving west towards the border with Laos.

"Be safe you two," Coby said to himself, hoping they'd be okay. Sitting there, he guiltily contemplated how his life would be so much simpler if Bud didn't return. He had to admit it would save him a lot of problems if Bud bought it on this mission. "Wake up to yourself!" he said out loud, hoping he was a better person than the type who would see gain in someone's death.

Coby and his wingman Captain Green tagged along with the main force until the predetermined point where they peeled off, running north out to sea. Behind them, inland from the coast, they saw the telltale shockwave from Hai Phong Harbor, as the B52s released their loads. Coby was just about to comment on the raid when he remembered they were radio silent until after the attack. Attracting Bill's attention by signalling, Coby pointed towards the shock waves. Bill in return, gave him the big deal sign, meaning their mission was far more important.

Reaching a designated point south of the Chinese border, Coby leading, wiggled his wings indicating Captain Green should follow him inland.

"Well here goes nothing," Coby muttered. The countryside below him, seemingly empty, silently watched their progress. Two hundred miles short of their target, things started to go wrong, as Coby's threat proximity radar began to beep. Knowing they had been detected, Coby dropped radio silence.

"Four bogies are coming toward us from the south!" he warned.

"Well, we are the diversion. Let's put on a show, shall we?" Bill answered. At Bill's reply, Coby armed two of his missiles and edged south. As the distance decreased, Coby heard the growl of the infrared sensors on his console from his two active missiles. It grew in volume, as they sensed and locked onto the incoming targets.

"Missiles away!" Coby warned, as two streaks of light left his wings racing south. Turning away from the missile's flight path, Coby saw Green launch his two missiles, then turn and follow.

"Let's get some height!" Coby suggested, climbing using afterburners. Two flashes from the direction of their missiles disappeared meant they'd hit something. Now hopefully there were only two enemy planes to deal with.

"Two less to worry about?" Coby stated the obvious to Bill.

"Yeah, but what happened to the other two?" Bill queried, as they continued toward the target.

"They may have bugged out and run for home, or they are waiting up ahead," Coby suggested, searching the sky. He came up empty, as his mind turned to Diana and what she would make of him being on a raid with Bud.

Her last letter indicated he'd hurt her again. Why he wasn't sure, as Diana had revealed little. He had a sinking feeling it could be connected to their so-called coffee together. Back at base, he'd been so angry; he'd nearly gone to Bud's billet and confronted him about it. The problem was if he did and there wasn't a connection, he would've revealed they'd been keeping in touch by writing to each other. He was pondering what he should do when he heard Captain Green scream a warning.

"Coby! To your right!" he yelled. Coby reacted instantly, flipped his plane over, diving. Behind him, Captain Green's plane followed, as the two Migs dived down towards them. When their missile had intercepted the incoming enemy planes, the two survivors must've gone for the ceiling, climbing far above them. This would've hidden them from their search radar. Now as they came in for the kill, Coby cursed his stupidity for letting his mind wander. Coming out of the dive, he saw Green trying to evade the two Migs behind him.

Immediately he saw these two planes were different than the three he'd tangled with before and shot down, earning him the Medal of Honor. Studying them closely, he concluded that they were the latest Russian fighters, not the old models the Vietnamese usual flew. The wings had Chinese flags on them.

"Fuck they're Chinese!" Coby said out loud.

"I don't care if they're English Coby! Get them off my tail!" Bill yelled back. Coby quickly thought of a plan.

"Turn right and dive Bill! I've got an idea!" Coby shouted as Bill, without hesitation turned right and dropped like a stone. While the Migs followed Bill, Coby turned hard left and dived, his plane shuddering as the airframe felt the G forces of the sharp turn. Ahead he saw Bill's plane coming straight towards him!

"Dive under me!" Coby screamed as Bill's plane filled his front window. The shock of their near collision, caused Coby's plane to stall, as the Migs behind Bill's plane, roared towards him. Firing his guns at the approaching planes, he could see the look on the two pilot's faces as they both turned sharply, climbing above him. They avoided his fire, but by doing so, lost their chance at Bill. Tumbling earthward, Coby reignited his jets, soaring up. He relocated Bill above him. Of the Migs, there was no sign.

"Shit Coby you're not getting senile, are you? How'd you miss them?" Green asked as they both looked around for the two enemy planes.

"Sorry, I was distracted by the two hits. Did you see where the two survivors went?"

"Nah, I was too busy praying! I've also got some bad news for you. I took a few hits in the engines. My power's down by twenty percent."

"You can't go on with your plane damaged Bill. Can you make it back?"

"I'm not sure Coby, but I've got to go right now to have a chance at all." Coby sat there thinking about the mission before answering.

"I've got to keep going, Bill. I'm afraid you're on your own!"

"I understand. Just be careful Coby and concentrate! That was a rookie mistake back there, even though you made up for it with that Kamikaze manoeuvre you pulled. That my friend was unbelievable!" Captain Green chuckled as he relived the move.

"Just remember when you get back that you only got one of those Migs,"

"If you don't make it, I'm claiming both! So, you better survive!" He laughed, turned away and diving for the coast. It was lucky that he did, as his radar warned that two enemy fighters were up ahead. At first, he thought they were waiting for him, but then he saw the explosions on the ground. In the excitement of the dogfight, Coby had travelled the distance to the target bunker.

Bud and his wingman had arrived while the Migs were attacking Coby's wing. The fighters must've been recalled when Bud's group started their attack.

Watching, he saw Bud's wingman diving on the bunker, which was shrouded in smoke. He'd just cleared the area after dropping his bombs when the two fighters jumped him. He didn't even get time to react, as his plane plummeted into the ground. Bud, seeing what was occurring, intercepted the two Migs chewing one to pieces. The other had got on his tail when Coby arrived. Coming in behind him, he saw the Mig let loose a storm of fire on Bud's plane, before he opened fire, cutting the Mig fighter in half.

"About time you got here!" Bud angrily bursts onto the radio.

"There were four Migs Bud, not two. They damaged my wingman too. He's running for home on reduced power!" Coby retorted. "Did you get the target?"

"Yeah, although you better drop your bombs, just in case,"

"No problems. I'll go down," Coby replied, wondering what Bud was playing at. To him, the target looked completely gone, that aside, Bud was in charge, so he dived towards the smoke. Coming in fast, Coby felt the plane getting plastered by anti-aircraft fire. Clearing the smoke, he dropped his bombs, on a giant crater. He could see there was nothing left of the base. Coming back up to Bud, he kept his anger under control.

"Did you hit it?" Bud asked, merriment in his voice.

"Yes! Lucky, I went down. You both only damaged it."

"Let's head for home," Bud answered abruptly, accelerating towards the coast.

For twenty minutes, they travelled in silence during their cautious approach to the coast. Once in sight, they turned south. The first sign of trouble was when their fighter's threat detectors beeped.

"I can see surface to air missiles are coming up fast behind us!" Bud warned Coby, betraying his nervousness by telling him something he already knew.

"Drop a pattern of decoys and head for the ceiling!" Cody answered, releasing his decoys and climbing vertically using his afterburners. The decoys were for all intents and purposes, large flares. Their job was to create heat, the target of the infrared guided missiles coming towards them. This time they did their job as four explosions echoed behind them, vibrating their airframes.

"How far to the coast?" Bud asked, as again the threat detectors started beeping.

"Dive into a valley below us as fast as you can!" Coby ordered, already doing it.

"Shouldn't we go vertical and climb again?"

"We're too high already Bud. They'll be on us before we can gain any height and the decoys don't work as well up here where the airs thin. Better we get as close to the ground as we can. It confuses their guidance systems," Coby informed him, watching his screens. Diving towards the trees, Bud followed Coby as the missile climbed passed them then turned to follow them. Straightening out at tree height, Coby knew the missiles were closing rapidly.

"Release your decoys now Bud!" He yelled, letting his go as well. Again, the decoys worked, as the missiles impacted the valley walls behind them.

"Shit that was close!" Coby bellowed, his forehead dripping with sweat. Bud, as usual, remained quiet. "Okay let's stay down low at tree height for a while." Bud silently followed. Unfortunately, this time, their luck ran out. As they cleared the valley and started their run south, a battery of anti-aircraft guns tipped off to their approach, opened up. Caught looking the other way, both fighters received multiple hits.

"I'm hit, Coby! I'm losing fuel from my left-wing tank!" Bud warned.

"Pump what you can into the right-wing. You won't save much, and you'll be lopsided, but it might make all the difference," Coby suggested. Bud, for several seconds, remained silent.

"It's done, although I'm not sure how much I saved."

"Okay let's take a run a little further to the east, down through Ha Long Bay. It'll add a bit more distance, but it's a lot safer and if nothing else, it's a beautiful area to fly through," Coby answered, trying to lighten the mood.

"They're out to get us, aren't they?" Bud chuckled, finally relaxing.

77

"We may have just killed their illustrious leader Bud. I can't see them letting us just go home without taking a few shots," Coby replied, as again their threat detectors started to beep.

"Looks like missiles, but I can't see them!" Bud yelled, looking around trying to see the threat.

"They're above us, Bud! Probably a couple of Migs launched them. So, climb, it's our only chance!" Coby shouted back, going to afterburners, rocketing upwards. Bud slightly slower, did the same, only to be hit by one of four fired missiles. Unperturbed, he looped a full circle, locking onto one of the incoming Migs. Giving it a long burst of cannon fire, Coby, saw the Mig shudder as Bud's rounds impacted. The Mig pilot must've thought Bud's fighter was finished and came in for the kill, only to become the quarry himself. Coby watched the enemy fighter burning from end to end, as it spiralled down into the ocean.

As he was just about to congratulate Bud when another two enemy fighters fired on them from above. Rolling and turning frantically, Coby tried to outmanoeuvre the smaller, faster opponents. While killing one, Coby received multiple hits from the other, as the remaining Migs, seeing two of their number shot down, decided to bug out. Relieved, Coby saw Bud's fighter climb and pull up alongside his.

"Coby, I'm finished!" Buds voice flatly echoed through Coby's headset. Coby had to admit Bud's fighter was in a bad way.

"Don't give up Bud! It looks bad, but you can make it."

"I'd like to believe that, but that last missile hit my left wing. Although it didn't do much damage, it's taken the rest of my fuel. I'm on vapor's," Bud informed him, voice tense.

"Just keep heading south Bud. We are nearly clear of the Bay. Every minute you stay up is another couple of miles closer to our side of the border," Coby reminded him, as smoke started billowing from Bud's plane.

"Oh, shit Bud! You're on fire!" Coby warned. Bud, seeing flames coming from his engine's exhaust, cut his engines. He then sent out a mayday as he slowly headed downwards.

"And I thought I had trouble with no fuel!" Bud sniggered, as Coby followed.

"There's a stretch of beach up ahead. Try landing there! I'll cover you."

"Forget me, Coby! Keep going!" Bud told him, aiming for the beach.

"Would you leave me?"

"In a heartbeat Coby. You know that."

"When you're down, I'll radio your position and head back to base. For now, I'll stay and fly cover."

"Thank you, Coby. For a black man, you're okay!" Bud sniggered, as lining up the sandy beach he lowered his wheels.

The Phantom accustomed to smooth bitumen or a concrete runway hit the sand hard and fell apart. The landing gear crumpled on impact as the plane became an overweight sled. Sliding sideways the right wing was ripped off causing the cockpit to somersault several times. Coby, feeling ashamed of his earlier thoughts, watched it end up on its side.

Bud, coming to after being knocked unconscious, slowly took in his situation. Unfastening his harness, he fell against the cockpit's roof section. Unable to unclip and push it out, forced him to pull the emergency release, causing himself and the roof section to fall free of the plane and hit the beach hard. Knowing the enemy could be there at any moment, he quickly scanned the area as he grabbed his survival bag and groggily started ran south along the beach.

A relieved Coby looking down saw him at last leave the plane. Making sure Bud was clear, he fired on what was left of the aircraft, destroying it. Reporting Bud's position, he was about to leave and return to base, when a group of enemy vehicles arrived at the northern end of the beach.

"Damn! They'll be on him in minutes!" Coby told himself, turning back. Coming in fast from the sea, he sent an avalanche of fire into the surprised enemy troops, Coby turned for another pass. He had destroyed all their vehicles when the unexpected happened. A lone soldier with an ordinary AK47 assault rifle opened fire. He got lucky hitting something important in Coby's plane's engine. At first, Coby thought he'd be okay, then his engine spat smoke and coughed. A shudder passed through the fuselage as fatally damaged; the engine caught fire.

"Fuck! I'm in for it now!" Coby screamed. Turning south, he killed the engines trying to put some distance between him and the enemy, while keeping above the coastline. His plane managed several miles before the fire spread towards his fuel tanks, forcing him eto eject. While dangling from his chute, he watched his plane become a flaming arrow, diving into the ground. The impact caused a massive explosion, which mushroomed, sending black smoke billowing into the air.

Landing a couple of hundred metres from his plane, Coby figured he was about three miles further down the coast from where he thought Bud had crashed. Unclipping his parachute, he pulled out his pistol looking around. The troops who had shot him down would be there soon. After what he'd done to them, he couldn't see them being his best friends when they caught him. Moving silently, but swiftly, he headed southeast towards the coast.

Digging his way through the thick vegetation, Coby, at last, reached a hilltop vantage point above a beach. Turning south, he jogged for two hours continually looking behind. Seeing it was getting dark, he reversed his course and headed north. Bud and Coby were following a set 'pilot down' program. Their instructions, if shot down, were to head south, then backtrack. The rescue people would expect to pick them up a couple of miles north of their last known location. It was a sound strategy, as long as you didn't run into the bad guys following you.

To avoid this, for the most part, they'd leave a clear set of tracks on the coast heading south. They would then hide their tracks when they turned inland. The trick was to get enough distance away from the coast to remain unseen, yet be free to travel at speed. Vietnam's coast has continuous dense foliage making navigation in the jungle difficult. Coby and Bud had both discussed this at briefings, suggesting the best idea was to let the enemy pass, then strike north. It was a lot simpler planning than actually doing it, Coby thought, as he watched a squad of twenty soldiers rush south along the beach beside him.

Waiting ten minutes just to be sure, he was about to head off, when an officer and a radioman came along the beach. Diving back to the ground, he saw the Officer hesitate and call on the radioman to stop as well. Coby had never been so scared in his life, as he lay amongst the undergrowth, waiting. The worst part was he didn't know if he'd been seen or not. Holding his breath, he waited, expecting at any minute to hear the approach of footsteps. That he figured, would be followed by a loud bang, as the officer discharged his weapon, into the prone scared to death fool lying on the ground.

Instead, he heard the sound of amusement as the two men shared a joke, before moving off. Waiting another ten minutes, Coby fearfully looked around, before standing and urinating.

"God that feels good," he whispered shaking slightly, as he started running north along the beach.

Trying to disguise his direction, Coby ran in the footsteps of the enemy soldiers who had moved south. It wasn't long before he reached the smouldering remains of Bud's plane. Continuing, he came upon the burned-out wrecks of enemy vehicles. The smell that wafted from the area confirmed many of the troops had been trapped in their trucks. Gagging, he vomited, before running further north along the beach.

With his compass and the help of a small torch, Coby figured he'd reach the pickup point. The sky had clouded over, and it was starting to get dark. Coby feared that Bud, if he was here, might shoot him by mistake; or depending on his mood, deliberately. Moving from the foliage onto the beach, he saw a dark shape move to his left.

"Is that you Bud?" he softly asked, his weapon pointed at the shape.

"Yeah, it's me, Coby. What the fuck are you doing here?"

"I saw a mobile patrol pull up to the north of you after you crashed. I softened them up a bit before one of the bastards got lucky. I crashed to the south about two miles inland."

"That explains the explosion I heard. They didn't follow you did they?"

"No, I'm pretty sure they didn't, although you can never tell."

"Do you think it's safe to use our beacon yet?" Bud asked sounding nervous.

"It's dark enough, and the light will only be picked up out to sea if we position it carefully," Coby answered confidently. Moving to a rock outcrop, they placed the two lights both of them had carried, just above the water level. They then gathered pieces of wood and debris washed up onto the shore, to shield them from the landward side. Moving back, they checked their work, finding the lights difficult to see from a distance.

The beacons were small, but powerful beams of light, which flashed a pre-determined signal. With luck, it would be spotted by their navy rescue boat sent to locate them.

"What now?" Bud whispered.

"We wait. It's all we can do," Coby then collapsed down onto the sand, feeling drained.

As the day turned pitch black, Coby understood the irony of being on a beach with the husband of the woman he loved. Feeling for his pistol, he remembered Diana telling him about her latest beating. It had occurred just after the medal ceremony, and Coby wondered if Bud had found out about their meeting. If he knew, there'd be no better time to get rid of him than right now. Feeling slightly afraid, Coby looked into the darkness studying Bud as he lay ten paces away from him. He appeared to be staring right at him.

It was getting near 2100hrs when Coby's overactive imagination started to hear the sound of what he thought was someone walking on the sand to the north. Seeing Bud react too, Coby, slightly relieved that he hadn't imagined it, saw the dark outline of someone walking casually along the beach towards them. Pulling out his knife, Coby got into a crouch position behind a solid piece of driftwood and waited. Bud had moved back up into the foliage bordering the beach, either to await the outcome of his encounter or to flee. Which, Coby couldn't be sure of.

A figure now outlined in the moonlight could be seen walking along the beach near the water's edge, with what appeared to be a small net over his shoulder. He stopped twenty paces short of Coby, tossing the net into the sea. 'It's a young kid!' Coby made out as the boy gathered in his net and walked towards him. The youth on reaching the driftwood stopped as if he'd hit a wall. 'He's seen me!' Coby assumed, as springing forward, he grabbed the kid. Covering his mouth with his hand, Coby told him to keep silent in Vietnamese. The boy nodded he understood, as Coby wrapped his belt around his hands behind his back. "What will I do now?" Coby asked himself, as Bud reappeared beside him.

"Kill him," Bud ordered, pointing his gun towards both Coby and the boy.

"There's no need for that! Once we are picked up, we can let him go," Coby explained, his hand straying to his weapon.

"I'm in charge here nigger! You do as I say, or I'll shoot you both!" Bud growled, raising his voice. Coby saw he was on edge and moved the boy behind him.

"That's not going to happen, Bud. Lower your weapon, before you do something you'll regret."

"I won't regret anything boy! I should've dealt with you after you first made eyes at my wife. Did you think I didn't know about you screwing my wife in Washington?"

"I didn't sleep with Diana, Bud. We met, but that's as far as it went."

"It doesn't matter boy! You've got this coming." He sniggered, as he pulled the trigger. Coby saw the gun jump in Bud's hand at the same time the bullet hit him. Catapulted backwards, he landed beside the frightened boy. Seeing Bud's attention turn to the boy, he rolled over covering him with his body as he made to draw his weapon. He pulled the weapon clear of its holster but had no time to fire, as his gun was wrenched from his hand.

"If you hadn't been trying to save that kid, you might've got a shot off!" Bud snarled, as he aimed at Coby's face. Coby didn't know what to say, pulling the boy closer, as a shot rang out from behind Bud. Bud's face seemed stunned as if he was trying to register what happened. He slowly toppled forward, face-down beside Coby and the boy. Not knowing what was going on and close to passing out, Coby told the boy in Vietnamese to run.

Crying, the boy did as he was told and began sprinting up the beach. He had travelled only a few paces when a voice called out in Vietnamese.

"Twain stop!" The sprinting boy froze.

"Daddy!" he sobbed, turning and running back towards where the shot had come from.

Coby looking into the darkness could see the outline of two men standing above the beach on a small dune. At the boy's approach, one dropped his rifle and embraced the boy.

Captain Chew was home on leave after being hit in both legs by mortar fire near the border to the south. He lived with his wife Kim and their son Twain, in a small fishing village on the south side of Hal Long Bay. Earlier that day the village had received word that two enemy airmen could be in the area after both were shot down. The message informed them that the two pilots were wanted for some heinous crime against the North and all the villagers were confined to their village. This was awful news to Twain. Since his father's return, Twain had wanted to try a new fishing net his father had bought him, while he was away.

There was always some reason why he couldn't go, and now with enemy pilot's close, he again was stopped from using it. Deciding the chances of the airmen coming north were zero, Twain decided to wait until dark and sneak out. Chew and his wife were having dinner at a fellow officers' family, so wouldn't know he'd gone. That night, as soon as his parents departed, he quickly seized his net and slipped out of the village.

His clandestine trip would have remained a secret, except his father's friend had asked to see his son's new net. When Chew returned home, he'd found both his son and the net were gone. Angry he'd told his friend what had occurred, as they'd both grabbed their weapons and started looking. They'd arrived at the beach just as Coby had captured his son. Waiting for their chance, they'd seen the black pilot shield Chew's son, before the white pilot fired.

Shocked at seeing the white officer approach the black pilot and his son with his gun aimed, Chew opened fire. In disbelief, he heard the black pilot tell his son in Vietnamese to run for it. Calling his son made him stop and run to him instead. Walking forward, guns raised, Vietnamese Officers saw the black pilot, although shot in the side, stand and face them.

"What do we do with him?" Chew's friend asked. Chew stood looking down at the dead pilot for several seconds, as out to sea the sound of a motorboat could be heard approaching.

"Nothing Soug. He saved my son's life. I'll not have his blood on my hands," Chew replied, as Soug beside him nodded his agreement.

"Go home pilot! Don't come back!" Chew said in broken English to Coby, as the two soldiers and the boy walked up the beach, disappearing into the undergrowth.

Coby stood there for several minutes unable to believe he was alive and free. Collapsing, he pulled out a field dressing from his leg pocket, wrapping it around his waist. Tightened it, stemming the flow of blood; he injected a small vial of morpheme into his stomach to ease the pain. Knowing he'd done all he could, he crawled over to Bud. Turning him over, he saw his lifeless eyes staring skywards. In a way, Coby now had what he'd wished for. His way was clear to be with Diana. Cursing himself for even thinking that, he closed Bud's eyes and covered his body with his emergency raincoat.

"What do I tell Diana now?" he whispered, as the sound of muffled footsteps made him look up. Standing over him looking down, were six blackened faces.

"Are you okay Sir?" one asked, his eyes drawn to the body beside him.

"Yeah took one in the side. Captain Van Clef was shot as well but died of his wounds."

"Where are the enemy soldiers?" another asked nervously. Coby sat staring at Bud for several seconds, before answering.

"Bud held them off after I was shot. I don't remember much. I guess they thought we were both dead? Or they went to get reinforcements?" Coby suggested. The soldiers looked at each other in amazement.

"We better get out of here then?" the first suggested, as they picked up Coby.

"Don't leave Bud! He's a hero," Coby choked out. The men nodded their understanding.

"You're both heroes, Sir. We wouldn't leave either of you here, under any circumstances," said the first soldier, clearly their commander, as the other soldiers carried Bud and Coby to their rubber raft.

STATESIDE

Coby's injuries proved far more life-threatening than first thought. Patched up in Saigon, he was airlifted back home to Washington. There he spent many weeks in Beersheba Hospital in the critical care wing. Hallucinating, he several times saw Diana standing beside his bed holding his hand, as Trevor looking broken, stood beside her, staring at him. Other times he saw his family and members of the 202nd. It was only after three operations that he became aware that the dreams were real.

From an orderly at the hospital, he found out that Captain Bud Van Clef's wife and son had visited him many times out of respect for his friendship with her husband. His family and Colonel Johnson had also come many times, just to sit and talk to him. Bud, he found out, had come home a hero. Bud's bravery while fending off Vietnamese soldiers to protect Coby, earned him the Medal of Honor.

He'd been carried on a gun carriage through their States Capitol, followed by the President, Diana, Trevor and Senator Van Clef. The 202nd had also flown over the Capitol, a spot in the formation empty for their lost comrade. Buried in the family graveyard on the Van Clef plantation, the country mourned, as the funeral was televised throughout America. For many, it proved the turning point in the war.

Coby, of course, missed all this, as he fought for life, still on the critical list. Coming out of his coma after a month, he opened his eyes to find himself alone in a hospital room. Blinking several times to clear his eyes, he saw fresh flowers beside his bed.

"Someone must love me?" he croaked, as an orderly poked his head around the corner in shock.

"My God you're conscious!" he cried out, pushing the nurse call button next to the bed. In no time the room filled with medical staff who thoroughly examined him, before calling his parents. Three hours later his family arrived. Emotions were raw, many crying, at what they saw as a miracle.

"Did the others make it?" Coby croaked out, while drinking water from a straw a nurse was holding for him. Why he'd asked, would forever haunt him. He had no idea where that question came from, but it was his first thought. Silence became a tomb, as everyone looked for someone else to say something first.

"No one else made it son. Bud's wingman died over the target. Your wingman Captain Green is missing in action, believed dead. Bud died defending you!" his father sobbed, having always felt bad about Bud.

"Did we get Ho Chi Minh?" Coby asked as the room gasped in shock.

"Can everyone leave the room for a few minutes thank you?" an Air Force Officer who appeared from nowhere, asked from the doorway. Although polite, it sounded more like an order. "And people, not a word of what Captain Coby just said, is to be repeated. It's a matter of national security," he warned, as Coby's family and the staff reluctantly moved outside. Once the room emptied, the Officer relaxed.

"I'm sorry Captain Coby to interrupt your time with your family, but the mission you were on has been classified."

"Why?"

"Two reasons. One we didn't get their leader. He was delayed and escaped the bombing. Two, several high-ranking Russian and Chinese Generals, were there as well as several of the North Vietnamese general staff. To prevent turning, this so-called police action into a full-scale war, we decided to pretend it didn't happen. Both Russia and China would have lost face over the death of their people. If the success of the raid became known, they'd be forced to take military action. I know it stinks, but that's the way it has to go," he told him with a shrug.

"Is there any word on Captain Green?" he managed to say, broken-hearted at the thought of his friend's disappearance or more likely death.

"I'm sorry Sir I wouldn't know."

"You don't have to call me Sir. We are both Captains!"

"I know that. It's just an honour to meet you Captain Henderson," the officer replied, before saluting and leaving.

Once the ghost officer had disappeared, his friends and family flocked back in, welcoming him back. The talk of the mission's purpose had been removed from the chitchat. After an hour of catching up, a nurse appeared at the door. Pointing out the time, his family slowly left, promising to return. In the end, just the nurse remained.

"Well hero, it's time for your tablets and a quick wash, doctor's orders." The nurse smiled, as another nurse joined her. Both nurses were attractive. One was a white nurse, with a pile of blonde hair tied in a bundle behind her head. She was cute and the younger of the two. The other nurse, who did all of the talking, was an African American. She was more than just pretty. With her hair cut short, she appeared all business, although her full figure made Coby hope otherwise.

Watching him, a smile creased her face, as if she had read his thoughts. Pulling back his sheets, both nurses tried not to smile, as they began sponging him, causing him to go red.

"I think I can do that myself," Coby murmured, moving to grab the sponge.

"Hey, we've seen it all before Captain. When you're well enough, you can do it yourself. For now, let us naughty nurses enjoy ourselves," the older nurse replied, causing the other to laugh hysterically. 'Yet you'd be a handful,' Coby thought to himself. In the end, he had to laugh as well, knowing the first thing lost in a hospital was your modesty.

When they finished, Coby thanked them, getting a seductive, "Anytime," from the first nurse. The other couldn't contain herself giggling.

"Hey, you didn't tell me your name?" Coby asked as they neared the doorway.

"That's easy Captain. It's Nurse," the elder of the two replied and then left him alone.

"Thank God, I'm out of bed at last!" Coby chuckled, ambling to his bedroom door. It had been two weeks since he woke and this was the first outing on his own. One careful step at a time he walked down the corridor adjoining his room. Several orderlies clapped as he passed, giving him the thumbs-up as well.

"Where do you think you're going Captain?" a Nurse's voice erupted as he passed their station. The orderlies suddenly disappeared leaving Coby alone to reply.

"I'm okay. I just need to walk around the ward for some exercise," he answered giving his best smile. The nurse scowled and grunted, which Coby interpreted as reluctant approval, so he kept going.

"Men are just boys with beards!" the most senior nurse exclaimed, the junior nurses agreeing with their superior, as Coby sheepishly moved around the corner out of sight. Checking behind him to make sure he wasn't being watched he shuffled to an open lift door, stepping in. As the lift moved slowly to the ground floor, he started to feel feverish, making several people in the lift look at him.

"Are you okay Sir?" a male nurse asked.

"Yes,ÅŒ, just getting some fresh air," Coby replied as sweat started to run-down his face. The male nurse didn't answer, but Coby could see he was worried. As the door opened the other occupants let him out first, their concern evident. Coby summoning all his strength walked into the foyer where several nurses from his floor were waiting to get in.

"Good morning nurses." He smiled, walking past them before going out the front door. In the glass door's reflection, he saw them watching him before they hurriedly entered the lift.

"Shit they'll squeal on me as soon as they reach the nurse's station!" he said out loud, trying to hurry into an adjoining park. Exhausted, he collapsed onto the first bench he came to. Knowing he'd pushed himself too far with this little escapade, he took deep breaths trying to calm down. Eventually, he felt a bit better and looked around. It was so good to be outdoors after months bed-bound in hospital. Rising above the pain, he soaked up the sunshine, peace and fresh air, so glad he'd escaped if only for a short time.

After several minutes, he began to feel faint again. The wound in his side throbbed. Bending forward, he steadied his head with his hands, as nausea gripped him, making him shake. How long he sat there alone fighting his waves of sickness, he wasn't sure. But as time passed, so did his pain and the uneasiness. The sound of birds singing in the trees drew his attention letting him again take in his surroundings. Breathing deeply, he felt each breath rekindle his spirit. A sudden thought came to him. 'I can't hear any sounds of war!'

There was no shooting or the thud of impacting ordinance through the ground. There was no roar of planes landing and taking off, no shouting men around the barracks, where he used to spend his down time. The only noise sources, was the road outside the hospital and the sound of birds in the trees. 'God I've missed this so much,' Coby confessed, his eyes awash with tears.

"Are you okay Captain?" a musical yet concerned voice whispered beside him. He didn't have to see to know that voice. It had been the only thing he'd thought about since his last trip to Washington. Looking up into the sun, he saw Diana's face silhouetted as if she was an angel. Smiling, overcoming the shock of seeing her there, he wiped his eyes clear. He was just about to tell her how her very presence lifted him when he remembered her husband Bud was dead.

"Diana, I don't know what to say," his voice broke, as she reached down to hold him. Behind them, a reporter seeing the shot of his lifetime snapped off a picture. With the caption, 'Fallen hero's widow comforts the man her husband died defending'. The image would portray Coby, a Medal of Honor recipient as a broken man. It would appear on the front page of every newspaper across America. It would lead the nation down a path to increasing skepticism over their involvement in Vietnam.

Of course, the truth of the photo told another story. Guilt over their secret liaison weighed heavily on both of them. Coby knew Diana deserved the truth about how Bud died. The problem for him was whether she would believe him. Throwing caution to the wind, he knew he must tell her the truth.

"Diana, I need tell you something. It must stay between the two of us."

"It's about Bud's death, isn't it?" she asked, surprising him.

"Yes, it is. How do you know?"

"Bud knew I had been with you. That night when I met up with him at the hotel, he asked how my afternoon was. I told him I visited my sister's house to check on it for her. Without warning he struck me, knocking me to the floor. He knew you were there; he had me followed. Blind with rage, he whipped me with his belt so badly that I was unable to leave the house for two weeks. Trevor witnessed the beating. He told him I'd been with a nigger. His last words before he left, was that he would see you dead.

"After that night, I found it hard to believe he would lose his life, saving yours," she told him and started to cry again. "So, what did happen that night Coby?" she sobbed.

He told her everything. He watched her watching him, knowing she believed every word.

"So why did you lie Coby?"

"I don't know. Maybe it was for Trevor or Senator Van Clef so that they could remember the father and the son they wanted him to be. I couldn't have him remembered as a man who wanted to kill a boy so he wouldn't be caught. It would sound so hideous, and many good men died on that mission. I wanted them all remembered as heroes. Bud would've tarnished what they'd tried to achieve."

"So, what about you and me Coby? Where does this leave us?"

"You're the wife of a national hero. We will wait until a suitable time has passed and be careful in the interim," Coby whispered, as if even talking about it could lead to their discovery.

"I want to be with you, Coby. I know it's too soon, but Bud and I were over with a long time ago."

"There's also Trevor, Diana. He can't know any of this. Let's at least wait till I've recovered, then we'll meet," Coby promised. With great care, Diana kissed him on the cheek.

"I will wait forever if that's what it will take. Let's go back to your room. I have a surprise for you." She smiled for the first time.

"What's the surprise?"

"You'll see?" she replied, helping him to his feet.

The walk back with Diana was both a relief and excruciating. Knowing she still wanted him and believed him was everything. The hard part was he'd pushed his body too far, and every step became a mission of its own. After exiting the elevator, Diana called for help as an orderly fetched a wheelchair. As he was pushed passed the nursing station, no one had to say anything. The judgmental looks the nurses directed toward him said it all.

By the time they reached his room, for the first time since he'd been admitted, he looked forward to getting into his bed. Instead, he saw someone was already occupying it. The sheets were pulled over the patient's head giving him a departed look, which made the orderly pushing Coby freeze in the doorway.

"What the fuc!" the orderly started to say but stopped himself because Diana stood beside him. Instead, he moved around the wheelchair and approached the bed. Pulling back the sheet as if the departed man might leap at him, the orderly jumped back when the patient in the bed sat up.

"Surprise!" Captain Green yelled, startling both the orderly and Coby. If he hadn't been in the chair, he'd have been on the floor, so shocked that he was. Captain Green seeing how pale and unwell he looked, quickly jumped out of bed and moved to him. "Are you okay?"

"Yes, I'm okay. It's just that I was told you were dead Bill!" Coby confessed, tears running down his face.

"No way! I just got a little lost that's all," Green replied, tears in his eyes as well, as he hugged his friend.

"God I'm so glad you made it Bill. It makes the mission more acceptable somehow."

"Yeah, we didn't even get the big guy, although we scared the shit out of the others!" Green happiness was contagious.

"Well, how did you pull it off? How did you get out alive?" Coby asked. Diana decided to leave the two of them alone for a while, excused herself, to find a phone. Both men watched her leave before Captain Green spoke.

"That woman's quite something, isn't she?" Green was watching Diana walk down the corridor to the lifts.

"Yeah, the orderlies say she's been visiting me while I was in a coma. Bud's a lucky man," Coby responded before he grasped what he'd said. "God that was a terrible thing to say. The poor guy's dead."

"You know as well as I do what Bud was like Coby. I won't be shedding any tears for that jerk. Diana on the other hand, I feel sorry for," Green admitted, pausing before continuing. "What happened out there, Coby? I hear he saved your life and is a hero. I don't believe that horseshit for a second!"

"Let it go, Bill. The truth will only hurt more people," Coby's eyes drifted towards the door.

"There's electricity between you two. I'd watch that if I was you," Bill said softly, seeing Coby take on a haunted look.

"Nothing happened between us, Bill. I would've loved if it had, but it wasn't to be."

"She's single now?"

"She's in mourning Bill. I'll keep my distance."

"Then you're a noble fool, although you always were." Bill chuckled, moving on. "Anyway, I now tell you honestly how I escaped, although I might embellish just a little," Bill conceded, as Coby swapped the wheelchair for his bed.

CAPTAIN GREEN'S ESCAPE

After leaving Coby, Bill set off for the coast, keeping down low to avoid radar tracking. From the coast a little north of Hai Phong Harbor, he headed out to sea, before gradually turning south about ten miles out. Without warning his cockpit filled with smoke. Checking his fuel, the needle still indicated the tanks were half full. Surprised by the amount he still had, he tapped the gauge. The needle, which must have been jammed, immediately fell to empty! Cursing, he guided the plane down towards the sea. Trying to radio his position, proved useless, as his communication equipment had stopped working.

Smoke continued to spread throughout the cockpit, making reading his instrument panel difficult. Cursing again, he knew he was now too low to jump. Taking a chance, he released the cockpit cover, hoping to clear the smoke. It didn't help his vision, as the hurricane-like wind ripped off his helmet. Temporarily blinded, he levelled the plane reducing the speed so he could see. With the wind reduced, he was able to steal a quick glance to get his bearings. He nearly shit himself when looking out the side of the plane; he saw he was just feet from hitting the water. He concluded that if he hadn't straightened up, he'd have hit the water at full speed.

Smiling at his good luck, he continued south feeling a little more optimistic. That euphoria ended as soon as the jet engines coughed and died. His plane lost altitude rapidly, hit the water hard and rolled. Bill was already underwater before he could unfasten his harness. Leave the sinking plane, with only his lifejacket and survival pack; he bobbed to the surface. Looking around, he could see nothing except water.

Knowing keeping his weapon was pointless, he ditched it along with anything else which would make floating easier. His first thought as he drifted aimlessly along, was that a shark might get him before he managed to drown. Miserable, he decided if he made it till dark, he'd use the stars to try to swim towards land.

"Why bother? The bastards will just shoot me!" he shouted angrily, trying to think of a way out of this mess. Coming up empty, he bobbed along praying for a miracle. Fortunately, the water was quite calm and warm. Bill became conscious of just how tired he was. Yawning, he accepted his lot and drifted off to sleep.

He wasn't sure how long he slept, but a noise made him stir. There, above him, rocked several boats full of Vietnamese fishermen.

"What are you doing?" a voice asked in broken English.

"Just swimming. I must've fallen asleep and drifted out to sea?" The young man who had first spoken, translated what he said, causing the others to burst into laughter.

"You come aboard please?" the young man suggested, which Bill, of course, tried to do.

Unfortunately, his time in the water had made his legs go numb. The Vietnamese finally pulled him aboard. Instructing him to change out of his wet clothes, the young translator explained how they'd found him. Because of the war, they had to go further out to sea and to the north, to avoid becoming targets. His rescue was brought about by them travelling further out to sea. Bill was the first American any of them had seen up close. The younger man with a spattering of English had for a time been in the army, but a shell fragment embedded in his leg made him unfit for service.

Deciding they'd caught enough including an American, they decided to return to their village.

To say Bill was stunned when they arrived was an understatement. The village was built, on a series of pontoons comprising forty-four-gallon drums. The whole place floated! It was hidden, in between several massive granite blocks that poked out of the sea all over Ha Long Bay. Hundreds of feet tall, they allowed the villagers to stay hidden from allied planes seeking enemy soldiers.

The whole village turned out to see the strange barbarian while the young ex-soldier described how they'd found him. Poked and prodded by the children, Bill faked being ticklish which caused an outbreak of merriment from the villagers. The problem now arose as to what to do with him? The young translator although having served in the army was against just handing him over. He told the villagers how many American pilots were tortured by their prison guards; many dying in captivity.

Although he had no love for the Americans, he had no wish to be involved in his death. The village elder, who had remained silent throughout the debate, put forward an idea. He suggested taking the American north to China, even to Hong Kong, where maybe the American could pay them for his rescue. The translator seeing this idea appealed to everyone, put it to Bill. Overjoyed with the idea, Bill told them he could get cash from his bank account and transfer it to Hong Kong.

He had for a rainy day over ten thousand dollars in his account. Translating what he'd said brought a gasp from the villagers. That anyone could save so much money, many found amazing. On a handshake between the ex-soldier and Bill, they accepted the deal for payment for his freedom. Of course, sailing to Hong Kong was not going to be an easy feat. It meant crossing a vast stretch of open water patrolled by both friend and foe alike. Summoning the best fishermen in the village, the elder asked if anyone could do it.

Silence descended over the group, until Duk Ning, the young translator, came up with a solution. Twenty miles to the south was the wreck of an American patrol boat. It had run aground while looking for an anti-aircraft gun on one of the islands. The North Vietnamese Navy had already salvaged what it could, but the boat was still there. Once hostilities ceased, the Navy intended to salvage the boat, for its use. Duk Ning and two of villages had been aboard the vessel searching for anything useful. They were surprised to find the ship's engines still intact and the fuel tanks practically full. All it needed was to be refloated. So, confident was the Navy that the Americans could not reach it, they left it in working order.

Bill, through the translator, pointed out that the ship was worth far more than he could give them, so why not sell it as well. This caused a lot of soul searching, as it could be considered helping the enemy. Bill assured them they could sell it to some wealthy businessman who could claim salvage rights over it, meaning the Americans couldn't have it back. This seemed, in the final analysis, to satisfy everyone. Taking four fishing boats and twenty men, plus a collection of drums, the group headed for the wreck. It took two nights to reach it, as travelling by day was out the question with so many planes in the air.

Spotting the patrol boat, Bill saw the captain had at full speed hit a sandbank adjacent to an island. Not wanting to visit Hanoi, the Captain had called in another boat and transferred his crew. Because of the sandy bottom, the hull was intact. All they had to do was float it off. While waiting for low tide, the men ran ropes under the hull, securing the drums to the ends. The next part was the most frustrating, waiting for the tide to come in.

In the first four hours of the eight-hour tide, the drums barely moved. The first sign that the plan might work was a creaking sound as the drums stretched the ropes. Bill was the first to see movement, as with a shudder it surged, the drums bobbing freely as the weight eased.

"I'll be damned! It worked!" He smiled as the villagers clapped wildly. Securing their fishing boats to the rear, they powered up the boat and headed north. For security reasons they couldn't return to the village with it, so Instead, they hid the ship in a large cavern four miles away. Four men were chosen to accompany Bill. Their job would be not only navigation but also the receipt of the money. Bill still saw many doubted he'd pay up. The village elder for some reason was sure he would.

Sitting with the elder one night, Bill asked Duk Ning to ask him, why he trusted him. The translator started only to have the elder stop him, indicating for Bill to follow him, while he sent Duk Ning on an errand. Entering what Bill took to be his own home, the elder indicated for him to sit down.

"This is just great; how do I find out anything from this old guy now?"

"You stop talking and listen to this old guy," the Elder said in clear English, as he sat down opposite.

"My God, you speak English!" Bill exclaimed, the elder touching his lips to indicate for Bill to keep his voice down.

"Many years ago, Bill, I was an envoy for the once King of Vietnam. I travelled to America, and despite your people's lack of culture, I found the American people honourable. Of course, I keep my past life hidden, as the Communist party dislikes any association with our royal family of the past. I came here over thirty years ago and established this village. It's the perfect place to remain hidden.

97

"You could come to Hong Kong with me. There you could get a visa for America with my help," Bill suggested.

"My home is here Bill. It mightn't be a palace, but I'm needed here, and that's what counts." The Elder smiled.

"You've saved my life, my friend. I won't cheat you," Bill promised.

"I know, but the villagers are naive to the ways of the world. Once you reach Hong Kong, you will have to help them return. They have not thought of that."

"That's right! If they sell the boat how do they get back? I didn't think of that either," Bill admitted, as the Elder stood.

"We won't speak again, so I wish you good luck Bill. Someday in better times, you might return?" he said offering his hand, which Bill shook.

"I'd like that, but I suspect it will be a long time."

It was another week before the time was right for the voyage to get underway. The patrol boat although full of fuel, would need topping up to make the distance. Having friends in the black market helped secure what they needed. Leaving a fishing boat at the cavern, the story would be that the four men were off fishing if anyone from the mainland visited. Duk Ning, as acting Captain, took first shift at the wheel. At the stroke of midnight, at full power, they roared out to sea. After two hours of running at full speed, Duk Ning cleared the coastal waters of Vietnam and reduced their speed to conserve fuel. Pointing to his chart, he indicated their position to Bill. Four days would see them in Hong Kong if the fuel lasted.

On the second day, they ran into their first problem. As they headed east, a warship appeared in the north. It was heading south. A closer look through the binoculars indicated the destroyer was Australian. As their paths would cross, Duk Ning asked Bill's advice.

"To turn would make them suspicious. Let's keep going," Bill suggested. Duk Ning left Bill at the wheel and disappeared down a set of stairs. When he returned, he handed Bill a naval cap and hurried to the rear of the ship. Pulling out an American flag, he ran it up the mast and returned to the wheel.

"Good thinking Duk! I forgot about the flag," Bill admitted.

"We Asians catch on fast." He giggled, Bill, joining in. As the Australian warship passed, except for some waving, both boats continued on their routes. Bill was surprised that the Aussies hadn't called them up to identify themselves, but, why would they? The North Vietnamese navy never ventured out for fear of being destroyed. The American Navy, especially its patrol boats, were well-known for their strange behaviour; hence the friendly waves.

"They most probably think we're off for a booze up, in Hong Kong?" Bill smiled, waving back as the larger ship passed. Twice more they had encounters with naval vessels although both times the ships were distant. On the fourth day, during their final approach to Hong Kong, they had their most worrying run-in.

A fighter plane, American by its wing markings, took two runs at them. Bill, with a sinking feeling, thought the pilot might be running the ship's bow numbers, which all American ships carried. When the plane turned for that second run, Bill thought how ironic it would be to be killed by a fellow American pilot. He was later to find out that the plane had indeed checked the ship's ID. Luckily the Captain who ran it aground had been planning his own mission to retrieve it, so the Navy hadn't written it off yet.

Coming into Hong Kong Harbor proved to be an anti-climax, as his supposed captors stood dumbstruck by the amount of shipping moving around the harbour. Motoring into an area reserved for private craft, they tied up at a wharf.

"Hey, you can't leave that boat there!" an official voice shouted from what appeared to be a clubhouse at the end of the wharf. A large, portly man of about sixty waddled down the wharf to stand next to them. He introduced himself as the President of the Hong Kong Yacht Club, which owned the wharf they were tied up to. After introductions, Bill observed him checking over the sleek lines of their boat.

"Sorry we didn't know where to moor it," Bill replied innocently.

"What's an American air force pilot, doing with a Vietnamese crew, on a yank patrol boat?"

"It's a long story. You don't know anyone who wants to buy a boat do you?"

"Now you're talking Yank. Welcome to Honkers. Here we buy and sell anything!" The man beamed, offering his hand.

"What's going on Bill?" Duk Ning asked suspiciously.

"We're in luck. It looks as if we've found someone to help sell our boat," Bill answered, as the President disappeared up the wharf.

"Already? We just arrived!" Duk Ning exclaimed in surprise.

"Things happen fast in the capitalist world Duk." Bill chuckled as the President reappeared with two men in tow.

The money transfer from his stateside account took three days to arrange. In that time, Bill went to the United States Consulate. To say they were amazed was an understatement. He didn't mention the boat of course, which had already changed colours and was now the yacht club's official vessel. Instead, he told them how the fishermen had managed, at great personal risk, to get him to Hong Kong. In the process, their own vessel had sunk, and a local yacht club boat had picked them up. The Ambassador had personally wanted to hold a reception for these brave men. Bill talked them out of it saying they were eager to return to Vietnam to continue rescuing down pilots.

"How do we get them back then Captain?" he asked.

"Easy! When you arrange to fly me back to Da Nang, we can drop them off on the way," Bill suggested to Ambassador, who seemed quite unsure.

"You can't land in Hal Long Bay Captain. There are no friendly airfields."

"You're right Sir, but there is plenty of water," he answered, leaving the Ambassador wondering about Bill's sanity.

Two days and a lot of begging saw Captain Green at the controls of a Catalina flying boat. It belonged to the US Navy's Search and Rescue Unit and was being ferried to South Vietnam to help with rescuing down pilots of all things. Duk Ning and his three friends had enjoyed their visit immensely. Presents filled the plane as the three men sat with Bill in the front cabin. The ferrying crew wasn't too pleased to see Captain Green flying solo across to Nam without them. When he told them what he planned, they changed their minds, returning to America on the next commercial flight.

Approaching North Vietnam in the dark, skimming the waves, Bill started to doubt the wisdom of doing it himself. Trying to work out their exact position was Bill's priority, which he was failing at. The problem was North Vietnam because of the bombing, had imposed a total blackout. This meant landmarks were hard to find in the dark. Fortunately, Duk Ning, sitting beside him, spotted the villager's island. Someone had left one light on in the village, barely visible amongst the mountainous terrain.

Turning south in no time they were over the island where they left the fishing boat. Circling to make sure no one was home, Bill brought the plane down and they slowly motored into the cave. Bill's secretive landing, caused panic to the cave's occupants. Five of their villagers fishing boats had tied up there for the night. At the sight of the American plane, most of them jumped overboard, swimming further into the cave.

Once the plane stopped, Duk Ning swiftly opened the outside door and yelled a greeting. The fishermen slowly returned and crowded aboard the strange aircraft, which was also a boat. As soon as the goods Duk Ning and his crew had purchased were unloaded, the fishermen said their goodbyes to Bill. It was somewhat emotional, making Bill realised these people had become his friends. Promising to return someday after the war, he started up his plane.

As he took off and headed south, Bill concluded that his time as a fighter pilot was over in Nam. He couldn't in good conscience fly missions again; not after what these people had done for him.

Two hours and a lot of soul searching, Bill prepared to land at Da Nang airfield. It was then that he saw the fires. From the air, it looked as if the whole place was burning! Surprisingly he got an okay from the airfield, as he brought the flying boat into land. As soon as he was out, the ground crew frantically towed the plane to between two blast walls.

"Welcome back Captain Green!" Colonel Johnson yelled out, having arrived in a jeep.

"Things have changed here?" Captain Green pointed out, looking at the surrounding area.

"Yeah. It's been going downhill since you went on that raid," The Colonel confirmed, watching mortar rounds impact the north, in Da Nang City.

"I'd better go change and meet you in the debriefing hut, Sir. I've had an interesting trip."

"There's no time for that Captain. Pack your gear. The air wings going stateside."

"But I just got back here Sir!"

"Well, you can stay if you like Captain. I sure the incoming fighter wing would welcome your experience with the local area. But the rest of us are going. So what's it to be?"

"I'll go pack."

"Yeah, I thought you'd say that!" The Colonel chuckled, leaving Green standing there pole-axed.

"That is quite a story Bill if it's true?"

"Of course, it's true, although the telling of it was easier than actually being there."

"And the 202nd is now stateside?"

"Yeah. They've done their time and I for one, am glad we're out of it. The war is lost, Coby. Our bombing is just prolonging it."

"Where are we stationed?"

"Just outside of Atlanta, about two hours' drive from your parents' home,"

"It will be good to catch up with the men." Coby smiled, seeing Bill's smile vanished. "What's wrong?"

"The ground crews stayed. Only the planes, the pilots and the command personnel came home. The rest have to stay till they're relieved. "

"That's not good enough! They have done their time too. How did that happen?"

"No one wants to go there, Coby. The High Command thought it was easier to leave them in place than replace them. Let's face it! They know the airfield, and they'll be needed by our replacements."

"And what happens when they're overrun?"

"I don't know Coby. You'll have to come back and find out," Bill answered, sounding unsure.

After Bill had left, Diana returned. Bud's death and Coby's injuries had hit her hard. Guilt and uncertainty over her relationship with Coby weighed heavily on her. What would happen next scared her. True, in the last few years Bud had been a monster, although he hadn't always been that way. Now with his passing, she remembered better times, when she loved him and enjoyed her time with him. He'd been so gentle, so adoring, wanting to make every day of her life a blessing and then Trevor had come along.

For some unknown reason, Bud didn't bond with Trevor, giving the impression that Trevor wasn't his. Somehow Diana had the feeling he thought she had cheated on him. Bud had been the only man Diana had ever been with, yet she sensed he didn't trust her. Why, she had no idea, having given him no cause to doubt her faithfulness. She knew it had something to do with his college friends, with whom he had spent more time in the last few years.

Rumors suggested they were all aligned with a white supremacist group. Diana, on the other hand, had a deep commitment to equal rights. She and Bud often clashed over her involvement, but he always seemed to, in the end, see the logic of it. One weekend when some of his friends stopped over, one of his buddies had made a point about white women being easily seduced, by the trickery of black men. Diana had laughed thinking it a joke.

Looking around, she saw no one else was laughing. Could it be he feared she'd slept with African Americans she met at her rallies? It would explain his murderous rage when she'd gone for a walk with Coby. Why had she gone at all she wondered so many times, knowing the answer was tied to her marital problems. She had to admit her need for someone to love her. It wasn't Coby's colour or good looks that had drawn her to him, although in his uniform, he did look striking.

In all honesty, it was the man she saw inside; an honest man, who was desperately lonely. Since that walk, he'd been in her thoughts and dreams constantly. Going for coffee at her sister's house had been Diana's desperate attempt to see him again. She hadn't wanted it to turn into a one-night stand, although if he'd taken her, she would've been willing. The truth was she wanted to be with him, to talk again and share that magic that they had created at the Van Clef plantation.

Coby, as usual, had been a gentleman. She understood his desire for her nearly drove him to the point of taking her by force. Shamelessly she admitted wanting him too. Even when she broke away telling him they must leave, she'd secretly hoped he'd overpower her again and put an end to her resistance.

When news of Bud's death arrived, she had grieved; not for the man he'd become, but for the man, she'd married. Putting on a brave face for her son and her family, she had become the hero's wife loyal even in death. It was hard for her, but any thought of Coby and the future had to wait. Trevor, her son, was her real worry. He had reached a crossroad in his life. Torn between the man he knew and the hero the press made his father out to be, he'd accepted the media's version.

Now at only six years old, he had stood beside his mother following his father's coffin, his face lined with sorrow at his parting. As he wept, the nation wept, his father in death becoming the father he'd always wanted. Still, his nightmares made him confront the past, reminding him that his distant father had once been another person entirely. Visiting Coby had not been Diana's idea. She had decided to keep away avoiding the possibility of her passion for him erupting in public. Heartbroken at the death of his son, the Senator Van Clef asked, if not pleaded with Diana, to visit Coby.

He wanted firstly to see how he was. Secondly, he wanted to get the details of his son's death from the man he saved. Like Diana, the Senator had doubts about Bud defending Coby to the death. He knew it didn't somehow fit with Bud's beliefs. With a guilty conscious she'd agreed to visit him. She knew the rest of the country would falsely see a hero's wife, giving comfort, while what drove her was excitement at seeing Coby. Over the past month, she had dutifully visited the man who had been saved by her husband. Sometimes she'd sit with him alone, other times with his parents, but always under the watchful eye of the media.

Twice she'd brought Trevor, wanting him to meet Coby. The problem was Trevor associated Coby with his father's beating of him and his mother.

'She's been with a nigger!' He remembered his father screaming. Although he was too young to understand, he knew Coby was an African American and involved somehow with his mother. After the second visit, he asked his mother not to take him again. Hoping as he grew older he'd understand, she conceded to his demand. Today when Diana had visited, she'd found to her surprise that Coby had regained consciousness and recovered enough to go for a walk. The nurses seemed upset that against their advice he'd left the hospital. Diana, her heart racing, had considered leaving at that moment. She had doubts about what might occur, and the media was everywhere.

One of the nurses, an African American, asked her as a favour if she could convince him to return. There was something in the way she asked that made Diana look at her more closely as if somehow, she was a rival for Coby's affections. Putting it down to her own overactive imagination, she agreed to go down to the ground floor and find him. This she saw won her some friends with the nurses. Down in the lobby, doubt started to creep into her resolve, as she exited the lift. She was about to give into the urge to leave when she ran into Captain Green.

He recognised her from papers, and after introducing himself, he asked her where Coby's room was. She told him Coby was out walking, but she promised to bring him back. Captain Green asked her to keep his presence a secret and said he would wait in Coby's room for them. Trapped by her own kind nature, she walked out into the park. When she saw him sitting on the park bench looking discarded and broken, she nearly forgot her role and ran to him.

With heart pounding in her chest, she stopped, clutched her heart and fought to control her emotions by taking several deep breaths. With what dignity she could muster, she walked towards him and called his name. He immediately swung his head in her direction, his face brightening with pleasure. Holding back tears she moved to him, hugging him, while behind her, the cameraman took his shot. If he kissed her then and there she knew it would be all over. Her emotional restraint was so close to breaking. Instead, because he was so weary from his injuries, he was unable to take advantage of the moment.

When they'd arrived back at the room, and Captain Green had hopped out of bed, she had left them to their moment together, supposedly to make a call. In reality, she had hurried to the toilet, collapsing in a cubicle, crying at her suppressed love for him. She had been there for several minutes when a light tap on the door made her sit up and wipe her face.

"Are you okay?" A female voice sounded worried.

"Yes. I just need some time alone," she answered, putting on her media face for the public. She opened the door, moving to the hand basin and washed her flushed face. A towel floating beside her meant the Good Samaritan was still present.

"Thank you. That was kind of you." Diana smiled, wiping her face, before reapplying her makeup.

"You're an inspiration to our country Mrs Van Clef! The whole nation mourns your loss." The same African American nurse who'd asked her to fetch Coby from the park, told her, as her own eyes filled with tears.

"Thank you, nurse, although I'd rather have not shared this moment. It hurts too much," Diana confessed crying again, as the nurse held her.

"Your husband was something special, a real hero to this country. Your loss must be unbearable," the nurse added, trying to comfort her.

"He was a monster and a racist, who beat my son and me for no reason. That's the hero the people didn't see." She sobbed for once in her life telling someone the truth. Seeing the horrified look on the nurse's face, she became aware of what she had said. "God I'm sorry. I should not have told you that. Please don't say anything to anyone nurse?" Diana begged.

"I won't Diana, and my name is Glenda. Just one thing, if he was such a monster, why didn't you leave him?" Glenda asked still holding Diana.

"In the past, I was going to, and then the war came along. I thought he might change, but I was wrong. I was going to when he returned. I couldn't do something like that by mail or on the phone. It had to be face to face," Diana admitted, the nurse nodding her understanding.

"You've got your whole life ahead of you. You'll meet someone else," Glenda assured her, helping her with her makeup.

"I already have, and except for this, we might've had something special. Now I don't know any longer," Diana confessed.

"If you love him and he loves you, then he'll wait no matter how long it takes." Glenda comforted her, walking her to the door.

"Thank you for everything Glenda. I needed someone to talk to desperately," Diana admitted, before putting on her media face and walking back to Coby's room.

"God, I hope it helped sister. I'm glad it's not me in your mess," Glenda whispered to herself, walking back to her station.

"You've been gone awhile?" one of her friends asked.

"I had to save someone's life." Glenda smiled, hoping she had.

"A penny for your thoughts? What are you thinking about?" Coby asked, seeing Diana's mind had drifted far away.

"Just what happens next for you and me? How can we make this work?" Diana asked. Coby, to ensure privacy, walked across to the door and closed it. Returning, he took her in his arms and gently kissed her. The kiss deepened, releasing their suppressed passion. Diana overwhelmed, ended up underneath Coby on his bed. Fully dressed she felt naked under the onslaught of Coby's hands roaming freely over her body. It was Coby this time who broke away and let her go so that she could sit up. Guiltily they both looked at the door.

"For a while, it will be risky, but we'll make it work Diana."

"What if someone had come in and caught us?" Diana pointed out, straightening her clothing and appearance.

"They didn't, although you're right! We'll have to be more careful," Coby kissed her lightly on the lips.

"Well then, you need to get better. We can't do much more than this here!" She giggled, knowing they would make it work somehow. A tapping at the door made them move apart, as Diana got up opening the door. Glenda stood there with a tray.

"Time for your pills hero." She smiled, as Diana said her goodbyes and walked out the door. Glenda looking back at Coby saw the look in his eye, as Diana left. "My God Diana, you'll need an ocean of love to make this work."

Once everyone had left, Coby settled down and listened to the latest news broadcast. The fires around Da Nang, which Bill had seen before leaving, were the start of the Tet Offensive. It was launched by a combined operation from the north and the south. The bombing of the bunker by Bud had severely affected the command structure of the north, meaning the Viet Cong in the south shouldered all the effort. They had some major successes, including seizing the American Embassy in Saigon. In the final analysis, though, the Viet Cong were decimated and never effectively operated as a separate force again.

Coby spent many sleepless nights worrying about his ground crew, knowing he could do nothing while he slowly healed. All he could do was wait and pray that they were all right. Over the next two weeks, Coby built up his strength waiting for the chance to get back into the cockpit of a fighter. Diana visited once more walking with him, keeping contact respectable for the media. He also had an unexpected visit from Senator Van Clef.

Diana had told him roughly the same story the media were broadcasting. Sure, now that it was true, he'd decided to visit Coby. The media, of course, was there too.

"I'm glad you made it Coby. If my son had to die in battle, I'm glad he managed to save you in the process." The Senator eyes filled with tears as he spoke.

"America has lost a good man in Bud Sir. I just wish he'd made it too," Coby responded, his voice showing he meant it.

"You've done your country proud Coby. Never hesitate to call me if you need anything." The Senator shook his hand. "Now if you reporters are finished, I'd like to talk to Coby in private," the reporters having got what they wanted, left.

"This is just between you and me Coby. How did Bud die and I want the truth?" Coby hesitated then answered.

"He was shot by an enemy soldier Senator. Does it matter if he was defending himself or me? Either way, we would've both died. He was a hero when he attacked that ammo bunker and then the command bunker on the border. He had his faults like anyone else, but when the chips were down he came through, that's all that counts," Coby told him, meaning it. The Senator, while absorbing the information, sat down beside Coby.

"Thank you, Coby. Bud was such a confused young man. I blame myself for that. I was always away from home working. I should've spent more time with him," the Senator confessed.

"So, what now Coby? Have you given any thought to the future?"

"Not past being a fighter pilot Sir."

"Well think about it son. The war in Nam is doomed. When it ends there will be cutbacks in frontline units; you can count on that. Best to think where you are headed now."

"I come up for re-enlistment in a few months. What do you suggest?"

"You're a good public speaker Coby. This country is going to see hard times after Nam, and we'll need honest people to look after the ones who have suffered the most. Why not enter politics and make a difference?"

"I do want to see equal rights in our Universities and schools Senator. Racism needs to go," Coby answered, thinking about it.

"That's the ticket, Coby. At the moment militant black groups are the only ones leading the push, and they're not respected. We don't want anarchy, where the black population feels they have to fight to get equality. What we need to do is debate the issues, get it out in the light of day, where people can see what racism really is. Maybe you can be the voice of reason that swings the undecided?"

"I'd like that Senator. I'll think about it."

"I'll talk to Diana about helping you. She used to help campaign for equal rights before she was married. She could be a great help?" This took the smile off Coby's face.

"Are you sure Senator? She's been through a lot."

"It will take her mind off her loss, Coby. I think it will be good for both of you," the Senator pointed out, unaware of Coby's embarrassment. Realising the time, the Senator quickly said his goodbyes, leaving Coby behind to feel confused and guilty.

At that moment, he understood how Diana felt about deceiving people. The problem was, the more he thought about it, the more it made sense. She had a background in law, something that he lacked. It would be a good fit. With Diana's organisational skills and his gift for making speeches, they would make them a formidable team. There was also the fact they could see each other publicly, without creating too much of a fuss. In time, if things went well between them, they could make their feelings public, after a respectable time had passed.

"And how long is that?" Coby said out loud, making a nurse in the hallway stop and look in.

"Are you okay Captain?" It was Glenda, the nurse who had first washed him.

"Yes, just thinking out loud."

"Then don't. This is a hospital, not the battlefield. Keep the noise down," she suggested.

"Yes General!"

"That's better." She smiled, moving away.

'I bet you'd be a handful!' Coby thought to himself as he watched the pretty nurse walk down to the nurses' station.

FLYING AGAIN

Coby received a hero's welcome at the new 202nd Airbase. Although they were all happy to see him return, he could see the pilots were apprehensive about their ground crews. Because of his time in service and his successes Coby now had the rank of major. He wasn't the only one to advance in rank, as General Douglas greeted him.

"Congratulation's General!" Coby's greeting included a crisp salute.

"Are you crawling to me, Major?" Douglas replied, returning the salute.

"Wouldn't dream of it, Sir."

"I suppose Captain; I mean Major Green has told you about the ground crews?"

"Yes, Sir. What's going on? Are they okay?"

"Word has come through that Da Nang Airfield is being constantly shelled. Flights in and out have been cancelled. Only the base's fighters belonging to the 66th fighter wing are using the strip at the moment."

"We need to get them out, Sir. They've done their time like the rest of us."

"I understand Major, but for now it's too dangerous to rotate them home. Once things settle down, we'll go get them," Douglas assured him.

"How is it over there?"

"Not good. The top brass is talking to the north. They are trying to get some peace deal, before bugging out. We're going to leave the south swinging in the wind and run, the poor bastards,"

"Any timeline?"

"Probably a year? That stunt of taking over the Embassy in Saigon rattled our Government. Old Tricky-Dickey Nixon wants another term in office, and with this war running he's got no chance. Funny thing is the Viet Cong are finished in the south. The north is the only force we have to contend with now."

"So, what do you think will happen to Da Nang Airbase?"

"I'd say they'll reduce the airfield's aircraft, moving them south where it's safer to operate. They'll leave a token force there to prove we're not beat. That's when we can airlift our men out."

Douglas smiled, trying to convince Coby and himself that it would happen.

"What, do we do in the mean time?" Coby changed the subject.

"We train and train some more and prepare for the day when we're needed most Major. I suggest you get changed into your flying gear. Let's see if you've still got it?" Coby snapping a salute, left to find his billet.

"Wheels up?" Coby said out loud, as his Phantom screamed into the air, rocketing up to thirty thousand feet. His take off had been average at best, and Coby knew many on the ground were watching. It wasn't unusual for a pilot shot down to develop a case of stage fright and have trouble getting into a cockpit again, let alone take off. Reaching his required altitude, Coby looked around making sure the sky was clear. He was just about to relax thinking himself alone when near the sun a shadow appeared.

"Shit no!" he shouted, flipping the plane over and diving. A quick look behind him revealed the other fighter, a Phantom, gaining on him. "Well you think you're good, do you? Try this!" Coby made three sharp turns, doing a split S manoeuvre. To his horror, the other plane stayed with him. Knowing any second his pursuer would get missile lock, he hit the afterburners, heading towards the stars. His shadow followed as Coby rolled his plane on its back and hit the flaps. This had the desired effect of shaking his tail lose, as he shot by.

Going to afterburners, Coby went after the other fighter, only to see him copy his every manoeuvre and hit the flaps. Coby caught by surprise sailed by as his nemesis again tried for a lock. Desperate, Coby repeated his tight turns only this time, on the third, he corkscrewed into a roll, his airspeed dropping when his plane stalled. For a split second, the other plane misjudged his intention and shot past. The pilot wondering which way Coby would roll out had been fooled. Instead of completing the roll, Coby upside down, accelerated. Locking the other fighter momentarily, he pressed the fire button.

"Gotcha!" Coby triumphantly shouted, over his radio.

"Took you long enough!" Major Green's voice replied, coming alongside.

"I was making you look good," Coby answered.

"Yeah, bullshit you were!" Bill chuckled. "You want to go again?"

"No, that took it out of me. Let's go back. I need a shower," Coby confessed, as together they dived for the airfield.

Once landed, Coby hurried to the showers, while Bill went to see General Douglas.

"How'd he go?" Douglas asked.

"He's still got it, although I nearly had him several times."

"Is he back to hundred percent?"

"Six months ago, he'd have got me straight away. Although I've improved, he's not the killer he used to be."

"Can he still cut it, is all I want to know Bill."

"Yes, of course, he can. He's just seen too much action too soon. It ages you," Bill admitted, knowing that despite his improved flying, it had aged him as well.

"We all have Bill. He, more than most, has been through a lot. I just have to be sure he's ready."

"I wouldn't lie to you, Sir."

"I know. Now go tell your friend he's back on the line, Major."

"Yes Sir," Bill saluted leaving. As he walked back towards the barracks, he looked back. He saw Douglas still at his desk, deep in thought.

THE RESCUE

Six months dragged by, as news from Da Nang grew dire. Despite Major Green and General Douglas's doubts, Coby was again on top, having defeated all challenges. Douglas was just about to announce that Coby would be stepping up and leading the wing when an urgent order came through. After fierce fighting, enemy mechanised units had just about encircled Da Nang. Three Hercules transports had been ordered to fly to Da Nang to evacuate the base personnel, including their ground crews. As a show of strength and support for their ground crews, the 202nd fighter wing would fly cover, while the Hercules landed and loaded.

The 202nd Air Wing flew west over the Pacific, landing in Hawaii. They then travelled north to the Philippines, which required refuelling en route. There they rested, after crossing the Pacific in a day. While they slept, their planes took on armaments and fuel for the last leg north to Vietnam. Leaving the Philippines at 4 am, the wing flew northwest, skimming the water and finally landed at an airfield south of Saigon. After showering, the pilots ate a hearty breakfast, before attending a briefing to discuss the operation. Their mission was simple. They had to get in and out as swiftly as possible and evacuate the ground crews.

In other words, they had to pick up everyone they could fit into three transport planes and get the hell out of Dodge. This, of course, was before the enemy reacted. General Douglas, who'd taken the place of a sick pilot and flown one of the fighters across the Pacific, had decided to go with them against orders. His superiors had ordered him not to go, warning him to stay on the ground. They feared the fallout at losing an Air Force General at this stage of the war.

"They can shove it. I'm going!" he growled, after receiving the message from the base commander. The messenger with this reply from General Douglas hurriedly returned to the Base Commander's office. Moments later the Base Commander appeared in person with two MPs.

"General Douglas, I have been ordered to hold you here if necessary or imprison you if you try to take off and go on this mission," the Colonel warned.

"I'm sorry. You're right Colonel. I apologise for my earlier attitude. Instead of going on the mission, I will fly instead to Saigon to argue my case at our Headquarters there. Then I can go on any backup mission if it's necessary?"

"That General is the right course of action Sir. I will inform headquarters that you are on the way," the Colonel answered, looking relieved. The Colonel left with his MPs.

The raid was planned at the unusual time of two that afternoon, in an attempt to catch the enemy napping. The General wished them all good luck and launched first, heading towards Saigon. Once his plane had departed, the 202nd roared into the air. Even south of the border they received ground fire, as they flew north towards Da Nang. Coby was one of the first to notice the General's plane joining them from inland.

"You're way off course Falcon One! Saigon is back the other way!" Coby informed him.

"You didn't really think I was going did you Falcon Two? That clown of a Colonel back there is the most gullible person I've ever met." He chuckled, as they neared Da Nang.

"Do you want to lead the cover group or the attack group Falcon One?" Coby asked. He knew arguing would achieve nothing.

"I'll take the attacking force. We'll soften up the opposition, while you cover the pickup Falcon Two," he replied, as half the fighters moved into a formation behind him.

"Good luck Falcon One. Give 'em hell!" Coby grinned, checking his weapons.

The first target for the General's group was the mountain peaks above Da Nang, while Coby led the other half, to cover the airfield. The General's planes plastered the mountain range above Da Nang with napalm. Sending a prearranged signal, the three transport planes came in low from out to sea. Once they had touched down, they quickly taxied to the maintenance area. No sooner had the planes stopped, then men started pouring from the hangars, scrambling aboard. There was no panic, but it was clear they'd had enough.

Spasmodic shellfire from the surrounding area showed that the napalm hadn't silenced all opposition. The enemy must have grasped that something was up. Coby knew the General's group would be getting low on ordinance, so decided to help.

"Falcon One we're getting bored. How about letting us get rid ourselves of these extra bombs we're carrying?" Coby suggested hearing some of the pilots' laughter.

"Sounds like a good idea! When you reach us, we'll take over your position Falcon Two," Douglas replied, as Coby's group flew toward the enemy positions.

Once overhead, Coby led them down, while the other wing left to protect the airfield. Fear for the first time, crept into his thinking, as Coby dived towards a gun emplacement. In the past, he'd never thought too much about dying. Like many pilots, he knew he had a job to do, and when your number was up, it was up. Now with Diana constantly in his thoughts, he found himself worried by the return fire, which scored the occasional hit on his plane as he climbed away. He didn't want to die here for nothing he concluded, turning for another pass.

"They're my friends down there, that what makes all the difference!" he said out loud, diving and dropping his ordinance on yet another enemy position.

For twenty minutes the battle of wills played out. The enemy cowered by the strafing and continuous bombing gave up, going silent, as they yielded to the Phantom's weaponry. On the airfield, the three transport planes, now fully loaded, struggled into the sky. Flying on the deck to avoid anti-aircraft fire, they flew out to sea, before turning south. Inside, their relieved ground crews looked down for the last time, at their old base. When they landed south of Saigon, the ground crews couldn't believe their eyes when their escort landed.

Many were speechless, their emotions evident, at the sight of their pilots returning for them. The strain of the last few months had worn many of them down both physically and mentally. The discovery that these men cared and were willing to risk their lives to see them free lifted their morale. After a barbecue thrown by the base personnel to celebrate the ground crews' rescue, the General welcomed them back to the 202nd. Shortly after, the ground crews boarded commercial airliners, to start their journey home to the States. Watching them take off, Coby, like many others, felt a debt had been paid to these men, who had been left behind. At dawn the next morning, the air wing again took to the skies heading back to the Philippines, then along their previous route across the Pacific, to home.

Soon after their return, General Douglas resigned. If it was for disobeying orders or because he'd just had enough, no one would ever know. At his farewell, he told the gathered pilots and the returned ground crews how honoured he'd been to serve with them. Coby would remember that evening, as the night Vietnam ended for him. In truth, it went on for another six months, but for him, it ended with Douglas leaving.

General Cobbs arrival was a surprise. Many thought Coby would get the nod having been an outstanding pilot and instructor. His intention to leave at the end of his enlistment period had swayed the brass into selecting someone else. Cobbs, a veteran himself, was well liked by the men and took over General Douglas' role with a minimum of fuss. He also managed to get one concession out of Coby, before he left, suggesting Coby should join the National Guard Air Force Reserve. Cobbs saw this as a way of passing on Coby's skills to other pilots, which would be lost and wasted if he simply left.

Coby at the time wasn't sure, but he joined anyway feeling a release from his day-to-day life mightn't be a bad thing. As Senator Van Clef had warned, the Air Force soon announced a reduction in fighter wings. Coby took this as a sign and resigned, going to the Reserve. This surprised many of the pilots who thought he'd stay on for a while.

"What will you do?" Bill asked Coby at his going away party.

"I'm going to run for a Senate seat in my State, Bill. I want to make a difference."

"Shit, you even sound like one them!"

"What about you Bill?"

"I'll give it another three years, and then I'll go fly a commercial airliner, make some money while I can. I'm a pilot Coby. Like you I'll join the Reserves so I can fly fighters once in a while. It's the only thing I was ever good at." Bill confessed, seemingly happy with his decision.

117

"Good luck Bill, I'll miss you."

"I'll miss you too. And marry that girl before I do!" Bill warned as they continued drinking.

POLITICS

It was a lot easier making the decision, than actually running for the Senate. For all his training Coby was unprepared for the aggressive nature of politics. A year after leaving the service he was yet to get pre-selection, let alone campaign. There were tough times after the war and Coby many times thanked Cobbs in his prayers, for talking him into joining the Reserve. It didn't pay much, but it kept him afloat while he got his political career rolling.

Starting off in his hometown, in a small office just around the corner from where he'd grown up, he made his first run for a seat in the local House of Representatives in his State. This was a shock for him, having thought with his medal of honour and his service in Vietnam, he could go straight for a seat in the United States Senate. Unfortunately, with the defeat in Nam, people wanted to forget everything to do with the war and that included war heroes.

Diana, who dropped in to see him from time to time, warned him it wouldn't be easy.

"Start off small and work your way to the top," she constantly told him, having seen how slowly the Government worked first hand. Senator Van Clef had told him that earning his way would require patience and persistence. In time it would happen. Both Diana and the Senator were an inspiration to him in those early days, providing him with the drive to succeed. There was, however, one other matter they'd avoided making an issue of and that was which party he should join?

He could be an independent, but in American politics, there were only two parties that mattered. Both Diana and Senator Van Clef were Democrats. They made no secret of it though, on purpose, they kept their distance so he could make his choice without interference. The Democrats he found were mostly opposed to war and had caused a lot of trouble for returning soldiers, by targeting them at University led demonstrations.

This made siding with them hard, as he thought they should've tried to keep their attacks on the Government, not on the returning soldiers. The Republican Party, on the other hand, gave him a lukewarm response to his plan to push for the end of all forms of segregation. This made him hesitate. In the end, he decided that his primary focus was on segregation, not on a war the country was trying to forget. Both Diana and Senator Van Clef were delighted when he reluctantly chose the Democrats.

Running his first campaign on a shoestring budget, Coby received support from many black unionists in the local factories. They saw him as one of their own, a man of the people. Being from the same area and financial situation gave him an insight into their worries and fears. His first clash came when he attended a debate hosted by a small local television station on equal pay and the approaching state elections. Five different candidates attended. Coby representing the Democrats was on the far right of the stage. The Republican candidate was on the far left. There were three independents; one of them was an African American, like himself.

His name was John Carson, and he had ties to the Black Panther movement. The group was what Van Clef had described as hard-liners. In other words, when they didn't get their way, they turned to the law of the street. Black power groups had become the voices of the downtrodden. They were fiercely anti-war, especially after Martin Luther King was gunned down when he loaned his support to the anti-war movement. They saw the black man as still a slave and encouraged their brothers to take up arms.

As soon as the debate started, Coby knew he was fighting for his life. The four other candidates saw the Democrats as the enemy, as the polls showed a win for them in the coming Presidential elections. Standing up to answer several questions, Coby was hammered by the four. At the end, tired of being the target, he went on the offensive. Pointing out each candidate's weaknesses in their augments, he told them honestly, what the Democrats stood for. Carson, seeing Coby was winning, lost his temper!

"You're nothing but a baby killer. Just a nigger soldier following the white man's orders!" he screamed, stopping the debate. The crowd hushed by his statement waited for Coby's answer or reaction. For a split second, Coby saw red. Every muscle in his body tensed, as he prepared to launch himself at

Carson. "It's what he wants!" his mind screamed, making him calm down.

"Was there a question in that insult from a man to my left? I think not! He advocates violence in the streets if he fails to get his way. He calls me a baby killer for doing my duty in the armed forces of this country. Is this what the black people of this country want? I hope, and I pray they don't! I believe that most of us want a good life and a home where we can raise our children as free and equal Americans. We can't stop segregation by dominating our protagonist, or we'll become like them!

Only through debating the issues can we truly be free. You follow a man like this one, and there will be no peace for any of us, no matter what colour you are!" Coby exclaimed as the room sat in silence.

It started slowly, as a grey haired old lady to his right stood and clapped. Others stood with her. In the end, the room as one got to their feet and clapped. Carson's reply was drowned out, as the clapping continued. Even the other candidates clapped. Carson, sensing the changed mood got up and left, causing a cheer. Coby, raising his hands, called for silence.

"People, like me you came here tonight to look to the future. Let's hear what the other candidates have to say, as this is what a democracy is all about." He told them, sitting down. The debate showed the people of Coby's electorate that he wouldn't be intimidated, that he would fight doggedly, but fairly, for his beliefs. The debate continued for another hour, but the judges from Coby's speech onwards considered him the winner.

Leaving the debate on a high, Coby walked to his car feeling confident about the night. He'd held his temper in check, and he believed he'd won the debate. Halfway to his vehicle, he noticed two large men following him. Remaining calm, he approached his car to find John Carson and two men waiting.

"Well, well, well, if it isn't the smart little nigger! Democrats pay you well to betray your people?"

"No one pays me anything John. And you of all people should know what an insult it is calling me a nigger. It's bad enough those white supremacists call us that. Why would a fellow black man do it?" Coby stood his ground waiting for John to answer.

"You made a fool of me in there! Did you think you could just walk away?" He sneered as his two friends moved in.

"You didn't need me to make you look a fool, John. You did that on your own," Coby retorted, waiting for the three men to make their move. John, smiling, moved in close, his hands balled into fists as he readied to strike him. While Coby was distracted, one of the other men kicked his legs out from under him. On the ground, the three laid the boot in, as Coby rolled into a ball trying to protect himself.

"How clever do you feel now smart-arse?" John Carson chuckled before his face took on a surprised look. The kicking stopped, as Coby saw two of his antagonists crash to the ground beside him. Carson recovering from his surprise turned to run. Unfortunately, he'd hesitated too long, and was seized by one of Coby's guardian angels. Lifted up, he was tossed him into a parked truck. He didn't get up.

"Are you okay Mr. Henderson?" It was one of the two men he'd seen earlier following him. Coby got unsteadily to his feet and leaned against his car for support before answering.

"Yes, thanks to you two I am!" Coby confessed, trying to tidy himself up.

"Our mum back there sent Bobby and me here to watch over you. She thought you underestimated that Carson fellow's anger. She said, Billy, take your brother and follow Mr. Henderson and make sure he's okay. We didn't think they were going to do anything at first, so we backed off. When we saw them knock you to the ground, we came running!" Billy explained.

"Well thank your mother for me. She saved my life. Do I know her?"

"No, I don't think so. She got up and clapped first. When you finished talking. She told us you were a good man and you'd go far." Billy smiled.

"Is your dad here?"

"No, he died in Nam a couple of years ago. He got a medal as you did, but not a big one like you got."

"He probably deserved the big one. Most of our soldiers do," Coby replied, as his two saviours shook his hand.

"Me and Bobby here just signed up for the Army. Thought we'd follow in our dad's footsteps." Billy grinned, as with a nod, the two ambled off back towards the hall.

"I hope you both do well! Your father would be proud of you both," Coby called out to them, as they waved a goodbye over their shoulders.

"Well, that debate went well?" Coby smirked, as he slowly climbed into his car. Body aching, he drove slowly home, glad the Billy and Bobby's mum had turned up.

Two months of talking till he was hoarse, found Coby four weeks out from the election. Delivering speeches was his gift, but running a campaign had him floundering. Working all day and well into night, he knew he was behind in the polls. He'd missed some important debates, mainly because he was so disorganised. Feeling the election slipping from his grasp, he was becoming despondent.

"Is this where I apply for a job?" A voice full of merriment called from the door. Coby speechlessly stared at Diana.

True to his word, Senator Van Clef had convinced her to help him. At first, she'd just wanted to give a little advice and keep her distance. When the Senator told her Coby was sinking, she decided it was time to come to him and volunteer to run his campaign. Telling him, she was only there to help and wanted it kept professional, wasn't what he wanted to hear. Nevertheless, knowing he was lost without help, made him agree. At least he would see her, and that was something.

As the clock ticked down, leaving only days till his electoral battle, Coby found himself at a Democrat rally for Senator Van Clef. Both he and Diana attended. Diana was there as a guest of her father-in-law, so Coby saw little of her. After the rally, they sat with Senator Van Clef who introduced Coby to as many influential supporters as possible. Diana, dressed in a simple black gown, looked stunning. Coby, hypnotised, had trouble avoiding staring at her. As the night drew to a close and the crowd was thinning, he approached Diana.

"How about we get a drink?" he asked, as his eyes wandered to her cleavage.

"It's too risky Coby. There are reporters everywhere."

"All I want to do is spend some time with you."

"I just don't feel comfortable here Coby."

"One drink isn't going to cause the downfall of America, is it?" He smiled. Looking at him she couldn't help but remember that stolen kiss at the hospital.

"Look, how about I meet you at your room in an hour? We can have some privacy then," she whispered, her eyes looking around the room.

"That sounds good to me."

"It's only for a drink Coby! You understand that, don't you?" she warned.

"Of course. I'll be on my best behaviour," he assured her. Faintly smiling, she walked over to the Senator, while Coby excused himself and left the party, hurrying to his room. Once inside he changed, putting on a casual shirt and pants. A knock at his door soon after made him jump. The clock confirmed she was early, as he rushed to the door. Pulling it open excitedly, he found the Senator's right-hand man Robert Charles, standing there.

"I'm not disturbing you, am I?" Robert asked, startled by the door being flung open.

"No, not at all! Come in," Coby answered, hiding his disappointment.

"The Senator wanted you to meet him for breakfast around eight if it's okay with you?" Robert asked. It suddenly occurred to him that Coby was expecting someone else.

"No problem Robert. You tell him I'd be honoured. And thanks for your help tonight. The Senator told me you'd arranged some of those introductions," Robert could see he meant it.

"No problem Coby. Someday I might need a job." He smiled, turning to go.

"And you would have it," Coby told him. Robert nodded before walking back to his room, just down the hall. Once there, Robert phoned the Senator to tell him Coby would be there. He tried to imagine what type of woman Coby would be attracted to. Most people would've thought it was none of his business, which was far from the truth. Coby would soon be, he hoped, a prominent member of his Party. He had to know what Coby was up to and into, to avoid any future trouble. The lift bell sounded, and he hurried to his door. Closing one eye he looked through the peephole to watch the corridor outside.

"If he or she is going to Coby's room they have to pass my door," he whispered, hoping it was a woman as even the Democrats avoided the gay issue at the moment. For a brief instant, the woman's tense face was visible as she glided by. It was enough! Shocked, Robert backed away from the door. Tripping over a coffee table, he ended up on the lounge. As he sat there, he tried to come to grips with what he'd just seen.

"Good God! What do I tell the Senator?"

Down the hallway, Coby had come to the conclusion Diana wasn't coming. Disappointed but understanding her position, he decided to turn in. He was just turning off the light in the lounge area when a faint knock sounded on his door. Thinking it could be Robert again, this time he opened the door with a more caution. Diana stood there looking close to crying. She moved inside past him, and he closed the door.

"I nearly didn't come tonight Coby. I was so scared that someone might see me coming to your room," she whispered as if terrified someone might be listening as well.

"I'm glad you did Diana. You've been so distant from me at the office; I was wondering if you still felt as I do," Closing the distance between them, he put his arms around her, holding her gently.

"We're in the public eye at your office. It's too risky!" she answered, enjoying the immediacy his arms provided.

"How about I make you that drink?" He suggested, reluctantly setting her free. The bar fridge yielded a small bottle of bourbon and two glasses into which he poured an equal nip topped up with coke. Diana meanwhile looked around Coby's room. It was a one-bedroom set-up similar to hers. The main room contained a kitchenette and lounge area, leading to the bedroom, which had a small bathroom off it. As much as she tried not to, her eyes kept going back to the bed. It seemed to grow, dominating the room and her thoughts, as she sought to keep herself under control.

When Coby had suggested, she comes to his room, for just for a drink, she'd sensed that tonight they'd lose control. She'd thought seriously about not going, feeling it was far too risky. On the other hand, she wanted to be with him, if not as man and wife, then as lovers.

"It's only for a drink," she'd assured herself, knowing full well there might be a bit of suppressed wanton passion, mainly kissing; but they could control themselves. "Yes, it will be okay," she convinced herself, making for the lift.

Pressing the up button to his floor, which was two floors above hers, she waited nervously. She'd considered for some time what she'd say if someone else was in the lift and who knew her when it stopped. The easiest thing was to say she was on the way to the Senator's suite, which was located four floors above hers. If that happened, she'd just press the Senator's floor button and visit him, covering her clandestine meeting. Instead, when the lift stopped at her floor, it was empty. Breathing a sigh of relief, she entered and lightly pressed his floor number. As the elevator went up, her doubts grew.

"You won't be able to stop! You're kidding yourself!" her conscience warned. Suddenly the lift pinged, announcing Coby's floor. Terrified she started to walk forward but froze in the doorway. The elevator doors unaware of her fear tried to close. Rebounding from its contact with her, the doors retreated. Startled, Diana almost fell out of the lift as she escaped onto Coby's floor. Scared, knowing her self-control was almost gone, she turned to re-enter the elevator, only to find the doors had already closed.

Knowing she couldn't just stand there, she walked towards his room, as if to an execution. Pausing before knocking, she felt her heart pounding in her chest as she waited. Moments later the door opened, and Coby cheerfully welcomed her holding her tightly. To her Coby's embrace became unbearable, as her suppressed wanton desires fought to break free. As she waited for her drink, Diana considered the gravity of the situation, feeling a serious urge to flee before it was too late.

"Are you all right Diana?" Coby's voice broke into her thoughts, startling her, returning her to the present.

"Yes, I just need a drink, but first I'll use the bathroom." She smiled, covering her nervousness, as she moved through the bedroom into the bathroom.

Coby watching her go waited patiently, sipping his drink slowly. God, he wanted her so much he admitted to himself. Hopefully, he would be able to keep things under control for her sake. Despite his promise to behave, he felt himself stir, knowing she was here in his room alone.

Diana, trembling, looked in the bathroom mirror. Taking out her comb, she tried to concentrate on tidying her ruffled hair. Looking at her breasts, Diana saw them surge up then down, as she fought for breath. Gulped down air as if she'd run a marathon, she tried to calm herself down. Sweat started to break out on her brow as she contemplated what would happen when she left the bathroom. Her whole body was on fire as she grabbed a towel wiping her face.

"God what can I do?" she murmured, her hands shaking, as she sat down on the side of the bath. "What I want to do!" she answered, as defiantly she stood. Taking off her clothes, she looked at herself in the mirror. Despite giving birth to Trevor, her body still looked good. In control her breathing steady again, she looked towards the door.

"Well it's now or never," she told herself, opening the door.

Coby in the kitchenette started to wonder what was keeping Diana. The bathroom door squeaking open, made him turn. Transfixed, he watched Diana emerge naked. To him she looked like a Roman statue, her body shimmering like white marble. As much as he tried to concentrate on her face, his eyes drank in her nakedness, her womanhood beckoning him. Placing his glass on the coffee table, trying not to rush or startle her, he moved towards her.

Stripping rapidly, he saw her stare at his nakedness. Without a word, she climbed onto the bed and lay down. Moving to her he sat down, marvelling at her beauty. Running his hands lightly over the contours of her body caused her to moan with pleasure, as he lay down beside her. Kissing her lips, he remembered their first kiss as his arousal grew. His touching now became more intimate as his hunger grew. Their kissing that had been so gentle and loving became more heated, more savagely passionate. Climbing above her, he hovered over her, as she pushed up against him.

"Are you sure Diana?" he asked, his heart pounding in his chest, knowing stopping now would just about kill him.

"Yes Coby, I've been ready since the first time I saw you." She moaned, pulling him down, as her legs wrapped around him.

Waking at first light, Diana carefully climbed out of bed. Coby lying naked with only a sheet covering his lower body, slept, his face half hidden by the pillow. Looking at his masculine chest cover with a thin layer of hair, Diana had the urge to touch him, wake him and make love again. The night had been everything she had expected and more. The first time had been about pent up lust, a letting go of their shared frustrations.

They had been like wild animals rutting for release, tearing at each other to satisfy their stored needs. After the initial satisfaction, they had made love, again and again, to satisfy their partner's every need, enjoying the time together. Just thinking about it made Diana hesitate about leaving. Looking down, she could see his hand marks on her body where he had held her savagely, as she raked his back with her fingernails. Smiling, remembering how wanton she had been, she forced herself to turn away and return to the bathroom for her discarded clothing.

Dressing she came back to the bed standing above Coby. Stealing a kiss, she left like a thief in the night, scared of the consequences if she was to stay. Back in her room, she showered, before resting in her own bed.

Coby rolled over to hear the alarm sounding. He'd set his alarm clock for seven before Diana had arrived, worried that he'd miss his breakfast appointment with the Senator. Reaching across, half asleep, Coby fumbled with the clock until he found the off button. Remembering the night, he turned to the empty space beside him. Diana was gone, and he felt an integral part of him was now missing. Last night had been a mixture of love, lust and passion all rolled into one. He felt emotionally drained; but he also knew if she was here now, he would have wanted her again.

He wiped his face and pushed back his hair, before standing and walking to the shower. Finished, feeling refreshed and clean-shaven, he dressed in silence. He was aware of how deserted the room felt now without her. "How long will it be until I can be with her again?" He asked himself. Seeing her at work would no longer satisfy his yearnings. They had talked during the night, mostly about their relationship. He wanted her with him, even if it meant giving up politics. She, on the other hand, felt he needed to follow his path and achieve what he saw as an obligation to his fellow man.

Coby, in the end, had to agree with her, knowing he would regret it if he didn't make a stand and try to change the country's attitude to segregation. Still, driven by his loneliness and need for her, he'd made her promise to share his love and bed whenever possible. It felt cheap somehow that they had to sneak around instead of proclaiming their love for each other, but for now, they believed that was all they were allowed.

"We'll work something out. We've got to!" he said out loud before leaving to meet the Senator.

"How's the campaign going?" the Senator asked, between cutting up his bacon and eggs. Coby had arrived at the restaurant, at the same time as the Senator and his assistant Richard.

"Good. The polls have me slightly ahead," Coby answered, his thoughts still wandering to last night, as he munched his cereal.

"Keep the pressure on Coby. Right up until the polling booths close, you're vulnerable. Many a politician has been left out of office by turning his or her back on the electorate when they thought they had it won."

"It's a lot more complicated than I thought. Just getting volunteers to man the hundreds of polling stations throughout my electorate, is a big deal."

"Wait till you're running for the Senate! Then you'll need thousands to man those polling stations! You'll be glad then that I had Diana give you a hand?" The Senator chuckled. Coby for the first time noticed Richard remained silent.

"Yes, she really makes a difference. I don't know what I'd do without her," he replied, watching Richard drop his fork nervously, before picking it up again. 'He knows! Somehow he knows!' Coby mused, remembering how he had just left before Diana arrived. For the next hour, they discussed the issues that affected the

State, before Richard reminded the Senator he had an appointment at ten. Excusing himself, the Senator left to change, while Richard remained.

"What the fuck are you doing with the Senator's daughter-in-law?" Richard growled protectively, once the Senator had left.

"I love her Richard. When enough time has passed, we intend to marry."

"How long has it been going on?"

"That's none of your business."

"As the Senator's PR officer and your party's political advisor, your personal life is my business. In public office, nothing is private for you Coby!" Richard forcefully reminded him. After thinking it over, Coby answered.

"A couple of years ago the Senator invited me for Christmas at his home. Diana and I struck up a friendship straight away. We met again at the medal ceremony in Washington for coffee. We kissed, but that was all. She's been writing to me since then, and I've been in love with her ever since the first time I saw her. I know it sounds crazy with her married at the time, but we were meant for each other."

"Did Bud know?"

"He was suspicious after the Christmas visit. He whipped Diana for just being with me, although that had more to do with my colour. When we met for coffee, he again beat Diana and his son for being with a nigger. So yes, he knew."

"Then why get killed saving you in Nam Coby? I know Bud was a racist, and he would've hated you for touching his wife let alone being in love with her. So why did he risk his life?" Richard asked as Coby sat there not answering. "It's bullshit, isn't it? He didn't save you at all, did he? Did you kill him?"

"No, I did not!" Coby angrily answered, making several patrons look their way. Richard warned him to settle down and waited for his reply. "We were waiting for the rescue boat when this Vietnamese kid stumbled onto us. Bud feared he'd inform on us and wanted to kill him. I stood in front of the kid, and he shot me. He made it clear he'd intended to kill me then and there. He was just about to finish me off when two Vietnamese soldiers appeared and shot him. One was the kid's father, so they let me go for saving him. I couldn't tell the truth, or my relationship with

Diana would've come out. There was also the Senator. He knew his son had faults and loved him regardless. I couldn't have him hurt by the truth; he's a good man." Coby looking exhausted, finished.

Richard sat there as if time was standing still. What he'd just been told could bring everything he'd worked for tumbling down in the blink of an eye.

"Who knows about this?"

"Just Diana and now you Richard, Bill, my co-pilot suspects something, but he won't talk."

"I suppose there's no way you'd break off your relationship with her?"

"I'll find another career, Richard. I love her, and that's the end of it!"

"Look there's no need for that. I for one hope you do marry her. You look good together. It's just the Democrats are heading into government on a platform of honesty. Nixon's finished, and the war has put the Republicans on the nose. Senator Van Clef is keeping it quiet, but it looks like he'll be the next Vice President. If it comes out that his son was a coward and you slept with his wife, we could lose the election!"

"What do you suggest?" Coby asked his eyes showing his growing uncertainty.

"Just keep it quiet until after the election. I know you want to do the right thing Coby, but in politics, the right thing can keep you in opposition for years."

"I just want Diana to be happy, that's all."

"I know Coby. Just be careful." Richard warned, glad it wasn't him.

As the Senator had predicted, Coby's fight for his right to represent the people of his state, went down to the wire. Senator Van Clef and Diana had insisted that Coby and his team of supporters continued to sell his message right up until the polls closed. Standing in the States Electoral Campaign Centre at midnight that night, Coby felt his future hang by a thread, as polling booths across his vast and diverse counties, painstakingly added up the votes. Once they'd tallied each county, they would send them into the Electoral Centre.

Both Coby and his main nemesis waited all smiles. Both confident of a win, they intently watched as the votes appeared on the wall-sized computer screen. Since eight that night, the two men had watched their other rivals fall by the wayside, while their two columns rose, the lead swapping periodically. It had always been down to either a Democrat or the Republican winning, as in United States elections, independents rarely make an impression.

For Coby, it was good to see the race narrow, knowing their pollsters had been correct in their predictions of a close two-party finish. Coby, sensing the moment of truth was nearly upon him, fingered the two messages he carried in his suit pockets. His right front pocket contained a message of hope for the future. His left, was his polite capitulation to his opponent.

"God, I hope I don't have to read that one," he said softly, as Diana standing beside him momentarily squeezed his hand.

"Don't give up! They haven't counted the Donnelly district yet, and there are a lot of votes for us there," she whispered back and moved away to check on her team.

"I'd be dead without her," Coby told himself, as he watched her rev up their supporters, assuring them of victory. Looking down at the desk where Diana worked, Coby saw her pad with the breakdown of ballot locations and the votes from each. She also had a graph showing what she thought they'd get from each area. As she had said, the Donnelly area had a large population, and she had sixty percent of the votes coming their way. Donnelly was a low-income area made up primarily of black voters.

'I shouldn't just depend on the black vote,' Coby thought to himself, hoping white people also trusted him. Looking at her predictions, she also showed Stanton Hill. This was a white area of middle-class income earners. Unlike Donnelly, this one had already been counted. Diana had calculated they'd receive forty percent of the vote. The actual figures showed he'd received a little more than fifty-two percent. "Maybe they are voting for me?" Then it struck him.

'No wonder she was confident, the swinging areas were going his way.' Looking across at his opposition, he saw his trade mark smile start to slip.

'He knows!' Coby mused, his own political smile remaining in place, as Donnelly's numbers hit the chart. A gap that hadn't seemed significant before widening. Coby's column surged ahead, leaving his opponent in his wake. The room exploded, as Coby's supporters saw the chart and cheered. Victory, at last, seemed within reach. The opposition's supporters, who up to now had matched cheer for cheer, remained pessimistically quiet. Their leader, who usually rallied them with a war cry, was also subdued.

Standing there surrounded by his supporters, he seemed to have lost stature, as if he had been abandoned and was alone. Coby knew that except for a few precious votes from Donnelly, he would be the one standing alone. Looking into the opposition's crowd, he saw the opponent's main financial supporter move up next to him. "You're fucked," Coby saw him whisper.

Approaching Coby, he removed a speech from his pocket, his lips moving, trying to get the words right. The crowd hushed as the two combatants faced off. Coby looked at his once invincible opponent, seeing the cracks of defeat etched on his face and felt for the man.

"Congratulations!" he choked out, as Coby put out one of his hands, raising the other in the air signalling for silence, stopping the man's humiliation.

"People!" he shouted. "Today this state seat picked one man out of two good men to govern. Either way, this county would've been lucky as in a contest like this, you're only as good as your opposition and in this man, I was indeed tested," Coby confessed, as cheers erupted in the room. His opponent at first surprised smiled and shook his hand.

"Thank you, Coby, for your generous words, but I've got to warn you. I'll be here again in two years!" he shouted, as the whole room cheered.

"I look forward to it," Coby answered, hugging the man.

Deep in thought, Coby drove home from his victory celebrations, both elated and disappointed. He had started his journey into politics with his first win. True it was only a State election, but a man had to start somewhere and his constituents and later his country, would judge him on how he performed here.

His disappointment was not with his victory. It was simply that Diana was missing from it. When the victory party had started, Diana who had stayed by his side all night, left early.

Tired from the campaign, she excused herself, giving him a quick peck on the cheek, no more and no less than the other women present. He had hoped that after the celebrations they could have been alone together. Instead, she had deserted him, leaving him depressed. Although they had agreed to keep their love secret until he reached the Senate, he had expected something more tonight. Even a passionate, quick stolen kiss in his office would have sufficed.

"Well maybe she's just cautious you fool!" he said out loud, knowing he wouldn't have been satisfied with just a kiss if they were alone.

At his apartment, which he rented above his office, he trudged up the stairs. Looking around the area where he'd parked, he entered his apartment locking the door behind him. He was aware that the racist segment of the community had warned him to stay out of politics. There had been no physical trouble, but threats were threats, and in the south, a black man took them seriously. Dropping his wallet and car keys on the side table, he was moving towards his bedroom, when he saw light squeezing through the crack under the bedroom's closed door.

Stopping as if he hit a wall, Coby tried to recall if he'd left it on. Knowing he hadn't, he looked around for a weapon. Spotting a baseball bat, he'd been presented with by a local baseball club for his support, he armed himself, before approaching the door. Turning the handle slowly, he braced himself, before flinging open the door. With a loud crash, the door smashed into the wall. Coby, leaping forward, was ready to swing, only to find Diana naked on his bed. Shocked she covered herself, as they both recovered from the surprise, calming down.

"Good God! You scared me half to death!" Diana giggled, short of breath, as Coby lowered his bat.

"I thought you were someone waiting in here, to do me harm!" Coby confessed, his heart still pumping, causing Diana to laugh hysterically.

"They wouldn't wait in your bedroom, Coby. They'd be near the front door where they could surprise you silly!" Diana pointed out, smiling. "Anyway, I thought you'd want a special reward for winning, so I snuck in here through the downstairs office. In the morning, I can dress and go downstairs and open the office at the usual time, no one should suspect anything."

"I owe this victory to you, Diana. Without you, I would've failed."

"Nonsense, it would've just been a lot closer." She sniggered, her eyes watching him, as she moved to the end of the bed, helping him undress. "I know we've got all night, but hurry my love, I need you right now!" she pleaded, as Coby naked, pushed her onto her back on the bed.

"That was a stroke of genius!" Senator Van Clef smiled, as he and Richard reviewed Coby's campaign.

"Which part Senator? The whole campaign went like clockwork," Richard replied, looking over the results.

"His speech when his opposition admitted defeat. Most would've put the boot in, rubbing their noses into their defeat. Instead, Coby saved the man from humiliation by supporting him."

"He'll go far, Senator. There's something about him that makes you remember him."

"Yes, this election proves he's got what it takes." The Senator smiled.

"I wonder what Coby would've done if we'd told him the polls warned us he'd be beaten convincingly. Diana knew, didn't she?"

"Yes, she did. When I told her about the secret polling the party had carried out, she just laughed. She told me the only poll that counted was the one on Election Day. She proved to be right."

"Just one thing Senator, why did the polling show he'd lose?"

"Two things, which the people at the moment are worried about. One is the war. Anything connected to the war is on the nose and Coby is connected. Two is his inexperience. Sure, he might've been a great fighter pilot, but what's he know about running a state? His opposition tried to focus on those two points throughout the campaign."

"Then why did he win?"

"Because Diana skillfully changed tack and avoided any fallout. Every time his opposite number started to zero in on his two weaknesses, she would hit the media with some plan Coby had come up with to help the state. The opposition was forced to come up with a better idea or try to downplay Coby's ideas. This took their focus off the attack. I can't believe what a perfect team they made Richard. I just wish Bud could've seen what they both achieved." The Senator turned away, wiping his eyes.

"She would've got Bud the Presidency Senator," Richard answered, trying to lift him.

"Unfortunately, no. Bud was always adamant that she wouldn't be involved in campaigning, which was a pity. He would've instead let her help Coby. It would have helped get him over a racism problem he had. They'd have made quite a team those three," Van Clef dreamed.

Realizing the Senator could only see his son through the imaginary vision Coby has created, Richard simply nodded.

"What next Senator?"

"Let's see how the party goes in the next election. If we win office, it will be my last term."

"But Sir!" Richard choked out.

"Don't start Richard! My mind is made up. In two years, I'm stepping aside. The State needs new blood, and that's where you come in. I want either you or Coby to run for my seat in the Senate." Richard tried to interject, but Van Clef stopped him again. "Hear me out, Richard. Both of you have what it takes, although it won't be easy. You're Mexican, and Coby's black, both of which will impact the voters, no matter what they tell you in public. Between then and now, you two have to prove your worth to them. Are you up to it Richard?"

"Senator I'd like nothing more than to run for your seat, but I'm an organiser like Diana, not a politician. Public speaking isn't my thing, although I'm an expert at writing speeches. I knew from my debating days that although I got the message across, I never persuaded the people to cross to my side. That is what Coby just did."

"I think you're wrong Richard. Maybe you just need more time to see yourself as I do. Putting that aside, if you don't want to run, I want you to help Coby. He'll need it if he takes on the big boys in

Washington." Richard stood there hesitantly, filled with indecision. Coby's career could crash and burn if his secret got out, ending Richard's career as well. On the other hand, Van Clef was asking him for help and Coby was a good man.

"I'll do it Senator. I'd be honoured."

Coby, representing his county, took his seat with the other members of their States House of Representatives. There, no matter what party they represented, they all tried to put forward their visions to advance their state's future. Since his first day in office, Coby had made it clear that he wanted equal rights for all. In schools, on public transport and at work, coloured people were still deprived of the very rights they'd fought for in Nam for the Vietnamese. Coby found that the courts, especially, discriminated against the poor. As the greater majority of the poor were coloured, Coby started there.

In his second week in the States House of Assembly, he presented a Bill to Parliament for the establishment of a legal aid service. It caused an uproar.

"How dare a new member to the chamber, demand millions of dollars of Government money be allocated to some lawyers so that they could work for the poor for free!" the opposition screamed. Undeterred Coby hit back putting solid augments behind his Bill. To Coby, it became a dogfight, but unlike flying, this one went down into the mud. He gave as good as he got, continuing the argument for over the next three months. In the end, the opposition capitulated, admitting the merits of the scheme.

Diana who had helped with the strategy watched from their office, as cars started to hoot their horns in the surrounding streets when the news broke.

"He made some waves today?" Richard, now semi-employed as Coby's public relations spokesman, chuckled from his desk opposite Diana's. True to his word, while he wasn't helping Vice President Van Clef at the White House, he was, on the side, helping Coby with his career.

"Yes, he's just made a lot of friends and a few enemies," Diana replied, watching the TV, which focused on the House of Representatives. In the front of the building, many white supremacists waved placards calling for Coby's resignation or worse. As Diana watched, Coby appeared at the top of the stairs where several microphones had been set up on a podium.

Coby walked to the podium to field questions from the waiting media.

Instead of bagging out the opposition, he praised them for seeing sense in helping the less fortunate to have an even playing field in court. Several members of the opposition, who waited behind him for their turn, were caught off-guard by his praise. When asked their opinion, they found themselves backing Coby's plan, demonstrating bilateral support. Diana had never been prouder of him. Not only did he get the Bill through, but he also made everyone a winner, guaranteeing the Bill's longevity. Diana was about to comment on the crowd's good behaviour when a man charged at Coby.

The police caught off guard gave chase, as the man drew a gun from his pocket. Coby saw the man draw a weapon and pushed the other House members beside him to the ground, just as the man fired. The bullet grazed Coby's left armed, spinning him down and sideways. As he steadied himself, the shooter again aimed.

"You deserve this nigger!" he screamed. Knowing he couldn't escape, Coby braced as the shot rang out. The man above him appeared to freeze, a look of intense pain spreading across his face. He dropped his gun on the step beside Coby, before crumpling backwards like a rag doll, down two flights of steps. Behind the shooter, a state trooper unseen by Coby had gone down on one knee, taken aim and fired, hitting in assassin in the chest.

Dazed and in pain, Coby slowly got to his feet, as the panicked crowd ran in every direction, trying to get away. Checking his arm, he found the bullet had passed straight through. It stung like hell, so he removed his coat to check it. Blood was pouring from the two holes on either side of his forearm. Ripping off, his one of the sleeves of his shirt, a second state trooper helped secure it around his wounds, helping to stop the flow of blood.

"Thanks," Coby said to the retreating back of the trooper who moved off to help hold back a group of white supremacists trying to get closer. Down below him, he saw the shooter lying on the stairs, watching him. Bleeding profusely from his chest wound, he lay on his side, a trooper watching him. Coby folded his coat as he approached the injured man and knelt down beside him. Because it was evident the bullet hadn't passed through, Coby held the coat against the entry wound.

"He tried to kill you!" the Officer who had fired, pointed out. He was amazed Coby would help him.

"I know, but I can't stand by and let him bleed to death," Coby answered. The trooper silently nodded. Holstering his weapon, he got down on the ground beside Coby to assist. Several minutes had passed before the paramedics arrived.

"We'll take care of him now Mr. Henderson, "one of the paramedics assured him, as the shooter was examined and in time loaded onto a stretcher, with Coby's coat under his head. Another paramedic reviewed and bandaged Coby's arm, before taking him to the hospital in a second ambulance. Returning to the House of Representatives in a taxi, Coby found the three Opposition members whom he'd pushed to the ground, outside waiting for him.

"That was brave of you to shield us, Coby! Thank you!" Adrian Holden, the leader of the Opposition said, shaking Coby's good hand.

"I just reacted, that's all."

"I don't understand why you helped that man! He tried to kill you!" Adrian said, bewildered.

"I don't know Adrian. He looked as if he was dying and I thought I could help?"

"You're a good man Coby, but you can't help everyone. Some don't like being helped. Let's get back inside and find you another coat?" Adrian smiled, as Coby walked with him.

"A shirt wouldn't go astray either." Gregory Chance another opposition member smiled.

"I forgot about that!" Coby chuckled, looking at his sleeveless, bandaged arm, as the others joined in.

"I'm sure we'll find you something! It's the least we can do," Adrian reassured him as they entered the House.

"I've got another Bill coming up, you know?"

"Don't push the friendship, Coby!" Gregory laughed, as they entered the chamber to a sea of people clapping.

Across town at their office, Diana screamed as the TV relayed the armed man running towards Coby and taking a shot. The TV then went blank, before transmission transferred to a newsroom where the shocked presenter reported Mr. Henderson had been shot. Grabbing her bag, Diana rushed towards the door.

"Diana stop!" Richard shouted, running after her. "Let me drive?" he suggested taking her keys. They had travelled half the distance to the House of Representatives when the radio reported a news flash. Its audience was reassured that no one had been injured, except the shooter. Senator Henderson, who had been shot in the arm, was in a stable condition and had left hospital to return to the House.

"Oh, Richard I'm such a fool! I should have waited instead of panicking!" Diana cried, sobbing across from him.

"You love him, Diana. There is nothing silly about that," Diana looked intently at him.

"You know! How long have you known?"

"Since you visited Coby's room at the Convention. Don't worry; I won't tell anyone! Mind you, if someone else had been in the office today, they would now know."

"I'm tired of keeping it a secret Richard. I want to be Coby's wife, not his secretive secretary he sleeps with when we think it's safe." She sobbed, as Richard stayed quiet. "Do you think less of us Richard?"

"I don't think less of you Diana. I think you're both in a bind, which will soon be over. And I might say, I've never seen two people more made for each other than you two are."

"Thank you, Richard, that's means a lot to me." She smiled, wiping her eyes.

"Do we continue to the House?"

"No turnaround! I'll ring him as soon as we get back to the office."

TREVOR

Trevor stared down at all thirteen candles, as his friends sang happy birthday to him. His mother, grandfather and grandmother stood to one side, allowing his tight knit group of friends to enjoy his moment, without too much parental restraint. Becoming a teenager meant he'd started his transition to adulthood. It had been a fun afternoon with his friends. The only problem all day was the unexpected arrival of that nigger, as his friends called him. Coby had dropped in to give Trevor a present, which he had to admit he'd liked.

Something about him had always worried Trevor. Maybe it was the way he tried so hard to get him to like him or the way his mother looked at him. They were always slipping away to talk politics, but Trevor suspected there was more to it than that. Ever since those hospital visits, his mum had become attached to the man his father had saved. Trevor figured his mother thought he might somehow be a replacement for his dad. Grandfather to seem to like him, which made the whole situation unbearable, as Trevor had no one to confide in.

"Blow the candles out Trevor! We're all getting hungry!" Jamie Benson yelled out. Trevor, with a big breath, took his frustrations out on the candles.

The party continued to midnight before his boys retired for the night. Being a weekend, Diana had arranged a sleepover in Trevor's room. Overcrowded with friends, they lay there fighting off sleep, as joke after joke broke the silence. Many had racist overtones, of which Trevor knew his mum would not approve; but it seemed harmless as the night stretched into the early morning. By two the room had grown quiet as sleep finally started to overtake even the most ardent sleep fighters.

"Trevor, what's going on between your mother and that black man?" Jamie asked out of the darkness.

"Nothing Jamie. She works for him, that's all. My grandfather asked her to," Trevor answered defensively.

"My dad says it's wrong for a white woman to be with a black man," Neil, another of his school friends spoke out. Trevor fought to find the right answers. In the end, he went for his usual defence.

"My dad died saving his life. My family is just doing the right thing by my father's memory," Trevor replied, hoping to end the discussion.

"Do you know for sure that's what happened? My dad told me your father hated Coby, so why did he die saving someone he didn't like?" Jamie snarled as room gasp.

"Your father's full of shit Jamie. If they were friends or not, they were both fighting for their lives. No one knows what happened that night. Trevor's dad was a brave man, and despite his colour, so is Mr. Henderson! Everyone knows that. They don't give the Medal of Honor to just anyone, so let's all go to sleep? I tired of this bullshit!" Lance, one of Trevor's closest friends intervened, stopping any further talk.

Shocked, Trevor lay there looking at the ceiling. Could Jamie's father be right? He remembered the beating he and his mother took that night when his father accused his mother of being with a nigger. Could Coby have been the black man? It made sense. So, if his father hadn't died defending Coby, how did he die? If Coby and his mum had been involved, did Coby kill him so that he could be with his mother?

He had to find out more. Who would know and more importantly would tell him? It boiled down to asking Coby. But what if he was wrong? Filled with doubt, Trevor finally drifted off to sleep, his life forever changed.

Vice President George Van Clef walked out of the White House for the last time. In a month, elections would start, and again the rival parties would vie for a chance to represent their States in the House of Representatives and the Senate. They had done well during their two terms in office, but George Van Clef was looking forward to retirement. Four years he'd been the Vice President, two years longer than planned.

He smiled as he thought of Richard who had given in to his badgering and was running for a seat in the House of Representatives. Coby would be running for his own seat in the Senate. Both were good men, and both faced insurmountable challenges. A Mexican, and an African American, as they were now called, were running for two different seats in his State. Coby would have another problem to handle as he wanted to marry Diana.

When Coby had come to him at his home where they'd first met, for "a talk" as he put it, George had known something important was coming. Usually, totally in control, Coby had seemed nervous almost anxious. George had been trying to work out what could upset him so when he asked him if he could he marry Diana. At first, George was too stunned to reply. Despite his hatred of racism, the thought of Diana and Coby together somehow didn't seem right after she had been married to Bud.

"Why are you asking me, Coby? I'm not her father!" George bluntly asked.

"Her parents are both deceased, and you will always be her father-in-law and grandfather to Trevor," Coby explained. While trying to come to terms with the shock, George saw a man before him who had always stood up for the down trodden and weak, someone who fought for a person no matter what colour he was. A man to be proud of stood before him, waiting for an answer.

"I'm sorry Coby! Of course, you can! It's just quite a shock to me, Diana being Bud's wife and all." George smiled, shaking Coby's hand.

"The colour thing takes a bit of getting used to, doesn't it?" Coby pointed out, knowing George must have his reservations.

"How did your parents handle it?"

"About the same reaction as you did. When I fell in love with Diana, I too had doubts. I suppose it's ingrained after hundreds of years of hatred."

"The barriers are coming down son. It's only a matter of time now."

"Should I announce it before the campaign starts?"

"That's up to you two. At least the engagement should be announced, to stop people thinking it's just a stunt."

"Good idea, although we should tell Trevor first before he finds out from someone else."

"How is he going anyway? Since he went to the same University as his father, we've heard very little from him."

"Good, although his University is one of the last hold outs on segregation. I might take Diana down there later in the campaign to see if I can change their position on segregating students."

"Good luck with that Coby! There's a lot of old money down in that corner of the State. They won't let their old way of life go without a fight."

"I can be very pervasive."

"Yes, you can! I saw that tonight."

Trevor stood beside his mother, as the priest performed the marriage ceremony. When his mom and Coby had come to him to tell him, he'd been too astonished to reply. Seeing his mother's hurt look, he had, in the end, agreed and even managed to smile. Swallowing his hatred for the man who may have killed his real father was hard. He doubted he'd be able to keep silent forever. Now, as he dutifully stood beside his mother, acting as if she was marrying a decent man, instead of a murderer, he found it a lot harder to appear happy.

Couldn't she see he was evil? Didn't she suspect his hand in his father's death? Looking around at the gathering he saw a mixture of black, white and even Mexican people standing there, some crying. What was his mother thinking? His friends at school had been horrified that his mother was marrying a coloured man. Trevor hadn't been too worried until students at the school started avoiding him. Even the teachers and especially the Dean appeared offended as if they were marrying Coby themselves.

To Trevor colour wasn't the problem. His father's death was. Yet now he stood tongue-tied, as the priest asked if anyone objected to the marriage. Now was his chance to clear the air and ask if Coby had killed his father! Instead, he remained mute, taking the coward's way out. A shout from the crowd startled him, as looking up he saw his mother kissing Coby, as the priest declared them married. Shame made Trevor fake sickness as he left the ceremony to sulk in his room. He'd been laying on his bed for maybe an hour when a knock sounded at his door. Coby stood there.

"It's about time we talked Trevor, man to man. I can see you're not happy with my marrying your mother. Is it because I'm black or is there another reason?" Coby asked, his voice flat, but not unfriendly.

"No, it's not that, although for my friends it's an issue," Trevor replied his voice shaking with both fear and anger.

"Then spit it out. Let's get this over with!"

"Did you kill my father?" Trevor snarled, his anger spilling out.

"Why would you think such a thing, Trevor?" Coby whispered, his eyes looking haunted.

"Jamie's father knew my dad from college. He said there's no way in hell my dad would save a black man," Trevor told him, intently watching Coby's reaction.

"He's right Trevor. Your father didn't save me. In fact, it was quite the opposite."

"He knew you'd been with my mum, didn't he? He had beaten us before he left for Vietnam. He said mum had been with a nigger; I guess, that, was you?"

"Yes, it was, but nothing physical happened between us, until after your father had died. You have my word on that."

"So, what happened?"

"A kid came along as we were waiting to be rescued. Your father wanted to kill the boy before he told the enemy where we were. I said no, and he shot me. It was then he told me that he knew I was in love with your mother. He was about to finish us both when two soldiers turned up. They shot your dad and let me go for saving the kid. That's what happened. I couldn't tell anyone for fear of ruining the lives of you and your mother."

"And you expect me to believe that?" Trevor accused.

"You can believe what you like Trevor. I made up the other story to prevent hurt to you, your mum and your grandfather. Your father was a good pilot Trevor and a hero; he just couldn't handle that his wife didn't love the man he was."

"I'd like to be alone now if you don't mind?" Trevor demanded, his eyes misting up.

"Okay, Trevor. I'll give you space to work it out for yourself. Just remember, I mightn't be your father, but I'm here to help, and I'd like to be your friend. If you have any problems, come to me. We can work it out man to man. Okay?"

"We'll see," Trevor answered. Coby sensed he hadn't convinced him at all as he sadly left.

Trevor now sixteen, stood within the crowd at his University chanting. Like the rest, he was watching for the Democrats new candidate, running for the Senate. The protest had been arranged, because of this candidate views on his University stand on segregation. Of course, he knew it was Coby, his stepfather, which made his position at the University untenable. Since the wedding he'd kept his distance from the man, his coming here he'd taken personally. All the students of course there knew, although to save his embarrassment, they kept quiet about it.

The faculty staff members were lined up in front of the administration building, while the majority of the students blocked the entrance to the University's front gates. This was deliberate, as the faculty staff could later say they were unable to speak with the candidate for the Senate because the students had blocked the road. Trevor's thoughts were interrupted as a howl erupted from the crowd near the gate, signalled that Coby had arrived.

Most assumed once he saw the angry crowd, he would turn around and leave, fleeing confrontation. Trevor knew they didn't know Coby at all. As the group of vehicles came to a stop, over the heads of the crowd, Trevor saw Coby get out. He looked at the students and walked forward into their surprised midst, heading up the driveway followed by his entourage. Two of the people in his entourage were tall black men like Coby. The others were too short to see over the crowd, although some appeared to be women.

When he reached the surprised faculty staff, Coby extended his hand for the Dean to shake. Caught off guard, the Dean's automatic response was to take his hand. The subdued crowd suddenly burst into life, hurling abuse. Coby continued talking with the staff, ignoring the huge crowd as if they weren't screaming at him. After several minutes, the noise level from group reduced, as they tired.

"My God, the cowards are giving up! We've got to do something!" Jamie shouted looking for support. Reaching down, he picked up a rock, handing it to Trevor. "When I give the word throw it at that nigger!"

"Jamie, I don't know if I should. He's my stepfather after all!"

"He's here to change our way of life Trevor. You're either with us or against us," Jamie growled, as Trevor's friends all stood watching him.

"Okay, I'll throw the rock. Just yell when you're ready," he answered, his guts in a knot as he stood waiting.

"Now! Throw it now!" Jamie's voice exploded from behind the brick wall to his right. Trevor, aiming for a window behind the Dean and his stepfather, tossed the rock, praying Jamie and his other friend, would be happy with his show of defiance.

When Coby first arrived at the gate, his first thought was for Diana. He told the driver to stop and turn around, but Diana stopped him.

"We don't run from bullies Coby. Let's get out and walk up to where those cowards are waiting!" Coby unsure got out first and gauged the crowd's reaction. As a test, he walked forward and saw their surprise. Bluffing, he continued as the unruly mob magically moved aside letting him through. Diana, with Richard and a small group of people, walked several paces behind Coby's two bodyguards who made up his entourage.

"Maybe it would be wise for you to wait here, Diana?" Richard proposed, studying the crowd. He'd come along to lend support. Nobody had warned him that he might have to walk through a crowd of angry, vocal students.

"We will be okay Richard. Look at Coby. They are letting him through!"

"Yeah, but that guy's invincible." He pointed out. With Diana at his side, they moved through the demonstrators.

Undaunted, Coby continued to move forward, parting the crowd like Moses parted the sea, till he reached the Dean. The Dean was visibly stunned by his appearance, as Coby relying on instinct reached out to shake his hands.

"Glad to meet you, Dean. This is quite a welcome!" Coby smiled, waving to the crowd as the yelling increased.

"They want you to leave I'd say?" the Dean retorted, as the crowd's noise level continued.

"Nonsense! They're getting used to my being here. How about we go inside?" Coby suggested as a window smashed, causing the noise level to cease. Coby, like the Dean, flinched at the sound.

"That was close!" Coby smile. As he watched, he saw the Dean's face bleach to an ashen grey.

"Oh my God!" the Dean shouted. Coby surprised, turned to see what he was looking at. Horrified, saw Diana on the ground covered with blood.

"Diana!" He screamed, rushing to her side he knelt down beside her. She looked at him, her mouth moved, but no words came. Blood was pumping out of a deep wound in her left temple. He ripped off his coat and pressed it against the wound.

"Someone call a doctor now!" Richard bellowed as several campus staff ran for help.

"Coby, I can't see! It hurts so much!" she managed to stammer as blood seeped through the fabric of his jacket. Frantic, he put more pressure on the wound to stop the continuous flow.

The police, who had been following Coby, had remained outside the University. Their choice to not interfere caught them off guard. They'd hoping the trouble-making black Senator to be, would leave when he saw the crowd. Seeing someone in his group was hurt caused them to surge into the University grounds. The crowd, witnessing what had occurred and the late police entry, melted away, many shame-faced.

"Call an ambulance!" Coby screamed to the police, sounding not entirely human. The police, feeling guilty for not intervening sooner, rushed to help. A doctor on the University staff hurried to Diana's side, as the police pulled Coby aside so he could work on her. Blood began to pool on the ground as the doctor tried to stem the bleeding.

"Coby don't leave me!" Diana groaned, her hand reaching for his. Her body jerked as she fought to live.

"I'm here love. Just lay still while the doctor looks at your wound," he gently assured her. His face seemed to age ten years in seconds. The facility staff seeing Diana in pain, guiltily moved inside, leaving Coby with his grief. Despite working frantically, the doctor finally stood up, shook his head and wiped his hands. Ashamed, he had trouble facing Coby.

"I'm so sorry. There's nothing more I can do," he said softly. Coby, moaned in pain, before dropping to the ground beside her. Reaching for Diana, he held her to him, as her eyes lost their glint, her hand then slipped from his grasp, as her body relaxed in finality. Heartbroken, Coby wanted to shake her and shout at her to stay, he didn't, knowing she'd lost her fight to live.

"No God don't take her from me!" Coby prayed, as Trevor appeared in the thinning crowd

"Mummy!" He cried, fighting his way to his mother's side. The doctor was relieved to be able to move back and stand with the police. Trevor, his face a mask of pain, looked down on the blood-covered body of his mother. He dropped to the ground next to her and hugged her, trying to bring her back to life. Coby emotionally distraught, collapsing to the ground next to his wife.

The media, of course, snapped away, recording Coby's soul-destroying suffering. The police seeing this invasion of privacy pushed the media back, shielding Coby in his grief.

"Did anyone see who threw the rock?" an Officer wearing gloves asked, as he picked up an object and placed it in a plastic bag. Silence followed the question as the two men sat beside the blood-covered woman. For twenty minutes the police spread out through the now scattered crowd, asking if anyone had seen anything.

On their return, the Officer in charge asked the two men to let them take Diana. Reluctantly both rose, as Diana lifeless body was placed on a stretcher and covered with a blanket. Coby pulled Trevor to him for comfort, till Diana's son gradually stopped sobbing.

"I threw the rock just to scare you, Coby!" Trevor moaned. "I didn't mean to hit mum or anyone!" Trevor blubbered his confession. Those within hearing froze.

"No Trevor! Tell me you're lying!" Coby groaned, pushing Trevor away as if he'd become a demon.

"It was an accident! I didn't mean to hurt anyone!" he cried out, as a police officer moved towards him. Turning him around, the officer, handcuffed him, before reading him his rights.

"Coby, I'm sorry! I didn't mean it!" Trevor wept in anguish, as the police led him away to a police van. Coby, unable to respond or even look at him, slowly stood as if turning to stone.

"Coby we've got to go," Richard whispered. He received no answer. With the help of another member of Coby's team, they lifted and carried him to their waiting car.

"She's gone, Richard. I never had time to trulyl love her. How can she be gone?" he asked, as they slowly drove away.

Trevor, under police guard, attended the funeral. George Van Clef like Coby, couldn't look at him, the pain was too great. Richard, seeing the state Trevor was in, held him while his mother was buried. After the funeral, Coby remained at the grave, unable to leave Diana. His whole life had revolved around her, and now he fought to find a reason to live.

"Do you think she'd want you languishing about here?" Van Clef's voice echoed behind him.

"Leave me, alone Senator. I've got nothing to say," Coby whispered, his will to live gone.

"So, you're just going to sit here and sulk are you? What about the election?"

"I don't give a shit about the election, let alone being a Senator at the moment, so fuck off!"

"Well, you do have some fight left after all! Do you think Diana would want you to throw your life away, instead of helping the people of this State? Get over it and get back out there Coby."

"You don't understand Senator! She was everything to me,"

"How dare you? I lost my son, then my wife and now Diana! How dare you think you're the only one who lost something? If you want to stay here and wallow in self-pity, then go ahead! I thought you had more guts than that, you coward!" One minute Coby was at the graveside, the next he was gripping George's throat. Looking at Van Clef's face next to his, his anger fled. Letting him go, he broke down and hugged him.

"I'm sorry Senator. I just can't see the future without her."

"Run for the Senate for her son. It's what she wanted you to do. There are too many people depending on you for change. Don't throw it all away." Standing there by Diana's grave, Coby realised Van Clef was right. Diana would have wanted him to help people and make the most of the opportunities.

"Let's go then," Coby suggested, as arm around each other's shoulder, they moved towards their vehicles.

"Hey! Stop calling me Senator! It's George or Ex Vice President!"

"You will always be the Senator to me," Coby answered, smiling for the first time in a long while.

Trevor was sentenced soon afterwards. The trial was just a formality as he had confessed his guilt. Because of his privileged background, his youth was not taken into consideration. He was given eight years in prison, the first three in a juvenile facility. Coby and Van Clef both attended, neither making a plea for leniency. After his sentencing, he had the chance to ask his family for forgiveness for what he'd done. Coby stood and replied.

"We forgive you Trevor, but we can't forget. You took away something special from this world, someone we all loved. For that you must be punished," Coby pointed out, then sat down his face emotionless.

"Thank you anyway, Coby. You won't see me again," Trevor promised. Crestfallen, he was led away, into captivity.

Coby won the election in a landslide. The people had witnessed his suffering and greatness in the face of unfathomable pain, and their hearts went out to him. Richard also won his seat although it was a much harder fought battle. In a way, Coby would always wonder about that election. Would he have been elected if Diana hadn't been taken from him? 'It would've just been a little harder,' he remembered her saying, smiling at the memory. Two years later, he won again, still by a fair margin.

He was known now as a tough, incorruptible politician, devoted to his State. In his third term, while pushing through a Bill for equal pay for all workers, regardless of colour, he hit a crossroad in his life.

As always, he had received the usual death threats, and as usual, he ignored them. That was until someone torched his electoral office. The FBI who handled this type of threat warned him not to proceed with a planned march through the Capital. Sitting down with Richard and the Senator, he asked their advice. Both confessed they had reservations about his marching, as security would be minimal. In the end, he decided to march, seeing it as a necessary risk for his beliefs.

On the day of the march, the FBI came to him, suggesting he wear a bulletproof vest. Declining their offer, he laughed off their concerns, pointing out no one else marching that day would have one. The march was completed without any incident. Coby addressed the crowd afterwards, to generate support for equal pay and to try to bridge the gap between the 'haves' and 'have nots'. Coby was overwhelmed by the crowd's support. Considering the march an outstanding success, he happily returned to his office. He was ringing the Senator to suggest dinner when from his desk, he saw a man enter the office.

"Can I help you?" Coby asked. Looking at his visitor's hands, he noted a swastika tattoo on one of them. Seeing where Coby was looking, the young man suddenly drew a pistol and fired at point blank. The left side of Coby's chest was hit, and he was catapulted backwards. On the floor, unable to move, he watched his assailant walk towards him, preparing to fire again. Shouts from outside and the sound of a siren approaching, made the young man hesitate, before running out the front door. Lying on the floor being drowned in pain, Coby heard the distant sounds of screams, as several of his female staff arrived from the rear of his office.

Prone and staring at the ceiling, Coby flashed back to when he was shot by Bud. Pain, agonising pain, again made him cry out, as he saw faces some white, some black and one Asian above him. Scared, he blinked his eyes to clear away the demons of his past. Faintly he heard the sound of screeching tires as the sirens stopped.

"Hold on Senator Henderson!" someone shouted near him. Suddenly his vision blurred and he lapsed into unconsciousness.

"Hang in there Senator!" reverberated through his mind. He opened his eyes to see the hazy shapes of two paramedics working above him.

"He's conscious!" one of them shouted happily to the driver, his huge grin making his face light up.

"I told you he was a fighter!" The other laughed, continuing to work on him. Confused, Coby tried to communicate, but his mind had trouble making his words come.

"Is Bud okay? Did you get here in time?" he asked, his mind returning to the past. Both paramedics looked at each other.

"What's he talking about?" one paramedic asked.

"Bud Van Clef was a fighter pilot. Got the Medal of Honor for saving the Senator here's life, when they were in Vietnam." The driver shouted, causing the paramedics to go silent.

"I remember that! Didn't Senator Coby get the Medal of Honor too?"

"Yeah, he did, and it will take more than some arsehole with a gun to stop this guy!" the driver barked above the noise of the siren. In the hospital driveway, they cut the siren and screeched to a stop. Opening the rear doors, the paramedics were momentarily blinded by camera flashes.

"Get back you vultures!" A cop ordered. He and several other police officers shielded the medics, as they rushed Coby into the Emergency Department through two giant plastic doors.

"You made it Senator! We're here," the paramedics reassured Coby as a nurse and Doctor appeared.

Coby, his vision blurred, focused on the nurse.

"Hey, I know you?" He groaned as the nurse attached an IV drip to his arm.

"Yes, you do Senator. But for now, just lay there quietly while the doctor looks at your wound." Her eyes misted while she assisted the doctor.

"There won't be any medals this time?" he coughed out, as the people around him looked at one other.

"No Senator. The war is over now," the Doctor quietly responded, adding a needle to the drip.

"Then why are we still shooting at each other?" Coby asked. This time no one answered.

GLENDA

Two days after the shooting, Coby opened his eyes and looked around. The nurse from his past was sitting and reading a magazine beside him.

"It's Glenda, isn't it?" he rasped, as the nurse jumped to her feet.

"You nearly scared me to death Senator! And yes, my name is Glenda."

"You were at the hospital in Washington when I came back from Nam?"

"Yes, I transferred back home to take up a position as head theatre nurse here." She continued to smile at him.

"I'm glad you did," he managed to say, as Glenda placed a straw in his mouth. The fresh water was like heaven to his parched lips. "Thank you, nurse."

"No problem Senator. So how did this happen?"

"The name is Coby. I attended a rally. I was warned not to."

"You're still stubborn then?"

"As a mule, I'd say," he joked.

"I was sorry to hear about your wife's death. She was something special."

"Yes, she was," he whispered faintly, as approaching footsteps echoed down the hallway. No nonsense knocking announced the four men who entered his room.

"Sorry to disturb you, Senator. My name is Agent Coulder. I'm the one who warned you about the march. We have some news about your shooting."

"At least you didn't say I told you so. Let's hear the news." Coby lay there expectantly.

"We tracked the shooter to a right-wing group. They're holed up in a farm outside the Capital. It seems these guys were even too wild for the local clan. They, in fact, told us where to look. Isn't that something?"

"So, what now?" Coby asked.

"We're sending a SWAT team out to convince them to come in for questioning."

"You tell those men to be careful Agent Coulder. The guy who shot me gave me no warning."

"Don't worry Senator. They know what they're up against. I know it's hard to remember, but have you seen the shooter before?"

"No, I hadn't seen him before, although I could identify him in a lineup."

"That's good. Anything unusual about him?"

"He had a swastika on his left arm." Coby noticed how the FBI agents looked at each other. He concluded that they knew the shooter.

"That is great Senator! Anything else?"

"No. He just walked straight into my office and opened fire. I'm just lucky the guy was a lousy shot."

"Yeah, we think the young man was put up to it by the leader of the group. Anyway, we'll keep you updated, but we're pretty sure you won't have any more trouble from this group."

"Thank you Agent Coulder, and again thanks for your help."

"No problem, although next time, please listen, Sir?" He smiled to soften the severe message delivery.

"Good luck with that Officer!" Glenda put in, making everyone laugh. "Well, it looks as if those bad guys won't be hurting anyone else?" Glenda pointed out, once the FBI had left.

"There's always someone out there who thinks a gun is an answer to everything."

"Yes, there is Senator. Remember that when you're out there causing trouble the next time," she sniggered, kissing him lightly on the forehead, before leaving. Coby watched her go and remembered his first assessment of her several years ago. Glenda still had a good firm figure and as she walked away, her bottom swaying rhythmically from side to side. Coby felt himself stir, for the first time in a long time.

"I owe you a kiss nurse," he whispered to himself, with a secretive smile.

"She's from the wrong side of town Coby. Your numbers will take a hit!" Richard warned Coby when they met at his electoral office. Coby had been seeing Glenda since his stay in the hospital over a year ago.

"I love her Richard. That's all that matters," Coby replied, his anger rising.

"Look, Coby, I like Glenda too, but the opposition will jump on her having a son out of wedlock."

"God Richard it's the nineties! People aren't as uptight as they used to be."

"You know I'm right Coby. Middle America still hasn't got over the war in Nam, let alone racial equality. I tell you you're best to wait and get married after the election."

"We can't Richard. Glenda's mother has cancer. She could go at any minute. It's got to be now."

"Then go for it. Just remember, you're going to have to pull out all the stops in the next campaign, or you'll be looking for another career like I had to."

"You can run again Richard. You lost your seat to an opponent who had money to burn. You can't do anything about the fickleness of the voters."

"Remember that Coby at the next election."

"Maybe he's right Coby. Maybe we should wait?" Glenda whispered. For more than a month Glenda and her son Michael had been living with Coby. Michael, at first, was a blank wall to Coby's attempts to befriend him. Now, after a lot give and take, they had a good relationship.

"No Glenda, I'm not waiting! Your mum told me that she wants to see you in a stable relationship for Michael sake. He needs a dad, and I'll do everything to see he gets one."

"What about your career? You love being a Senator!"

"We don't always get what we want Glenda. All Diana wanted was for her son and both of us to be happy and look what happened? No, I'd rather go out and find another job, then go through all that again, because I didn't do the right thing."

"It wasn't your fault Coby! Sometimes bad things occur, no matter what you do."

"I lied to him about his father, hoping to shelter him from the truth. Even though I still think it was the right thing to do, it shattered him when he did find out. Not only did I lose Diana, but he's also lost to me as well."

"Then why not visit him? He's nearly through his sentence. It might help you both?"

"I can't Glenda. It's too painful! Seeing him would bring back what he did, what he took away from us both. No, when he threw that rock meant for me, it ended our connection. Better to let it rest."

"I sometimes feel I'm sharing you with Diana."

"I must admit, for a while there, you were. But now I feel I've moved on. I will always love Diana, but you're the one I love now. Never doubt it." Reaching across, he pulled her to him and soundly kissed her lips. Without another word, Glenda pulled her nightie off over her head, threw it on the floor and straddled him and started kissing him wantonly.

"Show me then?"

Despite Richard's misgivings, Coby was re-elected, though by only a small margin. Coby's friendship with Michael took several careful years to mature, till they reached the point where he called Coby Dad. For twenty years Coby served the people of his State always honestly and supportively. Retired Senator Van Clef became Michael's de facto uncle, always giving advice and spoiling him rotten. As Michael grew into adulthood, he followed Coby into the Air Force and served with distinction. Van Clef one night confessed to Coby he'd kept track of Trevor, helping him find his way when he left prison.

Coby found his wound had healed concerning Trevor and told the Van Clef he'd done the right thing. The old senator told Coby that Trevor had changed his name and travelled overseas, trying to find his way. Once in a while, he would call Van Clef, asking how his family and especially how Coby was.

"I hope he's okay Senator. Although what he did was monstrous, he too has suffered," Coby grudgingly admitted.

"I know Coby, but now he's the only relation I have left, apart from your family, which I've adopted." He smiled. "Speaking of them, I hear Michael's following your footsteps?"

"Yeah, he's running for a seat in the Lower House. I think he could go all the way someday? Meantime, I hear you're the keynote speaker at the party's convention this year?"

"Yeah, they're dragging out an old warhorse to show the party's got soul," he chuckled before his face became serious.

"You know Coby, the nominations for President and Vice President are coming up?"

"Don't give me that look Senator! The American people are not going to vote for a black President. We have not come that far yet," Coby told him.

"Maybe you're right. But what about the Vice President? Like me, you can give whoever runs some much-needed support?"

"I'll think about it Senator, although I'm happy just representing my State," Coby admitted.

"Well bring Michael along anyway! It's funny, but he reminds me of Bud. Do you think that's weird?"

"No, Bud was a good looking all American boy and had a mile of charisma. Michael too was a star at college football. He's smart and good-looking. Of course, they differ slightly in complexion, but things are changing."

"Well, I'll meet you there. And think about what I said."

After Van Clef had left, Coby sat thinking about the nomination. Sure, it would be a big victory for equality, and that's what worried him. The lie about Bud's death kept coming back to haunt him. If he ran and someone found out, it could do serious damage to the party and the movement for equality. No, as much as he would like to, he'd decided to pass on it, happy with what he had.

The years rolled by as Michael joined his stepfather in representing their State in the Senate. Glenda retired from nursing and wanted to do the senior citizen thing and travel the world. Coby still enjoying politics kept putting off retirement. In the end, he found himself outmanoeuvred, by his wife. At a conference where Coby was asked to speak, Glenda dropped the retirement word during an interview. Rather than argue, Coby smiling for the cameras told them this might be his last term. In their room that night Glenda pretended to be innocent of all wrongdoing.

"You know the media! They always get it wrong!"

"I'm still in my prime! I can't believe I told them it was my last term."

"Maybe you're getting feeble and can't remember what you said?" She giggled, as Coby picked her up, throwing her on the bed.

"There are a few things I can remember!"

"Well, you'd better hope you're still in your prime then."

THE SEARCH BEGINS

"And here we are! This Trade talk and peace treaty with the Vietnamese was to be my swan song. I was picked to come here because of my military career and my familiarity with the Vietnamese people. Michael's here to not only support me but to keep an eye on me for his mother." He chuckled, before getting serious. "And now this?"

"That's the type of story that can make a nation cry, Senator!" Paul admitted, continuing to take notes.

"At the moment, I don't care! I just want to find Trevor!"

"We're not even sure he's here Dad. He could be anywhere."

"Michael could be right. There's no record of a Trevor Van Clef or Trevor Henderson ever coming here, although I'm sure he did," Paul pointed out.

"George Van Clef told me once, that he'd changed his name. I'd had better ring him."

"You could kill him, dad! He's in his eighties!" Michael warned.

"Son, we'll be lucky to stop him flying here!"

"Look, Dad, I'll stay here with Paul and look for Trevor! You fly back home and see grandpa, I mean George," Michael quickly corrected. It showed how much he cared for George.

"Is that okay with you Paul?" Coby asked, seeing the man wince at being included.

"I'll help you, as long as you know this is a job for me. I'm not family!"

"I trust you, Paul. Let's find my son!"

"You know Coby; you've got the gift for bringing out the best in people." Paul smiled.

"Tell that to Trevor."

Before Coby could leave, he had the Treaty to sign. Dressing in his off the rack suit, something that his constituents loved about him, he had the Embassy car pick him up straight from the hospital. His arrival at the People's Assembly, as the Vietnamese called it, caused quite a stir. No visiting politician from another country had ever attended their Government's Parliament House without first getting their consent. The media of course getting a whiff of it, rushed there to set up across the road. Coby saw no one was there to greet him, so he took out his camera and walked around the gardens, taking photos with his son like any visiting tourist.

"God dad you've got balls!" Michael chuckled, as soldiers appeared at the front of the building. Michael could see the media setting up across the road without permission, which surprised them. Within minutes two Vietnamese Army Colonels walked up to Coby and Michael. The men were no fools and recognised Coby and Michael immediately.

"Good morning Senators. What are you doing here?" The senior of the two by his attitude asked.

"Just sightseeing. Oh, by the way, is General Chew or his son Twain here? I've got to sign a treaty before I leave." Coby smiled to reinforce his friendly attitude to the matter.

"They are both in our assembly discussing that every document. I might be best if you return to the hospital and rest," he said sternly.

"Look, Colonel, it is Colonel, isn't it?" Getting a nod from both of them, Coby continued. "I have to leave straight away for home due to family problems. This Treaty means billions of dollars in trade to your country. Do you want to be the ones who stopped it?" The Colonels looked at each other, as the younger shrugged his shoulders. This meant the senior officer was on his own. The senior, talking swiftly to the junior officer in Vietnamese, sent him rushing off towards the Assembly building.

"It seems you are still a worthy adversary Senator," the Colonel replied, a tight smile appearing on his lips. It quickly disappeared as he continued. "I have sent my companion with a message that you are here waiting."

"That is good of you Colonel. Now, how about a photo of you and my son? What's your name?" The Colonel taken aback didn't know at first what to say, but after a short pause answered.

"It's Colonel Don Lap."

"Good! I always like to know people by their names. It makes the conversation more personal. This is my son Michael by the way," he added conversationally, as Michael shook his hand and stood next to the Colonel for a selfie photo. Behind them, next to the Assembly building, over fifty Guards in uniform appeared. Not clear what was going on, they stood watching the growing crowd of Vietnamese people line up beside and behind the media.

Twain Chew was addressing the assembly about why the negotiations with America had stalled when the young Colonel burst into the room. Twain watched him rush down to where General Chew his father was sitting. Tapping him on the shoulder to get his attention, he saluted him, before talking to him. His father suddenly stood up and looked towards the door, before turning back to face his son. It was clear to Twain that the message had surprised him. Waving to get Twain's attention, he signalled for him to stop talking.

"Mr. President, I think General Chew has something urgent to say?"

"You have the floor General!" The President declared. Standing up, the General cleared his throat before starting.

"Honored members of the Assembly. Both Senator Coby Henderson and Senator Michael Henderson are outside in the gardens taking photos with one of our Officers of the Guard. They say they are here to sign the treaty immediately.

"I thought General they were standing firm on no compensation for victims of the Defoliant named Agent Orange?" The President exploded, unused to surprises.

"It appears the Senator's stay in hospital has improved his disposition."

"Twain how long till the treaty is ready to sign, as it is?" The President asked excitedly.

"It is ready now Sir. All it needs is your signature and the two American representatives, which are now here."

"Good! General Chew, you seem to have some bond with this former adversary. Would you fetch them in here, while we make ready?"

"Of course, Mr. President, I'll escort them here immediately," Chew replied, his son Twain joining him. The Colonel who had brought the news followed behind them.

In the meantime, the media outside were lapping up the Senators' antics in getting photos with the Presidential Guards. A sense of 'something big was about to happen' gripped the media contingent when out of the Assembly Building walked General Chew and Twain, escorted by a Colonel. Behind them, the press noticed the fifty guards, hastily forming up in front of the Assembly's entrance.

"Senator Henderson. You and your son will both be the death of me yet!"

"Come on General! I'm about to sign a treaty giving you a couple of extra billions. Surely that's something to smile about?"

"Welcome to my country's Assembly Senators. No Dignitaries from the West have entered this building since before the war. If you follow me, you will find the treaty is ready to be signed by our President and the Representatives of America," Twain formally announced. The news crews who heard him surged forward.

"What's going on Senators? Why are you here without the Vietnamese Government's approval?" one shouted. Twain and his father, unused to the world media, wore stony faces.

"Members of the press, please remember where you are? Across from us is the resting place of Ho Chi Min, a man who led his country to victory. He is the father of this country, and despite our being on the losing side of that war, he deserves respect!" Coby's words silenced the media and crowd, as he continued. "As you know, I have been unwell, but that does not mean I would let this opportunity to establish a treaty with our former enemy for the betterment of both our countries slide. The General and his son here have worked closely with us in hammering out this treaty. They deserve more respect! Remember this is not America and their customs are far different to ours.

The sticking point on this treaty was our reluctance to help the people affected by our use of defoliants in the war. I served here as an Air Force Officer and I am shocked at the long-term effect spraying has had on the innocent. We owe it to these people to right this wrong. I called our President and explained the problem to him. He backs this treaty as does the majority of the American Senate members. Now if you please, I will now accompany these two gentlemen and get this treaty signed!" Michael and Coby walked with General Chew towards the Assembly.

Michael glanced back to see the news crews standing as if spellbound. By the time the two Senators entered the Assembly, Coby's translated speech had been seen and heard by the party members inside. As they entered, the whole Vietnamese Assembly, as one, stood and clapped. The noise could be heard by the press outside, who were at first unaware of what a significant occasion this would be. Coby, without any fanfare, walked up to the President and shook his hand. He then signed the two copies, as did Michael and the President of Vietnam.

Back outside speakers and a microphone had been set up on the stairs. The President, his voice full of emotion, read out the treaty's main points to the roar of the crowd who had gathered after hearing the American Senators had come to the assembly. He then read the treaty in English so the press could take it all in. To the Vietnamese, it was a new start with their once dangerous adversary. To the Americans, it represented closure for a war that continued long after the shooting had stopped. The story was beamed around the world. People of all nations saw this American step as a sign that even in defeat, the United States would always honour its commitments to world peace.

Michael, who had signed witnessed the treaty, was overwhelmed by the moment. He moved amongst the Vietnamese, hugging them and accepting flowers from the crowd. Swamped, he was pulled back by soldiers, who hugged him as if he was a brother in arms, instead of the representative of a foreign power. Hanoi hadn't seen such celebrations since the end of armed hostilities. Everyone knew it as a pivotal moment in history. After an hour of what the world would call emotional closure, Coby and Michael climbed into the Embassy vehicle for their trip back to the hotel.

"Dad as long as I live, I will remember this moment when our country shone brighter than the sun," he choked out, his eyes filled with tears.

"Yes, son it was quite a morning. I for one wish it had occurred years ago!"

"God, how did you get the Senate and the President to back you? I thought they were dead against admitting responsibility for the injuries caused by defoliants?"

"They didn't son. That was my idea." Michael appeared struck by lightning. He couldn't respond for several seconds.

"Are you fucking kidding me, dad? What have we done?"

"We've done the right thing son. Don't worry it will be alright."

"How can it be alright? The President will cancel the treaty, and we'll be denounced as complete idiots. That's if the Vietnamese don't shoot us first."

"The President and Congress will do nothing. To the world, they are the heroes of the free world. To say it wasn't their idea would make them look as if they'd lost control. No, they'll all accept the accolades and take full responsibility for the treaty. They have no choice." Coby chuckled.

Michael sat there trying to argue that what he'd done was wrong. It occurred to him that they had just changed the course of America's world policy on their own.

"You're right. The President would be embarrassed if it was found he was against helping the victims, although he won't be happy."

"I don't doubt it. I'll be retiring soon, so I'll take the heat. You can truthfully admit that you knew nothing."

"You didn't just do this so you could look for Trevor?"

"No, although it has cleared me to return to America. I did it, Michael, because I always intended to. My God have you seen those poor people. It shames me that we dragged our feet for so long!"

"What is the next step then?"

"I'm going home to see the Senator. You're going to visit our new friend General Chew and his son Twain."

While Coby went to the airport the next day, Michael rang Twain. Arranging to meet him for dinner that night, he also warned him Paul would be there. Twain, of course, was on edge wondering what the meeting was all about. Michael assured him there would be no surprises. Arriving at the tuck away restaurant in the northern suburbs of Hanoi as the sun was going down, Michael and Paul found themselves ushered into a rear private dining room. Twain was waiting for them accompanied by the Colonel from the Assembly gardens.

"You understand Senator that I could not meet with you two alone," Twain informed them.

"That's quite alright Twain. This is Paul. He works for the 'New York Times'. He's been doing a story on Coby's other son, Trevor. This meeting is about him, nothing else.

"That is good Senator Henderson. As you can imagine with the treaty just signed I was of course worried."

"I can understand and my name is Michael." He smiled as he put out his hand, which Twain shook.

"So, what is the problem?" Twain asked. The Colonel beside him stood mystified.

"Let's us all sit down shall we?" Michael suggested as they all moved to the table. "Paul here has been doing a story on Trevor. He has found out he was wrongfully jailed."

"Good God! Does your father know?"

"Yes, he is on his way back to America to tell Trevor's grandfather, the retired Vice President George Van Clef. He asked me to meet you."

"But why, what is it to do with us?" Twain asked.

"Trevor is believed to be living here in Vietnam under an assumed name. We were hoping you might be able to help, without causing a fuss," Michael explained.

"You have a journalist with you? How are you going to keep it quiet?" Twain smiled.

"Paul knows Coby's whole story including his time in Vietnam," Michael told him, seeing Twain bristle.

"That could cause some people here a lot of trouble Senator."

"I have no intention of revealing what happened during the war Twain. You have my word on that!" Paul jumped in, watching the Colonel. Twain seeing his look smiled.

"The Colonel is from our village, Paul. He knows the true story of the death of the pilot named Bud and of Coby's rescue."

"Good! Then everyone here knows the fallout from that episode could hurt a lot of innocent people, so it will stay out of sight. Paul has agreed to exclude that piece from his story," Michael explained as Paul nodded his acceptance of the condition.

"Excellent. My father risked much by letting your father go," Twain pointed out.

"As did mine in saving you Twain, though he would have done the same even if he'd been imprisoned."

"Yes, I know. Your father is a great man Michael. We know he didn't have permission to sign that treaty, but did it anyway, forcing his President and Government to follow suit," Twain told them, as both the Colonel and Paul nearly choked.

"You're joking!" both said at the same time in different languages.

"Yes, it is true! I reacted the same way when I found out!" Michael laughed.

"That is incredible! The American President has already taken full credit for it!" Paul told them, before bursting into laughter, as did the Colonel.

"Why did he risk everything to do such a thing?" the Colonel asked, astounded.

"He said it should've been done years ago. He wanted it over with," Michael confessed, proud of his dad. Twain sat there thinking of the guts it took to take such a chance, before moving on.

"Obviously I can't personally help you in your search, but I will give you every assistance. Colonel Don Lap here will go with you. Is that agreeable?" Twain asked.

"It is far more than we expected Twain. I am in your debt."

"No Michael, my country is in yours. I suggest now we eat or people will ask about this meeting." Twain suggested, as, on queue, a woman arrived with the menus.

While Michael was at his dinner meeting with Twain, Coby was touching down in Washington. To his surprise, as he made his way through customs, people started to clap, causing quite a commotion for the customs officers. In the end, they passed him through to quieten the waiting crowd. Exiting the customs area into the arrival terminal turn into a circus as the people there surged toward him, everyone trying to shake his hand. The news crew on hand, fought to get close to him, as the whole terminal became a scene of celebration.

Airport security, seeing the confusion, rushed out to form a barrier around Coby. He was escorted outside where he waved his hands and asked for quiet.

"My fellow Americans. I am overwhelmed by your kind words, but remember your President and your Congress are responsible for this treaty! I just signed on the dotted line." He smiled, as the crowd cheered. "Any questions?"

167

"Senator, there is talk that you didn't have permission to sign the treaty? Is that true?" This question made the crowd grow silent in surprise.

"Oh, come on people! Next, you'll be telling me there are aliens at area 51!" Merriment erupted from the crowd. "The President sent me there to get the treaty signed. You think he didn't know? God that's the best one of heard all day!" He joyfully chuckled, as everyone joined in. As if it had been rehearsed, the President with a large number of secret service agents arrived sending a roar through the crowd. With the aid of his security detail, he pushed his way through the crowd to stand beside Coby. Giving him a handshake and then a bear hug, the President waved to the crowd which had grown to several thousand, as the airport emptied out onto the roadway.

"Fellow Americans! Like you I welcome back a man who carried out the wishes of the Congress to the letter, in redressing a wrong. I stand with him now, as the American people stand shoulder to shoulder with the Vietnamese people in backing this treaty. Well done Senator Henderson!" he exclaimed, as the crowd erupted in celebration. With the help of his security, he ushered Coby to his car. Once safely inside, airport security fought to clear a path through the screaming, jubilant crowd, the President waving merrily all the way. Once clear, the President's mood changed.

"Are you fucking crazy? You've just cost America two billion dollars in medical aid!" he yelled, startling his secret service men.

"I couldn't give a shit Mr. President. It needed to be done!" Coby angrily retorted, making the President blink.

"No one talks to me that way!"

"Well, maybe that's your problem?" Coby shot back, as the agents in the front covered their mouths and coughed, suppressing laughter. Calming down, the President closed the glass wall between the back and the front.

"I could still kill the treaty in the Senate if I wanted to."

"You do that, and I'll announce I'm running for the Party's Presidential ticket. With the American people backing me and you proved to be a lair, I'd win easily."

"You wouldn't dare! It could split the party!"

168

"Then do your job and let me retire! You can find a way of saving two billion somewhere else."

The President sat there fuming. He didn't like being blackmailed. On the other hand, Coby was immensely popular. He believed Coby could win if he ran. There was also the poll that showed that with the treaty signing, he would get re-elected for a second term easily.

"Good luck with your retirement Coby. We won't be seeing each other again." The President seethed, as Coby's hotel came into view.

"Thanks for the lift Sir. I'll miss you?" He chuckled, as he got out the Presidential car, which immediately sped off. Coby noticed as it did, that all the secret servicemen waved to him, showing their support.

"Well, that was worth it!" He grinned, before turning to walk into the hotel. To his surprise, another crowd of people were gathered in the lobby. They clapped and shouted his name as he spotted Glenda and retired Ex Vice President Van Clef. In his early eighties, the old statesman still had presence. Glenda kissed him before the Senator hugged him. Looking into his eyes, Van Clef saw something.

"What's wrong Coby?" he whispered, smiling for the cameras.

"We need to talk right away! I'm returning to Vietnam," Coby softly replied, as they made their way through the crowd to the elevator.

"What's wrong Coby? You look like you've aged ten years? Did the President give you hell?"

"Yeah! He was pissed. I don't think he'll be shedding tears at my retirement party, but he'll honour the treaty!"

"Then what's wrong?" Glenda again asked.

"Let's get to the room first," Coby told them, his eyes warning them to be quiet.

Inside George Van Clef's room, Coby had them all sit down.

"Anyone want a drink?" Coby nervously asked.

"Spit it out, Coby! I can take it!" Van Clef told him, knowing it was something to do with him.

"In Vietnam, I ran into Paul Malcolm from the 'New York Times'. He told me that Trevor is innocent; that he didn't kill

Diana." Glenda stood frozen, not knowing what to say. George tears running down his face remained emotionless like a statue.

"Is he sure Coby? I couldn't take this if it's just another beat up!" he stammered, as he began to cry. Coby came over to him hold him.

"He's got a confession from the rally organiser. He's dying of cancer and was bragging about putting a rich kid in jail for what he did. He also found evidence that a piece of brick killed Diana, not a rock, which Trevor said he'd thrown. He smashed the window to our right, as he thought he did at first, before admitting he was the one who'd did it."

"The poor kid! All this time he's been trying to make up for something he didn't do! I've got to find him, Coby!" George collapsed into a seat.

"Trevor's believed to be somewhere in Vietnam. I've left Michael to search for him, with the help of some Vietnamese officials. What we need is his new name?" Coby told him, as he wiped his eyes.

"I'm going over there now Coby!" George declared moving towards the door.

"No Senator you're too old! With respect, it could kill you!" Coby warned.

"There's nothing on this earth is going to stop me apart from death Coby. I'll go with you or alone, but I'm going!" he growled and wiped his eyes. Coby looked at Glenda for support.

"Don't look at me like that! I'm going to! That's my stepson out there."

"No one is going anywhere until we find him. When, and if, Michael contacts him, then we'll work out who's going. For now, we wait," Coby told them. George looked deflated and seemed to shrink into his seat.

"How are we going to do this with close media attention? At the moment, you're more popular than Elvis!" Glenda pointed out to Coby.

"I thought we'd fly first to Thailand for a supposed holiday. From there we can arrange a private flight into Vietnam. Customs should be okay. As you said, I'm popular at the moment. Now, what's Trevor's new name, George?"

"Ben Clef. He didn't want to lose the family name entirely I guess." George briefly smiled.

"Good. I'll tell Michael. For now, we all keep a low profile, if that's possible?" Coby warned as he dialed Michael.

Michael and Paul sat watching the American news channel while they ate a late dinner. Across from them, Colonel Don Lap was busily writing down names. Since their meal, he'd been onto immigration, checking on long term Americans staying in Vietnam. They figured Trevor had been here for quite some time, so possibly he was now either a citizen of the country or here under a working visa. Because of his grandfather, they figured it would be the latter. After finishing his phone call, Don Lap joined them. They ate in silence the three watching Coby's televised arrival back home.

"He could run for President and win you know?" Paul put forward, seeing the media and the crowd's reaction to him.

"He told me because of what happened to Bud and the lie he told, he wouldn't," Michael answered.

"God I'd love to be in that vehicle right now, to hear the conversation!" Paul exclaimed as they watched Coby hopping into back seat of the Presidential limousine.

"Yeah, I bet it was heated! But what can the President do? He is already taking the credit!" Michael replied, a slight unease for his father's sake.

"Here he would be shot!" Don Lap pointed out, making them both smile.

"How did you go with immigration?" Michael asked as Don Lap handed him the names.

"Like public servants everywhere they had to stretch it out. No one gives you a straight answer. In the end, I told him I'd tell General Chew he wasn't helpful. That got things rolling!" Don Lap grinned.

"Would he have got involved?" Paul asked.

"No, not at the moment. The General stands a good chance of being the next President. He must keep away from any involvement with foreigners."

While they talked, Michael who had been browsing the names as he ate, dropped his fork when he saw Ben Clef.

"Ben Clef! It's got to be him!" Michael exclaimed.

"Yes, he loved his grandfather. He probably couldn't give up his whole family name," Paul said softly. Don Lap looking at the name and his notes in Vietnamese alongside.

"He works in a highland village in central Vietnam, with people who have birth defects from the defoliant Agent Orange. The report says he is very dedicated."

"Something told me, whatever he would be doing, would be for the betterment of his fellow man. The guilt he must carry must be overwhelming?" Michael admitted his eyes for the first time showing sorrow, at the thought of his stepbrother.

"That's if it is him, Michael? All we have is a name." Paul suggested making notes in his pad.

"Why didn't you include the story of what happened to Coby and General Chew during the war? Surely it would've sold many papers?" Colonel Don Lap asked, seeing Paul writing.

"I've been a journalist for a long time Colonel. Hurting people isn't my thing. Sure, you're right, it is a big story. But what happened to Trevor will tug at people's emotions and is by far the better story." At that point, Michael's mobile phone rang making the three pause their conversation. He saw Coby's ID.

"Dad! How did you go? How is the Senator?" Like Coby, Michael called him Senator too, even though it could be confusing at times.

"Good son. I've got Trevor's name. It's Ben Clef."

"Yes, we're with Colonel Don Lap. You met in the park outside the Assembly? He's helping us track down Trevor. As a matter of interest, we found the same name just a while ago. He works with villagers affected by Agent Orange."

"Good work son! We'll be there as soon as you locate him."

"Who's we dad?" Michael asked, as Paul and the Colonel both started to pay attention.

"Your mum and the Senator want to come with me. Believe me when I say I have no choice!"

"Are you sure Grandad is up to it?" Michael warned as Don Lap started choking on mouth full of food.

"He'd have come on his own Michael. He's as stubborn as me. When will you be meeting Trevor?"

"Tomorrow we'll travel into the Central Highlands to try to locate him. I'll ring as soon as I can!" Michael promised him.

"Be careful Michael! Mum sends her love," Coby told him before hanging up. Michael, putting down the phone, looked to his travel companions.

"Dad will return, with Trevor's grandfather and my mother. I suggest we head off tomorrow while there are only three of us."

"George Van Clef is coming to Vietnam? That is a great honour for my country, having an ex-Vice President visit!" Don Lap exclaimed, losing his usual bland face.

"Let's hope it doesn't kill him?" Paul warned, knowing Van Clef's age.

"Dad said it would've been worse if he'd try to leave him behind."

"You're probably right. He loves that kid. Even after what everyone thought he did, Van Clef still kept in touch with him."

"Well let's turn in. Tomorrow will be a big day," Michael suggested. The others nodded.

Taking a commercial plane to Da Nang, Don Lap arranged for a vehicle to be waiting. Michael found he had become quite well known to the Vietnamese people now. He was amazed that by signing that treaty, he had somehow won their hearts and minds. The financial support for the afflicted people was welcomed, but admitting responsibility was what the Vietnamese admired more.

They left the airport after forty minutes of shaking hands. Colonel Don Lap drove towards the highlands. Michael, like Peter, looked at their transport, which was an old Vietnam War vintage American jeep, complete with bullet holes.

"This jeep has been around?" Michael pointed out.

"You Americans build them tough," the Colonel commented happily, as he accelerated down a busy multi-lane road, which to them appeared as one lane.

"God, I can see the road through the holes in the floor!" Paul exclaimed, making the Colonel chuckled.

"It will do the job! Don't worry!" The Colonel assured as they headed out of town. Michael, beside him, was just about to comment on the Colonel's faith in the old jeep, when he noticed the Colonel was wearing a pistol.

"Is there a problem Colonel?" Michael asked indicating the sidearm.

"The mountain tribes have always been fiercely independent. They don't like unexpected visits from Government officials." This surprised both his passengers, who thought under communism that everyone obeyed.

"Why does the Central Government allow this?" Paul asked. Like Michael, he was mystified.

"During the war, the hill tribes were pivotal in turning the tide in our favour. It was a loosely based alliance based on mutual trust which the central government respects. Also, their numbers are minimal, so as long as they conform to our laws and governance, they have a certain degree of freedom," Colonel Don Lap admitted.

"So, we're free to visit these villages?" Michael reiterated.

"Yes of course, as long as we abide by their wishes," the Colonel warned, driving on.

For four hours, they drove through the smaller coastal mountain ranges alternating with wide flat valleys dotted with rice paddies. The valleys here had a reputation for good rice yields, and every inch that could be planted, was cultivated. In some places, the road thinned to allow for more rice fields, making it hard to pass trucks approaching from the opposite direction. Colonel Don Lap seemed unfazed by the oncoming traffic, turning and talking freely as vehicles passed within inches of theirs.

The valleys were soon forgotten as they headed up into the steep central ranges. The road became a single lane, mostly dirt and full of potholes. Paul, next to Michael, had until then talked incessantly. He became quiet as the sheer drops either side of the road made him hold his breath.

"Shit, tell me it's not far?" Paul asked. The Colonel shrugging his shoulders, continued as if he was driving a tank, instead of a fragile four-wheel drive. The road that appeared seldom used became a mud-pit as they moved into the thick jungle of the mountains. Don Lap switched to four-wheel drive pushing ever forward.

"Well at least being in four-wheel drive slows him down a bit?" Michael whispered. Paul seemed unimpressed by this news.

After clearing a blind hairpin bend, the rough country opened into a long thin canyon. Here rice paddies again dominated, before huts came into view. At their arrival, several armed and unfriendly looking tribesmen blocked their path. The Colonel as if meeting some friends, hopped out of the car and walked casually forward. The conversation seemed to be friendly until they heard Don Lap use the name Ben Clef.

At this point the Mountain men's attitude immediately went downhill, as weapons were pointed at Don Lap. Michael and Paul, though not understanding the language, felt the urge to run for it, as all eyes turned toward them.

"Shit I don't like this Michael! The way they're looking at us makes you wonder if he's doing a deal to save his arse?" Paul whispered. Suddenly laughter rang out. Don Lap pointed to them and signalled for them to join the group.

"What's going on?" Michael asked

"They thought when I mention Ben; we were here to arrest him. By their tone, I'd say he's highly respected around here. I told them you were his half-brother, which because you're black, made them think I was joking. They now luckily believe me!"

"What if they hadn't?" Paul enquired.

"My pistol holds nine rounds. Their five AK rifles hold thirty rounds each. You do the numbers!" He smiled, as he introduced Michael and Paul. To Michael's surprise, they bowed to him, shocking even Don Lap. Talking to them, Don Lap asked why they had bowed? They explained that they'd seen Michael sign the treaty on their television. It was evident their lifestyle wasn't as primitive as they assumed.

"It would appear you are a celebrity from the treaty signing," Don Lap told them.

"Have they seen my brother?" Michael asked as Don Lap translated.

"They haven't seen him for some time. Rumours were he was sick. They can take us to the Hospice where he works, but they say the track is hard for westerners."

"Tell them I would be honoured to walk with them," Michael replied, fetching a bottle of water. This caused another discussion between Don lap and the tribesmen.

"They want to know what is so important that you can't wait?"

"Tell them a great wrong was done to Ben. I am here to see that he knows the truth," Michael explained, as Don Lap again translated. The tribesmen looked at each other, before one who seemed to be the leader, softly spoke to Don Lap.

"He says Ben has always been a blessing to the people here. He has helped the people affected by deformities caused they believe from the spraying of the jungle during the war. Many wouldn't have made it, without his help, although some say he is haunted by demons in his dreams." Michael, stood silently unable to respond. Like everyone else, he had thought Trevor; now Ben was a monster. His gut-wrenching guilt now bubbled to the surface.

"Hey, it's not your fault Michael! No one knew the truth until now!" Paul whispered. He understood the shame connected with this story and related to the family's pain.

Finishing their introductions, tribesmen hurried to several huts nearby. Returning with what looked like old army backpacks the tribesmen all shook Michael's hand, while Paul, in the background, filmed.

"They say you are a good brother to come with this message of truth to heal Ben of his guilt. They say they will stay with you until your brother is found," Don Lap translated, as he too grabbed a backpack from the vehicle.

"Hey, there is no reason for you two to come!" Michael pointed out to Paul and Don Lap.

"As if we would want to miss this!" Paul replied putting on a pack.

After four tough hours of wading through knee-deep mud and traversing steep, unmaintained tracks, the group arrived in Syi Dun. It was a large village, with a population of just under a thousand. In the distance, at the far end of the village, was a massive temple. In bygone days, it would have been impressive. Now, still exhibiting damage from the bombing during the war, it was just a shell of its former glory. Villagers, when they saw the two American men with a Vietnamese Colonel stayed out of sight. Michael, saw several, watching from the safety of their huts, as the five tribesmen escorted them through the village. As they neared the temple, to either side sat groups of young people. Paul and Michael saw many of them had deformities. "Are all the villages as affected as this one?" Michael asked, astonished at the numbers.

"No. The other villages send their people here to be healed. This village shelters them until the doctors at the temple have time to look at them," Don Lap explained.

"Is Ben a doctor?" Michael asked.

"No. From what I was told, Ben organises everything and somehow keeps the doors open, although no one knows how he manages to do it."

"I'll bet my grandfather could shed some light on that!" Michael smiled, remembering how Coby had told him that he sent Trevor money from time to time. "I wonder if he knew what Trevor was spending it on?"

"Money goes a long way here Senator. What you spend in a week in America could last this village a month. Life is simple here, but good," the Colonel explained.

"Are you Senator Henderson?" a female voice asked in broken English.

"Yes, I am," Michael managed to get out, before becoming tongue-tied. In front of him stood a Vietnamese woman wearing a white coat over her clothing. In her hand, she held a stethoscope. What made him stare was that she was a beautiful and tall for a Vietnamese woman. Because Michael hadn't continued, silence stretched between them. The woman finally took the initiative.

"Well, there's a surprise! An American politician who for a change can't talk? You did better at the treaty signing!" She smiled.

"They weren't as beautiful as you are." Michael immediately became conscious of what he'd said, his face going red. Paul, beside him, nearly choked as he tried not to laugh. Don Lap also grinned at the 'gob smacked' American.

"Thank you for the compliment Senator, but we appreciate the money more." She answered walking past him.

"God, I don't know what came over me!" Michael mumbled once the doctor had moved away.

"Everyone else here does!" Paul laughed, the tribesmen joining in. It seemed that a woman's power over men was universally understood. Getting redder, if that was possible,

Michael fought for something to say. In the end, he gave up and walked towards the temple, surrounded by suppressed laughter.

Kim, a hundred paces ahead of him, giggled to herself. The Senator was very handsome and appeared quite innocent and inexperienced when it came to women. She had been in awe of him, approaching him to tell him how great a man he was. Instead, he'd showed his interest in her. What did she do now? She was no expert on the opposite sex either A little confused; she thought she'd ask her sister when she reached the Temple. Su Lye, unlike Kim, was a nurse with a lot more experience with the opposite sex.

Having spent most of her life training to be a doctor, Kim had lacked the time and inclination to meet someone or have a relationship. This American Senator for some reason had kindled her interest.

At the Temple, all Michael's pre-conceived ideas fled. Bomb damage from the war had not been repaired. Instead, hastily built walls and roofs of tin sheets covered the exposed sections. Inside was a scene from hell, as the floors were covered wall to wall with beds full of mutated people. Their afflictions varied from the lucky ones with a slight twist in their arms and legs, to severely bent and entwined structural disfigurement, which had led to amputation for some of these unfortunate people. Paul and Don Lap beside him also felt the shame associated with being normal.

"My God I just didn't know it was this bad!" Paul confessed, his voice laced with guilt.

"Yes. To our shame, we have hidden these people away," Don Lap admitted, feeling awkward for being able to stand unaided.

"Senator Henderson I presume?" asked a beautiful young woman in English. She was wearing a nurse's uniform and looked similar to the doctor Michael had seen earlier.

"Yes, that is my name, although I prefer Michael."

"Mine is Su Lye Clef, but Sue in your language is good enough for me too." All three men tried to hide their surprise at her surname.

"Well. Good morning Sue! These two men with me are Paul Luke from the 'New York Times' and Colonel Don Lap. The Colonel was good enough to escort me here.

"Well, you're all welcome. Now I suppose you'd like the ten-dollar tour, now America has decided to help these unfortunate people?"

"That would be great, although we'd heard an American runs the hospice," Michael replied following Sue inside.

"Yes, my husband did manage the hospice, but he is not here." She sadly smiled, leading the men into a recovery area outside a surgery.

Michael like the others stood frozen by her statement. Sue, as she was called, was now the only link they had to find Trevor. Not wanting to ruin the tour, Michael signalled to Don Lap and Paul to remain quiet, as they looked into the operating theatre. Inside, through the glass, Michael saw a team of two nurses and a surgeon working on a man's deformed leg. Michael recognised the doctor he'd seen earlier.

"What are they doing to his leg?" Michael asked feeling slightly squeamish.

"The leg was horribly deformed preventing him from walking. They have to saw the leg bone and restructure it using artificial bones. With luck, it will allow him to walk." Sue smiled proud of their work.

"It seems very basic, even though the cost of this procedure must be overwhelming," Michael pointed out.

"Yes, just this one operation used up most of our budget for this week. We hope with the treaty more money will flow to us?"

"I can guarantee it will nurse. I will inform General Chew himself of your work," Don Lap told her. He had been impressed by what he'd seen. Michael, looking toward the surgeon, saw her looking at him then quickly looked away.

"Well that's one I won," he whispered to himself, smiling as they moved on. The next section they entered was the critical care unit. This section was overcrowded with men, women and children, all needing operations. The three men were deeply shaken as they readied to leave.

"I can't tell you how proud I am of you people! What you do is unbelievable!" Michael confessed, turning away as he brushed his eyes.

"Yes, at first it can be most unsettling. I just wish my husband, Ben, had been here to meet you," Sue replied, holding Michael's arm, seeing how upset he was.

"You mean Trevor don't you Sue?" Michael smiled, watching her reaction.

"I don't understand what you mean?" she replied, her face showing her astonishment.

"Trevor is my stepbrother, Sue. That makes you my sister-in-law." Sue looked ready to pretend she knew nothing and then changed her position.

"What happened to Trevor's mother was a terrible accident. Trevor put that life behind him, Michael. He didn't want any contact with his family, and neither do I," she said sternly.

"He was innocent Sue. That's what I came to tell him. Paul here found out the truth only a short time ago. We want him to know." Sue putting her hand in her mouth to stop herself from screaming, collapsed in a faint. The female doctor who had Michael spellbound, burst from the temple rushing to her.

"What is going on here? Are you okay sister?" she asked hugging Sue.

"She's your sister?" Michael exclaimed, this making her his distant sister-in-law he thought. Sue, clutching her sister spoke in Vietnamese, her sister reacting the same way she had.

"Look, I know this is a shock. It was to me too. Coby, my stepfather, forgave Trevor a long time ago but kept his distance. He is grieving over what happened to Trevor. I wanted to personally apologise, for all the years I disliked him for something he didn't even do," Michael admitted, his eyes again welling.

"It is too late now Michael. It is best that you leave." Sue sobbed, as Kim pulled her to her feet.

"Can you at least tell me where he went? Anything you could tell us about him would be appreciated," Michael begged, as Sue stood silently watching him.

"His leaving has caused me great sadness for many reasons Michael. I do not wish to discuss them now." She said turning to leave.

"Look I'll leave a copy of my research into what occurred that day at the University," Paul interjected, handing his research to Kim

"Thank you, but for now we need time to digest what you have told us," Kim told them, leading Sue back inside.

"What now Senator?" Don Lap asked after the woman had gone inside.

"We're best to return to Da Nang so I can contact Coby and the others," Michael stated, wondering if he could have handled things better.

It was getting dark by the time they walked back to the village where they'd left their vehicle. Paul practically dropped to his knees and praised the Lord, when Don Lap said they should wait until morning. They found lodging with the tribesmen, but Michael had trouble sleeping, what with see-saw thoughts about Trevor and Kim. Both filled his dreams for different reasons. Trevor, he realised, had made a new life for himself and wanted nothing to do with them. That aside, Michael wanted to return to see Kim again. He could see she was committed to this hospice, but there was something about her that made him think the effort would be worth it.

"Should I see her again, knowing she'd never leave this place?" He mused wondering if it was a waste of time. "You're a politician! You'll think of something," he reassured himself and finally drifted into a deep sleep.

Morning found the three men still tired but looking forward to a shower and sleep in a soft bed in Da Nang. They waved goodbye to their guides after promising to return as soon as possible. The tribesmen assured them they'd be waiting. The drive back wasn't much better, although this time the road wasn't as wet. Paul cursed the whole way wishing he'd never touched the assignment. In the end, they arrived on the coast at Da Nang and booked into a hotel on China Beach. The first thing Michael did was to dive into a hot bath. He then fought off sleep to call his family. Since Vietnam was several hours and a day ahead of America, it was late at night States side. Finding Trevor was married but for some reason had left his wife and the Hospice for who knows where was important news.

Michael rang Coby. His voice said everything. Coby crestfallen, looked at Van Clef sitting opposite him.

"Michael you're best to come home. It will be a little while before we can return with the media watching us."

"Okay Dad I'll tell the others," Michael replied hanging up.

"What's wrong Coby?" Van Clef softly asked seeing Coby's face.

"Trevor isn't at the Hospice. He's married, and his wife confirmed he had left her." At Coby's words, Van Clef groaned. Glenda, worried, moved to hold him. Sobbing for several seconds, he suddenly changed. Sitting up, he wiped his eyes.

"I have a granddaughter-in-law, and for all we know, Trevor could return Coby. That's something!" He smiled his eyes still awash with tears.

"Yes! I too would like to meet her. Do you still want to travel there?"

"Of course! I would like to see this Hospice he created too," Van Clef told him.

"Good, I'll make preparations for us to leave, although it will take some time and we must keep our plans low key. We don't want a media circus following us."

"I'll leave that to you Coby, but I can't afford to wait too long," Van Clef warned.

THAILAND VISIT

Coby's travel plans didn't go as smoothly as hoped. Going overseas after signing a treaty viewed around the world by millions, made sneaking out of the country nearly impossible. Taking your wife and Ex- Vice President George Van Clef as well, caused pandemonium. At the airport, although he'd kept the purchase of the ticket low keyed, he had to inform customs where he was heading. The Secret Service, for one, kept tabs on Ex-Presidents and Vice Presidents, so they were the first to react. Explaining it was just a holiday in Thailand brought a mute response, meaning they didn't believe him.

Coby knew he was struggling and asked Van Clef for help. The Senator, furious, rang them. Explaining what was going on, he told them point blank to keep away from him, or he'd have the President all over them. Michael's return with Paul in tow soon after brought up more problems. Telling the Senator how challenging the track into the village was, found the old Senator unmoved.

"You made it! I'll make it!" he growled. Michael could see why Coby folded when trying to stop his going.

"Look Senator; I barely made it there and back. You won't make it!" Michael shot back, angry at being ignored.

"Hey everyone, let's settle down. Look I'm sure if we tell General Chew that the ex-Vice President wants to visit the village, they'll arrange transport," Paul suggested. Everyone looked at Paul, as Michael smiled, thinking how this reporter had become part of the family.

"I don't like using my old position for gain Paul, but I take your point," Van Clef answered, knowing he was right.

"Good that's settled. Now how do we get into the country without causing a riot with the press? Of course, I'm not including Paul in that bunch," Michael explained, as Paul smiled.

"We'll try losing them in Thailand. There we'll have the advantage of a private plane secretly booked. Then, even if they follow us to the airport, they won't have time to book a flight," Coby put forward.

"That might work Coby. And Thais, like the Vietnamese, want a trade agreement. We could use that as the reason for being there," Michael proposed.

"Okay, it sounds good. So how do we get the President to okay it?" Coby asked, knowing he wouldn't be the one talking to him.

"Leave that to me. I'll handle him. We go back a long way," Van Clef grinned.

Taking off from Washington's Dulles International Airport was, to Coby, a relief. Instead of the rousing welcome he'd received when returning from Vietnam, this time because of Van Clef's presence, they were ushered through a side door and spared the media circus. Traveling First Class, which Coby usually avoided, to avoid offending his constituents, kept intrusive stares to a minimum. Many of the passengers, instead, stole shots of the three political celebrities with their mobile phones.

"That wasn't too bad?" Van Clef smiled, as Glenda, beside Coby, felt her husband's tension.

"Maybe we shouldn't have all come?" she confessed.

"No George is right! Despite my worries about us all going, we should be there to meet Trevor's wife and with luck find Trevor. I can't even imagine the pain he's lived with. Now, to find out he's suffered for nothing, I think would be horrendous," Coby confessed.

"Well, I'm glad I came. Sure, the press will find out what we're up to sooner or later, but for now, I'm free to meet my grandson's wife, and that's all that counts to me!" George exclaimed. "Now who's for a drink?"

"How did you get the President to let us represent the Government again?" Michael asked the Senator.

"There are some secrets you're best not to know Michael. Let's just say I've joined Coby on his hit list!"

Landing in Thailand again caused a stir as the Thais scrambled to welcome the visiting American politicians. After flowers had been presented, the Prime Minister himself greeted them and the invitation to stay at the Grand Hotel in the Presidential suite, as Thailand's guest, was graciously accepted.

That night, over dinner, they confided in the Prime Minister explaining their reasons for being there. At first, he was both surprised and upset, expecting, like Vietnam, to have the trade agreement between the two countries finally worked out. Coby seized the initiative and took a copy of the draft trade agreement to look over on behalf of his Government. Sitting with Michael and the Senator later that night, they could see the main stumbling block.

America insisted on stopping Thailand's import of motor vehicles, which would put pressure on the American auto industry. It wasn't much of a problem really, as most of Thailand's vehicles were built and shipped to Asian countries. What Thailand needed was a sweetener to get over this hurdle. Studying Thailand's manufacturing sector, Coby saw huge potential for the export of motorcycles, an industry that was just taking off in America. Maybe this compromise would do?

Van Clef, knowing Coby and Michael weren't his most popular Senators at the moment, rang the President. To say he wasn't overly impressed to hear from George by phone was made loud and clear. George, unmoved by the President's negativity, told the President he should put their idea to his number crunchers and ring back. An hour later, the President's financial advisor rang in person. He told them he'd suggested a similar variation, so he had no resistance to their suggested change. The problem was just getting the trade treaty pushed through the Government's red tape that had held it up. George told him to send a copy of his final draft, which they promised they would get signed. Surprised by their willingness to help, he assured them he would send it, as soon as he cleared it with the President.

Twenty minutes later, again the phone rang. The President, this time, was more civil. He told them to go ahead and have the Trade treaty signed. He would announce it to the country the next morning at prime news time. He stopped short of thanking them.

Next, they placed a call to the Thai Prime Minister. The situation explained, initially, the response was lukewarm. When they pointed out the import of motorcycles rather than cars would be acceptable, the impasse was broken. Agreeing, he arranged to meet with them that night and sign the treaty. He also put them in touch with an aviation company, which could fly them discreetly to Vietnam. Thanking him, they prepared for the night.

The press this time had been told in advance by the President's office about the treaty signing at a banquet held in honour of Ex-Vice President Van Clef. After the formalities, George, Coby and Michael all signed the Treaty with the Thai Prime Minister. It didn't cause the stir the Vietnamese treaty had, although to the Thai people it signalled future stability, something they had all waited for.

Glenda found the attention a bit overwhelming as questions about Coby's so-called retirement abounded. Most thought Coby was setting himself up for a run at the Presidency. No matter how she denied it, many smiled believing it a ruse. Coby, in the end, stopped it cold with an announcement.

"Gentlemen! George Van Clef, Senator Henderson and I came to Thailand on our way to a family gathering. The President himself asked us to sign this Trade Agreement, which was well overdue. I will not be running again for any office, as I want to spend more time with my family. I have had too little time for them during my political career. So, let's enjoy the evening ladies and gentlemen. It means a lot to the people of Thailand and to us!" Coby exclaimed, quieting the media. With that statement, Coby's career in politics was truly over.

"I'm sorry you have to give it all up my love," Glenda whispered, feeling she had pushed him into it.

"Don't be silly Glenda! I can see now that this was the best way to get the media off our backs. Now we're just retired politicians enjoying retirement. Nobody should bother us, except for the odd photo now again." He smiled, as again the Prime Minister called them over for another photo opportunity.

The next morning, Coby wandered down to the front hotel foyer and found it empty of journalists. As he had predicted, their story about the treaty and his retirement announcement, negated media interest. He returned to the others, who swiftly packed. Their gear was then loaded into a mini bus, which with a police escort, headed for a small airport outside of the city. Being a private airfield meant they went straight through the front gates and right up to the plane. Customs, with the Prime Minister's help, had already cleared them, as they walked up the small set of stairs onto the small aircraft. The steward served them a soft drink, as the plane prepared for take-off.

"You know Coby; you just solved the States' problems with two different countries in less than two weeks! Can you imagine how good it would be, to get rid us of all that red tape that clogs up our government and just take the time to listen?" George pointed out, as he sipped his drink.

"I don't know Senator. Think about what a toll it has taken on our private lives. What we've done in the past weeks is great, but there have to be checks and balances, or monumental mistakes could be made when dealing with world issues on the run."

"You are probably right Coby, although millions of people in these two countries would argue with you right now." George looked very happy as they became airborne, flying east towards Vietnam.

Colonel Dan Lap had been warned by Michael and waited at Da Nang Airport. As he stood, looking through the Terminal window, he could see the old American corrugated iron huts, which lined the other side of the airfield. Mixed amongst them were the concrete blast tunnels once used for plane storage. They had even housed Coby's fighter wing. Now the noses of Vietnamese Mig jet fighters sat there. Nearby, several tourists snapped shots but kept a respectful distance from him, as his Colonel's uniform made him look unapproachable.

"Good morning. Are you from America?" He asked, addressing one tourist who sensed the ice begin to melt. Others surged forward and surrounded him. Many shook his hand, especially older ex-servicemen who felt a responsibility to right the wrongs of the past. After he'd been photographed from every angle, the crowd eventually moved on to join their flights.

"Keeping busy?" Paul asked as he came up beside Colonel Don Lap. Unlike Coby's family, Paul had been able to travel by a commercial flight, to give the family breathing space.

"Just playing the polite soldier to the tourist. You know it's funny, but I didn't think this treaty was such a big deal until I came here. The tourists, especially the Americans, seem to have accepted us now as equals, something that I never felt before," he admitted.

"Americans have big hearts Colonel. I know we can be overbearing and know alls, but most of our people just want to get along with our neighbours," Paul explained. The Colonel nodded and moved on.

"How did Mr. Van Clef take the news of his grandson's disappearance?"

"Not well, although he is overjoyed to have a daughter-in-law."

"She is Vietnamese!" The Colonel pointed out surprised.

"To Van Clef that doesn't matter. She's his kin now."

"That is good. Will he want to take Sue and her son back home to America?" the Colonel asked. Paul pole-axed, stood opened-mouthed at the Colonel's statement. "Is there a problem Paul?" the Colonel asked seeing Paul's shocked look.

"Good God Colonel! Didn't you think it necessary to mention she had a child?"

"Most married women have children Paul! I only noticed it when I checked their marriage certificate. The child was born only six months after they were married," the Colonel informed him as if announcing the arrival of a bus.

"This is a big deal Colonel! George Van Clef and Coby will go ape shit when they find out!"

"I will tell them as soon as they land."

"No! Wait till they reach the hotel. That way we'll have no problems with anyone collapsing," Paul warned. Outside the window, a small jet started its approach.

Coby watched Da Nang Airfield below with a mixture of sadness and excitement. On one side, he was sad for the death and despair visited on so many during the war. On the other, he felt again the excitement of launching from that field for the first time, so many years ago. He could even see some of the barrack buildings were still there, alongside the hangars and the concrete fighter bays. Of course, the Terminal was new, as were the planes, lined up beside it.

As their plane touched down and made its way to the terminal, Coby noted two Migs sitting on the tarmac waiting for take-off. Blinking, he looked again, to see they were the same model he'd shot down in that dogfight, which made him an ace and earned him the Medal of Honor!

"How can they still be flying that model?" he said out loud.

"Vietnam has a lot of war debt with China and Russia. I suppose they are all it can afford," Van Clef beside him, answered. Nodding his head in reply, Coby watched the two planes accelerate down the runway and climb into the air.

"Well, they still take off and fly okay. I suppose that's the main thing?" Coby admitted, as their plane with a bump, came to a halt.

Walking along the mobile covered bridge, Coby exited the tunnel to see Paul and the Colonel waiting patiently.

"Hello, again Colonel! Michael tells me you have been a great help. Thank you for doing this for us!" Coby smiled, firmly shaking his hand. Glenda and George had been held up at customs.

"It was the least we could do Senator Henderson. One thing Sir, General Chew and several high-ranking party members from the local area, are waiting outside the foyer to greet Ex-President George Van Clef," Colonel Don Lap warned. Michael could see he considered Coby very special.

It was then Glenda, and Van Clef appeared. At Van Clef's appearance, the Colonel snapped to attention saluting, as tourists and travellers, seeing the Colonel's reaction, immediately recognised Coby and the others.

"You do our country a great honour by your visit Mr. Van Clef," he barked, startling Coby and Michael.

"Relax Colonel! I'm retired you know." Van Clef chuckled. "As for visiting, I should have done this a long time ago. Now the Treaty's signed I hope many Americans and Vietnamese can visit each other's country so that we can grow closer." He beamed as the forming crowd cheered. This time it was the Colonel's turn to be startled. By the time their bags had arrived the large crowd had mushroomed. Colonel Don Lap found himself swamped. In the end, he signalled to an airport security soldier to get help.

Ten soldiers in dress uniform quickly formed two lines either side of Van Clef, as Coby and the others followed. Coby could see George talking to the soldiers as he walked along with them. Even though they couldn't speak English, he seemed to be getting through to them, as they smiled back. Exiting the terminal Van

Clef came to a sudden stop, causing everyone else to halt. Coby moved up beside him. Over a thousand soldiers were drawn up in four lines before them. In the centre, on a raised platform, stood General Chew and his son, with about twenty well-dressed men and their wives.

"Time to play the politicians?" Van Clef whispered to Coby, as Michael and Glenda followed. Walking straight to the raised platform, Van Clef waved to the crowds as they, in turn, shouted back. General Chew, with the others, stood to attention as Van Clef approached.

"Even though I know the real reason for your visit, I welcome you to our country," General Chew said softly, before moving to the microphone.

"On behalf of my country, I welcome Ex-President Van Clef and Senators Coby and Michael Henderson and Mrs. Glenda Henderson. I hope this is the first of many visits by the leaders and statesmen of our two countries, as together we live in peace!" General Chew exclaimed, complemented by the flash of hundreds of cameras.

"General Chew, I am overwhelmed by your welcome. My family and I are here not for political reasons, but to holiday and to see your beautiful country. With the treaty, I hope that as friends, we can move forward together and heal the wounds of the past," Van Clef replied. The crowd at first became hushed, as they took in his words. Slowly they responded until a deafening roar engulfed them all. As the noise subsided, General Chew turned to individually introduce his party members to Van Clef, Coby, Glenda and Michael. They all seemed humbled by Van Clef's words.

After the welcoming ceremony, General Chew offered them all a lift to their hotel. While driving, Coby broached the subject of returning to the inland temple with General Chew. He told them Colonel Don Lap had already arranged for a helicopter to take them all there.

"This won't affect you, will it General?" Coby asked, having heard from Paul about the General's plan to run for the Presidency. This caused the General and his son to smile.

"Senator, the best thing I ever did was let you go on that beach." He chuckled. "This official welcome today for you and your family will guarantee me a shot at running my country. Since the treaty was signed, many of the Assembly have called for more dialogue between our country and former enemies.

At the moment, China has great sway here. Not only do we share a border, but we also owe them a lot of money for aid during the war. Many feel that reliance on one super power leaves us vulnerable.

"When we signed the Trade Treaty, China seemed offended we hadn't asked them first. Many in the Assembly feel as I do that as an independent nation we should be able to make decisions for ourselves, without having to speak to them first. To survive, we need to form treaties with as many countries as we can, to secure our long-term independence. Our President at the moment is a good man but tends to be too influenced by China. I am confident I have the votes now to lead the Assembly."

"Well, I wish you good luck General. We'll keep a low profile. You don't need us rocking the boat for you," Van Clef promised, as they arrived at their hotel.

"Now we'll go in, and all look happy and share a cup of tea before I leave. If I don't get a chance afterwards, I'll wish you good luck now on your trip." General Chew smiled, before leaving their vehicle and waving to the gathered crowd. As at the airport, the crowd cheered while General Chew and Van Clef walked side by side into the foyer. A ceremonial tea awaited them, at which point the General excused himself and left. It was then the media's turn.

They all knew about Thailand, but this trip to Vietnam on a private jet left them all speculating about what was going on. Coby, in the end, held a press conference in a side conference room, so Glenda and the Senator could escape to their rooms.

"Look, gentlemen, I know you have a mountain of questions as to what's going on, so I'll start at the beginning. Trevor my stepson and George Van Clef's grandson was over twenty years ago, jailed for the murder of his mother, my wife. Paul here from the 'New York Times' looked into the case and made some convincing discoveries, which proved Trevor was innocent of causing the death of his mother." This caused an intake of breath from the media, who are seldom surprised.

"Didn't he plead guilty?" someone yelled from the group.

"Yes, he did. At the time, he had thrown a rock, which we now found only broke a window. Thinking he must have hit his mother, he pleaded guilty. Paul has discovered that an actual piece of brick was what struck Diana, his mother. Like everyone else, I too thought he'd thrown the rock that killed her, much to my own shame." Coby stopped to quickly sweeping his hand across his eyes.

"That doesn't explain why you're here!" another journalist yelled out.

"Trevor, after his imprisonment, left America and opened a hospice in the mountains of Central Vietnam. He helps the villagers affected by the use of Agent Orange during the war. We are here to meet his wife, as Trevor has left, where we're not sure." Coby stopped struggling to continue. The media recognising his pain, politely remained silent. "I know you would like to ask a million more questions, but as you can see this has affected us all. Paul can fill you in on the evidence he found, even though I'd say as a fellow journalist he'd like to be the one to write his own detailed story." This generated subdued laughter from the group. "Once we meet his wife, we'll arrange another meeting. As for now, we trust you can understand our request to give George Van Clef some space. He's been through a great deal." Coby left a hushed group of reporters behind him.

In the lift on the way up to his room, Coby noticed Colonel Don Lap's agitation.

"Is something wrong Colonel?"

"No Sir!" he answered, as if on a parade ground. Putting it down to nerves, Coby exited the lift with the Colonel following him.

"You can relax for a while Colonel. We can call you if we need something." Coby smiled.

"I will wait for Paul. We have something to discuss," the Colonel replied, eyes downcast. 'What's up with him?' Coby wondered. Entering his room, he found the Senator and Glenda waiting with Michael.

"I'd thought you'd be all resting?" Coby sat down.

"Paul asked us to wait for him. I'd say the Colonel here has some news?" Michael pointed out, as Don Lap eyes took on a hunted look.

"Okay Colonel, let's have it. I know Paul said to wait for him, but what's wrong?" Van Clef demanded.

"There is nothing wrong Mr. Van Clef. I found something out when going over Trevor's records." All watched him intently "Trevor's wife has a son. At the time, I didn't think it was important, but Paul thinks it is a big deal!"

"My God, I have a great grandson!" Van Clef exploded, startling Don Lap.

"I'm sorry I didn't tell you earlier," Don Lap apologised.

"Don't be silly Colonel! To you, it was just a child, but to us, it means Trevor left something of himself behind! This is great news for us!" Coby told him, as Paul appeared. Looking around the room he knew.

"The Colonel told you I believe?"

"Yes, why didn't you tell us sooner?" Coby inquired.

"He told me at the airport. I thought it best you find out in private."

"Good thinking Paul! I don't think I could've got through that welcome if I'd known," The Senator confessed.

"What do we do now?" Glenda asked.

"Since your absence, I have been busy Senator Coby Henderson." The Colonel barked, making them all smile.

"You have been a great help Colonel. What have you discovered?"

"I returned to the village with a message of support from General Chew who promised funds, and when possible, to visit them. Sue, as you call her, said you could return if you wished." The Colonel informed them as if it was a military mission.

"That is great news colonel. We are in your debt!" George told him, rising to pump his hand and then embrace him. The Colonel for the first time since they'd met him seemed out of his depth as an ex-Vice President hugged him.

"I will pick you up at seven hundred hours sharp! " he announced, then fled the room.

"He'll go far if he can lighten up a bit!" Michael chuckled, as they all sat down. Paul described his encounter with the media and left the family alone.

"Quite a day, wasn't it?" Coby acknowledged sitting down.

"Yes. I'd say the media let us off easily," Michael answered, knowing from experience how hard they could be.

"And we gained another member in our family! That makes all the travelling worthwhile!" George responded.

"I hope this meeting with Sue goes well. I want so much for us all to be friends," Glenda admitted, knowing Sue could decide to have nothing to do with them.

"Sue's got a sister too. She's a doctor and surgeon at the Hospice. She made me look like a fool when we first met. She came up to talk to me I froze when I saw how beautiful she is," Michael confessed, while the others smirked knowingly. "Hey, it's nothing like that!" Michael jumped in, trying to defend himself.

"Sure, it isn't! What's her name?" Glenda asked, her eyes watching her son closely.

"Kim. She's really intelligent, as well as beautiful mum. There's something else though; I just can't put my finger on it?" Michael mused as George burst into laughter.

"I bet you'd like to put your finger on it!" George exploded, as Michael flushed red, yet again.

Don Lap, looking immaculate in his uniform, marched into George Van Clef's room to escort them to the airfield.

"Did everyone sleep okay?" he asked as if reading it from a script.

"Yes, Colonel. We are all ready to go," Coby informed him.

"Good I have arranged a vehicle to take us to the old American barracks on the far side of Da Nang Airfield. Our helicopters are based there," he explained, all business.

"Thank you, Colonel. You have been most helpful," George replied smiling, laying on the charm.

"It is an honour Mr. Van Clef" The Colonel returned his smile as he held the door open for the elderly statesman.

"Well let's go meet my great grandson!" George smiled, leading the way.

Coby stared intently at the barracks buildings and billets where he'd once lived. Rust dominated many of the remaining structures although many had been completely removed. 'In a way, it still feels like home,' Coby mused following the Colonel.

194

The actual building that he'd been billeted in was gone. In its place sat a wicked looking Russian helicopter. With its camouflaged hull, it looked like a bird of prey, awaiting its chance to leap into the sky on a deadly hunt.

"It must be strange returning to where it all began?" Paul beside him asked.

"It didn't start here for me Paul. It started at the Senator's plantation where I first met Diana. Here I admit I learned a lot about life, death and friendship with the members of the 202nd fighter wing. Funny I thought I'd dread being, here again, seeing it in the hands of own old enemies. Instead, I feel a kind of relief that a part of my life I've kept suppressed, veiled and denied for so long, is now free. My guilt associated with that time of my life can now flow away from me," Coby confessed.

"That was beautiful! I'll write it down," Paul answered scribbling furiously, as Coby laughed.

"You really are a journalist through and through Paul! Any other time I'd be offended that I told you something from deep inside me and instead of honouring it, you ask if you can use it? On the other hand, we wouldn't be here without you! So yes, of course, you can write it down," Coby replied as the pilot of the helicopter, waved them aboard.

Flying over the jungle, seated next to the pilot, Coby was able to look down without fear of being targeted. The stunning changed from rolling coastal lowlands to rough, wild mountain ranges was breathtaking, but at the same time familiar to him. Coby vaguely remembered having a run-in with an anti-aircraft gun in this area. Someone had reported a weapon firing on the Medivac choppers as they returned to Da Nang. They had large red crosses on their sides, but still, the enemy shot at them. Bill had been the dumb bait coming up from the coast.

The anti-aircraft gun just couldn't resist firing at him as he skimmed the trees, flying up a valley towards the mountain range. Coby was following at ten thousand feet. Beneath, he saw the telltale sign of smoke from the gun, as Bill turned away sharply. Coby immediately dived on the weapon's position, releasing his bomb. To his amazement, it moved swiftly away, causing the bomb to miss! Angrily he came around for another pass. To his surprise, he saw that their target was a mobile-gun.

It had tracks like a tank so that it could traverse any rough terrain. Firing his cannon, he saw the vehicle hit, then stopped, although it continued to spew lead at him. Bill had turned and came in fast to drop his two five hundred pounders on the now stationary vehicle, then headed for the ceiling to avoid the blast. The explosion was spectacular as the weapon platform roared into the air. Their mission complete, they returned to Da Nang.

Coby searched for landmarks trying to relocate the spot. He had just about given up when he saw the road Michael and Paul had travelled with Colonel Don Lap. He knew it followed the same valley Bill had flown along. There, where he figured the vehicle had been destroyed, was the outline of a huge crater. The pilot seeing him look, spoke to Don Lap in Vietnamese.

"The pilot asked if you dropped that bomb?"

"No, it was my wingman," Coby answered, as the two Vietnamese converse.

"He says the crew when the gun was crippled, fled. They'd just reached cover when the bombs dropped. He was told it was a new prototype of a self-propelled anti-aircraft gun the Russians were testing." Don Lap smiled.

"Did it pass?" Coby replied.

"Obviously not. It appeared like most of the cheaper towed or stationary guns to have a problem with smoke from its munitions. It gave away its position when it fired, so it gave them no advantage," Don Lap informed him.

"You made a mistake there. That mobile gun was years ahead of what you had. True the smoke was still a problem, but except that I got lucky and stopped it, it would've got away or killed one us. Bill filed in a report, which led to American forces getting several batteries of them. They were pivotal in Iraq." The Colonel then told the pilot what he'd said. After thinking about it, he replied.

"He says it is most probably your overwhelming air superiority which helps the guns in the field. Sure, they're good weapons, but fixed weapons are more stable. Only America could afford to spend so much on a weapon."

"Tell the pilot he has a good point there. Although like in this country, it doesn't always work." Coby watched as the Colonel translated. Coby saw the pilot smile at him before he nodded in agreement.

The chopper, although noisy, continued effortlessly above the treetops, gaining height as they approached the central mountain range. Paul, who lived in fear of driving back to the village, enjoyed every minute, glad to be above that road. Glenda, who hadn't been in a chopper before, was most apprehensive. As time passed though, she became more accustomed to the noise and shuddering, enjoying the view. The Senator, as usual, remained unruffled.

"Are you enjoying the flight?" Coby yelled above the noise.

"It's great! Although I've been in the President's chopper and that's more comfortable!" He chuckled, before suddenly asking, "Hey is that the village?" He pointed toward a rising smoke plume, emerging from the jungle. Coby, shading his eyes and looked towards the smoke, as the temple's dome became visible through the haze that floated around it.

"That's it! The temple gives it away," Coby assured him.

Paul watched as all eyes were drawn to the village.

TREVOR'S FAMILY

Landing in the centre of the village caused great excitement. Although the villagers had been warned a helicopter would visit, most hid as soon as the noisy man-made bird dropped from the sky. As the giant double rotor ground to a halt, the villagers, singly or paired, approached to slowly encircle the flying machine. The Senator, of course, was first out. His face wore a mixed expression of sadness and expectation, as he looked around at the village where his grandson had worked so hard for these people.

As the villagers moved nearer, Coby saw the Senator examine the various forms of physical mutation. Despite his obvious trepidation, he walked forward shaking hands with all who would, ignoring their afflictions. Glenda too had trouble seeing such abject suffering which these people put up with daily. Wiping tears away, she followed the old Senator hiding her feelings as she did when a nurse, not allowing her horror to interfere with her greetings. Twenty minutes swept by before they reached the temple. As if awaiting inspection, the hospital staff stood stiffly to attention.

Sue and Kim stood at the front, Sue holding a small child. Coby found himself speechless, as, after a short greeting, he dropped to his knees to say hello to Trevor's son.

"What's his name?" Coby asked Sue, as he reached for the boy and cuddled him, much to the child's delight.

"Coby," Sue answered, her eyes misting over. Coby Senior was dumbstruck and looked to the ground, unable to converse.

"Let me hold my great-grandson!" George interrupted, taking the child from Coby, who walked away, standing off to the side. Glenda saw how upset he was, so she suggested the staff take her on a tour with Paul and Colonel Don Lap. This left Sue, Kim, Coby, the Senator and Michael on the front steps.

He looks a bit like you George!" Michael smiled. The boy was European in appearance, except for the jet-black hair like his mother's.

"No! Luckily, he looks more like Bud. I can see it in his eyes," the old Senator choked out, his face a combination of tears and smiles.

"Thank you for seeing us, Sue. You don't know how much this means to us," Michael explained, noticing the two women had said nothing except tell them the child's name.

"I was against it at first, as Trevor had always wanted to avoid any contact with his family. Of course, that was based on the fact he believed he'd killed his mother, which has turned out to be false. I decided that my son should know his father's family. That's why I allowed this visit," Sue confessed, as she watched her son happily pull on George's beard.

"That is very gracious of you Sue. I cannot find the words to tell you how sad we were that Trevor had left you. Despite what you may think of us, we always loved Trevor. It's just we thought wrongly that he'd killed his mother, someone who was special to us; someone we loved deeply," Coby explained as he dried his face and came back to stand with them.

"Would you like to come to our house for lunch?" Sue suddenly spurted out, as if the idea had just occurred to her.

"It would be an honour," Coby smiled, stealing little Coby from George.

"Yes, that would be great, but can we wait for Coby's wife, Glenda? She'd be a bit miffed if we went off without her," George added, watching Coby play with the young boy.

"I meant your whole group Vice President Van; I mean George." Sue smiled to cover her mistake.

"We are family Sue. You will never have to call us anything other than our names ever again," George put in, as Sue led the way. Giving Coby the 'you are hogging him look', made the younger man hand young Coby back to him again.

Meantime, Michael talked freely with Sue but avoided engaging Kim. They remained in a silent battle of wills, as their eyes constantly locked. Finally, when the group moved off, the pair dropped back, walking together.

"Tongue tied again?" she whispered.

"You're intoxicating Kim. I find myself out of my depth with you," he confessed. Kim missed a step nearly falling. The others turned to her.

"Are you okay sister?" Sue asked.

"Yes, just being a bit clumsy that's all," Kim replied, her face ablaze as if she'd been caught doing something wrong. Sue looked at her sister then at Michael, who had a similar 'caught out' expression on his face. Resuming their walk, Sue smiled, thinking how worldly yet innocent they both were.

"They're made for each other?" George whispered to Sue, as young Coby curled up in his arms, sleeping.

"Yes, my sister has never been so off balance with anyone," she replied. "He's not too heavy for you George?" she asked, watching him.

"I've waited all my life for this moment, Sue. But you're right he is getting heavy." He smiled, as Coby willingly took him from him.

"You were hogging him anyway?" Coby laughed, tickling the infant, as they walked around back of the temple.

There nestled amongst a group of weathered looking trees was a single level building made of the same mud type material as the temple. Unlike the temple, the structure although old, was intact, having survived the bombing. In its time, it must have served as a guesthouse for visiting dignitaries. Now it provided a home for Sue and young Coby. Sitting down in what they used as a lounge room, and with Glenda's return, the long-separated family sat watching young Coby sleep.

"I'll make some tea," Kim volunteered, moving to a far door. Looking at Michael she raised her eyebrows, indicating the kitchen. Taking the hint, Michael spoke up.

"I'll give her a hand!" Michael declared, following her out back as his mother tried to hide a smile.

"Your son likes to work in the kitchen?" Sue asked, having observed Glenda's smile.

"Not until now!" Glenda answered. The kitchen, by western standards, was primitive. With just a wood fired stove and a sink with a hand pump, it would've made many a wife scream in despair. Kim didn't seem bothered at all, as she stoked the fire adding timber lengths. Once the fire was burning merrily, she placed an old kettle on an iron plate above the flames.

"Should take about five minutes?" Kim spoke softly, as she turned to face the silent Michael. He was leaning up against the sink behind her and had been since he entered. He'd spent the whole time watching her work, his eyes glued to her petite figure. When she'd indicated for him to follow her, his mind had painstaking worked over a hundred reasons why she'd wanted him to go with her. One more than any other that came to the forefront was that maybe she wanted him as much as he wanted her. Now as she moved towards him her face said everything.

Kim, on the other hand, was about to ask how his family had their tea when she looked into his eyes. They were filled with longing. Spellbound, she moved closer, as if magically controlled by his intense gaze. Michael, seizing the moment, came to life. Without a word, he wrapped her in his arms, pulling her close. A moan escaped her lips, as she snuggled into his body. His lips clumsily sought hers. The kiss dissolved their misgivings and was overwhelming. Both stumbled backwards, upending pots and pans.

Pushing her, in the end, up against the wall to anchor their passion, Michael threw caution to the wind, as he started to unbutton her dress. A moan again escaped Kim's lips as Michael's hands roamed over her smooth thighs.

Whether it meant her acceptance or her refusal, it broke the moment, as Michael looked beyond his arousal, at his surroundings. Breaking their embrace, he took in Kim's near naked body, caused by his passionate exploration.

"God I'm sorry Kim. I have no right to demand anything from you! You're a doctor here, and I'm a Senator from America. How can we fall in love?"

"Hey, I've wanted that kiss since the first time you stumbled over your words," She giggled. "As for love, that is something that I never really considered until now. You're right though, distant romances usually don't work out, but I'm willing to try if you are?"

"What do we do now?"

"First, we take out the tea, then we'll see." She smiled, her eyes shining. After tidying her clothes, Kim fetched the tea, while Michael loaded up a tray of cups and saucers. Adding some milk and sugar, Sue led the way.

"Did you have trouble with the stove?" Sue asked, a small smile playing on her lips. Michael and Kim's antics had been heard.

"It took a while to get hot," Michael volunteered, as George burst into laughter.

"It sure didn't sound like it took long out here!" He grinned, the others breaking into merriment as Michael and Kim turned the brightest shade of crimson.

It was an enjoyable afternoon as the group walked through the village towards the helicopter. Sue seemed at ease, walking beside them, as Coby happily carried young Coby. George seemed lost as they approached their transport back to Da Nang. Standing there, the group waited for someone to say something as Kim whispered in Sue's ear. Sue, smiling, looked at her sister wondering at the true motive for her advice.

"My sister was wondering if you could all stay the night? Accommodation here is pretty basic, but you're welcome," Sue told them.

"This is a big ask, Sue. Are you sure it is alright?" George answered, not wanting to impose.

"Of course, it's okay. Surely we have more to talk about?" Sue pointed out.

"I, for one, would be honoured to stay, even if I have to sleep on the floor," George replied, already walking back towards the temple.

"I cannot stay Mr. Van Clef. I must return with the helicopter," Colonel Don Lap explained sounding for once disappointed.

"I too must return to Da Nang," Paul contributed. If he was being polite or trying to avoid travelling on the road, they had no idea.

"Well if you can pick us up tomorrow or arrange transport, we'd be grateful," Coby told them, as the two men with a wave, disappeared into the monster's belly. As they moved back, the remaining family members shielded their eyes as the huge bird staggered into the air, before dipping forward and flying away.

"Big bastard, isn't it?" Michael said to Coby who was busily covering little Coby's ears and eyes.

"Yeah, I think its nickname is Hind. The Russians have always loved big helicopters," Coby replied, moving up the road with Glenda after George and Sue. Michael walked behind with Kim at his side.

"Thank you, Kim. I suspect you were behind our staying?"

"Yes, I knew Sue wanted to ask. She just needed a nudge."

"Well, I'm glad you did. It gives us more time to talk."

"And that's all you want to do?" She smiled, skipping away as he tried to grab her. Pretending to walk forward, Michael suddenly changed direction, grabbing her as she squealed in surprise. As Kim tried to break free, Michael tickled her mercilessly, her laughter echoing around the village. Kim breaking free grinned at Michael.

"You won't catch me that easily again." She laughed suggestively, before resuming their walk. Ahead, the others had stopped to watch their horseplay. Combing back her hair with her hand, she walked on as if nothing had happened.

"I'd better go check the ward," she announced giving Michael a playful push and a grin. She hurried off to the temple, while Coby waited for his son.

"What's got into you, Michael? Remember you're a Senator, not a schoolboy!"

"Sorry, dad. She just she brings out the worst in me," Michael answered, still grinning.

"Or the best son. She's something else, isn't she?"

"Yeah, she's everything I want in a woman except her distance."

"What's being a long way from home got to do with it?" Coby asked.

"Would you have given up politics for mum?"

"In a minute Michael. There will always be time to serve the people. Finding someone special is a lot harder."

"You were married twice."

"And I consider myself one of the luckiest men alive son." Coby smiled, as the two continued toward Sue's home.

The strain of the last couple of weeks was starting to show on George. Finding he had a great grandson had been special, but knowing Trevor was out there somewhere, hurt him badly. After dinner, the group sat outside under mosquito netting, to make the most of the balmy night. Glenda, like the others vying for his attention, had volunteered to put young Coby to bed. Michael and Kim had excused themselves, deciding on a walk to help digest their big dinner. Coby thought it was strange since they'd spent most of the evening not eating, but staring at each other.

Once they'd left, George assured Sue that she and little Coby would want for nothing. Sue was adamant that little Coby, would not be spoiled by his relations. To this condition, she received a muffled promise that they'd all try. They interned, asked what her plans were for the hospice?

"Since George has promised to continue to supply money and with the Government now being financially supportive, I intended to repair the whole temple complex, increase the staff size and bed numbers," Sue explained.

"It's too bad, Trevor couldn't be here to see all this?" Coby sadly added when Sue had concluded.

"I had hoped to spare you this, but the reason why Trevor left had nothing to do with not loving me. Trevor developed an appetite for opium. At first, he smoked with the local tribesmen to cement a relationship with them. In time, it became a way of forgetting his pain. He knew the Government, and I had strict rules governing drug abuse in our Hospices. I gave him an ultimatum, either get clean or leave. He chose to leave!" Sue confessed, her eyes shining as tears fell. George lost for words, held her.

Of all of them, Coby seemed to take the news of Trevor's drug abuse the worst. Glenda, reaching across, held his hand as the room lapsed into silence. George, in the end, broke it.

"It must've been hard Sue, but you did the right thing!" He wondered if he could have ever done that to Bud.

"Do you have any idea where he went? If we could find him, Sue, we could perhaps get him help?" Coby suggested.

"To the local people, Trevor is a saint. He built this hospice from scratch and then arranged for the people who needed help to come here. In some cases, he carried them here himself. I came here after he'd advertised a position for a fully paid nurse to help these people. Kim came later after visiting me and completing her medical training. Even though they know of his addiction, the tribesmen would deny him nothing. He could be anywhere in the mountains, but you can be assured they are sheltering him," Sue acknowledged.

"Well, I'm officially retired. I'll stay till I find him," Coby announced. George was about to back Coby and stay when Glenda intervened.

"George and I will return to Da Nang tomorrow. As much as we'd both like to stay as well, George's health is being affected." George looked at her, before nodding his acceptance. That in itself showed how unwell he was.

"Good, we're all agreed then. I'll tell Michael when he returns," Coby told them, as the conversation changed back to Sue and young Coby.

On the other side of the village, Michael sat with Kim watching the village children play around a fire. Kim had already told Michael about Trevor's addiction. At first, Michael was upset, blaming himself for not looking for him sooner. After solemnly promising he'd search for Trevor until he found him, they sat by the fire, hand in hand, watching the children's innocent antics. Unlike most of the young adults, the children appeared to be normal or close to it, as time diluted the defoliant's poisonous genetic effects.

They were all still in a festive mood since the announcement of medical aid from America. Many saw a good future for their families, in contrast to the constant past struggle to simply survive. Michael became the centre of attention, as western people were rare in this mountainous area of Central Vietnam. Kim giggled merrily, as the children would sneak up behind and poke him, before running off.

Michael screamed each time, causing the children to become more daring. One time when a child came to close, he leapt for the child, who in horror shouted and ran in fear to her laughing parents. Just as at home, the parents soon noticed the time and dragged reluctant children off to bed, finally leaving Kim and Michael alone.

"God they're great kids!" Michael chuckled, as Kim smiled before he pulled her to him.

"You will make a great father," she whispered in between kisses.

"Guess I'll have to start looking for the right woman. Any suggestions?"

"I'm not sure? What type are you looking for?" she cheekily asked.

"I don't know for sure. Dark haired with a petite figure would be nice. It would be good if she had a career of some kind. Something that would support me when I'm thrown out of the office for lying to Congress and the President."

"Could that happen?"

"No, not at the moment thanks to Coby's guile."

"Your family is well respected as are you. I heard them say Coby could be the President of your country if he wanted to?"

"Yes, he most probably could have, but he won't. He's retiring at the end of this term," Michael explained, knowing why.

"You could too if you married someone acceptable in your country," Kim said softly, wondering if a relationship with her was the right thing for him.

"If I marry someone Kim, it won't be to win an election. It will be because I love her. To me that is all that counts," he answered forcefully, before softening his expression. "Would you consider coming to America with me?" The silence stretched as Kim sought the words to explain.

"I am needed here at the moment Michael. Maybe when more doctors arrive I could come?" she replied, her eyes misting.

"That is good enough for me, Kim. I'll wait till the end of time for you."

"It could be some time Michael. Sue needs me," Kim answered, wet trails appearing on her cheeks.

"If you love him you should go," a male voice sounded from the dark. What surprised Michael was it was in English. Beyond the fire, Michael saw an undernourished, bearded man about his height. He was dressed in the clothes of a local farmer, although his boots looked European.

"I like this guy. My name's Michael, what's yours?" As looking at Kim, he saw the shock on her face. Standing Michael moved towards him, offering his hand.

"My name is Ben," he answered, sounding unsure. Michael, on the other hand, looked as if he saw a ghost. Unable to speak, he moved forward, hugging Trevor. Trevor shocked, looked to Kim.

"Where have you been brother? Many things have happened in your absence!" Kim cried moving to him, hugging him too.

"Sure, looks that way. Can you explain why your boyfriend is hugging me?" Trevor inquired, getting uncomfortable.

"He is your brother!" she answered, as Trevor broke the embrace.

"I don't have a brother. What's going on Kim?"

"I'm so sorry Trevor. All those years I hated you for what you'd done to my step-dad, only to find it was a lie!" Michael confessed as Trevor stood looking completely baffled.

"My name is Ben!" Trevor answered, shaken by the use of his real names.

"He's Coby Henderson's stepson Trevor. The same as you are!" She told him. Trevor started to back away from them.

"No, it can't be!" Like a broken man, Trevor groaned, gripping his head with his hands.

"You didn't kill your mother, Trevor. You were set up."

"What's he talking about? Have you all gone crazy?" Trevor snarled, walking away from them. Michael hurried after him.

"Trevor, I know it's hard for you to believe me, but what I'm saying is true. Your friend Billy Weldon threw a piece of brick. He's confessed to it." Michael watched Trevor come to a halt and turn.

"I broke the window, didn't I?"

"Yes. Coby said he heard the window break, at the same time. It was your confessing that convinced them the sliver of rock you'd thrown, broke the window as well." Trevor unable to answer stood frozen like as a statue. The only movement were tears streaking down his face. "Dad, I mean Coby's, been looking for you since he heard. Both the Senator and Dad blame themselves for this mess!" Michael continued. This time when he hugged his brother, Trevor held him too. Time seemed to stand still until the three sat down again seeking the warmth of the fire.

"You know as bad as it's been, I don't regret anything I have done since leaving prison. Starting this Hospice and meeting Sue and having a son, have made life worth living."

"Where have you been?" Kim asked.

"Getting clean so I could come back. The local tribesmen, I suppose, got tired of my self-destructive pity. They locked me up and dried me out. I haven't seen or heard anything from anyone for about six weeks."

"So you don't know about the treaty?" Michael asked surprised.

"I heard something about a treaty with America. Has it happened?"

"Yes, they gave Vietnam Government, an assurance to financially support the victims of defoliants used during the war," Kim replied.

"My God that's fantastic! We'll get plenty of support for the Hospice. I can't believe they caved in?" Trevor smiled wiping his eyes.

"Well they didn't at first, but that's a long story." Michael grinned, remembering his shock.

"We've got all night," Trevor pointed out, so Michael explained what he'd missed.

"And you're saying the President took the credit?" Trevor exclaimed, finding the story unbelievable.

"Coby said when he returned from Vietnam and met him at the airport; his face went white as a sheet with rage!" Michael laughed, Kim and Trevor, joining in.

"Is Coby well?" Trevor asked, his voice concerned.

"Yes, although he's officially retired now."

"And the Senator is he okay."

"He's not young anymore and coming here has been hard on him."

"Wait a second. Are you saying Grandpa is here in Vietnam?"

"Yes, he insisted on coming with Coby and mum. They're staying with Sue tonight here in the village." Trevor looking scared stood up.

"I've got to go! I can't let them see me!" Trevor stuttered, his eyes looking terrified.

"Trevor, they came to find you. Coby, especially, is broken up about how you were treated."

"I'm a recovering drug addict Michael. Next week I might be back on the stuff for all they know."

"They don't care. You're Coby's son and the Senator's grandson. That's all that counts to them," Michael explained. Trevor stood thinking about it, but his hands started to tremble.

"Trevor, Su Lye is beyond worried. You can't just leave without seeing your wife and son?"

"I just don't know if I can face anyone Kim, especially Coby. There are a lot of things you don't know about me, Michael. When Coby married my mum, I was angry and said a lot of racist things about him. I also accused him of killing my first dad to marry my mother. It hurt him that I didn't believe his story."

"I forgave you a long time ago Trevor." Coby's voice resonated through the darkness. "You were young and surrounded by a lot of racist kids. Your mother was marrying a black man, whom your father hated. Who could blame you for feeling angry?" Coby choked as he moved towards Trevor. "I'm so sorry Trevor! You went to jail because we thought you'd killed your mother without looking at the facts. Can you forgive me?" Coby begged, standing now in front of his first son.

"Of course, Dad!" Trevor groaned looking wretched. "I can't believe I finally get to call you dad."

"I would've waited forever to hear you say it," Coby whispered, hugging him.

"Oh, dad I miss her so much!" Trevor sobbed, as Coby continued to hold him like the child he once was.

"So, do I to son. True I've remarried, but I will never stop loving Diana," Coby whispered. Michael seeing the pain Coby and Trevor were sharing, grabbed Kim's hand, and they moved away.

After some time, Trevor broke the embrace.

"What happens now Dad?" Trevor asked wiping his eyes.

"That's up to you son. You can come back with us or stay here. Either way, we will respect your decision."

"The Hospice is quite something, isn't it?"

"Yes, it's a real testimony to your hard work son."

"Look, as much as I'd like to go home, I'll need some time. Sue is devoted to helping these people as much as I am. There's also the problem of my addiction. I'm clean now, but you never know."

"We can wait. Talk it over with Sue. If you stay you're going to have a steady stream of relations dropping in," Coby warned with a smile.

"I can't believe the Senator's here. He shouldn't have come. He's not well enough!"

"You know him son. Nothing would stop him from coming once he knew the truth about you." Trevor seemed unsure about meeting George. But then he looked towards his home.

"Let's go see him then, but I'd like to talk to Sue first. I've got a lot of explaining to do."

"Whatever you want son. Let's go." Coby felt as if a huge weight had been lifted from his shoulders as he walked beside Trevor.

Entering through the back door of the kitchen, Trevor found Sue doing the dishes. Coby leaving them alone walked through into the lounge area. Sue stood motionless her eyes misting immediately at the sight of Trevor. Coby feeling the tension, left them alone, walking into the lounge room.

"I am so sorry. Can you forgive me?" Trevor stammered out.

"Trevor, I know you've been through hell, but I have to know this won't happen again!"

"I'm clean Sue. It's taken months, but it's out of my system."

"Till the next time?" Sue whimpered.

"There won't be a next time Sue. My demon has now gone," he assured her. He carefully pulled her to him.

"I can't go through that again Trevor, and little Coby needs a father, not a druggie!" She wept, her tears saturating Trevor's shirt. She had to be certain he understood how she truly felt.

"I can't promise you that it won't occur again, no druggie can. I can promise you instead that I will do my best and unlike before, I now have my family plus my father and his family." He assured as Sue wiping her face smiled.

"They have freed you, haven't they?"

"I hope so, although coming here and meeting you was the best thing I have ever done! I regret nothing since I left prison, except allowing my depression to make me seek a drug crutch," he confessed, before kissing her.

"We will start again my husband as if your life has begun afresh with the return of your family. Let us go to greet them, as

I'm sure they are waiting." She took hold of his hand and led him to the lounge room.

When Coby left Trevor and Sue, he first went to the bathroom to give Trevor some private time with Sue. Finished stalling, he went to the lounge room where George and Glenda were waiting.

"Did you find Michael?" Glenda asked.

"Yeah, he's with Kim. I'd say, they will be in much later."

"Well, I'm for bed. It's been a long day," the Senator yawned.

"What about a late-night tea Senator before you go?" Coby suggested, trying to keep them there.

"No, I've had it. I'm going!"

"It will help you sleep?" Coby exclaimed, making both George and Glenda look at him suspiciously.

"What's going on Coby? Why are you intent on keeping us up?" Glenda asked.

"Grandpa?" A voice sounded from behind them. They knew it wasn't Michael, making them all turn. In the doorway stood Sue and a man in early thirties. Wafer thin and dressed like a farmer, the room occupants stood in shock as George broke the spell and moved to him.

"Good God boy! They said they'd given you up for dead!" George cried, his face taking on a brittle, aged appearance. Without a word, Trevor gave George a bear hug, kissing him on the cheek. Looking at his grandson, George saw how worn out he was. "Where have you been Trevor?"

"I had a run of self-pity which led to drugs. Sue, whom I hope can forgive me, ordered me to get clean or forget about living here. It's taken several months, but I'm okay now." He explained, as Sue approached and kissed him.

"Did Coby?" The Senator's trembling began, as Trevor stopped him.

"Michael broke it to me. It takes a little getting use too."

"Can you forgive us?" the Senator whispered, his voice raw with emotion.

"You have nothing to forgive Grandpa. Despite everything, you always supported me; and Coby forgave me a long time ago. It was my fault for trusting that snake Billy Weldon, which caused this whole mess," Trevor admitted. Glenda seeing everyone was deep in thought, interrupted.

"I'm Glenda, Coby's second wife." She smiled, approaching Trevor. Trevor gave her a polite kiss on the cheek, which made them both smile.

"It's good to meet you, Glenda. Or should I say, Mum?"

"Whatever you're comfortable with Trevor," Glenda softly replied, giving him a quick hug.

"I'm sorry. I should have introduced you," Coby apologised to Glenda.

"That's okay! I can see your mind was elsewhere." Glenda smiled, moving to Coby and squeezed his hand. "Talking about elsewhere, where is Michael?"

"He was walking Kim home," Trevor volunteered.

"I bet!" The Senator chuckled.

"How about a cup of tea?" Sue suggested holding Trevor.

"Just don't send Kim and Michael to make it, we'll all die of thirst." Coby joked, the others joining in, except Trevor.

"It's a private joke. I'll fill you in later," George whispered to Trevor, as they all sat down.

While Trevor and his family shared that cup of tea, Michael did walk Kim home.

"Where are you sleeping?" Kim asked him, after yet another stop for a kiss.

"The lounge is mine," he smiled. "Unless Trevor grabs it?"

"You're lucky, my room is in the temple, besides the surgery. Here the doctor stays close to the patients."

"Well, at least it's private."

"It has been quite a night hasn't it?" Kim smiled, stopping at the temples front door.

"Yes, I now have a nephew and a brother." Michael grinned, feeling relaxed and happy.

"Yes, I'm sorry we kept the truth from you about Trevor, but he needed time."

"You have nothing to apologise for Kim. You were doing what you thought was right. There's nothing wrong with that."

Kim turning, unlocked the door, as the two of them walked inside. Kim used her keys to open the door beside the surgery, which led to one bedroom unit with a living area.

"Looks cosy," Michael commented as they entered.

"It is quite sufficient for my needs. Although a bathroom closer would be nice."

"Where is it?"

"There's a toilet out back, but if I want a wash or a shower, I have to go to Sue and Trevor's."

"That's a bit of an inconvenience?"

"Well, I suppose the monks who once ran the temple, washed in the stream near the village. I need a little bit more privacy and hot water."

"Where does that come from anyway? I saw now you heated the kettle with a wood fire, so how do you have hot water?"

"Trevor rigged up a pipe system that runs through the kitchen stove. It heats the water, which flows into a holding tank. From there he has a solar pump and batteries, which allow lukewarm showers at night."

"He really is clever, isn't he?" Michael smiled, moving closer to Kim. Pulling her towards him, he kissed her. She returned it eagerly.

"Why Senator Henderson, are you trying to seduce me?" Kim giggled, as Michael steered her towards her single bed.

"Yes I am, although the bed isn't exactly huge."

"I'm sure you'll think of something?" Kim smiled, as Michael started undressing her.

The next morning the family sat down to breakfast, as young Coby was constantly fought over for a cuddle. Where Michael spent, the night went unanswered despite the Senator's constant questioning. No one, of course, broached the subject about what was to happen next, as they all simply enjoyed being together. Kim was first to leave to do her rounds at the hospice. Of course, Michael volunteering to walk her there surprised no one.

After a kiss for all, Kim led the way to the front door. She opened her door, and her smile disappeared. It seemed the entire village had gathered in front of the house. Michael, wondering why she had ground to a halt, looked past her, at the silent crowd. Reacting, he moved protectively in front of her.

"What's going on?" he whispered, realising there were far too many people for just this village.

"Get Trevor and Sue!" Kim told him softly, while she walked out to meet them.

"Are you sure I should leave you?"

"I'll be okay, just get the others?" she asked before talking to the crowd in Vietnamese. Worried, Michael rushed back to his family.

"Trevor! Kim asked if you can come out front. There is a large crowd waiting outside your door!" Trevor swiftly rose from his seat and moved to the front door, followed closely by Sue.

"What's wrong Michael?" Coby and George asked at the same time.

"I'm not sure! The whole village, plus a lot of other people I'd say, are out there waiting," he told them. Outside, Coby and the others found Trevor speaking in Vietnamese to the crowd. Many seemed upset, as Trevor, looking like he was imitating Coby doing a speech in the Senate, spoke passionately to the crowd. Michael and Coby stood watching him debate, seeing him as the village saw him, as their benefactor and representative. After twenty minutes of what seemed like emotionally charged speeches by the villagers, they dispersed leaving Trevor, Kim and Sue crying.

"What was that about? Are we all safe?" Coby asked gripping young Coby whom he'd kept close in case of trouble.

"Quite the opposite. They were afraid we were all leaving. It was the villagers who were frightened," Trevor told them, wiping his eyes.

"When they found out Trevor's family had come looking for him, they thought you would take all of us back home with you and leave them," Kim explained, her eyes turning to look at Michael.

"I told them they were my family too. That I might someday leave them to visit you, but I would always return; that this is my home now," Trevor explained, holding Sue's hand. Coby like the others stood silently watching Trevor. He had hoped he'd come back with them. Now he saw Trevor had his own life and he was happy for him.

214

"You are your own man Trevor. What you decide to do with your life is for you to decide. I am happy with whatever you decide."

"Thank you, Dad. Of course, you can all visit whenever you like." He smiled, his eyes still locked on Coby.

"Count on it son!" Coby promised as they all moved back inside.

After things had settled down again, Kim finally left to do her rounds with Michael. He'd remained silent during the whole confrontation. She had been comforted by his defence of her when they'd first encountered the villagers, knowing he loved her as she loved him.

"You're quiet Michael. Is there a problem?" she asked as they reached the temple.

"I love you Kim and want to stay with you, yet I must leave soon," he confessed, torn between staying and leaving.

"Oh, Michael don't be sad! You knew this would be how it is. I must stay till there are more doctors to assist. Once that happens I will be free to leave."

"Then you are thinking of marrying me?" Michael exclaimed, brightening up.

"You want to marry me?"

"What did you think I wanted?"

"I wasn't sure. We haven't known each other that long Michael?"

"I know, but it feels right. I don't just want to sleep with you Kim. I want the whole deal. Don't you feel it too?"

"Yes, I do want to marry you Michael, but what will the people who vote for you think? Can an American Senator marrying a Vietnamese woman?"

"Who gives a shit what they think! It's none of their business. Then you will say yes?"

"Yes, I will say yes, but it will take some time for a replacement and more staff to be hired and brought here."

"I will wait forever as long as you promise to marry me!" Michael laughed, picking her up and twirling her around, making her shriek with laughter. Putting her back down, he kissed her before letting her go. "I'll see you later." He smiled, whistling out of tune as he walked back to Trevor's home.

"Congratulations!" Trevor yelled as he approached. Michael stunned, took several seconds to answer.

"How did you know?"

"Everyone knows. You two were talking so loudly and carrying on so much, that everyone heard." Michael at first was taken aback wondering how loud he'd been, before it came to him.

"You're kidding, aren't you?"

"Yes, but I'm right aren't I?"

"She won't leave here till she can be replaced. Only then will she agree to marry me."

"Is she worth the wait?"

"Yes, she is."

"Then congratulations again!" Trevor laughed shaking Michael's hand, as Coby appeared at the door.

"What's all the yelling about?" he asked. Trevor, grinning, pointed to Michael. "Well, Michael what's going on?"

"I asked Kim to marry me. She said yes, but only after she is free to leave here." Both young men watched Coby.

"You're a lucky man son. If she's half the woman Sue is, you should be prepared to wait forever."

"God, I said the same thing to her," Michael admitted.

"What else could you say?" Trevor put in.

"Let's go tell the others," Coby suggested, holding open the door for his two sons.

"Do you think I should wait till Kim's here?" Michael asked, getting nervous about telling his mum.

"Kim will be okay. Let's go tell them!" Trevor laughed, charging past Michael. Inside Glenda watched with amusement as her two sons carried on as of they'd been together since kindergarten.

"Glenda, I mean Mum, Michael's got some news!" Trevor exploded before Michael could say anything.

"Okay Michael, spill it! What's going on?" Glenda demanded.

"Mum I asked Kim to marry me. She said yes." He laughed as Trevor did his best to make it hard for him. Glenda at first was stunned, as Michael had always been the love them and leave them type. Over the years she'd tried to steer the right girls in his direction, but he always evaded them, coming up with a steady stream of excuses. "Is everything okay mum?" Michael asked when she hadn't answered.

"It couldn't be better happier Michael. It's just a shock that's all. You haven't known each other that long?"

"I know mum, but it feels right!"

"I couldn't be happier than son. After thinking you'd be single forever, you finally find your soul mate in the mountains of Vietnam!" Standing up, she moved to him and kissed him on the cheek.

"It surprised me too. Since the first time I saw Kim, I've been hooked," Michael admitted, hugging his mother.

"What's going on?" Sue appeared from the kitchen.

"Michael has asked Kim to marry him!" Trevor told her.

"About time! I thought he would've done it sooner!" Sue told them, seeming unfazed, as she disappeared back into the kitchen, followed by a mystified Trevor.

"Well the only ones left are the Senator and young Coby, and he like his mum won't act surprised." Coby chuckled. "Where is he anyway?"

"Went for a walk down along the river. Would you mind fetching him?" Glenda asked Coby.

"No problems. I'll take Michael. It's about time we had that father-son talk!" He sniggered.

"Never too late Dad," Michael replied, following him outside.

They followed an old, well-worn trail, which had been here for hundreds of years. It gradually zigzagged its way down to the river, creating the impression of a gentle valley slope, whereas, in reality, it was a clever deception, a far cry from the reality of a deep ravine.

"He shouldn't have come this far on his own!" Michael pointed out, sounding a little puffed.

"He knows his limits. Speaking of limits how many people are you inviting to the wedding, and where?" Coby asked starting to feel the walk as well.

"God, I haven't thought that far ahead. I suppose in America if that's okay with Kim?"

"Well if you want the Senator there, it will have to be in the States. He couldn't handle another trip like this I'd say,"

"Who couldn't handle another trip?" the Senator barked from up ahead. He was on his way towards them carrying young Coby. Coby had trouble replying, feeling as if he'd been caught out.

"Ah Senator, Michael has something to tell you," Coby stammered, changing the subject.

"What's going on Michael?" George asked, as Michael too hesitated.

"I asked Kim to marry me!"

"That's great news, Michael! She's quite a catch." George shook Michael's hand before kissing him on the cheek.

"Unfortunately, it can't happen, until she can find someone to replace her here," Michael added.

"Well, life wasn't meant to be easy son. At least it gives you time to prepare. Hey, how about we have it at the plantation? We haven't had a wedding there since Bud's." the Senator stopped himself. Memories of his son flooded back.

"That would be perfect Grandad. The only problem I can see is if Kim wants it to be here," Michael answered, ignoring George's slip up.

"Wherever it is, I'll be there!" the Senator choked out, as they retraced their steps along the trail. Coby, following Michael and the Senator, kept a close eye on George. He walked along behind Michael having given Michael the job of carrying young Coby. He seemed indestructible as he rambled on about the joys and responsibilities of being a husband.

"He'll outlive us all," Coby whispered, thinking about how this humble, righteous man had impacted his life. Right from the start, he'd been with him, guiding him and he'd always steered him true. "What will happen when he isn't here?" his inner voice asked. "What would my life have been like if I hadn't met this man?" As if sensing Coby's train of thought, the Senator turned giving him a direct smile.

"Are you keeping up or do you want a rest?" he asked before turning back to the trail.

"Would you like me to piggyback you, Senator?" Coby replied, his breath betraying his fatigue, as the Senator chuckled.

"Did I ever tell you that in my twenties I was a seasoned tracker? I even spent a couple of months tracking through Nepal, reaching the base camp at Mount Everest?" The Senator sniggered, his strides and stature showing he was enjoying this hike.

"No, but watching you walk now makes me believe it," Coby answered, as the three men ambled along.

On reaching the temple, their happy mood evaporated when they found Colonel Don Lap, Paul and another man in a business suit, waiting. Behind them, spread over the area in front of the temple, was a company of soldiers. At their appearance, the Colonel barked out some orders, the soldiers immediately spreading out around the temple area.

"What's going on?" Michael asked, as he passed young Coby to the Senator, and moved in front of the two older men.

The Colonel was about to speak, but instead, he pointed to Paul, indicating he should tell them.

"John Bridges, the President, has been killed," Paul told them, his upset evident.

"Good God. How did it occur?" Coby asked, truly shocked.

"After the boost in the polls from the treaty signing, he held a rally to announce his run for a second term in the White House. His motorcade was ambushed that night when it left to return to the White House."

"I thought the Presidential limousine could survive anything?" Michael put in.

"Most attacks yes, but this time they used a huge bomb in a fuel tanker. Eighteen secret servicemen were killed as well!" Silence settled over the group, as Coby thought of those secret servicemen who had given him the thumbs up after the President had dropped him off.

"Who did it?" the Senator growled.

"Many groups have claimed responsibility, but it looks like some radical group in the Sudan was behind it."

"Why the soldiers Colonel Don Lap?" Coby asked, seeing the Colonel was constantly searching the surrounding area.

"General Chew is worried that this group might have found out two high profile Senators and ex-Vice President Van Clef are here. After our treaty, he doesn't want anything happening to any of you while holidaying here," the Colonel informed them.

"Where is Glenda?" Coby asked as the man in the suit stepped forward.

"Senator Coby Henderson, I am Agent Stevens of the secret service. Your wife is secure inside with four of my men Sir. As are Trevor, his wife and her sister. I would suggest that you all pack immediately as an Air Force plane is waiting at Da Nang to take you all home."

"Is this really necessary?" Michael asked. Agent Steven's looked around before answering.

"It has been a close kept a secret, but the Vice President is unwell and was about to resign. The President had been asked to pick his successor but never got around to making a decision. As you two are serving Democratic Senators and you hold the majority in the house, the Senate has asked that you return immediately to Washington to vote for a new President and Vice President."

"There's no time to think about it. Let's collect our gear," the Senator ordered, as the men silently entered Trevor's home.

"Dad will you be all right?" Trevor asked as Coby entered the house.

"Yes, it's just precaution. Once the new President is chosen, we'll return," Coby assured him, noting two agents in the lounge area. Glenda then appeared from the room she and Coby were staying in, carrying their bags.

"I've packed everyone's overnight bag," she announced, trying to force a smile.

"Sorry about this everyone!" Coby exclaimed as the whole family gathered.

"No one is blaming any of you," Trevor assured him. "A great evil has been done, and you're needed. We will wait for your return." He smiled, hugging each of his departing family members, followed by Sue and Kim.

"What about these four? I'm not leaving them here defenseless!" Michael spoke up.

"Colonel Don Lap's men are staying here for now Michael. We are in no danger," Kim told him, gripping his hand. Michael seemed torn between leaving Kim and going.

"Go, Michael! I will come as soon as I can," she promised, as Michael kissed her on the lips.

"Geez are we all getting one of those?" the Senator asked mischievously, causing everyone, including the agents, to smile.

"Not a chance!" Michael replied, as picking up his bag and swiftly walked outside with Kim.

Michael, feeling his world spinning out of his control, took those first steps away from the security of Trevor's home. He felt his connection with Kim somehow diminish. The tribes-people seemed to share his indecision, as they lined the roadsides, waving sadly as they passed. Even these remote people had picked up the troubled undercurrent. The Senator, unfazed by the situation, continuously waved to the villagers, promising to return, as soon as he could. At the landing pad, they were guided by the soldiers onto three helicopters that stood waiting ominously on the far side of the village.

"Keep them, safe Colonel!" Michael shouted to Don Lap above the noise of the choppers.

"With my life, my friend." He smiled, offering his hand, which Michael shook before boarding. Coby was the last to board the beast. As the doors slammed shut, Michael blew a belated kiss to Kim who stood, holding tightly onto her sister. Trevor continued to wave while Sue and Kim shrank in size, as the chopper rose swiftly, heading for Da Nang. For many reasons, Michael felt he was leaving happiness far behind.

PRESIDENT HENDERSON

Landing just short of the main terminal, the group, were ushered towards Air Force One.

"What the hell is that doing here?" Coby asked an Air Force Major, waiting at the door.

"You're not the only ones we're picked up Sir. There were seven other Senators and their families either on holidays here or on business. This plane is the most secure we have, and the Vice President insisted it be sent," he explained, pointing for them to board. As they climbed the staircase, Coby had just reached the entry platform, when he stopped. To the south, the old Air Force structures no longer caused the same emotional turmoil he had felt before. This trip had helped, quell the anger and sadness, he'd felt about the unnecessary loss of so many brave men and women during the war.

Trevor's exoneration had also closed a gaping wound, reuniting his broken family. The distance he knew would be a problem, but it was not insurmountable. This tragic development had cut short their reunion, but fortunately, they'd all reached an understanding. Michael, he could see, was upset at leaving Kim. Unfortunately, in politics, that was part of the job. In the rear seating section, Coby saw the seven other Senators' families sitting watching television. The Senators were further forward, lounging near the bar. At the ex-Vice President and Coby's appearance, they all stood.

"Mr. Van Clef. Welcome aboard!" one of the Senators exclaimed, the others raised their glasses.

"I judge you've been waiting a while?" George replied, seeing some of them were a little unsteady on their feet.

"Several hours. They wouldn't let us leave without the treaty makers," another remarked, while others chuckled. The Senator seemed unimpressed with the alcohol-fueled joviality.

"I thought under the circumstances laughter would be the last thing I'd hear on this plane," Coby answered for him, stopping their merriment.

"We are all shocked by what occurred Senator Henderson, and I apologise if we offended you. We've just been sitting here under guard waiting for you for several hours. Having a drink seemed a plausible option," Senator Banks from the State of Ohio interjected. Silence followed.

"You're right Senator! I may have reacted a bit strongly. Like you, we were rushed here after receiving the news from the people who picked us up," Coby apologised, alleviating the situation. Nodding his understanding, Senator Banks introduced Coby, Michael and George to the group. Most, despite their drinking, were appalled and worried by the assassination of the President. Of the seven, only three were Democrats, so a discussion on the election of a new President would have to wait.

George after some discussion about what was going on, left the group, citing his weariness at travelling as his excuse. He was given the Presidential room to sleep in, much to the surprise of the gathered Senators. Michael knew his grandfather had been well respected by the secret service when he was Vice President. Apparently, they hadn't forgotten him. After several hours of discussion, the Senators all sought sleep, knowing the next day would be a long one. Coby was heading for his allotted bed, when the Major he'd talked to earlier, intercepted him.

"Can you come to the Communications Room with me Sir?" he politely asked.

"What's up Major?"

"The President would like to speak to you, Sir." The Major whispered, as Coby nodding his acceptance, followed the Major. Michael behind him saw the exchange and decided to tag along. Reaching the Communications Room, Coby and Michael entered to see several Air Force crew members present as well.

"Senator Henderson, the President, is on the line," the Major formally told him, handing him a mobile phone. Michael who was trailing behind noticed the secret servicemen had taken up station beside Coby. Raising his hand for silence, Coby asked for the call to be put on loudspeaker, which surprised the men working there.

"Go ahead Mr. President," Coby said out loud, putting the phone down.

"Coby, it's Benny. I judge you are up to speed on what's happened?"

"Yes Sir, and I have the phone on speaker so my son and the crew here can hear as well." He warned the President.

"You always were careful Coby. Well, let's get on with it. I've been racking my brain trying to think of whom to nominate. Your name keeps coming up."

"I'm retiring Mr. President. It might be best to select someone younger," Coby replied. Michael saw the looks on the men faces at Coby refusing the Presidency.

"I'm aware of that Coby, but this is an emergency. I'm not well, and the doctors say I have maybe two years to live, although, with treatment, I may live much longer. For now, the people need a face they can trust, and the financial sector needs stability in the markets. You're known as an honest man Coby. How about it?"

"How long would it be for?" Coby asked capitulating.

"Only until the next election and that's only eight months away." The President seemed to be pleading.

"Then if the Senate supports your nomination, I'll accept," Coby assured him, as the Air Force personnel around him clapped.

"Looks like the men are with you, Coby. When you land, you'll be taken to the White House and sworn in," the President informed him, surprising the people there.

"I thought it had to be debated?"

"Already done Coby. Even ill, I can still talk the Senate into doing anything!" He chuckled, and the crew around Coby held back laughter.

"I'll be dammed! You conned me!"

"Good! I'll meet you in Washington, Coby. And welcome aboard!" The President chuckled as the line dropped out.

"Congratulations Mr. President!" The Major snapped to attention, the crew the following suit.

"Thank you Major, but you're a bit premature?"

"I wanted to be first, and I'd say it's a done deal, Sir," the Major replied, as all the men present shook his hand.

Michael was the last to shake his hand, his eyes betraying his pride.

"I know you didn't want it Dad, but you deserve it," Michael told him, as three secret service agents appeared.

"Sir, as senior agent, I would like to congratulate you on behalf of the secret service."

"Were you there that day?"

"No Sir, only two agents survived," he murmured.

"If I'm made President, I want the two survivors on my detail, no matter how badly they were hurt. I also want to arrange a day at the White House, so I can personally thank the families of the Agents who were killed and injured. Can you arrange that for me?"

"Yes, Sir! It would be an honour," Agent Steven's whispered, as Coby and Michael moved on.

"Now there's a man worth dying for," one of the agents confessed.

"Let's hope it doesn't come to that," Stevens answered, as he returned to the Communications Room, to send word of the new President.

"That was well said Dad," Michael whispered, as they walked towards their rooms.

"They deserve it. God! Only two survived out of the whole escort! The service must be devastated."

"Are you going to tell mum now?"

"Yeah. I'm not looking forward to that."

"I'll see you in the morning." Michael half choked on a snigger as he opened his door and disappeared inside.

"You chicken shit!" Coby smiled, before opening his door to find Glenda waiting.

"I suspect you've got something important to tell me?"

"They want me to be President until elections can be held."

"So, you answered in the negative, of course?"

"Well, the President was convincing. I couldn't say no!"

"I understand Coby. But it better only be until the election!" she warned.

"I promise!"

"Like you promised to quit politics?"

"This is different!"

"It certainly is."

In his room, Michael thought about his father being President. Sure, it was a great honour, but what about Kim? How did this affect their marriage and their long-term future? A knock on the door stopped his thoughts. Opening it, he found the Senator there.

"Can I come in?"

"Yes of course Grandad. What's wrong?"

"I heard from the secret service that your dad's been nominated?"

"Yeah, although it could still be vetoed by the Senate."

"Bullshit! He's in; no one would challenge a retiring President," he pointed out.

"I wonder who the Vice President will be?"

"I'd say Benny will stay on as Vice President, to make sure Coby's okay."

"That sounds like a good idea," Michael answered, drifting off.

"What's worrying you son?"

"Marrying Kim. It will be hard to arrange with Dad being President."

"Nonsense. Coby will be there no matter when or where you hold it. Although considering the situation, I'd push her to get it over with straight away."

"Why?" Michael asked mystified.

"We can travel on Air Force One while Coby's President? God, this plane is so comfortable, compared to the domestic ones." George grinned.

As the Senator had foreseen, Coby once he'd landed in Washington, was rushed to the White House. The Speaker of the House, plus the Attorney General were waiting with most of the dealmakers of the Democratic Party. One familiar face was Robert. He now headed up the Democratic Party's PR machine. Catching Coby's eye, he signalled for him to meet before the ceremony started. After telling Michael he'd be back shortly, he followed Robert to a side room. Coby closed the door behind them.

"I thought you said you'd never run for President?" Robert started.

"And I never would. This is different."

"This reporter doing the story on Trevor, I suppose he knows everything?"

"Yes, he does, and he promised to keep the piece about Bud and me out of it."

"And you trust him?"

"A hundred percent!"

"A lot is riding on this Coby. It's not just politics; it's the country itself. The death of the President has hit the people hard. They're frightened that these terrorists will strike again."

"Have we identified the perpetrators?"

"Yes, the CIA is waiting for the new President to be elected before they carry out the briefing."

"Then let's get moving?" Coby ordered, walking to the door.

"It doesn't worry you that your first duty as President will be to kill people in revenge?" Robert whispered.

"My first duty is to protect the American people. Those people murdered a great many Americans. I don't seek revenge for them Robert, I seek justice," Coby explained, moving back outside.

"You've still got that patriotic fire Coby," Robert pointed out.

"Till I die, Robert," He left Robert digesting Coby's remark.

Coby's swearing in was broadcast around the world. Standing with Glenda, he asked for a minute's silence for the fallen, before starting his acceptance speech.

"Fellow Americans it saddens me that in accepting the Presidency, I do so knowing a great man and his protectors, have paid the ultimate price. Despite locking horns several times with the President, I found him to be a good, honest, hard working man and I am humbled to be asked to fill his large shoes. People, when good men do nothing, evil spreads. Today I promise the American people that the perpetrators of this murderous attack will be brought to justice, no matter where they are.

Any country that gives these men shelter is an enemy of this nation and will pay the price a hundred-fold. I wish I could have come to you today with my vision for America's future, but alas these faceless cowards must be taken care of first. Today we stand shoulder to shoulder with our neighbours and friends in denouncing this senseless violence. As long as our country stands, we will never be bullied into submission!" Coby shouted as the crowd cheered.

Michael and Glenda were the first to congratulate him, followed by visiting dignitaries and Senators. Once the ceremony was over, he signalled to a secret service agent.

"What's your name?" Coby asked.

"John Bronson Sir."

"Glad to meet you. Now John, can you call the CIA Chief and tell him I want him in my office immediately, as well as the Joint Chief of Staff of all the armed forces. It's time we found those cowards," Coby told him.

"Yes, Sir. I'd be honoured," John answered, then talked into his headset.

"Mr. President," John whispered, as Coby started walking towards the White House.

"Yes, John."

"The CIA chief said to say he has another engagement!" John whispered.

"Tell him it wasn't an invitation John. It was an order." Coby smiled, but to John, it seemed hostile.

"Yes, Sir!" John replied, sending another message.

By the time Coby did a tour of their accommodation with Glenda, then walked to the Oval Office, the Joint Chiefs of the Armed Forces and the CIA chief were there waiting. As Coby entered, they all stood.

"Relax everyone. I suggest you all get comfortable. You've got the floor, Mr. Horton," Coby pointed to the CIA Chief. Standing, the CIA chief gave the impression he was not happy to be here.

"After the incident, the FBI did a great job of identifying two of the terrorists. Both are from Northern Sudan and aligned with a group calling itself 'The Right Hand of God'. Using an inside contact, we have located the organisation's base. It's located on the border with Southern Sudan, in an old army headquarters bunker complex. The Iranians, we understand, are financially supporting them with training and weapons so they can raid Southern Sudan. We are not sure why or how they got here, but they must have planned this for some time." Horton finished his briefing and sat down. The room then darkened so that slides could be shown. On the wall appeared the camouflaged bunker in a desert location. Several hundred men could be seen training around it.

"So, Northern Sudan and Iran are backing this terrorist group, and they've set up shop in the south. Is everyone here sure that's these are the people we're looking for?" Coby asked.

"Yes, Sir." Several voices answered. Coby looking to the side saw Jim Benson the head of the FBI hadn't answered.

"What about you Jim?" Coby asked as all heads turned towards him.

"Yes, Mr. President I think this group was involved. The problem is it's just too neat. The only two bodies found, just happened to be unburned so we can identify them. Everyone else involved in the attack was burnt beyond recognition. I don't like it, Sir. They knew too much about the President's movements." He answered, seeming angry.

"Mr. Horton. Have you worked out how the terrorists knew of the Presidential route?" Coby asked.

"No Sir. Although they could have got lucky and guessed it. The events location was well known," Horton answered, giving Benson a sidelong look.

"This group deserves to be wiped out for its attacks on Southern Sudan, let alone this attack. I want that training camp and bunker obliterated gentlemen. But I also want whoever planned this attack. Like Jim said it's too neat. I also don't believe in luck, Mr. Horton. There has to be someone here involved. I don't care if you have to turn over every rock in this country or the Middle East, find who is responsible!" Coby ordered.

"I don't like the reference to my luck comment Mr. President. That was uncalled for," Horton snapped back.

"Look, Horton, I don't give a shit if I mucked up your day to be here. You're the head of our overseas Intelligence Service, and all you've got is what the FBI told you. This group in Sudan could be involved, but running it, I don't think so. I'll take out that bunker because we know they supplied men for this attack, but I'll want more proof before we relax and think we're safe. If you can't handle it, leave your resignation on your desk. Now if there aren't any more questions, I suggest we all get on with our jobs," Coby growled. The room remained deadly silent until Mr. Horton stood and left. After his exit, General Graven came forward.

"How hard do you want them hit Sir?" General Graven asked.

"Do I know you General?" Coby replied.

"Yes, Sir. At one time, I was in charge of the security units at Da Nang airfield."

"Yes, I remember now, although it was a long time ago," Coby smiled. "What would you suggest we use General?"

"Eight Tomahawks Sir. Nothing's going to get out of that area after they hit."

"You have a go General."

"Welcome aboard Sir!" He grinned, saluting before leaving. In turn, the other officers present did the same.

"I think you made a friend there," Benson said, as he made to leave.

"Wait, Jim! I like to talk to you alone for a second if you don't mind?" Nodding his acceptance, Benson waited until Michael arrived. Pointing to the chairs, both men sat while Coby paced. As usual, two secret service men stood near the door.

"Horton worries me. Talking about luck when we all know it wasn't, scares me!" Coby confessed.

"Rumors are he has a lot of friends on the hill?" Michael whispered.

"I don't care if he knows God. I want the men responsible found!" Coby snapped. "Sorry. It's just that good people died. I want those who planned it, not some dirtbag who pulled the trigger."

"Chances are he'll resign to make out he was pushed?" Benson replied.

"Who is your second in command?" Coby asked Benson.

"John Taylor. Why?" Benson replied.

"Do you have faith in him?" Coby asked.

"Yes. When I retire I was going to ask that he get the top job," Benson replied.

"Good. Tell him he has the job. You're going to head up the CIA," Coby informed him. Benson, shocked, stared at the President.

"Sir, can you even do that?" Benson whispered back.

"Watch me!" he smiled. "Well, how about it?"

"I course Sir. Can I take some key personnel with me?"

"Yes you can, and from now on I want to integrate the FBI, Homeland security and the Agencies. There's been too much hoarding of information and not enough sharing. We can't let petty differences affect our security."

"What about the secret service?" Michael asked, looking towards the two men standing guard at the door.

"They stay as they are. Of all the services, they have proved themselves. Now let's go sell this coming action," Coby suggested moving to the door.

"You can pass that onto your boss, men," Coby told them.

"He already knows Sir," one of the guards answered.

It wasn't as easy as Coby at first thought. Horton had a lot of friends who weren't happy about their friend getting fired. Going to the House the next morning, Coby told them of the changes, pointing out the need for greater cohesion amongst the agencies that protected them. Many wanted a vote. Coby said they could, but if they didn't agree he'd stand down as President. Most couldn't believe he'd dare after just being appointed. His steely gaze warned them he wasn't kidding. After that the Senate folded, giving him what he wanted.

His next stop was a press conference. Breaking with protocol, Coby marched straight into the room, giving the press no warning. As they tried to stand, he waved them back down.

"Gentlemen I won't mince words. We have identified two of the terrorist, and our response is on the way as I speak. People, unfortunately, will die, although they chose to attack our country and will now reap what they sowed. I have appointed Mr. Benson the Head of the FBI to the position of Director of the CIA to weld our agencies into a more efficient Intelligence Group. We must stop the petty infighting and get the job done. Any questions?"

The room for several seconds remained silent until a raised hand indicated the first question. Coby pointed to him to start.

"Mr. President. Rumors are you had a falling out with Mr. Horton over 'the terrorist got lucky' comment from him. Is that true?

"Yes, he did say something along that line, about the terrorists getting lucky, but he was fired because when I asked him to meet me, he was too busy. I am the President handling the death of my predecessor and many innocent Americans. There is nothing more important than that to me. Next question?" Coby asked.

"Mr. President. John Forest from the Globe. Public opinion polls put your popularity with the people at an all-time high for any President. Will you run in eight months' time?"

"No John I will not." This caused a rumble of talking amongst the press. "Look people! I am getting old and was looking forward to being with my family, which as you have heard has been through a lot lately. I took this job to steer this country through a bad time, until the next election. Then the people can elect their choice. My first act will be to kill people, something that no President should have to do. That said, our country cries out for justice. Until I have fulfilled that promise, I must stay the course. Any more questions?"

To everyone's surprise, no one raised his or her hand.

"Then thank you for coming! I have work to do," Coby told them and left.

"That was quite something Mr. President," Robert told him as they walked back to the Oval Office.

"They're worried, Robert. If the terrorists can strike once, they can again. No one wanted to ask that question."

"Do you think they will?" Robert whispered, sounding worried.

"Unless we stop them, yes," Coby replied. Robert was stopped at the Oval office door by security. "Sorry Robert, I have a security briefing."

"No problem Sir," Robert replied, staying outside as Coby and his security entered. Once inside, he saw the look of defeat on the faces of the gathered men.

"Okay General, spit it out!" Coby ordered, sitting down.

"We just used a satellite to check the target. The base is now deserted. Someone tipped them off that we were coming."

"Then we have one or more moles in our chain of command. I want them found gentlemen before they strike again!" Coby warned.

"Everyone connected to the information on the raid and the attack is being checked, Sir. We'll get whoever's responsible," Benson assured him.

"How long will that take?" Coby snapped.

"I can't give you a timeframe Sir. It could be tomorrow or a month. We're talking about thousands of personnel Sir." Benson snapped back, making the General and his staff looked towards him. Benson, seeing the looks, became aware his mistake. "Sorry, Sir. I shouldn't have answered like that."

"Never apologise for setting me straight. That goes for all of you. I am not infallible, and I want your honesty when you know I'm wrong. I'm just worried men. The enemy is out there somewhere, and we must find them."

"We will Sir," General Graven answered.

"In the meantime, flatten that base. They mightn't think we're onto them if we don't destroy it," Coby pointed out.

"That's good thinking Sir. I'll order the strike," Graven told him.

"There's something else I'm working on Sir, to flush them out." The new head of the FBI John Taylor added.

"What is it?" Coby asked.

"We're waiting for them to attack. I suggest we get in first."

"And how do we do that?" Benson enquired.

"Leak a target they can't resist," Taylor suggested.

"Jesus that might work John. But what's the target?" General Graven asked.

"How about something like the meeting between the President and the families of the Secret Service? They'd go after that for sure?" Taylor suggested. Coby watched the two secret servicemen bristle.

"There is no way in hell that will happen gentlemen! Until these terrorists are found, the meeting won't occur," Coby growled.

"It was just an example, Sir. Although it will have to be something just as big and include you, to lure them out," Taylor replied.

"Unfortunately, you're right. So, let's all think about it," Coby told them, the meeting at an end.

Though he was ready to turn in for the night, Coby found the Senator and Michael waiting for him. Glenda was still coming to terms with living in the White House and having staff to make her coffee.

"I can't see why I can't make a simple cup of coffee myself!" she exclaimed after the staff had left.

"It's their job, Glenda. They take it seriously if you don't let them do it!" The Senator smiled, enjoying his coffee.

"You've got to admit it's good Mum?" Michael pointed out, getting an angry look in return.

"He's right honey," Coby answered receiving a glare as well. "Anyway, how was your day?" he asked, changing the subject. The Senator chuckled in delight over in the corner.

"It was different but fun," Glenda admitted. "Being the first lady has its benefits I'll say that."

"Has anyone heard from Trevor?" the Senator butted in. By their faces, he could see no one had.' "I'm worried about them over there, and I miss them," he confessed. He seemed to have aged since their trip.

"They're safer over there than they would be here," Coby accidentally muttered, before realising it.

"What's that supposed to mean?" Glenda asked holding her chest, sensing something was wrong.

"Nothing, just speaking without thinking," Coby covered.

"Bullshit! What's going on?" the Senator asked. Coby decided foxing wasn't going to work, so told them honestly.

"Look there's a chance this terrorist cell will strike again."

"I thought you were taking care of the threat by bombing their base in Sudan?" the Senator snapped back.

"We did. When the bombers got there, they were gone. We believe they were tipped off by someone in the chain of command," Coby confessed. He was worried, and his family knew it.

"Bloody hell! The people think we're on top of it. There will be hell to pay if they attack again!" Michael warned.

"Are we in any danger?" Glenda asked.

"No of course not. Although this could be a good time for the three of you to visit Trevor and his family again," Coby suggested.

"There's no way in hell I'm leaving!" Glenda barked as the Senator rose from his chair to back her. As he made to talk, he suddenly grabbed his chest.

"Senator! Are you okay?" Coby asked, as Michael who was beside him, swiftly grabbed and lowered him back into his chair.

Glenda, shocked, knelt beside him, as Coby shouted to his guards. The two secret servicemen burst through the door, guns drawn. Taking in the scene, they called for an ambulance.

THE SENATOR

Two hours later they were at the Walter Reed Army Medical Centre. Coby waited with Glenda and Michael, as a surgeon arrived at the door. Coby's two secret servicemen removed his facemask to check the doctor's identity before he could approach Coby.

"Sorry about the security, Doctor!" Coby spoke first.

"No problems Mr President. Look there's no easy way to say this. Mr Van Clef has had a heart attack. It's a bad one. If he has other family, I'd get them here pronto. I'm sorry!" the Surgeon sadly added.

"How long?" Coby got out.

"Maybe a week but I can't guarantee even that length of time," the Surgeon confessed. Seeing their grief, the surgeon left them to themselves.

Coby, like the others, stood paralysed. He'd thought the Senator would live forever. George had always seemed indestructible. He moved to Glenda and Michael, embracing them both, sharing the grief they were all consumed by.

"You've got to get Trevor here Coby!" Glenda sobbed. "He's got to see his grandfather again before he's gone!" Glenda continued, as the three pulled themselves together.

"You're right. I'll contact Colonel Don Lap. He left a number in case of an emergency. I can have my people arrange transport for whoever wants to come," Coby told them grabbing his phone. He contacted his office and spoke to Robert who immediately got things moving.

"Thank you, Robert. I appreciate it," Coby told him

"Is it okay if I visit him?" Robert asked, his voice wavering. Coby had forgotten how much the Senator meant to Robert.

"Robert, you don't have to ask. Have someone else see to Trevor's arrangements and come now!"

"No. I'll make sure Trevor knows, then I'll come," Robert told him hanging up. At the door, a nurse hovered with his guards. She told Coby they could see the Mr Van Clef. The three followed her while behind them, the secret service passed on what they had heard to their headquarters. Outside the hospital, army units took up positions around the hospital.

An ambulance leaving the White House was news. The army blockading a hospital caused a media frenzy. By the time Robert had arrived, security had been moved out to half a mile from the hospital buildings. Getting out of his taxi, Robert proceeded towards the checkpoint surrounded by a sea of noisy reporters.

"Mr Roberts, can you tell us what's going on?" Several reporters cried out as Robert stopped before them. As the party PR spokesmen, Robert had to say something. Stepping up to the microphones with millions watching, Robert couldn't speak. Silence overwhelmed the reporters as they waited for him to start.

"Ex-President George Van Clef while visiting the President, has suffered a massive heart attack." Robert barely got the information out, as the subdued reporters came to life.

"Will he be okay?" Several asked at once.

"No," Robert answered before hurrying toward the barrier and disappearing inside. Behind him the media came to life, broadcasting the news.

Inside Coby, with Michael and Glenda, sat beside the Senator. Robert looked like an emotional wreck when he arrived. Going to the Van Clef's side, he held his hand.

"You know he once told me, that he wished I'd been his son. It was one of the greatest moments of my life," he admitted, as Coby came to stand with him and put his hand on his shoulder

"I meant it!" the Senator croaked from the bed, startling all of them.

"Bloody Hell Senator! You scared us all!" Coby exclaimed, as shocked as the others.

"Yeah being a Vice President trains you to frighten people." He smirked, before coughing. A nurse immediately appeared at the door. Moving to the Senator, she checked his vitals.

"How are you feeling Sir?" she asked, unaffected by the presence of the President in the room.

"I've felt better nurse. Can I have something for the pain?" He winced, as the nurse put his oxygen mask on his face.

"I'll get the doctor, for you Sir. In the meantime, the oxygen might make the pain retreat a little. Best try and relax." She smiled as she hurried away. The Senator seemed to go back to sleep.

"Jesus, we should have the nurses running the army! They are scared of nothing!" Robert pointed out once she'd left.

"Yes, their dedication to their work is inspiring," Coby admitted as the group moved closer to the bed. As if sensing their scrutiny, the Senator's eyes sleepily opened. After looking at his surroundings, he finally spoke.

"I judge it's bad by your looks?"

"You'll be up in no time Sir," Robert grinned holding the Senator's hand, although his eyes gave it away.

"Robert you've always made me proud, but lying is not your strong point. Tell me the truth!" Robert tried to answer, but the words wouldn't come.

"Senator, you're right. It's not good," Coby told him, watching the Senator's eyes swivel to him.

"How long? Days or weeks?"

"Around a week," Coby answered, the corners of his eyes stinging.

"Does Trevor know?" The Senator croaked, his eyes glued to Coby.

"Robert has already contacted him. With luck he'll be here soon," Coby assured him.

"Thanks, all of you. These last few months have been some of the best of my life. Finding Trevor was innocent has lifted a great weight from my soul," he murmured before he started coughing uncontrollably, causing the gauges on his monitor to jump wildly and sound an alarm. The doctor and the same nurse appeared.

"Might be best if you let the Mr Van Clef rest for a while," the doctor suggested. It sounded more like an order.

"Yes Doctor," Coby replied, leading Robert and his family outside. As they sat in the waiting room, it was Robert who finally broke the silence.

"What if Trevor doesn't come?"

"He'll come. Trevor has his problems, but the Senator's everything to him." Coby assured him.

"What do we do now?" Michael asked.

"I have to, unfortunately, return to the White House. I'll return when I can. I would suggest at least one of us is always here." While the others worked out a schedule, Coby left. The media and crowd numbers had grown. His immediate thought was what a target the hospital would make.

"Is the hospital secure?" he asked one of his Secret servicemen.

"The army is handling the visible security out to a half mile. From there local police and the FBI have a cordon out another mile. No one will get through Sir," Ben his senior guard replied.

"Thanks, Ben. And tell your boss to pass on my thanks to the men involved," Coby told him.

"Will do Sir," he answered, as they came to the media barrier. Coby's car was waiting, but instead, he approached the medias wall of microphones.

"Good evening gentlemen. I'll make this quick as it's been a long night. Ex-Vice President George Van Clef has suffered a massive heart attack, and unfortunately, I am told has only a short time to live." This brought a gasp from the gathered crowd.

"Will his grandson return to the states?" a reporter asked. Coby knew the story of Trevor's innocence was now widely known.

"He has been contacted, and I hope he'll arrive soon," Coby replied seeing another hand go up. "Okay, what's your question?"

"Why is the security here so heavy?" At the reporter's question, many turned to see who had asked it.

"I'll answer this question, but it's the last. There are two reasons. One. George was a popular Vice President, a loved Senator and a great man. Many will come here to support him in his last hours. Second, there is still a threat out there as the terrorists responsible for the death of President Bridges have not all been brought to justice. The security is heavy as a precaution only to keep the people safe." Coby assured them.

This answer caused an avalanche of questions. Coby, feeling tired, left the microphones, ending the interview. As he was entering his car, he saw Robert running towards his vehicle. He was, of course, stopped by security. Coby climbed back out and signalled for him to be let through.

"Trevor and his wife are coming!" he exclaimed, standing beside Coby.

"That is great news, Robert. Thank you for telling me," Coby answered.

"I managed to get through to him, via Colonel Don Lap. The connection wasn't the best. Trevor had hoped their son could come too, but Kim wasn't keen on it."

"The Senator will be happy just to have Trevor here Robert. If you can, find out when he's arriving for me. And thanks again."

"He was like a second father to me Coby; I mean Mr President," Robert stammered out.

"He loved you too Robert. Can I give you a lift?"

"No, Mr President. I'll stay with him for a while yet. I just wanted you to know about Trevor." He explained before he turned and walked back towards the Hospital.

"We'd better go Mr. President," Ben suggested. The men in the car all looked discomforted by Robert's emotional stance.

"Yes, we better return to the White House. This Country, no matter what personal problems we have, must move forward," he said, seeing the driver nod before driving off.

A hundred yards away at the barrier two men watched the President's escorts and his limousine drive away from the hospital. Both were dressed in heavy jackets, with scarves and hats, which hid their features. One of them raised his hand as if it was a gun. Pointing at the President's vehicle, he followed its progress.

"Bang!" he said out loud, smiling.

"Put your hand down you fool and watch what you say. They have cameras everywhere!" the other growled, merging with the crowd, away from the barrier.

"You worry too much brother. The pigs know nothing."

"And that's how I want it to stay. Let's get back to the warehouse," he ordered, adjusting his hat, revealing for a split second the swastika tattooed on his left arm. Behind them, a security camera momentarily studied them, before moving on.

For the next two days, Coby kept busy. The country had been through a lot and needed strong leadership, although his thoughts were constantly returning to the Senator and Trevor. Visiting the Senator when he got time was becoming more difficult as the crowds grew. Many had gathered there to pray for George. Others saw it as a chance to air their views to the media. The Secret

Service was becoming increasingly anxious, with these visits. The possibility of an incident occurring grew more likely as time passed. Constantly changing their approach helped, but in the end, there was only a handful of roads that led to the hospital's entrance.

It was just edging past ten in the morning on the third day since the Senator had his heart attack. Coby was about to attend a security briefing when the front gate guards reported the Ambassador to North Sudan with other two dignitaries had demanded a meeting with the President. This was highly unusual as most made appointments to make sure they saw the President and of course had the media there to witness their visit.

"Who and why are they here?" Coby asked, wanting to get to the security briefing.

"One is the Ambassador. He was at your swearing in ceremony." Coby nodded, remembering the well-spoken man. "The other two dignitaries are here to attend a series of meetings as part of an Arab summit we are hosting. As to why they are here, we did just bomb their border area, where the terrorists were training," Robert informed him.

"Yes, terrorist or not, we did violate their country's sovereignty. Okay, I'll see them in the Oval Office now. Can you arrange tea and coffee for us all Robert?" Coby asked Robert, who with a nod disappeared.

"He practically runs this place," Coby smiled, his two secret service guards nodding. "Can Security escort them to the Oval Office?" he added wiped their smiles away.

"Yes, Sir we will pass it on. Once the three men have been searched, they will be let in," the senior guard informed him.

"Is that necessary?" Coby asked.

"We know the North Sudanese Ambassador Sir. We do not know the other two men with him. Our boss thinks since we bombed their country, it might be prudent," the senior guard answered.

"You're right. My apologies!" Behind him, the guards looked at each other in surprise at his apology, before dutifully following him.

FRIENDS

When the Ambassador entered the Oval Office with his two companions, they all stood silently looking around. Coby was at his desk writing. At their entry, he got up and walked around his desk to greet them.

"Ambassador, it's good to see you again." Coby smiled, shaking the Ambassador's hand.

"Thank you, Mr President." He smiled before continuing. "These two men are two of our diplomats, Mr Chirr and My Defog. Both are here for the Summit," the Ambassador politely informed him, his voice taking on a formal tone.

"It is a pleasure to meet you both," Coby replied, shaking each man's hand. "I've arranged tea and coffee gentlemen if you will be seated." Coby pointed to three seats and noticed the Ambassador look to the other two men before they all sat down. Once they had been given their refreshments, Coby began.

"I judge this meeting is about the attack on the terrorist base on your border?" Coby asked them.

"Yes, Mr President. Although we can see why the United States carried out this raid after the death of President Bridges, it would've been nice to inform us first. The bombing has caused great resentment amongst our people," the Ambassador firmly told him.

"You are absolutely right Ambassador. I take full responsibility for that Sir. At the time, my anger at what had occurred made me see red. I can assure you no more military actions will be carried out in your country, before informing your government first. If you wish I will appear on your country's media and offer my regret at the action taken without permission," Coby assured him. For several seconds the three men sat in silence, caught off guard by Coby's apology and gesture.

"That is good of you Mr President to offer, but like you, we are glad the terrorists are gone. I will inform our President of your apology. Like me, he will see it was an honest mistake made in anger at what had occurred." The Ambassador smiled.

"That is good of you Sir. Now I have another pressing engagement; so I'll show you out." Coby smiled and led the three surprised men to the door and then to a pickup point from which they would be returned to their vehicle.

"You were born for this Sir!" Robert smiled, waving to the Ambassador as he left.

"It just makes good sense to sometimes admit you were wrong," Coby answered, as they both walked back towards his office.

"And you will warn them if we have to attack another terrorist position in their country?"

"Yes, I will Robert, if for no other reason, then to see if they can be trusted."

"You think we can't trust them?"

"The terrorist base was in their country, and they did nothing Robert. True, they may have been unable to take them on for many reasons, but until I'm sure, we'll wait and see." Reaching the Oval office, they found the Security briefing group, were all there. Waving the people gathered to sit back down, the meeting began.

The progress in the search for the terrorist was going slowly. The FBI had indeed spotted the two men at the hospital and had several photographs of the hand gesture. So far, they hadn't been able to track them down, but the swastika on the arm of one ruled out links with Islamic extremists. Or did it?

"Could it be a partnership of convenience?" Michael suggested. He and Robert had been added to the security briefings to provide two different perspectives to the investigations.

"Maybe, but I don't know if it would be workable? Let's face it, white supremacists and Islamic terrorists aren't exactly buddies," General Graven reminded them.

"As unlikely as it is, it does point to a white person leaking the information. Up to now, we've been profiling Moslems with an extremist background, or Americans with links to the Middle East. Maybe we should widen the net?" Benson put forward, and Coby nodded his support.

"That tattoo on his left arm. Surely there can't be too many people with a swastika on their arm?" Robert added.

"You'd be surprised Robert," Coby murmured, remembering when he was shot.

"Still it's a lead. I think we should put some resources towards it," John Taylor suggested.

"You know, as funny as it seems, there's something about these two men being near that Hospital. If they are part of this group, they were there for a reason," Robert added

"Should we move Granddad, I mean Mr Van Clef?" Michael suggested, sounding worried.

"No, he's very weak, and he hasn't much time anyway," Coby confessed, as the room grew still.

"The problem is, there are over ten thousand people outside keeping vigil for Mr Van Clef. It's quite a target," Benson warned them.

"What about blocking vehicles approaching with concrete bollards? We can still let the people through, just no unauthorised vehicles," John Taylor suggested.

"Will they stop a tanker?" Robert asked.

"I can assure you that the ones we use will stop anything but a tank," General Graven promised.

"Good. Then deploy them immediately and put more plainclothes men in the crowd John. I know it might scare them off, but I'd rather that than have a bomb going off in that crowd!" Coby exclaimed as the meeting ended. After the others had gone, Coby sat with Michael and Robert.

"It's getting scary, isn't it?" Robert whispered as if the terrorists could hear him.

"Yes, it is Robert. What bugs me is being on the defensive all the time. We need to get out ahead of these scumbags," Coby warned, showing the stress he felt.

"Changing the subject, has Trevor arrived yet?" Michael asked as Coby looked at his watch.

"Should have landed by now. Glenda was picking him and Sue up."

"I'm glad they're here. The senator didn't look good this morning," Robert volunteered. He'd been spending most of his free time at the hospital. The room lapsed into silence as they absorbed Robert's observation.

"The Senator's tough. He's not leaving unless it's on his terms and he's good and ready," Coby stated.

"Well let's go visit him? When Trevor arrives, I think he'll hog him?" Michael suggested.

"Not true brother!" a voice called from the doorway, Trevor was standing there, freshly shaved and dressed in dark blue suit.

"Thank God you made it!" Coby gasped, his voice breaking, as he walked to Trevor.

"Nice office Dad!" Trevor smiled, breaking the embrace.

"One of the perks of the job. Where are Sue and your mother?" Coby asked.

"Outside. Mum said the security wouldn't let all of us in."

"Bullshit. No one would stop Glenda coming in here," Coby replied making the others laugh. Walking to the door, he looked outside and found Sue standing with Glenda, who was holding little Coby.

"Surprise!' Glenda smiled, passing little Coby to him. The Secret Service seeing there was no problem started to leave.

"Thanks, men!" Coby called to them, getting several nods and a "No problem!"

"Those guys would do anything for you Dad." Trevor smiled, watching his father's exchange with the Secret Servicemen.

"They're good men. A lot of Presidents didn't give them the respect they deserved," Coby answered, knowing they'd put their lives on the line over the years for many a President who didn't deserve their loyalty, including the former one.

"This is a great honour to enter the Oval Office," Sue stuttered, nervous about their location, let alone company.

"It is impressive Sue, but it's just an office. The people are what America is all about," Coby informed her.

"Still I will remember this always as a great honour Mr President," Sue answered.

"We are family Sue. I will always be Coby or Dad to you," Coby replied. Sue happily gave him a kiss on the cheek.

"Look, Dad, I know you're busy, but I like to go visit Granddad." Coby could see Trevor was worried.

"Of course! You go with the others. I'll follow as soon as I'm finished here," Coby assured him, walking them to the front door.

Michael, because the Senate wasn't sitting, conducted Trevor to their transport. As they waited near the front door, Trevor noticed Michael's nervousness. The motorcade, which would take them to the hospital, was accompanied by a very large contingent of Secret Servicemen.

"Is something wrong Michael?"

"No. Why would you ask?"

"You look nervous, and we've enough men guarding us to invade a small country!"

"Our Mum's the President's wife, and we're the President's sons, and I'm also a Senator. Security has to be tight," Michael answered, as they all climbed into the Presidential limousine. Trevor looked at Michael before smiling.

"What's so funny?" Michael asked.

"Kim said you had trouble keeping a straight face when you lied." Michael's face at first looked angry, before softening.

"You're right. I'll have to put in more practice!" Michael smiled, relaxing. "We're just worried the terrorists who attacked and killed President Bridges might target the Hospital. Coming here for Dad is becoming a real risk, let alone managing the crowds of people outside."

"I thought you took care of them?" Trevor whispered, not wanting to worry Sue and Glenda, who were busily playing with little Coby.

"They were tipped off. We believe we have a mole," Michael in turn whispered. Trevor momentarily glanced at his family, before answering.

"Michael is there," he started, when Michael stopped him.

"They're safe Trevor. Dad and I wouldn't let any of you come if we thought you weren't." Michael assured him, as Trevor nodded his acceptance.

"We're approaching the Hospital, Mrs Henderson," Bobby, one of the Secret servicemen, informed them.

"Thank you, Bobby," Glenda responded. Trevor watched the Secret Serviceman nod to her, give a brief smile and return to his solemn alert look. Pulling up at the hospital Sue and Trevor moved to open the door to find it locked.

"Let us look around first Sir," Bobby warned. Getting an okay from an agent outside Trevor felt the door open.

"The name's Trevor," Trevor told him, getting a small smile in return, as the agent indicated he was listening to his radio. Finished, he replied.

"You're the President's son. It will always have to be Sir', Sir," Bobby informed him, making the others in the car hide their smiles. Trevor, lost for words, looked outside. Open-mouthed he stared at the size of the crowd. Michael stepped out first, followed by Glenda, who despite the Secret Service warnings moved toward the crowd. Accepting flowers from the children there, she thanked them all for coming. While she kept the crowd amused, Michael moved an overcome Trevor and Sue inside.

"Who are the people with Senator Henderson?" a reporter yelled from the crowd.

"That is my stepson Trevor and his wife, Sue. The little boy is Coby junior." Glenda smiled, as cameras clicked wildly trying to capture a shot of the now distant family.

"His wife looks Asian?" Someone in the crowd shouted.

"Yes. She is Vietnamese. My son met her in the central highlands. They were both working at a Hospice there. It set up for local people affected by defoliants used during the war."

"Why are they visiting Mr Van Clef?"

"Trevor is George Van Clef's grandson. He was Broderick Van Clef's son," Glenda told them while moving towards the hospital. In the crowd, one of the two men observed earlier, noted this information before moving away.

Once Trevor entered the hospital, he forgot all about the crowds outside. His focus was on seeing his grandfather. Michael leading the way pointed to a lift. Entering Michael pressed the second floor, before turning to Trevor.

"You'd best you prepare yourself! The Senator is not as you last saw him."

"What do you mean?" Trevor replied.

"He's paralysed down the right side of his body, and his face on the same side has dropped slightly where the muscles have collapsed."

"Thanks for the warning Michael, but where we work, we've seen much worse," Sue answered, as Trevor wiped tears away from his eyes.

"I always thought he'd live forever!" Trevor confessed as the door opened. On the second floor, Trevor noticed the heightened security. As they approached the Senator's room,

Trevor saw he'd have to go through a security check before being able to see George. Glenda, holding little Coby, waved to the guards as they all walked right through the barrier without hesitating.

"She was born to be the First Lady," Michael whispered beside him, guessing what Trevor was thinking, as they entered the Senator's room. A hush fell over them as they allowed Trevor to approach his grandfather first. The Senator, sensing his grandson's presence, opened his eyes, his lips forming a small smile.

"I knew you'd come!" he murmured, as a nurse gave him some water using a straw.

Trevor was glad Michael had warned him. His grandfather had wasted away and looked nothing like the man he remembered carrying his son on his shoulders. Now he looked light enough to be carried by Trevor. His skin, which had always been so tanned and healthy from working on his plantation, now was a pasty, ashen colour. Steeling himself, as he had with countless patients, Trevor leant down to kiss his grandfather's cheek.

"How about a hug? I won't break son!" His grandfather smiled as Trevor gently lifted him, hugging him, much to the annoyance of the nurse. "Hey at this stage does it matter?" the Senator croaked seeing the nurse's look.

"I'll leave you to have some time together," the nurse informed them in a stern voice, as if they were naughty children, before leaving.

"Boy, does she remind you of anyone?" Coby said from the door, as everyone looked at Glenda.

"We have a job to do!" Glenda sniffed, hiding a smile.

"I thought you had work to do Dad?" Michael put in.

"What and miss out? No way, the country can wait for a little while," Coby confessed, moving to Glenda, as Trevor remained with the Senator.

The conversation became one sided, as the Senator talk less and less, the others filling the silent void. Little Coby spent most of the night crawling over the Senator's bed, trying, in his own way to coax a smile out his great grandfather. It was getting late. Coby was the first to leave after a Secret Serviceman appeared at the door.

"Sorry I've got to go," he managed to say, not wanting to.

"I'll see you back home shortly," Glenda told him, as Coby was escorted outside.

"He's under a lot of pressure?" Trevor said out loud without thinking. The others nodded.

"He's tough! He can take it!" the Senator spoke from the bed, his eyes closed.

"God, I thought you'd gone to sleep!" Michael admitted.

"I'll have plenty of time to sleep later. I just like to lay here and hear you all talk. I'll miss you all!" The Senator's coughing continued intermittently. At first, they all thought he'd gone back to sleep when suddenly the warning beeps sounded from his monitor. The alarm meant his heart had stopped beating, the line going flat.

"Grandpa! Are you, all right?" Trevor shouted as they all rushed to the bed. Within seconds a Secret Serviceman appeared with a doctor and nurse. Immediately everyone was moved back, giving the nurse and doctor room. As they all stared at the monitor, they saw his heart beat start again and grow stronger.

"He's stabilised again, but it might be best to let him rest?" the Doctor suggested. Behind them, the Secret Serviceman left.

"Can I stay here the night?" Trevor asked.

"Of course. I'll have housekeeping bring you a blanket," the doctor promised, as he and the nurse left.

"Sue and little Coby can come with me, Trevor. You all can't stay here," Glenda pointed out, as Sue agreed. She kissed the senator and her husband goodbye.

"I have to go too. I've got a big day in the Senate tomorrow," Michael sadly admitted leaving with Glenda.

"Just you and me now Granddad." Trevor smiled, holding his hand as Robert entered, with a guard. Checking the room, the guard left.

"I'm Robert. You must be Trevor?" Robert introduced himself.

"Glad to meet you, Robert, although I remember you standing with me at my mums' funeral. It's good though to finally put a face to the Senator's foster son. The way he talks I'm amazed he didn't adopt you!" Trevor replied shaking his hand, as Robert went quiet unable to speak. Pulling himself together, he answered.

"He's a special person Trevor. I'd do anything for him." Robert stammered out, as the two men settled down beside the Senator's bed.

"Jesus Robert, are you crying again?" the Senator coughed, surprising them both.

"You know me, Senator! Always finding something to be upset about!"

"I did think about adopting you, but your parents would've been upset." The Senator chuckled before coughing.

"Hey take it, easy senator! We have got all night to talk." Robert smiled, holding the Senator's other hand.

"Have we?" the Senator answered, going silent.

After a meeting with several Senators and two Ambassadors, Coby was tired and headed for the West Wing and his bed. Glenda was there, playing with little Coby. All thoughts of sleep disappeared as Coby climbed onto the bed to play with his grandson.

"God I'm glad Trevor came and brought little Coby." He smiled and saw young Coby yawn, before snuggling up on his pillow.

"Yes, just in time I'd say. After you left, the Senator stopped breathing. He started up again, but it was frightening," she confessed.

"I know it sounds terrible, but I hope he goes quickly. He wasn't the type to worry about moving on. How long do you think he's got?"

"It was a miracle he didn't go tonight. It won't be long," Glenda told him as she quietly wept.

"It's different when you know them isn't it?" Coby asked her.

"Yes. When you work in a hospital, you think you've become as hard as a rock, seeing patients die all the time. Then someone you know goes, and it becomes personal, so quickly, it overwhelms you!" Glenda sobbed, as Coby held her.

"Well let's hope," was all Coby got out, as the phone rang. Both stared at each other, as Coby reluctantly picked it up.

"Yes. What is it?" he asked, as Glenda got out of bed and began to dress. "We'll be there as quickly as we can." Coby dropped the phone. Wiping his eyes, he stood up and dressed as well.

At the hospital, no one had to ask what was happening as the Presidential motorcade screamed into the front entry. Many of the crowd, who were either asleep or in silent contemplation, jumped to their feet, rushing to the barriers. The President and his wife could be seen running into the hospital, accompanied by Trevor's wife.

As before, they exited the lift and rushed down the hallway to the Senator's room. Outside in the hallway stood Michael, Robert and Trevor.

"The doctor's in there now. It's not good Dad!" Michael stuttered. Trevor and Robert were too upset to talk. When the doctor appeared, he gestured for them all to go into the Senator's room. His eyes betrayed his commiseration.

"Thank you, Doctor," Coby said as they all entered the room. The Senator had developed a raspy breathing noise as if his lungs were full of fluid. Every so many breaths' he'd cough, making his whole body shake alarmingly. Glenda had told Coby earlier that the nurses called this 'the death rattle'. Standing there, hearing it, he fearfully understood what they meant. In the corner, next to the Senator stood the nurse, who the other day had been cross with them.

Adjusting his pain relief, she quickly bent down and kissed the Senator on his forehead, before moving towards the door. Coby could see her eyes were glistening with tears. Putting out his hand, he stopped her.

"Thank you for everything nurse," Coby whispered.

"It was a pleasure, Mr President. He was such a great man." The Nurse sniffed and left quickly. Her swift exit caused one of Coby's security guards to put his head inside the door. Seeing everything was okay, he withdrew.

"Are you there Bud?" the Senator suddenly yelled out, startling them all.

"No, he's not here Granddad," Trevor answered, wiping his eyes.

"God, I miss my boy!" the Senator coughed out, before blinking rapidly as he looked around the room. "I judge since you are all here, this is it then?" He coughed again.

"You'll beat this Senator! You always do!" Michael replied, forcing a smile. The senator looked at him for several seconds before answering.

"Kim was right, Michael. You are a bad liar!" his voice becoming clearer, as the others chuckled at his comment. He'd just thought of an answer when the Senator spoke again. "I hope you're going to marry that girl! Women like her don't come along often."

"I'm working on it, Senator!" Michael replied, wondering if his face was that easy to read.

"Good. You know I love you all, don't you?" the Senator confessed as another bout of coughing struck him. Looking towards Coby, he continued. "You're the best of the best Coby. Since Bud died, I always considered you and Robert my sons. You've both made me so proud. And then there are my two grandsons and their wives and little Coby. I'm so glad I lived to see you all together as a family. And last but not least, there's Glenda. You filled a void in Coby's heart and my life. You included me in your family when many wouldn't have, and for that, I will always be grateful!" The Senator stopped talking and closed his eyes.

"It is we who were the lucky ones, Senator. Your love for us all, and especially for Trevor, despite what occurred, brought us all back together again as a family. You've been a better father to me than my own, and no one could ask for a better father-in-law," Glenda told him. Coby beside her wondered where she got the strength to be able to talk to him without crying. He couldn't say anything without breaking down.

"Thank you, Glenda, and thank you all. It's a pity, Bud..." That was all he managed before his monitor alarm went off again

"Granddad!" Trevor yelled out, grabbing his hand, as the nurse and doctor entered. Seeing Trevor gripping the Senator's hand, they both moved to the other side of the bed. Coby, Robert and Glenda moved to be with Trevor, Michael and Sue.

The doctor took out his stethoscope and placed it on his heart while his eyes locked with Coby's. His head shake was all Coby needed, as he gripped Glenda.

"I'm sorry Mr President. He was a great man." The Doctor told him as he and the nurse left, leaving the family to their grief. The doctor outside fronted the media, calling the time of George Van Clef's passing.

After everyone had said their goodbyes to the Senators, Coby seeing Trevor was taking George's death badly, asked Michael and Robert to take Sue and Trevor home. While they did that, he would meet with the media contingent outside with Glenda.

Coby was so glad Glenda was there beside him, as they walked out the front door of the hospital into an uproar. People having heard the news wept, while others prayed, glad his suffering was over. Many sang hymns while others, there for their other agendas, yelled abuse.

"Are you alright?" Glenda asked him, squeezing 'his hand, as they neared the microphones.

"I am now." Coby gave her a smile, walking on alone. Raising his hands hushed the crowd.

"Fellow Americans. Today a giant of a man has left us. To know George Van Clef, was one the greatest rewards of my life and I will always treasure the time we had together. For most of his life, he served this country in the Senate and later as the Vice President. I, like you, believe America is the better place because of his efforts." This brought cheers from the crowd and some difficult to hear boos. "George gave everything for this country, including a son and if George was here now, he would thank you all for coming, even the people booing." Some of the crowd laughed. "I too thank you for being here for him and like you; I will pray for George. God bless America!" Coby concluded then moved to his car.

Coby inside collapsed into Glenda's arms, as the motorcade quickly moved away from the Hospital. Behind them, two men watched, their emotions hidden. Seeing the crowd breaking up, they like many others hurried away trying to beat the crush.

"Well, that's a pity. A couple more days and we could really have hurt them. I suppose we'll have to target the funeral?" the taller one suggested.

"Don't talk, just keep moving," the man with the swastika arm tattoo, angrily replied.

"Your brother told me you were a bit over the top!" he sniggered.

"That's why he's not here. So, shut up, or you can help him chaperone those Arab dogs."

"Take it easy Wade. I was just trying to be funny."

"Well, it didn't work. Look, Jed, you're okay, but a lot is going on at the moment. My inside man thinks they're onto us, so better to be safe than sorry."

"Okay, now I understand. If you'd told me all that before we left, I would've understood. Let's get back to the others." Jed the taller one said hurrying away. Behind them, two FBI holding video cameras and a long-range sound recorder quickly packed up, so they could hurry back to their headquarters and update their boss. Further away from the hospital another group of agents, having been alerted of their departure, spotted and began to tail them.

"So, they're connected to this terrorist group?" Coby asked.

"No Sir. We think they both plan to double-cross each other once they have achieved their objective," Benson answered.

"Which is?" Michael asked.

"Destabilizing the country," Benson warned.

"They tried that with the last President. It didn't work," Robert pointed out.

"It nearly did. The share markets were rattled by the assassination, although I think the quick reaction by the financial sector surprised them. If we have another and people get spooked and start to think we're vulnerable, then we could have a big problem. There's also our standing overseas. If our enemies believe we can't protect ourselves, then they might strike at our interests there, further hurting us," John Taylor warned.

"What's the plan then?" Michael asked.

"We let slip where the funeral is and wait," Benson told them.

"Look, it's going to be a small affair; only the family and a few close friends. I can't see it being worth the risk," Coby pointed out.

"That's your affair Sir. We're going to announce a state funeral through Georgia's Capital City's main street. It will be too good an opportunity to miss," General Graven added.

"I don't want people hurt General!" Coby snapped, not liking the plan.

"No one will get hurt Sir. It's only to lure them out. If we haven't got them before the proposed funeral day, we'll cancel the whole affair leaving them with no target," Benson reassured him.

"The only problem is you will have to go through the motions of going to Georgia's Capital before the funeral to give it credibility," General Graven pointed out.

"Okay. You have my approval gentlemen, but make sure you get them. We can't afford another attack!" Coby told them before the meeting broke up.

"This is risky Dad. What if they find out the truth and target something else or you when you go there? The death toll, if they use the same type of tanker bomb, could be horrendous," Michael whispered after the others left.

"Your right son, but what else can we do? We've got to stop these madmen, and at least this idea gets us out in front of them. What worries me, son, is the Senator asking to be buried next to his wife and son, in a private service at his plantation. I want to honour that request. This announcement of a state funeral means that if these terrorist are caught, for the public good, we might have to go ahead with it." Coby answered. Looking towards the door, he noticed the Secret Servicemen conferring.

"Is there a problem Bobby?" Coby asked.

"The boss isn't happy with exposing you and your family at a State Funeral, real or not!" Bobby answered.

"Tell him thanks, but we have to flush them out with a big target."

"He knows that, but he's still not happy Sir," Bobby replied, moving outside.

"Jesus! Those guys really baby you Dad!" Michael smiled, Robert and Coby chuckling.

"Letting someone you have to protect become a sacrificial goat is not something they would usually consider, let alone allow. The Secret Service was formed to keep the US Government's top people safe, to ensure the country has continuous leadership.

That said, they're still upset with the loss of President Bridges. I respect their position on this, but we have to get these guys and quick."

"Mum won't be happy. The Senator's death has hit her hard," Michael warned as they left the Oval Office accompanied by Coby's minders.

"Let me handle her son," Coby replied firmly, generating a grin from Michael.

"Yeah, sure you will Dad!"

THE WAREHOUSE

"I tell you they're onto us!" Wade shouted, banging on the table at the same time.

"Take it easy Wade. As yet we're not sure. Has anyone heard from our inside man?" Colin Benet, the group's leader, asked.

"No. The last thing we got from him was the date of the state funeral. After that, he warned us he was going dark for a while. Said the Feds were nosing about," Jed replied.

"I don't like it, Colin. Since we checked out the hospital, I've had the feeling we're being watched."

"Shit Wade. You're getting all worked up about nothing. If the Feds knew we were involved, they'd be all over us," Brett, Wade's brother, shot back.

"Aren't you supposed to be watching our friends Brett?" Collin asked.

"They're all praying frantically in their church of rugs. You know what they're like! They'll be there for another hour at least!" Brett smiled as the group laughed.

"Just remember those ragheads have seen a lot more action than most of us. Don't think they don't know what we're up to," Collin warned.

"Then why have them here?" one of the men asked.

"They are our fall guys. When the next one goes off, they'll take the heat, not us." Collin smiled.

"What are they getting out of this arrangement anyway?" Jed asked.

"Propaganda. Each time we strike, we leave them behind to be identified. They get the blame, and back in the Middle East, they are heroes fighting the infidels. It does much to bolster their standing, brings them more supporters and backing," Collins informed them.

"I can't stand them! It's un-American to be associated with them," another man growled.

"Hey! They killed that arse-licking Jew Bridges and a dozen or more of his lackeys. Which one of you wants to drive a petrol tanker full of fuel and explosives?" Collins asked. Silence followed his statement. "That's what I thought. Wade, what do you suggest?"

"We keep a low profile. No one leaves or comes here without making sure they're not being tailed. I propose that we set up a watch post down the road from here. For the last block there's only one approach, so a man with a mobile phone positioned there can warn us if someone comes calling. Other than that, we wait for more Intel on where the funeral is."

"Sounds good. How's the bomb coming Billy?" Collin asked a skinny short guy in the back row.

"I've got some refinements to make, but it will be ready in another three days," Billy answered excitedly.

"Are we doing another petrol tanker bomb?" Brett asked.

"No! This one's special." Billy sniggered.

"What makes it so special?" a guy sitting near Billy asked. Billy had a reputation for being a little strange.

"It's a dirty bomb. The fallout will be massive!" Billy giggled. Looking around Billy saw his brothers-in-arms seemed confused and a little scared by his answer. He decided to start over. "The bomb I'm building is made up of nuclear waste. I managed, with the help of a friend, to steal several pounds from a power station, which is off line while being updated. It will seriously increase the range of destruction and deaths." Collin could see a lot of his men seemed uncomfortable with that.

"Are we in any danger, with it being here?" Collin asked. He was unaware of what Billy had been up too.

"No! The bomb is secure. You did say you wanted something special Collin!" Billy replied sounding upset.

"Yes, Billy I did. I just didn't realise how resourceful you could be. Can you tell us how big the explosion will be if we detonate it in the State Capital when the state funeral is held?"

"The explosion won't be much bigger than the tanker bomb was. It will maybe take out a block, killing maybe a thousand people. The radiation, which will be released when the bomb goes off, will make the entire city unlivable and kill thousands more! "Billy proudly told them, as if he'd won an Olympic medal.

"Shit! That's a lot of innocent people, Collin!" Wade pointed out.

"We knew when we started this campaign to free America from the blacks and the Jews, that many people would die. This will weaken our enemies and put us on the road to White Rule again!" Collin shouted, the others cheering their support. "And remember. All the Arabs will die in the next bombing and take all the blame with them," Brett added, increasing the cheer, many clapping excitedly. Wade, off to the side, stood quietly.

"What have we got ourselves into brother?" he whispered, walking outside.

Under the floor in the basement below them, Mohammed Bengali listened to their allies' planning. Progress back through the crawl space his men had dug for him was slow, but eventually, he got to their room. For over a year they had been here assisting these southern racists, who attacked their own people. Now they planned to wipe out an entire city to further their cause.

"And they call us terrorists!" he said out loud.

Gathering his men, Bengali took in the missing members of his group. In their first attack in which the American President died, they had lost ten men. Another two of them had volunteered to stay behind to martyr themselves so that they could be identified. Now as he explained the infidels' plan to the remaining thirty men, he decided it was time to implement his own plan. What surprised him, was that despite the Infidels' plan which would ultimately lead to the death of all of them, Bengali's men were jubilant, thinking of the blow they would deliver against the Infidels. Many took out their prayer mats, to pray and ask for God's help.

"You seem uncertain Commander?" Subel, Bengali's second in command, voiced his concern.

"Yes. Although we will hurt our adversaries in this attack, I fear the Americans will obliterate our country in response," Bengali pointed out.

"Our brothers and sisters will gladly sacrifice their lives to see America humbled." Subel smiled, welcoming the coming attack.

"Yes, my brother they would, but I was thinking of a better target for their sacrifice."

"What would be better than taking out another President and a city?"

"Washington. It is their Capital and their symbol of freedom. It is also the home of their President," Bengali told him.

"Is it even possible?"

"With God's help, anything is possible. Tell the men to be ready themselves. We have much to prepare," Bengali instructed him. After Subel moved away, Bengali, in private, pulled out his mobile and dialled a preset number.

"It is me. The time has come to take control. Warn our brothers that Washington will be the target. I will update you as to the time of the attack," Bengali advised and hung up, not waiting for a reply.

DAN

Three days out from the day of the state funeral, the FBI earned their money. Checking the phone records of an employee in the defence department, they discovered a link back to a White Supremacist group. From this group, they identified the three men outside the hospital. One, Wade DuPont, was a decorated ex-marine, believed responsible for a string of bombings across Alabama.

It wasn't long before they'd tracked down the group to a warehouse outside Georgia's capital. Briefing the President, Benson got an immediate order to arrest them all. One hundred men from several FBI special weapons teams were brought in to carry out the raid. Examination of the warehouse proved there was only one approach to the warehouse, down a single road.

"I don't fucking like the look of it at all! They'll see us coming a mile away!" Field Agent Dan Tenant pointed out to his commander Joe Denison. Agent Tenant was well known for sharing his opinion.

"Okay, Dan you've got a point. Any ideas anyone?" Denison asked the room full of agents.

"Send someone down the road on a recon. He can pretend he's lost."

"Sounds good. Any volunteers?" Denison smiled.

"Agent Tenant will do it!' someone at the back yelled out.

"Fuck you!" Dan yelled back, which was followed by an outbreak of merriment.

"Settle down everyone! What about it Dan?" Denison asked, trying to hide a smile.

"Yeah, I'll go. Safer than sending one of this bunch of newbies!" he replied, getting cat calls in return.

"Do I have a death wish?" Dan asked himself, as he drove sedately down the road to the old industrial centre.

"Did you say something Dan?" a voice sounded in his ear.

"No. Just thinking out loud," he replied, watching the road ahead. Turning the last corner to where the dickheads were supposed to be held up, he spotted someone sitting in an old pick-up truck at the corner.

"Looks like they have a lookout at the approach to their street," Dan whispered into his headset.

"The boss asked should we move in?" the same voice responded.

"Wait a sec. I'll try to talk my way in," Dan answered. Coming up to the parked truck, Dan slowing down, opened his window. The driver of the truck was hard to see. He was leaning forward on the dash, probably asleep.

"Hey, friend? Can you point me towards the interstate?" Dan asked, his hand holding his weapon just below the window. Getting no answer, he tried again.

"Hey wake up!" Dan shouted. Still, the man didn't move. Climbing slowly out of his vehicle, he approached the truck. He'd been wrong about him sleeping he concluded, seeing the back half of the man's head was gone.

"Got a guy here who has been shot in the head boss!" Dan informed his commander.

"All units move in now!" Denison ordered. Behind Dan, FBI vehicles screamed around the corner, racing down the street past him, towards the warehouse.

"Shit. What a bloodbath!" Dan stated the obvious, as he walked through the warehouse. Everywhere he looked he saw bodies, as their forensic team searched for answers.

"What do you think happened, Dan?" Denison asked from behind Dan, making him turn.

"Looks like a falling out between thieves? I'd say our American supremacists sadly underestimated their Arab buddies!"

"Yeah but why now? You'd think they'd find common ground for attacking the Funeral parade?" Denison answered.

"Anyone found alive?"

"No. They gutted the wounded!"

"This was well-planned boss. Even though these Nazi dickheads were arrogant, they would've been watching the Arabs. Something must've made them put the knife in?"

Denison for a second didn't answer as he listened to his headset receiver.

"They've checked all the bodies. Wade DuPont isn't here!"

"Shit, if we can catch him, we might find out what happened here!"

"We have an address ten miles from here. Take two men and if possible bring him in alive. I know it won't be easy but try. He's our only lead."

"Will do, Boss," Dan promised, hurrying away.

"Where's Dan going?" Agent Glen Nixon asked as he approached Denison.

"Gone to run down a lead on Wade DuPont."

"Is that wise? He's a little on edge!" Nixon pointed out. Dan's brother had been a Secret Serviceman attached to the late President's detail the day he was killed. He'd been burned alive.

"He'll do his job. The guy's been through a lot, but he will always put the country before his problems."

"Jesus, I hope you're right?"

"I am. Now help the other agents search for a bomb or at least find out where it was constructed. It must be either hidden somewhere here, or the winner of this gunfight took it with them. So, get moving!" Denison ordered. As he moved towards the command vehicle, Denison started thinking about what the agent had said. Dan had been through a lot, maybe to the point of breaking. Yet he'd handled the approach to this warehouse without a hitch. Still losing your brother was big.

"God! Don't kill him, Dan!" Denison prayed silently, heading after Nixon to join the search. It would be another twenty minutes before traces of radiation were picked up.

THE REACTION

"Are you sure?" Coby barked into his phone, as Michael and Robert stopped talking to watch Coby. "Tell the press the State funeral is cancelled immediately. And call in every Police Officer and National Guard unit you can. I want that bomb found even if you have to close every freeway and Interstate in the US. Am I understood?" Coby waited as the person on the line continued. "Good. Keep me informed," Coby answered, putting down the phone.

"Not good news?" Michael asked.

"The raid was too late. It looks like the extreme Islamic group butchered the white supremacists and made off with their bomb."

"Why would you close the freeways? Is it another fuel tanker bomb?" Robert asked.

"Far worse, it's a dirty bomb!"

"What? A Nuke?" Michael whispered.

"No. It's a standard explosive bomb surrounded by irradiated material. When it explodes, it spreads radiation over a large area killing anyone exposed."

"Holly shit! These guys must be completely crazy!"

"The ones who made it were, and now they're all dead. The ones with it now, are far more dangerous, because they're smart. They waited until the bomb was completed, before taking down the other group. That shows someone intelligent has planned it," Coby explained, pacing up and down beside the window.

"Any idea of their target?" Michael asked.

"No. It could be anything, from a city to something of national importance, like a port," Coby put forward.

"Could we locate it by the radiation?" Michael suggested.

"That's good thinking son." Coby smiled picking up his phone. "Get me General Graven at the Pentagon." A few seconds had lapsed before the General came onto the phone.

"Good morning Sir," the General answered.

"You've been told about the bomb by now?"

"Yes, Sir. We're deploying everything we've got."

"What about searching for the radiation signature? I heard our satellites are good at that."

"We're on it, Sir. They're being recalibrated and repositioned to cover the entire country. Don't worry we'll get them, Sir."

"Thank you, General. I'll leave you to do your job."

"Before you go, there's another problem Sir!"

"Go ahead."

"I heard you ordered blocking of the freeways and interstates. I think you should rethink that."

"Why?"

"We think it will tip our hand that we know the bomb is moving," the General pointed out.

"That's good thinking General. I didn't think of that!" Coby whispered to the others what he had said. "I'll leave it to you General. Do what you think is right." Coby thanked him and hung up.

"The General's already on to it son. And the idea about not blocking the roads is good thinking." Coby told Michael and Robert.

"Should've known they'd be on to it." Michael smiled.

"It's always good to check. When you've got a situation like this, people sometimes forget the obvious."

"So what do we do?" Robert asked.

"We wait. For now, it's all we can do," Coby replied, as the door to his office flew open. Four secret servicemen moved into the room.

"We're leaving Sir!" one of the men told Coby.

"I judge your boss heard about the bomb?"

"Yes, Sir. He sees Washington as a potential target."

"The FBI seemed to think Georgia's Capital was the target?" Coby answered.

"The Supremacist group had their own agenda for picking Georgia Sir. Our boss thinks the Islamic terrorists would consider Washington as their prime target."

"He's right Mr President. We've got to get you airborne, as well as your family!" Robert exclaimed, a sense of danger filling the room. Coby looked at the men around him.

"I can't leave my office because of a terrorist threat men! It would cause total panic. But you can take my family to Camp David. They can visit the Vice President whose convalescing there at the moment. It's something the people will accept," Coby suggested. The Secret Servicemen around him didn't reply, as they listened to their communications headsets.

"Sir, the risk is too high. The country can't afford to lose another President." The agent's voice took on a desperate edge.

"I can't run from these thug's men. You know I can't."

"Then don't. Let's go ahead with the Senator's funeral at his plantation where he wanted to be buried. You can announce that you've found a note from the Senator that stated he wanted a small service instead of a state funeral. It would get you away from Washington, without causing a panic. If this city is their target, they'll wait until you return," Robert pointed out. Coby stood thinking about their idea before answering.

"Okay. Announce it immediately Robert. Until then we stay put. I won't leave the people of this city to face this alone!" The Secret Servicemen nodded their acceptance before leaving.

"Jesus, I thought they were going to drag you outside Dad!" Michael exclaimed.

"Yeah, they're rather convincing when they want to be." Coby smiled before continuing. "Michael, can you go tell your mother to get ready to travel?"

"Bullshit Dad. I'm not doing it. You're the President, you go tell her!" Michael barked.

"Thought I'd give it a try," Coby confessed, leaving the room.

"I'm not going anywhere!" Glenda growled, standing arms crossed, staring Coby down.

"Look I know you want to stay, but we've got to get Trevor and his family away from here!"

"I don't want to be seen as the President's wife who ran away at the first sign of trouble Coby."

"You won't be running away. You will be just be going early to spend some time with the family at that Senator's home, before the funeral. I'll meet you there in a couple of days for the service." Glenda stood watching him for several seconds before answering.

"Okay we'll go, but I'm not happy about leaving you here alone!" Glenda pointed out, her eyes betraying how distraught she really was. Coby relieved, brought up another problem.

"Thanks for doing this love, but there's another thing I might need your help with. I need Michael to go with you as well. It will look like it's on the level to anyone watching if he's there. I just don't want to argue with him about it."

"He won't. I'll tell you why?"

"No way dad. There's no way in hell you'll get me to leave you alone here in Washington!" Michael exploded.

"Look son! I'll be joining you and your mother in a couple of days tops! I need you there, son!"

"Don't bullshit me, dad. I'm not going!"

"Kim will be there," Coby added. Michael blinked several times before answering.

"Are you kidding me?"

"No son. She has just flown in. She's travelling there to meet you and the others as we speak."

"Okay. I'm not happy, but I'll go!" Michael relented his anger dissipating, as Coby tried to hide a smile. "I still think I should be here with you."

"I know son. Kiss Kim for me." Coby grinned, as Michael shot an angry look his way, before leaving.

WADE

Agent Tenant looked at the block of units, his eyes looking for anything out of the ordinary. This seemed to him a waste of time considering the state of the units. Built in the fifties, Dan doubted if a paintbrush had ever touched the filth covered walls that made the other tired unit blocks in the area seem like new. The only thing he could see that had been upgraded at the block was the ugly steel grills that covered most windows.

"Shit what a dump! No self-respecting ice addict would live here, let alone one of the clan's finest!" Bob Donnelly, one of the Agents companying Dan, pointed out.

"Could be different inside?" Robby Williams the other agent chuckled, his pistol already in his hand.

"Wade Du Pont is a clever son of a bitch. This is a perfect hideaway for him. Just as you said, his type wouldn't have anything to do with the vermin that live here." Dan smiled drawing his weapon as well. "Just remember, we need this dirtbag, so don't kill him!" Dan warned before moving towards the entry door or the big hole where the door used to be. The address placed him on the top floor of this 4th level quaint apartment block.

"Don't touch the stair rails," Robby whispered, seeing excrement had been smeared all over them.

"The building is not the only thing in need of demolishing," Bob sniggered, trying not to laugh as they reached the third level. Here Dan stopped them, as he saw that someone had sprinkled broken glass over the floor.

"Could be just a drunk dropped twenty bottles or someone wants to hear us coming?" Dan smiled, carefully weaving his way through the glass, followed by his companions. Reaching the fourth level, the Agents approached the closest unit. There were letters carved into the door instead of numbers.

'Fuck Off' Dan figured was not the owner's real name as he tried the door, finding it locked of course. There was a series of four locks combined. Dan stood back thinking about the best way to gain entry.

"Think we should get a sledge hammer?" Bob whispered.

"No time," Dan answered. Pulling out his automatic, made the two other agents move back, as Dan shot the hinges of the door.

"Federal Agents!" Dan screamed out, as the three agents charged inside. A quick check found the unit empty as the agents checked and yelled, "Clear!"

"Well at least we know it's his unit?" Bob pointed out, as the place was filled, with explosives and weapons.

"Yeah, the guy likes his toys alright. Call the boss Robby! Tell him no one was home and to send a forensics team over here pronto!" Dan ordered as he started going through Wade's desk.

Mohammad Bengali watched the news with a growing sense of anger. The American President would leave Washington in three days to attend Van Clef's funeral in Georgia. Unlike the earlier plan, it would be a private funeral.

"Is there a problem my brother?" Subel asked.

"Yes, the President will leave Washington in several days. We won't be in position till after he leaves!" Bengali fumed.

"If he is here or not, we can still destroy their Capital."

"That is true, but I want this to be the death blow to the Americans. Killing the President in their most secure city would show how vulnerable they all are to God's wrath!" Bengali exclaimed, bringing a cheer from his men.

The attack on the clan members hadn't gone as they'd planned. They had thought that once they launched their assault, the white supremacists would panic allowing Bengali's much more battle-hardened men to gain the upper hand quickly. Instead, they'd fought bravely, inflicting severe losses to his group. Now, including Subel, he had only seven men left. Even the bomb-maker Billy, a weasel of a man, had managed to damage the detonator, while killing two of his men.

They still had the weapon and with a little help would be able to activate it. Subel had some knowledge of bomb making and had secured parts from an electronics store, to repair the damage to the detonator. To do this, they had left the warehouse and travelled towards Washington. The problem was the need for a place to work on the device. Currently, they were staying in a camping area on a large lake west of Washington.

Bengali had to admit the bomb maker Billy had been clever. He had not only designed the weapon; he had concealed it in an RV making its transport anywhere in America easy. When they had arrived at the lake, Bengali kept his men hidden in the van while he and Subel booked in. They had hired a remote shack towards the far end of the lake, ensuring them privacy. There they waited till dark, before moving the weapon from the RV to the shack. To get it inside wasn't easy. Because of its size, they had to remove a window of the shack, so that Subel could work on it inside.

Bengali, having no idea how long it would take to make the required repairs, had booked the cabin for two weeks. With the news that the President would be gone to attend the funeral, it gave them plenty of time to await his return. To allay suspicion, Bengali had his men take it in turns to go fishing at the lake while keeping watch. For two days they had no problems, which Bengali prayed continued.

"How it is going with the weapon?" Bengali asked Subel.

"Slow. Billy was a complicated man. He built this bomb with built in fail-safe. I have the frequency it worked on, so realigning the detonator should not be difficult. The problem will be testing it without blowing us all up. I have had to dismantle it to be able to test it safely, which with his fail-safes is extremely dangerous."

"Can you do it?"

"Yes, I have succeeded in the dismantling the weapon completely. Now after I make sure the detonator works I will rebuild it." Subel smiled.

"Good work. How long till it's ready?"

"Another two days at least."

"Then we will have to wait till the President returns," Bengali pointed out, disappointed.

"Relax my brother. God is with us. We will not fail," Subel reassured him, moving back to the weapon.

When Wade DuPont arrived back at his apartment block, he was dead tired and a little worried. He had been scouting the route to be used for the funeral procession through the Capital, checking out suitable spots to park the weapon. Everything seemed okay, and he'd found several sites he considered perfect for what they intended. His worry came from the fact he couldn't raise the warehouse.

True they'd all gone dark, not using or answering calls on their phones, but his brother had been expecting him to call him and he wasn't responding either. His first thought was to go straight to the warehouse to check on his brother. Instead, he decided to return to his apartment and arm himself first, just in case. He knew it was risky returning to his apartment, but he was confident his druggie-infested location had remained off the grid. Looking at the apartment block, he smiled, reassured.

"Shit no one in his right mind would live here!" he said out loud, chuckling to himself as he approached the front entry. He was about to enter when instinctively he stopped. Standing in the hole where the door had once been, he felt the darkness close in on him.

'It's quiet? Too quiet,' he warned himself as he stood frozen in the doorway. The derelict block was full of lowlifes, who only surfaced during the hours of darkness, so where were they?

Committed, knowing running wouldn't help, he moved inside as the stillness made the hairs on the back of his neck rise. 'It's a trap you fool!' an inner voice shouted. Rather than heading up the stairs, he went down towards the garage. No one came down here, he knew, without fearing for their lives. The car park was nothing more than a shooting gallery for the scum who lived here Wade admitted to himself, as he reached the bottom level.

Drawing a small pistol, which he concealed in his back pocket and he cautiously made his way through the garage. Just like above, it was deserted. He'd made it half way to the driveway out ramp when red dots appeared all over his jacket.

"FBI! Drop your weapon!" a voice called from the darkness, causing him to freeze. Standing there, he raised his gun, pointing it at his head.

"Fuck you Flatfoots. I ain't going to prison." He challenged, as the room filled with light.

"I thought you'd want to know what happened to your little brother and the other dirtbags at the warehouse!" a voice yelled out to him. Wade turned towards the source.

"Did you arse-holes kill them all?" he snarled, his eyes, black with hate.

"We were too late. Your Arab friends gutted them like fish," Dan happily told him. Wade, surprised, stood for several seconds as if trying to work out what he should do. "Are you going to let them get away with it and take the coward's way out chicken

271

shit?" Dan chuckling. Several agents looked sideways at him, before refocusing on Wade. Wade angrily glared at Dan.

"You'd better not be lying!" he screamed out, before dropping his weapon on the ground and laying down. Startled, the agents around him at first hesitated, before rushing forward and securing his hands and then searching him. After they'd finished, Dan walked up to Wade.

"You can get the chair or help us get those Arab fuckers. What's it to be?"

"The bomb was in an old dodge RV. Did they take it?" Wade defeated answered.

"They must have. It wasn't there when we arrived."

"How did my brother die?" Wade softly asked.

"He took a few of them with him," Dan replied, as Wade was led away. Once he'd been moved to a waiting vehicle and secured, Bobby spoke up.

"His brother died running, away didn't he?"

"Yeah, but I want him angry at those Arabs. This way he'll help us for revenge." Dan smiled again and walked towards the exit.

"How did you know he'd head down here?" Bobby asked as they approach their car.

"He was a Marine. I figured when he entered; he'd know something was up. You can't have this many cops in a place like this without giving it away. To me, the car park seemed the only escape route he could take."

"Clever. Do you think he'll keep helping us?"

"Yeah. It will give him time to figure out how to escape," Dan warned, as they drove back towards the warehouse.

By the time they arrived the bodies had been tagged and bagged. Wade, of course, wanted to see his brother. Dan went with him and opened the plastic bag containing his brother. He'd been shot in the head and mutilated by his killers. Wade was visible upset, close to tears.

"He was ugly, anyway wasn't he?" Dan goaded him. Wade handcuffed and wearing ankle shackles, still launched himself at Dan. Ready Dan punch him in the stomach, before knocking him to the ground.

"You've got no fucking morals you pig. If I get loose, I'll kill you!" Wade screamed, before starting cry, upset by his brother's death.

"My brother died guarding the President, Wade. Your lowlife trash killed him for doing his job. Next time you come at me, you won't be breathing. Do you understand me?" Agent Nixon seeing what was occurring, worried Dan was losing it, moved towards him. Dan observed his approach, raised his hand to warn him off. Nixon uncertainly waited. Wade lay on the ground not answering. He'd been against the bombing of the late president's motorcade for that very reason - because the secret servicemen accompanying him would die for just doing their jobs. Slowly he got up and faced Dan.

"Okay. I'll play ball until we get the bastards who killed my brother!" Wade promised, his eyes locked on Dan's.

"What can you tell us about the RV?"

"It's an old piece of shit, but mechanically it sound. It's also got a GPS tracker installed."

"Do they know?" Dan asked, wondering if Wade was on the level."

"No. I got Billy our tech guy and bomb maker to install it, so we could make sure the Arabs drove it where we wanted it to go."

"What about the bomb?"

"Billy had some friend working at a nuclear power station up state. They took enough spent rods to make a dirty bomb."

"How big is it?"

"Billy said the explosion would take out a block. The fallout would cover a city the size of Georgia," Wade sheepishly admitted.

"How the fuck did you guys get so low?" Dan exploded.

"I don't know. When it started out, it sounded like it might help the cause. After the first bomb, I knew we'd done the wrong thing, but with my brother involved, I couldn't get out." Dan looked at him again wondering if he was telling the truth.

"What's the GPS code to the RV?" Dan asked changing the subject.

Michael guiltily sat in the chopper beside Trevor. Sue, Glenda and little Coby were behind them. He knew he should've stayed in

Washington with his father, but the opportunity to see Kim again made his heart overrule his brain. Other organs had helped to decide as well he decided, remembering his last night with her.

"What are you thinking about?" Trevor asked, seeing his smile. Michael caught off guard hesitated, making Trevor smile. "I thought so." He laughed making Michael go red.

"What's so funny?" Glenda asked. She was nursing little Coby and had seen Michael go red as Trevor laughed.

"Michael's off in romance land." Trevor laughed harder, as Sue and Glenda joined in. Michael, a skilled speechmaker, remained tongue-tied and embarrassed, which made the others laugh even more. In the end, he joined in with the good-natured humour.

"God this is ridiculous! Every time I think about her I go mute!" Michael admitted to himself.

"Trevor was the same you know." Sue smiled. "When I was working with him he just kept looking at me instead of talking. I thought at first he was going to fire me and then I figured out he had more on his mind than working with me." She giggled, causing Trevor to go a little red as well.

"Well that makes me feel a little better," Michael answered with a grin.

From the window, Michael could see the Van Clef plantation below.

"Trevor! Take a look!" Michael told him pointing out the window. Trevor moved to look down. Tears formed in his eyes, as he saw his family home again.

"You know, I never thought I'd see it again. Even though, I know my real home is in another country far away from the life I had here, I always loved this place!" Trevor choked on tears as Sue held him.

"So, you will be staying in Vietnam?" Glenda asked.

"Yes. Sue and I are happy there helping the mountain people. We make a difference, and it will always be our home."

"What will you do with your grandfather's home?"

"That the Senator and I already decided. In Vietnam, he told me he wanted Coby and you, Glenda, to live here if you wished to. That way when and if I return, it will be waiting for me." Glenda sat there not knowing what to say.

"That is very generous of you Trevor, but how will you keep the Hospice going? It must cost a lot to run a place like that." Michael replied holding back tears.

"Granddad left me a substantial trust fund to run the hospice. There is also the money supplied by the American people through the treaty, which should start flowing to us soon."

"Sounds good Trevor, but remember you have a family now and we will always help you." Glenda tearfully told him.

"Thanks, mum, but for now I can manage," Trevor assured her.

"When will Kim arrive?" Sue asked changing the subject.

"I'm not sure. Her email said she'd be here today sometime. The secret service, which has an advance unit already at the plantation are expecting her. They will contact us when she arrives," Glenda informed her, as the chopper dipped, starting its approach toward the plantation's front lawn.

Michael, closest to the door, moved to open it. A firm hand on his shoulder stopped him.

"Sir. If I may?" a stern voice warned, as a Secret Serviceman moved to take up a position near the door.

"Sorry about that!" Michael apologised. The Agent nodded as he climbed out to scan the area. When satisfied, he signalled to Michael that it was safe, for the others to leave the craft. Entering the Senator's home seemed strange without the presence of their dearly loved friend.

"Feels weird coming here without the Senator, doesn't it?" Michael said, breaking the gloomy silence.

"Yes, he filled this house with love and laughter, although I still feel his presence in his home," Glenda softly answered, wiping her eyes.

"Hey! Granddad wouldn't want us to mope about. Let's find our rooms, get changed and enjoy the moment together," Trevor exclaimed.

"You're right. Let's all meet back down here in say thirty minutes and have something to eat. We can then go through the arrangements for the funeral," Michael suggested, the family members all agreeing.

Michael closed the door to his room and sat down on the bed. He missed the Senator and felt down for leaving Coby in Washington. Two hands on his shoulders made him jump, before looking around.

"Surprise!" Kim whispered, kissing him.

"God, you scared me! How come the Secret Service didn't mention you were here?"

"I asked if I could surprise you. They thought it would be funny too. They seem to have a sense of humour under those frowns."

"I've been so lonely without you!" Michael confessed, his pent-up grief bubbling to the surface and overflowing.

"I'm here now Michael," she whispered, pulling him to her and holding him. In time, he broke away and kissed her deeply. They sat silently together, thinking about what was happening around them.

"Is your dad coming here soon?" Kim asked, only now comprehending how strongly the Senator's death had affected Michael.

"In a couple of days. He has a lot of problems at the moment," Michael admitted. A glance at the clock confirmed how quickly time has passed.

"Damn! I've arranged to meet the others downstairs in fifteen minutes. Best I grab a quick shower and change."

"Good idea. I need one too!" Taking off her clothes she walked into the bathroom, leaving Michael staring after her. "You'd better hurry Michael. You wouldn't want to be late!" she called as Michael swiftly stripped and hurried after her.

THE TERRORIST

"Sir. We have their location!" John Taylor exclaimed.

"Good work John. Where are they?" Coby enquired.

"At a small lake west of the Capital. It seems one of the Clan members has decided to co-operate. The vehicle they're in has a tracking device. We are moving in now."

"Can you take them out, without their detonating the bomb?"

"That I cannot guarantee Sir. We're in unchartered territory here, and we have limited Intel. I promise you, Sir, we'll do our best. Have we your permission to proceed?"

"You have my full backing John. Have you informed General Graven?"

"He's in the loop, Sir. The Army's supplying logistical support, but the FBI team on the ground has the lead on this one."

"Okay, John. Tell the men involved how proud I am of them." Coby told him. John expressed his gratitude before the line went dead. Sitting alone in the Oval Office, Coby thought of a hundred things that could go wrong, as Bobby and another Secret Serviceman entered.

"Hey, the dangers are not here yet men!" Coby informed them.

"We know Sir. There's another problem."

"Shoot."

"A lot of things could go wrong Sir. We suggest you join your family in Georgia."

"Why, if there's no danger, should I go early?"

"We have worked out, that fallout from a bomb going off at the lake where the suspects are could cover half of Washington, including the White House."

"Look, men, I'm not leaving! The FBI has this well in hand. If and when things get out of hand, we'll leave."

"You're taking a chance, Sir."

"I know, but that comes with the job. Do your families live here?" Coby asked the agents.

"Yes, Sir," Bobby answered.

"Well if they're staying so am I. Let's get through this situation shall we?" The men, with a nod, left. Moments later Robert entered.

"Just got your schedule for today. There are only two important appointments. One is the Japanese ambassador at ten. He wants to talk about the trade deal again. The other is with the United Arab Council. They want to talk about the unrest in the Middle East. That's at two this afternoon. There are small meetings in between but nothing major," Robert told him. Looking closely at Coby, he saw he wasn't listening. "Did you hear what I said Mr President?" At his raised voice Coby jumped.

"God I'm sorry Robert. My mind was miles away."

"No problem Sir. I'll start again."

"Can't you call me by my name Robert, when no one's around. You're a friend, and I've known you for years!"

"Okay, I'll call you Coby. What's wrong Sir? I mean Coby?" Robert asked, sounding confused, before sitting down.

"The Secret Service thinks I should run and hide in Georgia with my family instead of staying here."

"I don't think they would've said it like that."

"No. You're right they didn't.".

"There is nothing wrong with going to the Van Clef plantation early. You've been busy lately, no one would judge you for doing it."

"And what if they do detonate the bomb and the fall out hits Washington?"

"Then Washington is their target?"

"Shit I shouldn't have told you that. But yes, the terrorists are holed near a lake west of here. The FBI is moving in as we speak."

"Then stop worrying. They know their stuff so let them sort it out. In the meantime, you can take me for a ride to Georgia. I too would like to stay once more at the Senator's home myself."

"Okay, we'll go. Let's again go over what's on today before we do." Coby visibly relaxed after his decision was made. After checking over the day's schedule again, Robert left, leaving Coby to prepare for his first meeting. Outside Robert found the Secret Servicemen waiting.

"I've talked him in to going this afternoon Bobby," Robert whispered.

"Thank you, Sir," Bobby replied, passing it on to his controller.

AT THE LAKE

"The attack will be today outside the White House." Bengali softly spoke into his phone.

"Allah be praised!" came the answer, as the phone went dead. Bengali pocketing the phone approached Subel.

"Is it ready Subel?" Bengali asked watching his two men fish from the wharf out front of their hut.

"In about another hour. It cannot be rushed brother," Subel replied, Bengali noting a trace of anger in his voice.

"I am sorry brother, but time is running out."

"I thought we were waiting for the President to return from the funeral?"

"We were, but I just saw the news, and he is still in Washington working today. We can drive there in two hours and detonate it near the White House where he will be this afternoon, at two. The Arab Summit delegates most who support America will be there as well. It's the target of the century!" he exclaimed.

"Then in an hour have the men ready. We will load it and drive straight there." Subel smiled, as Bengali embraced him.

"This day will be celebrated by our brothers across the world for a thousand years!" Bengali yelled out, only to have one of his men signal for him to be quiet.

"What is wrong Wahid?"

"Someone is approaching along the water's edge," he replied, as Bengali rushed to the window looking along the shoreline. There, dressed in long grey waterproof pants, carrying a fishing line, with a bag hanging over his shoulder, walked a middle-aged man.

"Subel keep working on the bomb. The rest of you, take up positions around the hut, but stay out of sight. Jamal and Turin both speak English, so we'll let them handle this," Bengali instructed, as they all prepared.

Bengali hidden inside the front veranda door watched the man approach. Now and then, he'd stop and throw his line out, before ambling along towards his men, fishing on a wharf near their hut. Reaching them, Bengali watched him shake hands with his men who introduced themselves, before talking for over ten minutes. The men in the cabin stood or sat silently watching, waiting for any sign of attack. As time passed by Bengali smiling told his men to relax, as the man continued to talk.

Finally, with a wave of his hand, the man continued on his way, still casting his line as he made his way slowly along the shore until he disappeared around a bend. Once Bengalis two fishermen were sure he was gone, one approached the hut, entering.

"Is everything okay Jamal?" Bengali asked, still watching the shoreline.

"Yes, although I nearly killed him for talking so long! The man was a bore!" Jamal replied, the others chuckling.

"What did he say?"

"He was complaining that there were no fish here. He said he'd been ripped off in coming here."

"Where was he from?" Bengali asked.

"From Washington and he is of all things a cop," Jamal smiled. The room went quiet as Bengali stood thinking.

"Did he say he was here alone?"

"No. There are three other police officers staying here with him. They came straight from work and are staying at hut number ten on the far side of the lake. He was doing a circuit to try and find a good spot. The others are having a drink, and he invited us to join them," Jamal explained.

"Anything else?" Bengali asked.

"No. Other than fishing we discussed nothing else," Jamal answered.

"Good. This is every good. Get Turin, Jamal. I have a job for you two." Bengali smiled gathering his men.

The cop fisherman walked into the hut throwing the fishing rod and bag into a corner. There waiting were Wade and Denison with six other agents.

"You took long enough Dan!" Denison snapped, as Dan went to the fridge.

"Fuck you think they'd stock the hut with beer?" Dan answered, before taking out a coke and opening it. Denison seeing yelling at him wasn't going to help, waited, while Wade quietly chuckled. After a deep swig, he answered. "I had to take a long-time boss. What did you think I'd do, just walk up to them and ask if they had a Nuke in the hut? They had to think I was a fisherman or it wouldn't have worked."

"Okay, I'm sorry. Do you think they thought you were a cop?" Denison was worried that the terrorist would spot how clean-shaven and short-haired Dan was, like everyone else there. "Of course, I told them I was," he replied, stunning them all.

"Have you lost it?" Denison screamed. "Fuck they're most probably leaving right now?" Denison exploded, looking to his communication officer. "Any moment?"

"Not yet, but four of them are loading the truck with what I'd say are weapons," he told Denison.

"Can I explain?" Dan interrupted.

"Go ahead," Denison growled.

"These guys aren't fools. They'd spot any of us as cops, by our appearance in a second. I told them I was up here with three other cops from Washington, that we'd come straight from work to do some fishing. They bought it hook line and sinker Boss." Dan chuckled at his own joke.

"How does that help us?" Denison asked.

"They have to get into Washington to do any real harm. Why not dress up as cops, especially as no one will miss these four cops for some time. I'd say they're getting ready to give us a visit." The whole room stood or sat there stunned.

"That's brilliant! You've split their group up." Wade smiled, causing the agents to look his way.

"And even better, they have to leave the bomb at the hut while their transport comes here." Dan pointed out, as Denison started issuing orders.

Bengali watched his four men depart, waving to them. Taking a quick look around, spotting nothing, he walked back into the hut. With only four men left including himself, he decided on only one man on the wharf, as lookout, fishing. Subel was finishing up his rebuild of the bomb, so all they had to do was wait for the return of his men and their new uniforms.

"God is great!" He said out loud, as his men return his call.

"All is ready brother!" Subel shouted, throwing his tools away.

"Good work Subel. Cover it with the tarpaulin we brought with us. We will move it outside as soon as the others return," Bengali ordered, as the sound of gunshots rang out. Silence descended over the hut as they all listened.

"Something is wrong! They were told not to shoot unless they had no choice." Bengali warned as his men all grabbed their weapons. Subel feeling a touch of fear picked up his rifle and moved to stand beside Bengali.

"What do you think brother?" Subel whispered as the shooting subsided. Looking at the lake, Bengali for the first time realised he could see no one at all. At this time of the day the lake was usually filled with boats!

"Detonate the bomb!" he screamed out, as Subel looked around for the detonator, only to see it on the table discarded, where he left it when he picked up his rifle. He was just about to get it when the hut became a sieve, as round after round impacted the wooden walls passing straight through into the men gathered there.

Dan and Wade lay with ten other agents in the forest that backed on to Bengali's hut. Dan was in charge, something he liked. He loved his boss Denison. Although he was smart, he wasn't much of an on the spot thinker. Dan had improvised at the hut, getting his idea of suckering them from his talk with the two lookouts. He'd gauged these men to be intelligent, which led him to make up the cop story. More stupid men might've started shooting when confronted by a cop, even one on holidays. These two had hardly reacted, which spoke volumes about their training and brains.

Dan knew Denison had been impressed, by his summing up of the situation. Now while Dan took out the main target, Denison's group would deal with the four heading for hut ten. Looking sideways, he saw Wade watching the hut with his binoculars. Being the only one who knew what the terrorist leader looked like, he'd been included in Dan's group.

"Can you see him?" Dan asked Wade.

"For a second I did. I'd say there are three inside, including their leader and the dope fishing on the wharf.

"Why call him a dope?"

"His line isn't in the water, and you can see the empty hook floating above the water. Not much of a lookout."

"I take your point," Dan replied, seeing Wade return to watching the hut. "Can I depend on you in there?" He watched Wade lower the glasses.

"I want these bastards Agent Tenant! I know it doesn't seem much to you, considering what I've already done, but if I stop this attack, I'll feel a little better about looking at myself in the mirror." Wade confessed, Dan, nodding his understanding. Reaching across, he undid Wade's handcuffs, his ankle bracelets having already been removed. Rubbing his wrist, Wade looked at Dan.

"Thanks, and I won't run." He smiled as Dan smiled back.

"We'll see," Dan chuckled thumbing his headset. "All units get ready!" he warned as his team took up their positions. 'Greg would be proud of me,' Dan said to himself, taking the safety off his rifle.

GREG

Dan's brother had always had a hard on to be in the Secret Service. Both after leaving school had joined the Marines like their old man. A year younger than Dan, Greg surprised Dan by leaving the Marines after just one tour of Iraq. He had immediately applied to join the Secret Service and was accepted straight away. Dan, on the other hand, had stayed for another two years in the Marines before joining the States Police Force, starting out as a footslogger walking a beat.

His advancement had been slow, until, by accident, he'd busted a major drug ring. He'd been sitting in his patrol car having, of all things, a doughnut, when around the corner came a car on the wrong side of the road. Giving chase, the passenger had fired several shots at him, making him call for backup and get angry. Ramming the car, he managed to flip it onto its roof. He pulled up, and he reached their car before they could get out.

The passenger, who'd shot at him, did try to make a run for it. He received a pistol-whipping for shooting at him. Then, after he'd found the gun, Dan dragged the driver out.

"Why the fuck did you shoot at me?" Dan screamed at him.

The driver was only about sixteen panicked. Thinking Dan was going to kill him, he spilled his guts, telling him everything.

They had four million dollars hidden in the boot and were on their way to meet their boss, to buy a shitload of heroin. A new Asian gang, which had moved into the area, had guaranteed twice as much junk for the same price they were paying to a Cuban gang. Dan took down the address and called the local FBI, fearing the police radios might be monitored. The FBI had been so excited; they sent thirty agents to the address.

In the raid that followed, two agents were wounded, while the drug dealers lost four men. One hundred kilos of heroin and a mountain of money were seized, making it one of the biggest busts in the city. Dan expected to be at least promoted to sergeant or receive a medal, for his part in the raid. Instead, he got nothing. He found out later; his senior officers weren't happy with his going to the Feds for help. The local Feds hearing this approached and offered him a job. He hadn't looked back.

When his brother was burned alive protecting the President, Dan lost it. Taking a few weeks off, he came back angry at the world for taking away his brother. Over time he'd settled down, but he still wanted payback for his brother. As he lay in the forest across from the hut, he knew that time had come.

Across the other side of the lake, Denison lay in a similar position, watching hut ten. Two of his men had volunteered to stay inside the hut, giving the impression of normality, as the RV approached. Pulling up, two men from the rear of the van climbed out and approached the hut, while the other two covered them. For some reason, one of the men walking towards the hut glanced towards Denison's men's position and froze. If he'd seen movement or light had reflected of someone's scope, no one would know as he screamed out, running back towards the RV, followed by his companion.

"Open fire!" Denison screamed, knowing the element of surprise was gone. The four were down in seconds, not even getting off a shot. Denison should have been happy, except they had planned for no shooting, as it would alert any terrorists left behind.

"Move in Dan!" he shouted into his radio, as shooting could be heard from across the lake. "God, I hope he gets them all!" he prayed, turning to his men. "Go check that they're all dead and find out who the fuck gave us away!" he ordered, running to his car. Behind him, his men moved forward, knowing whoever had fucked up, wasn't going to admit it.

When Denison yelled for Dan's team to 'move in', Dan, without hesitating, gave the order. Ten weapons instantaneously let loose a barrage of metal. Dan had made it clear that they were to keep shooting until they were sure all four targets were down. The lookout on the wharf was the last, as he wasn't near the weapon and he had nothing but a fishing rod in his hands to worry about. Dan could still see him standing there in shock as the hut disintegrated. In time, he woke from his fright and reached for his weapon, which was hidden under the seat beside him. It was a fatal mistake, as he was catapulted backwards of the wharf by a well-aimed shot from one of Dan's snipers.

Jumping up, Dan shouted for everyone to move forward. Once the shooting had stopped, the agents left their rifles and pulled out their pistols, advancing at a run.

"If anyone's alive shoot them!" Dan yelled out, reaching the door. Kicking it in proved unnecessary, as the shooting had flattened it already. Pouring into the house, the agents covered each other searching the house.

"I count two down. Where's the third man?" Dan yelled, advancing on the rear bedroom. Beside the bomb under the tarpaulin lay Bengali.

"Now you will all die Infidels!" Bengali yelled out. Dan, knowing he was too late spun around, as two shots rang out. Paralyzed by the shot that hit him in the neck, Bengali died, unable to press the trigger in his left hand. In his right hand, Dan saw a pistol.

Behind him up against the wall stood Wade holding one of the terrorist's pistols.

"I can't believe you guys missed him lying there," Wade grinned, before toppling forward, facedown on the ground. The room full of agents froze as Dan rushed to Wade. Bending down, he turned him over. Besides his heart, a blood red stain was spreading over his chest. Dan immediately put his hand over the wound.

"Get an ambulance!" Dan screamed out, as one agent rushed outside.

"Forget it, Dan! I'm fucked," Wade spluttered out.

"You saved a shitload of people today Wade, including all of us here," Dan told him.

"Does it earn me a favour?"

"What do you want?" Dan asked.

"Keep my brother's and my name out of the list of bad guys involved in this mess. Do that, and we're even!" Wade coughed out.

"I'll do what I can Wade and thanks," Looking into Wade's unblinking eyes Dan knew he couldn't hear him. He took off his FBI jacket and covered Wade's face before getting up.

"Three down. With the dickhead on the wharf that makes four. Stand down!" Dan shouted as the agents lowered their weapons.

"Fuck that was close Dan!" One of his men struggled for breath, as he took huge gulps of air.

"God we're lucky Wade saw that dirtbag!" another pointed out, as the others in the room nodded in agreement.

"Yeah, we were! But the bomb wasn't! Everyone out now!" Dan ordered. Turning, the other agents saw several holes in the bomb. It was then Denison arrived.

"Have you got it?" he shouted from his car.

"Yeah although it has some bullet holes in it," Dan yelled back. Denison, going to the boot, returned with a Geiger counter to check the hut.

"No dangerous levels of radiation registered, although as a precaution, I suggest everyone should strip off and shower. It looks like we got lucky!" Denison admitted, before seeing Wade on the floor. "What happened?"

"We all missed one of the terrorists hidden under the bomb. Wade grabbed a gun and shot him before he could detonate the bomb," Dan told him.

"Jesus, why he'd do that?"

"Wanted us to clear his brother's and his name from involvement with the clan and the terrorists," Dan explained.

"It's the least we can do. Anyway, I'd better call the Director. As you can imagine, he's been waiting for this call.

"Agent Denison, you have gone above and beyond on this one," Director Taylor proudly told him, more than impressed with the securing of the bomb.

"Two things Sir. One, the entire raid was the result of Agent Dan Tenant's planning. I couldn't have done it without him boss. He deserves all the credit. Two, the Clan Member Wade Du Pont saved millions of lives today. I want him and his brother's names taken off the list of traitors. Wade should be buried with full military honours, after all, Wade, was a decorated Marine.

"You're right. He deserves some credit. The agent whom you said deserved credit, why is his name familiar?" The Director asked.

"His brother was one of the Secret Servicemen who died with the President Sir."

"Jesus, that's a bad deal. Tell him he has the nation's thanks for what he did."

"Thank you, Sir. We're waiting for the army engineers now. Once they've taken the bomb, we'll return to Washington."

"I look forward to reading the report," Director Taylor replied before hanging up.

ENEMIES WITHIN

Coby was walking out to meet the Middle East delegations, when Bobby beside him, moved in close.

"The FBI has secured the bomb. All the terrorists are dead Sir," he told him, trying not to smile.

"That is great news! Pass on my thanks to all involved Bobby!" Coby smiled, suddenly lighter.

Coby greeted the delegation and escorted them into the White House's main dining area for an informal talk and meal. Once seated, Coby noticed two members were missing.

"Weren't there fourteen delegates?" Coby asked the Egyptian representative.

"Yes, Mr President. At the last moment, the two delegates from Northern Sudan had to leave. It appears their President is ill and has called them home to handle a situation he has there."

"How unfortunate. Well, let's get this meeting underway." Coby smiled and began their discussion.

Polite applause signalled the end of the speeches, as everyone sat down for dinner. Once the delegates started eating, Coby signalled to Bobby.

"Yes, Sir."

"Bobby. The two Northern Sudanese representatives were suddenly recalled. Check with the CIA and the FBI. See if our departed friends from Sudan knew about the bomb!"

"I'll find out Sir!" Bobby answered, moving away.

Directors Benson and Taylor were at that moment in a meeting with General Graven, when the Secret Service rang Taylor. After listening, he passed on to the others the relayed information.

"The President's getting a handle on the job, isn't he?" Benson smiled.

"Yeah. It's too bad he won't be staying on," Graven replied, the others nodding.

"What are the chances of these two delegates leaving just before the bomb was about to go off?" Taylor pointed out.

"We'll need hard evidence before we can go after them," Benson warned.

"What about this guy Bengali's phone? Can we find out who he rung?" Graven asked.

"He rang only one number, and we have no idea who it is."

"Can we track it?" Benson asked.

"Yes, but we'll only know where it is, not who," Taylor replied.

"Yeah, but what if it's on a plane?" Graven pointed out.

Taylor, understanding, dialled his headquarters.

"Ten minutes passed before Taylor's phone rang. Answering it, he looked towards Graven, smiling. Thanking the person on the other end, he hung up.

"They rang the number. Someone picked it up, but when my people asked who it was and they didn't answer. They then smashed the phone."

"What was its location?" Benson asked.

"Three hundred miles east of our eastern coast. The only plane near that position is a privately owned North Sudanese jet, flying to England. Their flight plan shows they'll refuel there, before continuing to Khartoum. It is believed they will land at a military airfield north of the city."

"Don't tell me! Let me guess. Our two delegates are on that plane?"

"Not much of a guess General, but yes they are. I'll contact the President," Taylor replied, again picking up his phone.

Coby was just finishing lunch when Bobby approached him. "Sir, I have a call for you from Director Taylor."

"Thank you, Bobby. I'll take it in the Oval Office." Coby smiled at the delegates.

"Sorry gentlemen, but duty calls. The Senate wants to argue about something to do with money." He smiled, as the delegates chuckled. Shaking hands with several representatives, Coby made his way casually outside. Once away from the meeting, he hurried to his Office. Sitting down Coby had Taylor's call was put through to him. Listening to what Taylor and his people had found out Booby, his secret service agent, watched the Presidents face turn from a smile to anger.

"Those two-faced liars! They were in my office with their Ambassador showing their support. What do you suggest?" Coby asked Taylor.

"That's above my pay grade, Sir. General Graven has an idea though."

"Put your phone on speaker Director Taylor!" Coby ordered.

"Sir, General Graven can hear you. Director Benson is here as well Sir," Taylor informed him.

"Okay General. What do you suggest?"

"Both gentlemen have diplomatic immunity from prosecution and are at the moment outside our country's airspace. We also don't have an extradition treaty with Northern Sudan, which seems to be behind the attacks. I suggest we take care of them off the books," Graven advised.

"How?" Coby asked.

"The carrier group Nimitz is, at this moment, entering the Med. We can have them to scramble a couple of jets and take care of this problem over the Atlantic. If anybody accuses us, we have deniability."

"Good thinking General, but not this time. No, I want the North Sudanese Government to get the message loud and clear. This gentleman is what I suggest," Coby replied, laying out his plan.

"Are you sure Sir? That's quite a statement!" Benson warned.

"Does anyone want these guys or for that matter, anyone else, to think they can try this type of attacks on America again?" Coby asked. No replies were forthcoming from the three men. "Good! General you have a go!"

"Yes Sir," Graven answered, sounding a little unsure.

Coby hung up and saw Robert standing outside his office with Bobby.

"You can let him in Bobby," Coby shouted out, startling them both.

"Did things go well?" Robert enquired.

"Yes, they did. How about we take an early mark and head out to Georgia?" Coby asked.

"My bags are packed."

"How about you Bobby?" Coby smiled.

"Always Sir!"

"Then let's get that chopper, here shall we?"

THE FUNERAL

As George Van Clef had requested, only his family and a few close friends gathered at his home for the service. The Minister kept the service short, knowing how emotional the Senator's family and friends were. After a quiet get-together, one by one his friends left until only Coby, his family and Robert remained.

"I will miss this place," Coby confessed, as they all sat outside on the veranda, which overlooked the pool. Coby remembered the first time he saw Diana lying next to that pool. His life had changed forever from that brief meeting.

"She was quite a woman, wasn't she?" Glenda whispered beside him, making Coby jump.

"Sorry. You're not jealous, are you?"

"No. I was once, but now I know you're mine, although she will always be a part of our lives," Glenda told him as she held his hand. Across from them, Trevor watched Coby, remembering that day when he had first seen Coby trying to rescue him from what he thought was danger. To Trevor, it seemed several lifetimes ago. So much had happened.

"Now we are family!" Trevor said out loud, seeing Coby look in his direction and nod to show his understanding.

"Here's to family!" Michael called out, pulling Kim and Robert to him, showing Robert he belonged as well.

"And to the Senator! A man who put family before everything and saw people for what they were, not their colour. For that, we will always love him!" Coby said softly but clearly, as he held back his emotions.

"To the Senator!" they all answered.

Sue had just taken little Coby to bed when Bobby entered the room. The conversation, which was getting louder, immediately stopped.

"Sir. The call you wanted to make, must be done within the next twenty minutes," Bobby told him, waiting.

"Sorry, everyone! I have an important call to make," Coby told them before standing up and leaving.

"What's that all about?" Trevor asked, sensing the mood swing in Glenda and Michael.

"Some things it's best not to know," Robert answered, as the room temporarily grew quiet before they resumed their conversations.

Coby walked out to the front of the Senator's home and was escorted to a mobile command centre operated by the Secret Service. Inside he found a video link had been set up to General Graven command centre. Around him stood ten Secret Servicemen and beside them sat two heavily bandaged men, who tried to rise as he entered.

"Stay where you are men. You've earned those seats!" Coby told them, as the men relaxed.

"Everything okay General?" Coby asked, seeing the soldiers in the General's command centre snap to attention.

"Yes Sir. Our surprise is ten minutes out."

"Good. Put me through to the North Sudanese Ambassador."

"You're connected, Sir!" Bobby informed him. Coby picked up the phone while everyone around him waited expectantly.

"Are you there, Mr Ambassador?" Coby spoke into the phone, which echoed around the room and the General's command centre.

"Yes, Mr President. I judge by the hour it must be important or you wouldn't have woken me." The Ambassador did not sound happy.

"It is Sir. I told you that before we launched another attack in your country, I would give you advanced warning," Coby answered, his tone sounding angry.

"Yes, Mr President I remember! When will the attack take place and who is the target?" he answered, his voice sounding unsure.

"The targets are the men responsible for the attacks on President Bridges and the failed attempt on Washington yesterday. These terrorists killed many good men and are about to be brought to justice," Coby forcefully told the Ambassador. On the other end of the phone, nothing could be heard but breathing.

"Are you still on the line Ambassador?"

"Yes, Mr President. Where are they exactly?"

"They are about to land at a military airfield just outside of Khartoum."

"I must warn you that an attack on our country and our armed forces will be treated as an act of war!" the Ambassador shot back.

"Good. Then we will reply with a nuclear weapon, like the one your country tried to detonate in Washington yesterday," Coby snapped back. The Ambassador could be heard breathing heavily again, before answering.

"I was told they were going to use a conventional bomb, Mr President. I know nothing of a Nuke." The Ambassador rambled, clearly understanding that he'd been left in Washington to die.

"Bring your family to the State Department immediately. We will give you immunity, in return for a statement from you about this attack on America." Again, the phone went silent for several seconds.

"We are leaving now," the Ambassador answered before the line went dead.

"Well done Mr President. There can be no denying their involvement now," General Graven spoke out.

"How long General?"

"We're switching to a drone over the air base now," Graven informed him.

Coby and the people gathered in the room, watched the General's control room disappear from the screen to be replaced with a clear morning shot of an airfield. The only difference from this airfield to an American airfield was the Russian built Mig fighters that lined the runways. As they watched, a small Lear jet touched down and taxied to a mobile set of stairs. There, waiting, was a crowd of people some of whom started to clap, as the door to the plane opened. It was at that moment; lights started flashing around them.

The crowd appeared confused by the warning lights and started running in all directions away from the plane. Airfield staff more disciplined ran to their battle stations. Several pilots by their clothing could be seen running to the fighters. One even started to taxi. At that moment, ten brilliant lights lit the entire area, the screen whiting out. It was then that the picture disappeared and refocused on the General's command centre.

"I'd say the entire airfield is gone, Sir. Six tomahawks would have been sufficient Sir. Ten means there's nothing there now but a large hole in the ground," General Graven informed them. Behind him, Coby could hear and see the soldiers clapping.

"Today we have righted a wrong carried out by cowards hiding in the shadows. Good work General Graven and thank your staff for a job well done," Coby told them as the staff cheered in the Senator's office and the Command Centre.

"Thank you, Sir," the General answered before the screen became blank. Once the noise had died down, Coby turned to the injured men in the chairs.

"I know this won't bring your friends and fellow agents back, but at least you know the ones responsible have been brought to justice," Coby told them, shaking each of the men's hands.

"Thank you, Mr President! It was an honour to be here," one answered before the two men were helped outside.

"That was much appreciated Sir," Bobby told him, before following the others outside.

Alone, Coby walked back to the house and entered the Senator's office. He sat down and thought about the emotional roller coaster his family had been on over the past year. Glenda had told him of Trevor's offer to let them live here while he continued his work in Vietnam. Although they had their own home near where his parents had lived, there was something unique about the Senator's home. Among the Senators family photos, his attention was drawn to one. It was Bud receiving his Silver Star.

"I hope you found peace, Bud!" Coby whispered. Next to it was another of Diana sitting with Trevor near the pool.

"God, I miss you so much my darling. Our family here is now complete, and I hope one day to see you again." He softly pledged, remembering better times.

"Are you okay Mr President?" Bobby asked from outside the room.

"Yes, Bobby. Just reminiscing about better times," Coby answered and then stood.

"Your family is waiting for your return Sir," Bobby softly told him. Coby was surprised by this assertion, as he'd never had a Secret Servicemen say anything unrelated to their job before.

"You're giving advice Bobby?"

"Wouldn't dream of it, Sir!" Bobby answered, a slight smile on his lips.

"Well thanks anyway," Coby told him as he walked out to join his family.

"Hey, where have you been? You didn't start a war or something?" Trevor sniggered, as the others remained silent. Trevor feeling he'd said the wrong thing went to answer. "Hey, Dad I was only joking!" he got out in a strangled voice before Coby came up and hugged him.

"I know son; you don't have to apologise. And I didn't start a war. Well, maybe a small one?" He smiled, which encouraged them all to express amusement with him. Coby, happy to back with his family, sat down to enjoy more conversation, about any random topic that occurred to them.

Just before 1 am, Glenda reminded them of the time. Knowing the following day would be a long draining one, they all called it a night. Carrying their crockery to the kitchen, Coby volunteered to wash, while Trevor dried. On their own, the silence between them was palpable. Coby broke the silence.

"What sill you do now Trevor?"

"Back home. We have a great deal yet to do," Trevor answered, piling plates into an overhead cupboard.

"Will you be okay son?" Coby asked him, his voice having a slight tremor.

"Yes, Dad. Don't sweat it," He responded, a small grin on his face, at his father's nervousness.

"It's just with the Senator dying, the drugs, and finding out the truth; you've been through a lot."

"Yeah, you're right. The last few months have been a roller coaster that's for sure. But I've got my Dad and a family back now. Grandpa dying was a shock, and I've got to admit I thought about lighting up, but I didn't. So, relax dad, I'm here for the long run!" he assured him and gave Coby a quick hug. Coby stuck for words return to his plates before answering.

"That's good son." He paused for a little, before saying, "You know I was thinking; after I move into my son's house, I might go on an official visit to Vietnam. There's to be a swearing in ceremony for President Chew. After that, I think I'll visit the highlands to see how American tax dollars are being put to work!"

"Maybe you could suggest Senator Michael Henderson accompanies you, to keep you on the straight and narrow?"

"Not a bad idea as he seems to have become an expert on Vietnamese relations!" Coby joked as Trevor grinned.

"What's going on in there?" Michael asked as he entered the kitchen holding Kim tightly to him, making Trevor and Coby both grin.

THE RETURN

With two months left of his term in office, President Cornelius Henderson looked out at Hanoi International airport. Unlike before, he had no reservations about this visit as he adjusted his tie. From the window, he could see the guard of honour, this time stretching from the terminal to Air Force One.

"Jesus! There must be over ten thousand soldiers lined up out there!" Coby exclaimed.

"Hey watch your language!" Glenda warned him, as she slipped on her shoes.

"Sorry," he apologised, as Bobby appeared at the door.

"Everything is ready Sir," he informed Coby, waiting by the door.

"Are you getting any time off while you're here Bobby?" Coby asked.

"Yes, Sir. While you're travelling to the highlands, I am staying in Hoi An, for a few days.

"What on your own?"

"No, my wife is flying in tomorrow. She'll meet me there." Bobby smiled.

"Why don't your wives travel on Air Force One with us?"

"Security Sir. It would place an Agent in an awkward position if he had to choose between his family and the President."

"I see your point. Still, it can't be cheap having her fly here."

"It's cheaper than two of us Sir." Bobby smiled, walking outside.

"I'll miss him! He's a good man," Glenda admitted, as she checked her outfit in the mirror.

"Yes, he is. Have you met the new guy?" Coby asked, again looking out the window.

"You mean Dan?"

"Yes. I had him transferred from the FBI to the Secret Service as a reward for service to his country."

"He seems a little nervous and his swearing legendary I've heard!" Glenda sniggered.

"Yes, he's a little rough around the edges. You know his brother died with President Bridges."

"No, I didn't. God the poor man!" Glenda replied, feeling for him.

"When I leave office, I'm entitled to have two Secret servicemen as security. I was going to ask for Bobby and Dan if they want to stay with me."

"That would be great, although they might want to stay on the President's detail. It seems they all competitively vie for those positions." At that moment Dan entered.

"They're waiting for you Mr and Mrs President." Dan stumbled over the words, making Glenda smile.

"Thanks, Dan. We'll be right out," Coby told him, as Dan not certain what to do next, turned, hesitated and then proceeded outside.

"What did he do, gun down some bad guys? He seems more like a cop than an agent?" Glenda surmised.

"He saved Washington and millions of lives by killing a group of terrorist hell bent on blowing it up with a dirty bomb," Coby absentmindedly answered as he adjusted his tie. Straightening, he looked towards Glenda seeing her staring at him fearfully. "I shouldn't have told you. I'm sorry Glenda!"

"This was why we left Washington, wasn't it?"

"Yes. At the time, we weren't sure what the target was. I couldn't lose my family again," Coby confessed, as Glenda came to him, holding him.

"I had no idea it was that serious. Once this trip is over, you can tell me all about it. For now, we have people waiting!" Glenda pointed out, as hand in hand they walked to the plane's front door. The crowd numbering close to half a million, burst into cheer as he and Glenda walked down the stairs.

"Fucking hell!" Dan at the bottom of the stairs spat out, watching the crowd, unaware Glenda was beside him.

"Yes indeed!" Glenda replied, smiling.

"Sorry Missus President," Dan blurted, going red.

"It's Glenda, Dan. From now on it's all you're allowed to call me!"

"Thank you, Glenda." He smiled back, as Coby unaware of the exchange, walked along the first line of soldiers, doing what he did best, meeting the people.

THE END